IRA SPIRO:
BEFORE COVID

A NOVEL

Dan Naturman

Luciole Books
New York - Toronto

This book is a work of fiction. Names, characters,
places and incidents are products of the
authors imagination or are used fictitiously. Any
resemblance to actual events or locales or persons,
living or dead, is entirely coincidental.

ISBN: 978-1-7374779-0-7

Cover designed by Dwayne Booth
Book designed by Donna Cavanagh

CHAPTER 1

To the extent that such things can be measured, studies have shown that New Yorkers are, on average, less satisfied with life than most Americans. Compared even to the average New Yorker, however, Ira Spiro was a noticeably angst-ridden person. He had come to accept that he simply was not destined to experience prolonged periods of great joy or even, for that matter, moderate contentedness. Yet some moments were certainly better than others and, as he made his way down Amsterdam Avenue towards home, the perfect weather, 75 degrees and cloudless skies, a peanut butter smoothie with just the right amount of agave and that boost of endorphins that one gets after a good workout at the gym conspired to make Ira feel about as good as Ira was capable of feeling.

Ira was no gym rat, but he tried to go at least three times a week. It was a paradox with Ira, albeit hardly unique to him, that, although he was more likely to greet a new day with trepidation than eagerness, he was terrified by the thought that at some point in time there would be no new days to greet. Debate might exist as to the health benefits of dark chocolate or vitamin D supplements, but all seemed to agree that regular exercise is a good way to extend one's allotted time on planet

Earth, and Ira felt an increasing need to do just that as the years passed. Forty is far from an old man, and in any case, that landmark birthday was over a year away, but Ira was already dreading it and was considering, at least half-seriously, turning off his phone and fleeing the country as it approached so as not to have to endure unwelcome birthday wishes.

- Holy shit! screamed a young man in his twenties as he rode past Ira on his Trek bicycle in the designated bike lane.

The scream deviated Ira's attention from the window of a new shop he had been peering into, wondering how it would ever stay in business selling nothing but artisanal marshmallows. The man on the bicycle abruptly braked, skidding to a stop several feet beyond Ira. He dismounted and then turned around and walked with the bicycle along the sidewalk, smiling and excited, until he caught up to Ira.

- I can't believe this. I'm a huge fan! he said to Ira.

Ira had suspected that the loud "Holy Shit!," audible for at least a block in all directions, might well be due to the bicyclist having recognized him, rather than, say, his excitement upon noticing a new place to get artisanal marshmallows.

- *Jackson Taylor's Christmas Party* is one of my favorite movies ever! gushed the young man.

- Thank you, replied Ira. I appreciate it.

- I'm Ben.

- Nice to meet you, Ben, said Ira, shaking the hand Ben had extended to him. By the way, if you're gonna ride your bicycle in New York City, maybe you should wear a helmet. I'd hate to see you crack your head open. I only have so many fans.

- Yeah right, responded Ben sarcastically. You're amazing! Oh my God I can't believe I just met Ira Spiro! Where can I see you? Are you doing any stand-up these days?

- Actually, yeah. I'm back at it, said Ira. I'm at the Comedy Den in Greenwich Village regularly.

- Awesome. I've been meaning to get down there, said Ira's increasingly enthusiastic fan. Can I take a picture with you?

- Sure. Why not?

Ira positioned himself close to Ben, putting his arm around him as Ben held his own arm outwards, holding his phone in the selfie position.

- Wait, will this be going on Instagram or something like that? inquired Ira.

- You don't want me to do post it? replied Ben with a hint of disappointment in his voice.

- No no, it's ok, said Ira, reassuring him. Just don't write a smart-ass caption like "He stunk of whiskey."

- Promise I won't, declared Ben with a laugh.

- Ok, snap the pic.

The selfie completed, Ben thanked Ira and rode away on his bicycle with a big smile on his face. Ben had met one of his favorite comedians and the star of his favorite movie, and he was actually nice!

Indeed, Ira had always been nice to fans but not always quite so friendly and willing to talk. Three years prior, when *Jackson Taylor's Christmas Party* was a surprise hit in theaters, Ira was constantly being approached on the street by fans. Not only did it interfere with him going about his day, but it also made him uncomfortable to be treated that way. He didn't quite trust it. Was it real or some kind of gag? Were people actually that excited to see him? Ira didn't view himself as a particularly impressive person. He realized that he was a funny comedian and that he wrote, perhaps, a pretty good movie, but he always felt that if you added up all of his talents and positive qualities and subtracted the negative ones, the aggregate score would be about average. Among other defects that would lower the final tally — he

3

wasn't particularly courageous, he was bad at relationships and he couldn't digest lactose.

During the period of his life when his movie was becoming popular, Ira had briefly tried sporting a beard and mustache. It didn't help much, however. Ira was still quite recognizable. He was tall and thin, about 6 feet 2 inches and 172 pounds. This lanky silhouette came from his mother's side of the family, of mostly Dutch, English and Scottish ancestry. His mother herself was about 5ft. 10 inches tall, and her father, Ira's late grandfather William Deridder, was 6'7." As for his other physical features, they came mostly from the Spiros, Jewish immigrants from Eastern Europe. He had his late father's wavy hair, though Ira's was medium brown, not black like Steven Spiro's had been. Their faces were quite similar, narrow with deep-set eyes and prominent noses. Father and son also both had full lips and a pronounced square chin which, in addition to his nose, was the subject of occasional taunts by Ira's schoolmates growing up, and even once by an eighth-grade math teacher who got big laughs from the class when, in mid-discussion about polygons, had said that "the sum of the angles in a rectangle, like Ira's chin, was 360 degrees."

In the years since the movie, Ira's career had lost most of its momentum, for a variety of reasons. Ben was only the second person to approach him that day, and it was already late afternoon. Ira found this relatively low level of attention tolerable and even at times enjoyable.

Entering his apartment, Ira plopped his gym bag unceremoniously down on the floor next to the front door before planting himself in front of his laptop computer. He was in the mood to watch music videos on YouTube. He could, of course, watch them on his internet-enabled television, but he preferred his YouTube videos inches from his face and in non-full-screen mode. This made it possible to scroll through the comments and, if the desire arose, to google facts

4

about the particular video he was watching. Even without these ancillary benefits, however, Ira still felt YouTube was a pleasure best meant to be enjoyed while staring at a computer or even a smartphone.

Ira tended to go through phases with YouTube videos. The recent 100th anniversary of America's entry into World War One had precipitated no less than two weeks of scouring the video-sharing site for documentaries on the Great War and old interviews with veterans. However, for the previous couple of days, it was with the sights and sounds of the early MTV era that Ira wished to inundate his senses. Music videos were a staple of Ira's online video diet, and in particular he returned to '80s music fairly regularly, simply because that era was a relatively happy time in his life.

Ira's apartment was a two-bedroom on the twentieth floor of a high-rise building on the Upper West Side of Manhattan. He had purchased it two and a half years before at the urging of his then-girlfriend Harlee Shaw. Ira would have been happy with a much smaller place, but Harlee was one of the most sought-after actresses in Hollywood. She herself had beautiful homes in New York and Los Angeles, and it was out of the question that the man she was dating would live in a one-bedroom or, God forbid, a studio. She was willing to date several rungs below her on the show biz ladder given Ira's potential, but there were certain conditions, so Ira laid out 1.5 million in cash for the apartment.

Harlee then insisted that her interior designer friend Giovanni, from Barletta, Italy by way of West Hollywood, do the decorating. Giovanni had a habit of sparing no expense with his clients' money, which explained the pricey lithographs on Ira's walls, including a couple of Picassos and a Miró. A designer coffee table in the living room set Ira back nearly eight grand. It featured a thick round slab of polished white calacatta marble set on a brushed aluminum frame. Ira was also the proud owner of a Victorian mahogany bookshelf that cost almost as much as the coffee table. The bookshelf and a few other vintages pieces were completely out of place in an apartment otherwise decorated at the leading edge of modernity. Giovanni was expensive, but not necessarily any good. The kitchen, though small, was custom built with generous use of Italian marble and exotic hardwoods. The appliances were all top of the line including the stove and oven that Ira never used. The closest he generally came to cooking was making a sandwich, and even that was a rare event. Getting food delivered was just too easy in New York and dining-out options too plentiful.

Harlee's decorative contribution to the apartment was a cylindrical multi-shelf display case in which she had Ira put a shooting script for *Jackson Taylor's Christmas Party* as well as the Best Original Screenplay Oscar he had won for that film. Rude though it might be to decorate and run, she broke up with Ira not long after. In the years since there had been no new awards to add to the display case, and Ira had since moved it, with the script and the Oscar statue, from the living room to the guest bedroom, where Ira ventured even less often than the kitchen.

A corner of the living room served as Ira's office, where Ira was seated at his L-shaped $3,000 metal and glass desk staring at his MacBook Pro. After having watched music videos for several new wave songs and a couple of U2 songs from "The Joshua Tree" album, he clicked on and sang along to the video for the 1986 Van Halen single "Dreams." That video featured the aerial acrobatics of the Navy's Blue Angels, leading Ira to change themes and start watching air show videos, which is what he was doing when he heard a sound that seized his attention and ended his relative state of tranquility.

An envelope being slipped under a door doesn't make much noise, but its volume seemed far greater to Ira given its significance, just as a mother might hear her baby crying above the roar of a raging storm. It was the bill for the monthly maintenance payment for his apartment. Even though he owned the place without a mortgage, he still had to pay 3,500 dollars a month for the upkeep of the building. Elevators needed to be serviced, boilers repaired and doormen paid. In addition, the lobby was undergoing a complete renovation.

For the moment he was above water, but for how long? His only income was the hundred dollars a set he made performing at the Comedy Den a few times a week, something he recently started doing after over two years of making no money at all. He could move to a smaller apartment and buy some time, but even then, sooner or later he'd be running on empty if he didn't start making real money again. His financial anxiety had become intense in recent months as his savings dipped to disquietingly low levels. At that moment, hearing the envelope being slid under the door, he felt moved to take action.

Ira paused the video of the Royal Canadian Air Force Snowbirds as they were flying in an inverted wedge formation in the skies above Winnipeg.

- Siri, call Dave Rothman.

Ira called Dave Rothman from time to time just to shoot the breeze. They were friends in addition to being talent manager and client. In fact, they were barely talent manager and client anymore as, apart from performing at the Comedy Den, Ira was all but out of show business.

- Spiro, what's good?

- Hey, Dave. Any offers for personal appearance work come in lately?

- Yeah. And I say you're not available. Those are my standing orders, right? No more high pressure headlining shows.

Only about half of Ira's money came directly from *Jackson Taylor's Christmas Party*. It was his first screenplay and his first lead role in a film, and he was thus paid relatively modestly. The film was a great success, but Ira did not get a piece of the profits. However, the film gave him a decent amount of fame, and fame can usually be transformed into revenue, especially if one is a seasoned stand-up comedian. Ira performed in theaters and at private corporate events for five and sometimes six-figure sums. Ira had never been at ease on stage, but the pressure of people paying big money specifically to see him made each performance an ordeal. After a disastrous performance at a theater in Denver, he stopped performing altogether until his recent return to the Comedy Den.

- Dave, I think I'm ready to go back out there. Any good offers?

- Wait, you wanna do a show? asked Dave with a mix of shock and excitement. What's happened? You finally get into therapy like I've been hounding you to do for years?

- What do you got? responded Ira, ignoring the question about therapy.

- A few things. Got a call from an Orthodox synagogue the other day.

- Is that gift I got you still on your wall, Dave?

On the wall next to Dave's desk was a framed word image that Ira had given him as a belated birthday gift years back. It said, in beautiful cursive calligraphy, "NO MORE ORTHODOX JEWISH GIGS."

Orthodox Jewish organizations have frequent fundraising events and often hire comedians. However, at least in Ira's experience, they generally preferred jokes centered around Jewish themes, which Ira could not deliver given that, though Jewish on his father's side, he was raised with almost none of the religion or culture. He wasn't raised with much Christianity either, even though he would one day write a movie about Christmas parties.

Once, back when Ira was still mostly unknown, after about twenty laugh-free minutes into a show at a wealthy Orthodox synagogue on Long Island, the Rabbi stood up and said to Ira "Ok that's

8

enough thank you" before announcing to the crowd that they'd be bringing out dessert and coffee. A thunderous, and for Ira terribly insulting, round of applause followed the dessert and coffee announcement. Fortunately, the synagogue had paid in advance, as a fight to get the money might have ensued otherwise. At that point, Ira told Dave he would do no more shows for Orthodox Jews. Dave continued to present offers to Ira for such shows, however, until Ira felt compelled to give Dave the aforementioned framed image which he insisted Dave mount on the wall next to his desk.

- Yes, it's still on my wall, answered Dave. Wasn't sure the rule still applied. I got some other stuff. Let me check what I have and get back to you.

As bad as the show at the Orthodox synagogue in Long Island was, it wasn't nearly as humiliating as the show in Denver which all but put an end to Ira's live appearances. He was thinking of the Denver show as he went back to his Royal Canadian Air Force Snowbirds video. The show in Denver had scarred him, probably for life. Ira would write about it in the opening chapter of his memoir which, though he would start working on it only a couple of months later, was not even a thought in his head at that moment. The memoir would ultimately be called *Ira Spiro: Before Covid*.

CHAPTER 2

IRA SPIRO BEFORE COVID: A MEMOIR - CHAPTER 1

A chronological documentation of one's life is more the realm of autobiography than memoir. The two terms are often thought synonymous, but memoirs are more focused on emotional development and growth as opposed to a simple recounting of one's experiences in the order in which they happened. Incidentally, though I'm speaking like an authority on the matter, I kinda don't know shit. This distinction is something I learned about recently. Anyway, since this is a memoir, I'm going to begin with one of the key events in my adult life, rather than talk about the circumstances of my birth or about my early childhood. It's an incident you may have read or heard about at the time, but I will endeavor to provide some details you are not aware of.

It was about 7:15 pm, forty-five minutes before showtime, when the limo pulled up to the Bellco Theater in Denver, Colorado. I experienced a brief but intense jolt of breathlessness when I saw the long line of people waiting to get in and the marquee which said "TONIGHT - IRA SPIRO - SOLD OUT." The first time I had performed stand-up comedy was at an open mic night in a tiny club in Manhattan for free. In fact, I had to pay for the privilege of performing. Thirteen years later I was about to do a sold-out show at a five thousand-seat theater for an average ticket price of fifty dollars. It would be my most lucrative night of performing ever. I had considered making the trip in a private jet. Not because it made any sort of financial sense. Chartering a jet with transcontinental range roundtrip from New York to Denver would have cost about seventy thousand dollars, which was nearly a third of what I would be netting for the show. But the biggest names in stand-up all traveled in private jets, and I wanted to be part of that prestigious group. Ultimately, however, I decided not to treat my credit card with that level of aggression and opted instead for first-class tickets for me, my opening act Karen Lee and my manager Dave Rothman.

- This is gonna be so much fun! Thank you for including me Ira Spiro superhero, enthused Karen Lee.

By the way, you may have seen Karen's recently released stand-up special, *Say When,* which is streaming online. If you haven't, check it out. It's a delightful hour of dysfunction and insecurity.

- You excited, Ira? asked my manager Dave.

- Dave, you know me. I'm excited after the show. Beforehand it's all nerves.

- I don't know why. You always do great. Can't wait to see you in action!

My manager and opening act were surely in good spirits as I assume were all the people walking into the theater to see the show. I would have happily traded places with any of them. I've always been anxious before shows. In my early years doing stand up I assumed the stage fright would disappear one day, or at least diminish. This turned out to not be the case, and, in fact, it seemed to be getting worse as with increasing fame I had felt more and more pressure to deliver a killer performance. In the previous couple of years, I had gone from headlining small comedy clubs to performing in theaters and doing private shows for large corporations. The reason for that change was the release of my film, *Jackson Taylor's Christmas Party*. The film was not an immediate hit, but slowly and surely gained in popularity, especially after it won the Oscar for best original screenplay, or should I say, after I won the Oscar for best original screenplay.

The limo dropped us off at the artist's entrance in the back of the theater. We were greeted by three men, the Director of Operations for the theater as well as two security guards, who led us into the green room backstage. My manager Dave immediately attacked the sandwiches and cookies that had been laid out for us. Karen Lee poured herself a glass of wine. As for me, I can never eat just before a big show, or even several hours before a big show. That's when the anxiety typically starts, eliminating my appetite. A drink would have been nice, but I have low alcohol tolerance, and even one glass tends to reduce my sharpness on stage noticeably.

The stage manager, a woman in her thirties dressed all in black, wearing a headset and carrying a walkie-talkie, came in and introduced herself. I believe her name was Audrey. Anyway, that's what we'll call her. Dave gave Audrey the rundown of the show, all the while chomping on mouthfuls of Pirate's Booty cheese puffs that he got from the generous bowl of snacks next to the sandwiches and cookies. I never could figure out how Dave managed to stay relatively thin despite being nearly 50 and in a constant state of munching. Karen, Dave explained to Audrey, was to be introduced from the house PA system and then would perform for twenty-five minutes. Then she would in turn introduce me, and I would go on stage and perform for about an hour.

As is typical before an important show, I needed to be alone to collect my thoughts, so I excused myself and went to the dressing room just down the hall from the green room. On the Ira Spiro scale, I was at level 4 anxiety. Level 1 is my base level. I'm always a little anxious, even when lying on a beach drinking a margarita. Level 0, no anxiety at all, is a purely theoretical notion for me. As I see it, we're hurtling through the darkness of space in a godless universe. Who could be

13

completely relaxed given such a reality? Level 2 is more intense, but I can still enjoy interaction with others and laughter is possible at this level. At level 3 I prefer solitude. Listening to music is helpful at level 3. At level 4 even music is no longer pleasurable, although moving around tends to give me some measure of relief. The dressing room was modest in size but there was room for pacing between the couch at one end and the bathroom at the other. Level 4 anxiety was not uncommon before shows at this point in my career, but thankfully, once onstage, it usually dropped to a manageable level 2.

Dave, holding a bag of Fritos, briefly popped his head into the dressing room to let me know that the show had started. Karen had just hit the stage and was about to regale the audience with tales of annoying family members, ex-boyfriends and the angst of never feeling pretty enough. Does any woman ever feel pretty enough? I've always been grateful to be a man and relatively free to look like crap.

I'd be going on in about twenty-five minutes. Current anxiety level: 4.2. I had never been quite this nervous before a show. It wasn't the biggest crowd I had ever performed in front of. Just the year before I had opened for Jim Gaffigan when he sold out the arena at Madison Square Garden! Eighteen thousand people! The Bellco was far smaller, but this time I was the draw. The whole thing was astounding. Thousands of people were paying good money to see me, a gangly coward who once, as a teenager, climbed down the ladder of a high diving board at a swim club in New Jersey because, when he got to the edge and looked down, he was too scared to jump off.

Five minutes before showtime Audrey came to get me. By this time Dave had gone into the showroom to watch from the back. The anxiety was climbing toward 4.3 as Audrey walked me backstage. I waited stage right as Karen finished her set. She was killing it with her closing bit about her boyfriend being frustrated with her because of her horrible phone sex skills.

14

- Thank you, that's it for my portion of the show, she said after finishing the phone sex bit, prompting the audience to erupt in a thunderous ovation.

Karen savored the moment as she stood there bathed in the adoration of the crowd. She was done. I was jealous.

- And now, she continued, it is my pleasure to introduce the person you all came to see. Are you ready for him?

Again the crowd erupted in applause.

- The writer and star of *Jackson Taylor's Christmas Party*, here he is, Ira Spiro!

I came onstage to a swirling symphony of cheering and clapping. "Calm down, people," I thought to myself. "I'm just a lactose intolerant neurotic who can't change a tire." I gave Karen a hug and kiss on the cheek and grabbed the mic as she left the stage. To the best of my recollection, this is how the show went from there:

- Hello Denver! Good to be here in the marijuana capital of the United States!

The anxiety started going down as is typical once I start my show and focus on my performance.

- Where are the marijuana lovers in the house? Where are the 420 folks?

The response to this question was, as expected, enthusiastic cheering. I noticed in particular a young college-aged guy near the front of the house. He was white but had dreadlocks and was wearing baggy green cargo pants and a t-shirt with the image of Homer Simpson smoking a joint and wearing a rastacap. Needless to say, he was rather excited by the subject I had broached.

- Potheads are funny. Y'all think weed cures everything. Diabetes. Parkinson's. Everything! If your computer crashes a pothead would be like, "Dude let me just blow this smoke on it. Oh wait is that a Mac? You need a sativa for that."

The crowd enjoyed this. My first laugh during a performance is always a relief, and I was down in the level 2 anxiety range as predicted.

- You guys legalized recreational pot use in 2012. I think it's also legal now in Alaska and Oregon. Here in America, different things are legal depending on where you are. I was trying to explain this to a guy I met in New York the other day from Denmark.

The guy with the Homer Simpson t-shirt let out a big "wooh."

- Are you from Denmark or something? I asked him skeptically from the stage.

- Nah, dude. Been there though.

- I said Denmark, not Denny's!

My response played on the fact that his physical appearance and crackly burnout drawl did not exactly scream "world traveler", and it caused a loud, joyful reaction from the crowd, including from the burnout in question. I then went back to the joke I had started, continuing where I left off.

- I was telling this guy from Denmark that in America laws are different depending on where you are. Say you're in Los Angeles, I explained to him. Something that's legal there might not be legal here in New York. I asked him, "Is it like that in Denmark? Like if something is legal in Copenhagen would it necessarily be legal in say, you know, for example, ahhhh, some other city in Denmark. There's more than one right?"

I should mention that that never really happened. I never had such a conversation with a Dane or anyone else. Many of my jokes never happened in quite the manner presented in my act, if they happened at all. Please bear that in mind while reading this memoir as I may not always point it out explicitly.

- It's been quite a year, I continued. I'm famous now apparently. Not household name famous but too famous for public bathrooms. My public bathroom days are over. I don't wanna be reading on Twitter,

"Ira Spiro just clogged the toilet at Best Buy. What did he eat at that Christmas party?"

This reference to my recent (and only) film was not lost on the audience who greeted it with generous laughter and applause. I followed it up with a couple more jokes about the inconveniences of fame before trying to transition to another topic.

- Was living in LA for a while. I live in New York now.

- How's Harlee? a bespectacled young man, sitting not far from the guy who claimed to have been to Denmark, shouted from the audience.

He was referring to my then-girlfriend, Harlee Shaw. At the time Harlee wasn't quite the superstar actress she is now, but she wasn't far away from it, and I anticipated the possibility that someone would bring her name up during the show. I had a response ready.

- Make a deal with you. Let's leave significant others out of this. Don't ask me about my girlfriend, I won't ask you about your sock.

The audience loved that line, and, once again, no one more so than the young man to whom it was directed, thrilled to be part of the show. As I think about it, it would not have worked if it was a woman that had shouted out "How's Harlee?" I hadn't thought of that possibility. I suppose I could have said, "Don't ask me about my girlfriend and I won't ask you about your vibrator," but implying that a woman has no human sexual options is far harsher than implying that a man doesn't, especially if the woman is not traditionally attractive. I would have felt bad saying it, and the audience would have felt bad laughing at it. Had the heckler been a woman, I likely would have just ignored the comment.

- So like I said I live in New York. Home of presidential candidate Donald Trump. Can you believe this guy's running for president?

More than a few boo's could be heard after my mention of "The Donald" as he came to be known in the '80s. Denver is a fairly liberal town, especially the younger people that are more likely to go see comedy shows.

- The whole world is obsessed with this election. But of course, we're the United States. People are obsessed with everything that goes on here. Other countries, no one cares what's happening. I was talking to this dude from Bulgaria the other day. What can I say, I meet a lot of foreigners in New York. Anyway, he's like (in generic Eastern European accent) "You know, we just elected our first female Prime Minister, but I'm sure you've heard this." I'm like, "Don't be too sure." I said to him, "Do you have any idea how slow a news day it would have to be in America for that to make the news here." You'd be watching the news - "Our final story tonight, Bulgaria just elected its first . . . oh wait a minute this just in, there's a cat stuck in a tree. We go now to Scranton, Pennsylvania where a cat is stuck in a tree."

Big laughs. The show was going very well. So far so good. By the way, the Bulgarian guy from this joke was no more real than the Danish guy from the other joke. I should also mention that Bulgaria had not just elected a female Prime Minister, but the audience didn't know that, which kinda proves the point of the joke.

I continued my act and it was going great. How much of it was due to the quality of the performance and how much was due to the excitement of seeing a famous comic in a theater with five thousand other people I cannot say. I do know, however, that I was killing harder than I had ever killed before. And yet my anxiety level started creeping up. Anxiety had never been a major factor for me during an actual performance, but there it was. It was coming at me like a crazed fan that had breached security and jumped up on stage. I was trying to fight it off as I started a joke about a French girl I once dated. In real life her

18

name was Charlotte, but for the joke it was Virginie (pronounced roughly like the word "virgin" and then "ee").

- That's actually a common name in France, I said to the crowd. "Virginie." I guess it's French for "Virginia." Virginie's not a name in English. I suppose it could be an adjective. "You have a comic book collection? Wow. That's kind of virgin-ee. That's a bit no-date-to-the-prom-ee."

As the words to the joke came out of my mouth, I noticed a group of people up front wearing the "Ira Spiro at the Bellco" t-shirts they must have bought just before the show in the lobby. There was also a young girl several rows back wearing an "I love Ira" t-shirt that looked as though she had made it herself and a man near her that seemed to be in his forties who, in the middle of March, was wearing the exact reindeer and snowflake print suit and tie that my character, Lawrence Hummel, wore in one of the scenes of *Jackson Taylor's Christmas Party*. My God these people loved me, I thought. Yet I was not reassured by the love. The anxiety mounted

- So sometimes I'd be out with Virginie and her French friends and she'd be talking to them and switching between English and French.

"What if I couldn't finish the show?" I wondered. Everyone would be so disappointed and I'd be humiliated.

- She'd be switching between English and French. And I don't think it was random. Like one time her friend was like . . .

Before I could finish the sentence I found myself at anxiety level 5 — full-blown panic attack! This had only happened to me one time before, after twenty minutes stuck in an elevator during the blackout of 2003. At least then there was only one witness, a Latin American man who was delivering pizzas. The memory of 9/11 was still fresh in my mind, and I remember asking him if he thought this might be a terrorist attack. *¡Càlmate! ¡Càlmate!* was all he kept saying

19

to me, perhaps lacking sufficient competence in English to say "I rather doubt that your grandmother's condo in New Jersey would be a target of choice for Al Qaeda." Thankfully we were pried out by a janitor before the screaming and crying started, as, make no mistake, it surely would have if a few more minutes had passed without rescue. This time, however, there were five thousand people watching me unravel. They didn't know yet what was going on, and some started laughing assuming that my stopping mid-joke with the color disappearing from my face was somehow part of the act. I had this sensation that I was about to explode. I couldn't hold it together any longer. I needed to get off stage.

- I'm sorry. I think I have food poisoning.

Food poisoning seemed a lot less embarrassing than admitting to a panic attack. After all, anyone can get food poisoning. Only nutcases get panic attacks. I was thankful to have had enough presence of mind to come up with that "ad-lib." I put the microphone in the stand and left the stage, hearing the confused crowd murmuring behind me.

- Are you ok, Ira? asked Audrey as I rushed past her making a wrong turn toward the control room.

I turned back toward her and told her I needed to get to the dressing room, which I found after a few more wrong turns. When I arrived Karen was waiting by the door.

- Ira, what's going on?

- Not feeling well, I answered. Gotta throw up.

- What's the problem? asked my manager Dave, who had just arrived from inside the theater.

Karen informed him of the situation. I had to throw up, or so she believed. I ran to the bathroom inside the dressing room, closing the door behind me. After a couple of seconds, I made the loudest most authentic vomiting sound I could. I don't do impressions or characters

20

on stage as they are not my strong suit, but I will say I can do some mean barfing noises.

The panic had dissipated by this time and was not yet replaced by utter despair at the thought of not having been able to do my damn job. I faked another round of throwing up before emerging from the bathroom and seeing Karen, Dave, Audrey and the house manager of the theater, let's call him Todd, standing there.

- Are you feeling better? Can you go back on? asked Todd.

- No I don't think so, I replied. I need to get back to the hotel.

When Karen, Dave and I arrived at the Marriott I ran to the lobby bathroom, pretending I had to throw up again and was unable to make it to my room. I was trying to make the food poisoning story as convincing as possible. Back in my room, I called up my girlfriend Harlee Shaw. She didn't pick up and I left a message explaining what had happened. Then I went on Twitter to send a message to my 1.5 million followers:

- Got sick on stage in Denver. Heaving my guts out at the Marriott, I tweeted.

The next time I looked at Twitter was a couple of days later when I logged on to cancel my account.

The last thing I wanted to do was stay in Denver. It was the scene of the greatest disaster of my career, and I needed a change of scenery fast. I had no desire to spend five hours cooped up on a commercial airliner with members of the public, many of whom were perhaps aware of what had just happened, news traveling fast in the social media era. So I chartered a Gulfstream 5 one way from Rocky Mountain Metropolitan Airport in Denver to Teterboro Airport in New Jersey for later that night. I figured in a couple of hours I could credibly tell Dave and Karen that I felt well enough to travel and that we'd be flying back private.

I wanted to get home so badly, and avoid the public so badly, that I dropped 35k for the Gulfstream after having made nothing for my much-abridged show at the Bellco, for which the theatre had to refund every dollar. Of course, I still had to pay the theater the fifteen thousand dollar rental fee, and I owed Karen five thousand as my opening act. I could have gotten an opener for far less, but it's always more fun to work with a friend and of course, since she's a friend, I felt the need to be generous. Though not obligated to do so, I felt so bad that I gave Dave a check for his ten percent commission on what he would have made. He ripped it up, thankfully.

When packing to leave for the airport, I neglected to put the outfit I had worn at the show in my suitcase, preferring to leave behind any tangible reminder of what had happened. According to a picture of me clutching my stomach and heading offstage that I recently found online, the outfit consisted of dark brown denim pants, a blue shirt with a white diamond pattern and, I assume, a pair of shoes, though they were not visible in the picture. I never wear a watch, but even if I had been wearing a ten thousand dollar Rolex, I might well have left that behind at the hotel as well. As I said, I didn't want any reminders of that evening, and what's more, the thought had crossed my mind that it would be bad luck to wear those clothes in the future, permeated as they were by the evil spirits of onstage calamity. They would be found by housekeeping and placed in the lost and found for a period of time after which, having remained unclaimed, they would be thrown away or given to charity. Hotels, I had heard, never call up guests to tell them if they've left something behind. The reason is that people often lie to their significant others as to their whereabouts, and hotel management tries to avoid awkward scenarios where an unsuspecting wife says, "What do you mean my husband left his tie in his suite this weekend. He told me he was at his parents' house!"

CHAPTER 3

Ira's debacle in Denver was picked up by several print and online publications in America, and even some overseas media covered the story, including a popular comedy blog in England which declared, "Yank Comic Ira Spiro Forced to Leave Stage Due to Dodgy Stomach Bug." Ira did his best to ignore all of this, and he closed his Twitter account before seeing any of the comments and jokes people were making about the incident. Several people tweeted that Ira's next tour would be sponsored by Tums. One person said it would be sponsored by Phenergan, which was more accurate as Phenergan, unlike Tums, actually is effective against food poisoning, but since the drug is less well known the tweet got few likes. Another person tweeted "@IraSpiro no one expects you to bring the house down, but at least keep your food down." The tweeter in question was, in fact, Ira's friend and fellow comedian Tony Powell. One mean-spirited individual tweeted that since Ira couldn't finish his show the audience shouldn't get their money back, but rather should have to pay extra. The opposite sentiment was expressed by @IHeartIra, Ira's biggest fan on Twitter, who said that seeing only twenty minutes of Ira Spiro was still a better show than a full hour of any other comic. @IheartIra tweeted frequently in the intervening years how much he wished Ira would return to touring as a stand-up. The wish had, thus far, gone unfulfilled. The incident had shaken Ira's confidence and, as mentioned, he stopped

23

doing stand-up altogether, only recently returning to do low-pressure fifteen-minute performances at the Comedy Den where he was one of several comics and not the focal point of the show.

The Sunrise Cafe was the restaurant above the Comedy Den. It was owned by Brian Rezak, the same person who owned the Comedy Den itself, and the comedians frequently hung out there after their performances. Sometimes they even stopped by when they weren't performing just to spend time at what had for years been the center of the New York City comedy scene. Out-of-towners often stumbled on the American bistro-style restaurant with the low-key rustic decor while exploring Greenwich Village, completely unaware it was affiliated with a well-known comedy club just downstairs. How surprised they were to see many comedians they knew from television and film there, sometimes calmly talking with their friends, other times being boisterous and drunk.

Seated at one of the tables on a typically busy Thursday night were Tony Powell, author of the "keep your food down" tweet, and Karen Lee, who had opened for Ira on that fateful night in Denver and had just gotten off stage minutes before. Tony and Karen were discussing a recent bad date Karen had had on Bumble when Ira walked into the restaurant. Tony, noticing him out of the corner of his eye, called out to him.

- Lawrence Hummel! shouted Tony, loud enough to startle half the customers in the restaurant.

Lawrence Hummel was the character Ira played in *Jackson Taylor's Christmas Party*. In part because of Tony's loud bellowing announcement, several customers recognized him as he walked across the restaurant, including one woman who walked over and asked for a picture. Ira politely obliged and then walked toward Tony and Karen. Tony stood up to greet him.

24

- Give me some love, Spiro, said Tony, stretching out his arms for a hug in typical lightly inebriated Tony Powell fashion.

Ira, though not a huge fan of male-on-male affection, gave Tony a quick hug.

-Ira Spiro superhero! said, or rather sang, Karen, in an improvised melody, as Ira sat down at the table.

Though Karen herself would have disagreed, it was thought almost universally among the male comics, and a lot of male comedy fans, that she was quite attractive. But to Ira, with her dark curly hair, at least on the rare occasions she didn't use a straightener, and her olive complexion, not to mention her occasional use of Yiddish expressions, she seemed too much a younger version of his cousin, Shari Spiro, to be an object of sexual desire. Not that Ira didn't have a crush on Shari as a kid, but the cousin-crush phase of life doesn't usually last into double digits, and Ira was nearly 39.

- You on the show tonight N****?

Tony had a habit of using the N-word quite liberally, using it to refer to people of all races. As an African-American he was, Ira supposed, authorized to do so, but Ira found it somewhat jarring, though by this time he was more or less used to it.

- I'm not on the schedule, but I'm gonna hop on the next show. I got a joke I wanna try out for a corporate gig I have coming up.

- Hold up. You doing a corporate gig? Like a full-length show?

- Ira that's so great! added Karen.

- Ira back y'all! shouted Tony for all in the restaurant to hear, after which he downed a shot of tequila. This is the biggest news around here since Kevin got a customer's order right, he quipped.

- Very funny Tony, said Kevin, a fifteen-year veteran of the Comedy Den waitstaff, as he crossed in front of their table carrying a tray of nachos, cheese fries and chicken wings smothered in an orange-colored hot sauce the approximate hue of his hair.

25

- Love you, Kevin.

- Don't say it unless you mean it, Tony, said Kevin en route to deliver his tray of unhealthy fried fare.

Tony was a favorite of pretty much all the waiters and waitresses, as he was always full of fun, festive energy and, most importantly, he tipped well, which was the main criterion by which the staff judged the comedians they regularly interacted with. In addition, several of them, including Kevin, appreciated Tony's lean sculpted physique which was a product of both natural endowments and frequent workouts at an upscale Manhattan boxing gym.

- Where's the gig, Ira? inquired Karen.

- Maryland. Ocean City. Some big insurance company. It's for their annual something or other.

- Yeah those big companies are always having annual something or others, said Tony. Sounds lucrative. What they payin' you, Spiro?

- I can't believe you're asking that Tony. What a schmuck, said Karen in a playful tone.

- It's a nice chunk of dough, responded Ira to Tony's indiscrete question.

- How much, Spiro? You know I get curious when I'm drunk! Karen, how many men you been with?

- Still a virgin Tony.

- The butt counts Karen!

- You're being just plum silly Tony.

- Plum silly is as plum silly does. Now talk to me Spiro, continued Tony, pursuing his previous line of questioning. How many digits? Mid-five-figures?

- Probably a lot more than that. Wait, we still talking about how many men Karen's been with?

26

- You're the best, Spiro! said Tony with a big laugh. Kevin, get this man a tequila shot, he shouted to Kevin, who was now taking an order at a table no less than fifteen feet away. And one for me and Karen.

Mid-five-figures is the kind of money Ira used to get for a gig and often more back when he was a hot name in show biz. An Arab sheik once paid him to perform at his birthday in Dubai for 100k. But as he was no longer in the spotlight, his price had dropped.

- Since you're not gonna stop hounding me, they're paying me twenty-five grand.

Karen, feeling she hadn't gotten her share of laughs in the conversation, jumped in.

-That's amazing Ira, you can finally get a decent coffee table!

Getting the laughs she needed, Karen excused herself to go the bathroom.

- Damn good money, said Tony. Who negotiated that for you? Your man Dave Rothman?

- Yeah Dave.

- Dave can negotiate. He a tenacious N****.

Had Ira responded to this by saying "Yes he is," he would be, it seemed to him, agreeing that Dave is, indeed, a tenacious N****, thus indirectly using the N-word. Perhaps Ira was overthinking things, but he decided to respond in a different way.

- Dave is definitely tenacious!

Kevin, the russet-haired waiter, came over with the three tequila shots Tony had ordered via long-distance shout. Neither Tony, nor Karen nor Ira had to pay for drinks at the Sunrise Cafe, but Tony slipped Kevin a much appreciated twenty-dollar bill. At that moment Doug Greco, who was M.C.'ing the show downstairs, came over to Ira.

- You wanna go on next, Ira?

- Sure Doug. That works.

- Ok, should be in about two minutes.

- Cool. I'll come down now.

- Hold up Spiro, said Tony. You got a couple minutes. Do this shot with me first.

- I don't drink before I go on. I get all slurry in the speech department, said Ira as he got up to follow Doug downstairs to the Comedy Den.

- You and Karen leaving me alone with three tequila shots? This could end badly.

Ira waited at the bottom of the stairs in front of the entrance to the Comedy Den showroom as Doug did a few minutes of jokes to "reset" the crowd after Stu Healy, the previous comic, had performed. Stu was a musical act. He played guitar and sang funny songs. Stu had ended his set with a song about a guy with a panty-sniffing fetish. It was sung to the tune of U2's "With or Without You" and was called "With or Without Poo". To summarize the song, this particular panty-sniffer wasn't all that fussy. It was beyond lowbrow, but always killed with the audience, and Ira himself couldn't help but laugh whenever he heard it. After something that outrageous Doug needed to get the crowd back into traditional stand-up mode before bringing Ira to the stage.

Ira took a quick look at a piece of paper in his pocket where he had written the new joke he wanted to test. It was a joke about flying. New York City-based comics generally avoided airline jokes, as they were seen as hackneyed. The prejudice against such jokes was not entirely rational. It was quite possible to craft a well-written joke about airlines, but the whole subject was considered overdone and too "1980's." Crowds still enjoyed them, but among most of the Comedy Den comics, it was something to avoid. That said, one could never have too many airline jokes when doing corporate shows. In general, performing at corporate shows meant being as inoffensive as possible.

28

The audience was made up of people who work together and thus have to behave professionally with each other. An obscene or politically incorrect joke would make everyone uncomfortable. "Can I laugh at a sexual joke in front of a female colleague?" they would wonder. "Can I laugh at a racial joke in front of a minority colleague?" Jokes about something as banal as airline travel, on the other hand, fit the bill perfectly. Not that any joke about flying was necessarily appropriate. Early in his career, Ira had written the following joke:

I was flying on Delta a couple of years ago during the Super Bowl, and the pilot would announce the score periodically. That's how important the Super Bowl is here in America. I wonder if they announce different things on airlines in other countries. Like you'd be flying on Aeromexico and hear, "Señor y señoras this is your captain speaking. I have news about the cockfight. Pedro the rooster, winner and still champion".

That joke was only in Ira's rotation a short while. It was too politically incorrect for corporate shows and too airline-based for most anywhere else.

- Ladies and Gentleman, are you ready for your next act?

Doug was about to announce Ira. Ira put the scrap of paper in his pocket and started walking into the showroom. It was a tiny room, which often surprised people given the importance of the club in the stand-up comedy universe. The one hundred twenty or so people in the audience sat in two rows. There were wooden chairs at small round tables in the front and large booths against the wall in the back. The stage, approximately five feet by five feet, was about six inches off the floor and about two inches in front of the front row. Club owner Brian Rezak had decided against a brick wall behind the stage, a frequent comedy club feature, and opted for wood paneling and a neon "Comedy Den" sign.

- You know him as the writer and one of the stars of *Jackson Taylor's Christmas Party*. Please welcome to the stage Ira Spiro.

One could gauge a comic's level of fame by the amount of applause that followed the announcement of his name at the Comedy Den. Three years prior, Ira would have been enveloped in thunderous cheering as he made his way toward the stage. The response in more recent times, however, was about mid-way between the aforementioned thunderous cheering and the base level of applause afforded to any comic, even those who were largely unknown, such as Stu Healy. It was an enthusiastic response to be sure, but a controlled one. Sometimes a comic would come in that was so famous that the initial applause were moderate, as the audience didn't quite believe the person was really there, and then the room would erupt in an explosive frenzy when he or she actually hit the stage. Such was the reaction when the late Robin Williams would stop by the club to perform. Such would be the reaction if Eddie Murphy ever showed up.

- Keep it going for Doug Greco! said Ira to the audience, giving the MC the standard "outro."

As the applause died down Ira launched into his set.

- Hey, I won an Academy Award three years ago. Best original screenplay. This year I'm up for another award. Worst career leveraging of an Academy Award. I'm right up there with post-Oscar career decline legends like Roberto Benigni and that woman who played Nurse Ratched in *One Flew Over the Cuckoo's Nest*. No, I'm kidding things are going great. Quick question. What are Oscar statues selling for on eBay?

Audiences love when people who have been in films or on television, whom they perceive as all being rich and living exciting lives, show vulnerability, and they responded with eager laughter to Ira's out-of-the-gate self-deprecation.

- I was dating this girl from France. She spoke English but made a lot of errors. Her use of prepositions was particularly dicey. She'd say things like "I am going AT 'ze store." Or "Last year I came IN America." Instead of saying "came 'to' America" she'd say "came 'in' America." That's actually a common mistake. I know cause I was in Paris and some French dude asked me "When did you come in France?" I'm like "I haven't yet. I'm a little tired from the jet lag. Maybe when I get to the hotel if they have wifi."

The audience loved that joke as they always did. It was one of Ira's surefire crowd pleasers.

- Anyway, we broke up. I'm single now. 38 and single with no kids, which is good cause summer's in a couple months. Summer is hard for parents cause the kids are around all the time. Parents love their kids, just not in excessive doses. My parents sent me to summer camp. Wasn't even my idea. One day they said "Ira, guess what. You're going to camp this summer!" I said, "Do I have to?" They said, "It'll be fun." I said, "Really?" They said, "Yeah, we'll have the house to ourselves. Some peace and quiet for a change. It'll be great!" I went to sleepaway camp in Maine the year I was going into fifth grade. Got beaten up by an older kid. He wasn't a camper. He was the bully from my neighborhood. Came up on visiting day.

Normally, Ira might do a few more tried and true bits before testing a new joke, but the audience was fully on his side by this time. As Ira found trying out new material unpleasant and stressful, there was a lot to be said for getting it over with.

- I flew to Vegas recently. Flying's not what it used to be. Everything used to be included. They'd give you something to eat, a deck of cards, a blanket. Now you gotta pay for all that stuff. On my way to Vegas, they made me pay fifty bucks to check my bag. Everything is extra. I'm surprised they don't have a slot for your credit card next to where the oxygen mask comes down. You're falling out of the sky, and you're trying to swipe your card. (Ira flails his arms over his head simulating trying to swipe a credit card in an out-of-control aircraft).

The joke didn't get enormous laughs nor were enormous laughs expected. But it did well enough to include in Ira's corporate gig repertoire. Now it was time to finish his set and get out without Tony seeing him, lest he be pressured into drinking that shot of low-end Comedy Den tequila.

CHAPTER 4

It was early afternoon on a Friday. Although his corporate show in Ocean City, Maryland wasn't until the next evening, Ira decided to go down the day before. He wanted to separate the stress of travel from the stress he always felt the day of a show. He'd rent a car and drive down, have a nice meal at the hotel, maybe have a swim in the pool and take a long soak in the hot tub, then watch a movie, go to bed and wake up on show day without having to worry about getting to the destination. Packing was an easy affair as he'd only be gone two nights. The most essential items were his clothes for the show. Ira was generally indifferent about his outfits, but certain occasions called for a greater sartorial effort, and a well-paying corporate gig was such an occasion. He packed a light blue Ted Baker paisley shirt, a pair of Alden brown suede loafers, and a two-piece navy micro-dot suit by Ermenegildo Zegna. Another non-optional item, along with the usual toiletries, was a couple of Xanax pills. Ira did not want a repeat of the panic attack he had suffered at the Bellco Theater in Denver. Given that Ira hadn't done comedy outside of New York City since then, many had already assumed that there was a psychological issue at play, and if he tried to claim yet another case of food poisoning on stage, no one would believe it. But .25 milligrams of the popular anti-anxiety drug, taken about a half-hour before showtime, would hopefully eliminate that danger.

Ira went into the bathroom and slid open the medicine cabinet. Laid out before him were anti-histamines, band-aids, aspirin, a thermometer, a few two-packs of Nyquil, cologne and several toothbrushes. He got a new one from his dentist after each visit but never used them, preferring his electric one. One thing he did not see was his bottle of Xanax. He could swear he had a few left. Then he remembered he had taken some three months before on a flight coming back from Florida after a quick visit with his mother who had been injured riding a moped in Key West.

Ira hated flying. Despite the favorable statistics, he was always nervous slicing through the stratosphere in a metal tube, and the flight from Florida that day was particularly turbulent. One pill was insufficient to stave off an impending anxiety attack, so he took a second and then, when it seemed like even that wasn't doing the job, a third. His next memory was being awoken in Florida by the flight attendant. He got off the plane still in a benzodiazepine fog and had to sit at the arrival gate for about an hour until alert enough to navigate his way out of the airport. A fan had sat down next to him to talk about comedy for several minutes but, when thinking about the incident afterward, Ira was still unsure if the conversation with the fan was a dream or not. Since the fan had not taken a selfie to post on social media, there was no tangible proof one way or the other.

Apparently, Ira had neglected to get a new prescription. Since he'd never get hold of his doctor at that hour on a Friday, he needed to figure out another way to get his hands on some Xanax. "Ok," he thought. "I'll text Stephanie."

"Where the hell is she?" thought Ira as he sat at the bar nursing a club soda with lime. Stephanie was supposed to meet him at Alistair's Pub at 6:30 pm and it was now almost 7. Not that he was too surprised. Stephanie was seldom on time for anything unless it was an audition. Ira thought to himself that she would likely also be sufficiently motivated to show up on time for a film or TV shoot, but since she never actually booked any acting jobs, that was a matter of pure speculation. Ira had abandoned the idea of leaving for Maryland that night, but better to arrive the day of the show with Xanax than the day before without.

Two hands suddenly reached around from behind Ira's head and covered his eyes.

- Guess who!

- I don't know. Could it be Stephanie Delsano? responded Ira.

- Apparently you still recognize my voice, said Stephanie, taking her hands off Ira's eyes and wrapping her arms around his neck.

- Well yes, and also who else but Stephanie Delsano would cover my eyes and say "guess who" at the bar where I was supposed to meet her, at the time I was supposed to meet her, give or take a half-hour.

- What do you mean? You said to meet you at 7, Stephanie protested.

- 6:30. Check the text, Ira insisted.

- Sorry. I would have been here at 6:30, but I was tied up on the phone with my father.

Ira didn't see the need to point out the contradiction of Stephanie first saying she thought they were supposed to meet at 7 and then saying she would have been there at 6:30. What purpose would it serve?

- How's your father?

- Annoying. Still trying to convince me to go back to school. Can't wait till I'm a famous actress and don't have to listen to his shit anymore.

With that, Stephanie released Ira from her grip, hopped on the stool next to him and ordered a vodka tonic. Ira had made it clear to Stephanie in the text that he just wanted some Xanax, for which he was willing to reimburse her, and then was planning to head home for a good night's sleep before driving to Maryland in the morning. Stephanie, it seemed, was trying to turn what was to be a brief transaction into a date.

- Do I look pretty tonight, Ira?

- Yes you look pretty. Like always.

- As pretty as pretty can be?

- Of course, he said, wondering how long this line of questioning would continue.

- Am I the fairest of them all?

If not the fairest of them all, Stephanie was fairer than most. In fact, she was breathtaking. She had chopped off her long tresses and was sporting an adorable deep brown bob that perfectly framed her exquisite face and gave her the look of a 1920's silent film star. She wore a white shoulderless mini dress that hugged her generous curves. Physically, Ira found her perfect. On the other hand, there was a reason he had ended the romance. Stephanie was emotionally unstable, at times professing her undying love for Ira, at other times her intense disgust at the very sight of him. In truth, Ira found both sentiments equally disquieting.

- The very fairest, responded Ira. So, do you have it?

- Have what? asked Stephanie, after guzzling a huge mouthful of vodka tonic like it was Gatorade after a hard-fought first half.

- What do you mean "have what?" The Xanax!

- Oh shit. I forgot.

- Forgot? That's kinda why I came all the way down here to the Lower East Side!

- Have a drink and then we'll go to my place and get it. What are you drinking?

- I'd really prefer not to drink tonight, protested Ira.

- Maker's Mark, neat, Stephanie shouted out to the bartender, mistakenly remembering that as Ira's preferred drink.

In reality, Ira had no preferred drink. When he did drink, it was usually a glass of red wine as he had read that red wine is good for cardiac health. Ira slowly sipped his way through his glass of bourbon while Stephanie tore through two more vodka tonics, talking about her recent auditions and her anger at her father for trying to encourage her to study nursing and forget about acting.

At about 8:30 they were back at Stephanie's apartment on Ludlow street. The last time Ira was there Stephanie had thrown him out after a heated argument. Stephanie was furious that Ira was unable to help her get signed to a talent agent. The truth is Ira himself was not even signed with a talent agent at the time and even if he were he could have done little more than pass along Stephanie's acting reel. His endorsement would have meant little. His name was Spiro, not Spielberg.

Stephanie's apartment was what one might expect of a struggling actress in her mid-twenties. It was a grimy studio on the fourth floor of an old tenement building. The white paint on the walls was cracking and dotted with nicotine stains. The bare wood floor was uneven, subtly sloping such that if one placed a ball on it next to the bathroom at one end of the apartment, it would slowly roll toward the window on the opposite end until its journey was interrupted by one of the numerous obstacles laying about such as an article of clothing, a theater script or a pizza box of not necessarily recent vintage.

An already inebriated Stephanie returned from the tiny cluttered kitchen into the living room/bedroom with a lighted cigarette in her mouth and holding two bottles of beer, one of which she handed to Ira. Ira put the bottle on a desk next to Stephanie's television without taking a sip.

- So what do you wanna do now Ira? she asked after taking a long drag of her cigarette.

Looking at Stephanie in the dim light of her apartment, there was little room for doubt as to what her intentions were — her head gently tilted to one side as she stared intensely into Ira's eyes. She finished off the rest of her beer in one gulp, put the bottle down on the desk, crushed out her cigarette in an ashtray perched atop of a stack of headshots, grabbed Ira around the neck and kissed him. When Ira had broken up with her she cried and screamed and wished him a painful death. A couple of months later she texted him that she had found someone new and was hoping they could remain friends. He had thought, perhaps naively, that indeed they could be just friends.

- So you're no longer seeing that guy?

- What guy?

- You know, that guy you were seeing. I think he's a DJ or something.

- Bradley? No, that's been done for a while.

- Well, like I told you, I wasn't really looking to hang out too long. Do you have that Xanax? Ira asked hesitatingly, knowing the question would likely be met with some measure of anger.

- So that's your plan? You're just gonna drink my beer, take my Xanax and leave?

- I haven't touched the beer, thought Ira.

- You know what, I'm fucking done with you, she screamed while punching Ira as hard as she could in the shoulder.

- Sorry. I probably shouldn't have texted you in the first place, said Ira moving toward the door, rubbing his shoulder.

- Wait, don't leave, said Stephanie, softly grabbing Ira's hand.

Even by Stephanie Delsano standards, this was an abrupt change of mood. Within seconds she had transitioned from hostility to tenderness. Once more she moved in for a kiss. Two opposing forces

38

battled within Ira. He was wildly attracted to Stephanie, as nearly any man would be to a woman with the physical gifts she possessed. At the same time, she was a psychological runaway train, and he was wary of getting back on board. Stephanie's beautiful face and body likely would have won the day, but Ira was anxious about his upcoming show, and thus a sexual encounter was of far lesser interest to him than it otherwise might have been. Of course, if it weren't for his upcoming show, he wouldn't even be there.

- Stephanie I'm gonna go now, he said, pulling himself away from her magnificent soft lips.

- Are you serious?

- My mind is elsewhere. I'm sorry. I have a big show tomorrow. Ira knew better than to ask for that Xanax.

- Alright I'll tell you what. Don't ever fucking text me again or call me or whatever. Fuck you!

The smell of garbage mixed with a sweet, sugary odor from the crepe shop next door greeted Ira as he walked out of Stephanie's building into the New York City twilight.

- *Jackson Taylor!* shouted some random guy through the open window of a cab passing by on Ludlowe Street.

Did he even like the movie? Simply shouting out the title was hardly an indication one way or another, but not wanting to be rude to someone who might be a fan, Ira waved back in his direction then started walking northbound towards Houston Street with no particular destination in mind.

Ira was glad to have extricated himself from an entanglement with Stephanie, but he was still without Xanax. "Maybe I don't need it," he thought as he made his way past the crepe shop. "No. I can't take the chance. I have to get some." Could he leave a message for his doctor and have him call in a prescription? He wanted to leave early in the morning. Maybe his doctor could call it in to a pharmacy in Maryland. "Is that even possible?" he wondered. "To call in a prescription out of state?"

He decided he would go to the Comedy Den. Surely someone there would have something — if not Xanax, maybe a related drug such as Klonopin or Valium. Comics, like actors, are not in general known for stellar mental health or their disdain for psychoactive chemicals.

As Ira walked into the Comedy Den he saw Tony Powell, Karen Lee, Brian Rezack the owner, and a young comedian named Jeff Bunton at the table in the corner. They were involved in what seemed to be a spirited discussion. No doubt it was about some political issue or another. Brian liked political discussions and enjoyed lively debates with the comics. He was originally a lawyer but inherited the club when his father died a few years earlier. Knowing how much his father cherished the club, Brian decided to keep it in the family rather than sell it. Becoming more and more involved in its daily operation, Brian eventually abandoned his law practice, but the argumentative litigator in him remained.

- Ira Spiro! shouted Tony with his characteristic enthusiasm.

- Ira, have a seat, said Brian. We're discussing immigration. Here's the question. How do we balance treating people that come here illegally with humanity with our desire not to encourage more illegal immigration?

- Not sure, Ira responded. But when are we deporting Bunton back to Canada?

- Thank you! I've been asking that for years! added Tony.

Jeff Bunton laughed, taking things in the intended lighthearted spirit. That was enough comic banter for Ira, opting to cut to the chase.

- This is unrelated, but anyone here have any Xanax?

- Why you need Xanax, N***?

40

- Cause pot's not an option, Tony! It makes me paranoid.

- I have some, but it's at home, offered Jeff.

- I ain't goin' to Toronto.

- My home is Brooklyn now, Ira. Green card coming soon!

At this point, Brian was getting slightly annoyed that the conversation had strayed from the intellectual debate on immigration he had been enjoying.

- So what's the green card process like? asked Brian, trying to steer the discussion back in the desired direction.

- Jeff got that Canadian universal healthcare Xanax, interjected Tony, thwarting Brian's attempt.

- Yeah, added Karen. His mom ships him a bottle every month with a bag of ketchup potato chips.

Everyone laughed at Karen's joke, except Brian who, in addition to being annoyed about the new direction of the conversation, did not know that ketchup potato chips were a beloved Canadian favorite. The comics knew, as they traveled frequently and had all performed at one or more of the numerous comedy clubs in that country.

- I love those, said Jeff. Nothing like relaxing on the couch with a bag of ketchup chips and a good curling match on TV.

- Hey Ira!

Blake the waiter was calling to Ira from over by the bar a few feet away. Ira excused himself from the table and walked over to him.

- I have Xanax if you need.

Blake wasn't a comic, but he was in a band. Musicians are another group not known for their disdain for psychoactive chemicals.

- Oh great. You have some on you?

- I only have one, but it's a two-milligram bar.

Blake reached into his pocket and pulled out the bar of Xanax. The bar was striated in four sections, meant to be broken off if the whole dosage was not desired.

- Here you go, said Blake, handing Ira the bar.

- Great. How much do these cost?

- It's ok. I feel like I owe you. You're the best tipper in the place. Well, you and Tony. And Jerry Seinfeld once tipped me two hundred dollars on a burger, but besides them.

- Okay thanks, Blake. And I'll keep the good tips coming.

As he walked out of the Comedy Den he felt the ping of a text message coming from the phone in his pocket. It was, as he suspected, from Stephanie:

- *I'm masturbating* :)

Ira turned off his phone and hailed a cab.

CHAPTER 5

It was an hour before showtime. Ira had arrived at his suite at the Royal Atlantic Hotel and Conference Center in Ocean City, Maryland around 2 pm after a five-hour drive. The combined stress of a show and traveling was indeed intense, and the ride down was marked by heart palpitations and a tension headache that necessitated a stop for Advil at the Clara Barton rest stop on the New Jersey Turnpike.

He felt a bit better once at the hotel and ate a late lunch, took a brief nap and spent the next several hours trying to distract himself as best he could by surfing the web and listening to music while his anxiety level steadily intensified with the approach of showtime. He had not attempted a long stand-up set since that show in Denver that ended with him pretending to vomit in the bathroom backstage. "What if I have another panic attack?" "Will the Xanax work?" These were the thoughts running through his mind as he sat on the bed, already dressed for the show in his Zegna suit, paisley shirt and brown suede loafers, watching the video for Billy Joel's 1989 hit "We Didn't Start the Fire" on YouTube. It was one of his favorite Billy Joel tunes, and he had been upset when he learned that Billy Joel himself had said he thought it was a terrible melody in an interview with Billboard Magazine.

"We didn't start the fire. It was always burning since the world's been turning." Ira sang the iconic chorus along with Billy,

43

usually finding singing helpful in reducing anxiety. In this case, however, it was proving insufficient. He needed to get out and move around a bit. Ira was approaching level 4 on his personal 1 to 5 anxiety scale.

Halfway between the door to his hotel room and the elevator, Ira decided that he may have left the door open, allowing anyone at all to walk in. Whenever Ira thought he hadn't locked a door or had left a space heater on or something of the sort, it turned out to never actually be the case. Not to mention the fact that there was nothing much to steal in the room anyway. But obsessive-compulsive symptoms are not logical, and Ira's always flared up under stress. He went back to the room and, of course, the door was closed and locked. However, he took out his key and opened it, suddenly feeling an overwhelming need to verify that he had turned off the faucet in the bathroom, which, of course, he had. Seconds after leaving the room for the second time he turned around and went back once again to make sure the door was closed. He pulled on the door hard while saying the word "closed" three times out loud, something he was sure to remember if again he came to wonder whether he had indeed closed the door.

Ira took a walk around the hotel grounds. Strolling by the pool he noticed the hot tub next to a man-made waterfall. Perhaps he would grab a cocktail and sit in it after the show. With all the stress gone it would be a formidable hot tub experience.

Ira checked the time on his phone. A half-hour till the show. Time to take the Xanax. He took the pill out of his pocket and broke off a quarter of it. There was a bar on the other side of the pool. He went and asked the bartender for a cup of water, leaving him a couple of bucks for the effort. Ira was always a good tipper, but after becoming famous he got into the habit of tipping even more, lest someone take to social media and announce to the world that he was a cheapskate.

- Thanks, said the bartender. By the way, big fan of *Jackson Taylor*.

- Oh thanks, responded Ira.

Unlike the guy who shouted "*Jackson Taylor!*" at him from the cab on Ludlow street the night before, the bartender explicitly stated he was a fan. Still, Ira wondered whether, given the matter-of-fact tone of his words, he truly liked the film or was just saying it to be nice.

Ira stepped away from the bar area before taking the Xanax so no one would see him popping a pill. To the extent possible, he tried to keep his neuroses a secret. Being extra cautious, the night before he had verified, with the help of Google images, that what Blake the waiter had given him was indeed a two-milligram bar of Xanax.

It was time now to head to the conference room where the show was going to take place and check in with Rose Corbett, the event planner.

- Hi, is this Rose Corbett? said Ira into his cellphone.

- Yes this is Rose.

- This is Ira Spiro. I'm here.

- Where exactly are you?

- I'm standing right next to the "Chesapeake Conference Room" sign.

- Okay great. I'll come meet you in just a second.

People were milling about, casually but smartly dressed, all wearing name tags and most with a cocktail in hand.

- Hey, Ira Spiro, said Bill Defeo, a man in his mid-thirties, as he came over towards Ira. Really looking forward to seeing you perform.

- Thanks Bill, responded Ira, glancing at his name tag.

- Well, just wanted to say hi. Break a leg up there.

"Break a leg," though a common expression among actors, is rarely used by comedians, but it is commonly said to them by members of the public who assume it to be an all-purpose showbiz phrase.

- Thanks, Bill. I'll try!

As Bill Defeo headed off with his glass of scotch, a woman in her early forties approached Ira.

- Ira!

- Rose Corbett?

- In the flesh! So how's everything? Your hotel room okay?

- Yes. It's very nice. Thanks. No complaints.

- Oh good. Yeah, it's a really nice hotel. So, some info about the event. This is the Warren Insurance Group. They're insurance brokers. They deal mostly in casualty and life insurance products, and this is their annual retreat. They have offices all over the northeast so this is a chance for everyone to get together and get to know each other a bit. They really look forward to it all year, so everyone is really in a good mood and ready to laugh.

- Ok great, said Ira. So, I'm doing forty-five minutes?

Indeed Ira's manager Dave had told him he'd be doing a forty-five-minute performance, but, nonetheless, Ira nourished the fervent hope that Rose would say something to the effect of, "You know what. They've had kind of a long day. Let's keep it short a sweet. Thirty minutes tops."

- Yep, forty-five minutes, was Rose's unwelcome response. But if you're having fun you can do a bit longer if you want.

- Sounds perfect, responded Ira, forcing a smile and trying to hide his profound disappointment as best he could. He planned to be offstage not a millisecond after forty-five minutes and in the hot tub with a strong drink shortly after that.

- So, Steve Warren, the CEO, will introduce you at about 8 pm. Your manager gave him your introduction. Meantime, just hang out and I'll come and get you at about five minutes to 8. If you need anything let me know.

- Will do. Thanks, Rose. Nice meeting you.

- Nice meeting you too Ira. Look forward to having a good laugh!

Ira decided to poke his head into the conference room to see what the setup was like.

- Shit! he said to himself out loud.

Ira was hoping to ease back into headlining shows with a somewhat smaller crowd, but there must have been around fifty or sixty tables in the room with about ten seats placed around each one. They had put up a stage facing the tables and on each side of the conference room were enormous monitors showing, at present, Ira's name and publicity photo. Most people were already at their seats engaged in drinking and conversation. Ira thought of the contrast between how relaxed and happy they all seemed and the anxiety he was experiencing that was making it difficult to even stand still. His breathing became heavy, and he was starting to feel lightheaded.

Ira felt himself inching helplessly toward another panic attack. His heart was racing, he was sweating and there was a slight tremble in his right arm. He went to the bar outside the conference room and asked for a glass of water, neglecting to leave his usual tip, as he was preoccupied and it completely slipped his mind. Ira had no choice. He needed to take more Xanax. He walked over to the elevator bank where no one was standing and furtively took what was left of the pill out of his pocket. Such was the state of his mental distraction that he took the entire remaining 1.5 milligrams.

Steve Warren, a large man in his fifties with blonde hair mixed with a generous amount of gray, stood on stage speaking to the crowd as the two video images of him projected on the large screens at each corner of the room did likewise.

- Before we get to our special guest, I just want to thank everyone for another great year.

Ira was standing next to Rose Corbett off to the right of the stage. The Xanax was starting to kick in, and he was feeling somewhat calmer. He was eager to get on stage and get the performance over with. He handed his phone to Rose in order to be as unencumbered as possible on stage.

- Would you mind holding this until after the show?
- Of course. I'll be standing right here when you get off.

Ira thought of those words. "When you get off." What a glorious moment that would be, and he was separated from it by a mere forty-five minutes. And yet, those mere forty-five minutes were like an alligator-filled moat placed between him and that shining castle of psychic tranquility on the other side. "You can do it," he said to himself.

- Has everyone been having fun this weekend? continued Steve Warren from onstage.

A big cheer filled every corner of the Chesapeake Conference Room.

- Well it's about to get even better because we have a very talented man coming to the stage in just a few moments. He wrote and starred in the film *Jackson Taylor's Christmas Party* for which he won the Oscar for best original screenplay, and he is a long-time stand-up comedian who has entertained audiences all across the country. Please give a warm welcome to Ira Spiro.

The audience energetically cheered and applauded, anticipating a great show to top off a great weekend. As Ira walked on stage he felt his body get heavy and was hit with a sudden wave of fatigue. He clicked the start button on the small electronic timer in his pocket. It was set to vibrate after forty-three minutes, leaving him a couple of

48

minutes to finish up his performance. Ira and Steve Warren briefly shook hands, and then Steve walked off the stage and took a seat at a table near the front.

- Thank you Steve for that wonderful introduction. Great to be here tonight. Everyone doing good?

The audience again cheered with gusto.

- Look at this great crowd. Steve Warren throws a hell of a company retreat.

The audience gave yet another cheer.

Ira seldom planned out his performances with any great precision. In general, he simply chose from his repertoire of jokes on the fly. He always knew what joke he was going to start with, however, before taking the microphone. Upon checking in, Ira was given a map of the hotel property and noticed that the gym and spa were in a separate building from the guest rooms, which inspired the following joke: "This is a beautiful hotel, isn't it? They got a great gym and spa here too, but it's a little inconvenient to get to from my room which is in a separate building (slight pause before punchline), at the Red Roof Inn down the street." He at first thought the newly written bit would be a good way to start things off, but then figured that at his level of success the idea that he'd be staying at a Red Roof Inn was so unbelievable as to render the joke ineffective. Instead, he opted to get things rolling with one of his oldest bits. A joke about his first name.

- By the way, Steve is also my father's name, he announced to the audience. My father's name is Steve and my name is Ira. The names are getting more old-fashioned with each generation. If I have a son his name will be Baldric of Lincolnshire.

The audience laughed. So far so good, but the effects of the two milligrams of Xanax Ira had taken were beginning to manifest themselves in slower than normal speech. He was doing his best to fight through the fatigue as he continued with his act.

- I never met a single other "Ira" born after 1960. Like if you played that word association game with someone, where you say a word and they say the first word that comes to mind, it would be like:

Dog! - Cat!

Ice! - Cold!

Ira! - Polio!

More laughter from the crowd.

- By the way, Steve, I'm impressed. You got a lot of people working for you.

Steve nodded and smiled from his seat near the stage.

- Here's something Steve Warren never hears - "Sir would you like to upgrade to economy plus."

This was an all-purpose rich guy joke that Ira had told at many previous corporate events when the head of the company was present. It was the last thing he remembered about his set that night.

The lights were low, but it was bright enough for Ira to see where he was after waking up. It took him a few seconds to realize that he was on a couch in the back of the Chesapeake Conference Room. "What happened?" he wondered. He reached into his pocket and pulled out the timer. It read "6:57:23" and counting. Ira calculated that it must have been about 3 o'clock in the morning. Realizing he had no Xanax left on him, he thought, "Oh my God, I took the entire two-milligram bar!" Ira had an awful feeling that further details of what exactly took place might be found online. He looked for his phone before remembering he had given it to Rose Corbett before going on stage. Next to him on the couch was a Royal Atlantic Hotel and Conference Center pad with a note written on it:

I left your phone at the front desk. Call me tomorrow if you wish to discuss what happened at the show.

Rose Corbett.

Back in his hotel room after retrieving his phone, Ira nervously entered his name into the Google search bar. There was nothing online about the show. That made sense. It was the middle of the night. By tomorrow morning the internet might well be buzzing about Ira Spiro. Even as the embers of fame cool, a sufficiently scandalous or humiliating experience can rekindle them anew, though generally not in any useful way.

Ira knew he would likely get no sleep until he knew more details about the ill-fated Warren Insurance Group comedy event. Of course, he might not get much sleep after that either. Xanax would help, but his limited supply was obviously all gone. It was out of the question to call Rose Corbett at that hour, but she had likely contacted Ira's manager. Dave was generally not up in the middle of the night, but it was worth a shot.

- You have reached Dave Rothman. Please leave a detailed . . .

Ira hung up, not needing to hear Dave's entire voicemail greeting. He spent the next several hours vainly trying to sleep and watching music videos, mostly from the '80s. He also watched an hour-long Discovery Channel documentary on the evolution and death of the sun.

What psychological mechanism lead Ira to make such a viewing choice is open to speculation. Perhaps he was in some way comforted by the idea that in seven billion years the sun, reaching the end of its red giant phase, would have expanded in size so greatly as to engulf the Earth. If even the Earth itself is ephemeral then everything that takes

51

place on it is meaningless, including Ira's apparent Xanax blackout that night on stage.

Indeed, as he was watching the documentary, Ira thought about just how temporary everything is, and how so much of what we deem of great importance will be gone long before that moment when the Earth is vaporized in a nuclear furnace. In a thousand years, Ira imagined, the United States would likely no longer exist, nor the English language as we know it, which would be as incomprehensible to the people in the next millennium as Old English is to us. In ten thousand years there would probably be no separate races or ethnic groups after intermarriage had done its work, and Ira doubted any of the Abrahamic religions would survive that long either. Unless one of their respective Messiahs showed up by then, it seemed a good bet that everyone would have long since just assumed they weren't coming and moved on. In a hundred thousand years, thought Ira, there may be no more intelligent life forms on Earth, which, he joked to himself, didn't necessarily preclude the possibility that Instagram would still be popular.

At about 6:30 am, Ira again put his name into the Google search bar. There it was, an item from TMZ.com - IRA SPIRO FROM JACKSON TAYLOR'S CHRISTMAS PARTY PASSES OUT AT PERFORMANCE IN MARYLAND. There was a video accompanying the headline. Someone in the audience had filmed him and put it online. Ira didn't want to watch, but he needed to know precisely what occurred and, as he would find out anyway, he nervously clicked play. Whoever had filmed him had actually filmed the video of his performance that was simultaneously playing on one of the two large screens that were set up in the conference room. Apparently, he or she was sitting closer to the screen than the stage.

The video started at some point after Ira had told the "Steve Warren never hears 'Sir would you like to upgrade to economy plus'" joke.

- My name is Ira. My father's name is Steve. My name is more old-fashioned than his.

- You already said that! shouted someone from the audience.

Ira was horrified watching himself repeating a joke he had already told and, making matters worse, in a slowed and slurred voice. There had been a chair next to Ira on stage which served as a resting place for a bottle of water in case he needed a sip during the performance. But that evening it would serve another purpose. In the video, Ira is seen moving the bottle of water to the floor and sitting in the chair as he continued his routine.

- I was on a plane in January. The pilot announced the Super Bowl, the winner of the Super Bowl. That's how important the Super Bowl is in America. Maybe in other countries they say other things. The Mexicans like cockfighting. This is your Captain Pedro the cock. Hola señor y señoras.

Ira had completely botched that joke, which was not appropriate for a corporate event in the first place, and his speech had become barely intelligible. There was another minute or so of complete babbling before Ira fell asleep in the chair. This was followed by a lot of commotion in the audience as people were utterly confused, some thinking maybe it was part of the act.

- My wife is a doctor, yelled out someone seated near the person filming. At that point, a woman went on stage and began to examine Ira.

- He's just asleep, she yelled.

Rose Corbett went on stage and was able to wake Ira sufficiently to be able to walk him off the stage. The camera phone panned as she walked Ira over to the couch in the back of the room where, apparently, he would remain for the next seven hours.

- Let's all move to the bar area, Steve Warren could be heard saying off-camera. The open bar will continue out there.

The video continued for another few seconds as Ira settled onto the couch and fell back asleep.

After watching the video, Ira packed for the trip home, leaving his expensive shirt, shoes and loafers on the bed so as to never have to see them again. Throughout the day more stories about Ira appeared online. And of course, there was Twitter. Several people tweeted along the lines of "Normally it's the audience that falls asleep when Ira performs." Though untrue — audiences usually enjoyed Ira — this was the obvious joke to make and many made it. Referencing the waiter who gave Ira the Xanax, his friend Tony Powell tweeted, "I blame @DrummerBlakeSamson #IraSpiro." Coming to Ira's defense once again was @IHeartIra who tweeted "Ira will come back better than ever!" There was also a tweet, completely unrelated to the incident, from Stephanie Delsano - "Ira Spiro needs to come out of the closet."

CHAPTER 6

Ira walked into his apartment after a brief trip down to the lobby of his building to grab his mail. Dave Rothman had sent back his twenty-five hundred dollar commission check, ten percent of the twenty-five thousand he was supposed to make for his performance in Maryland. As with his performance in Denver, Ira felt obligated to pay the commission even though he made no money for the show, and as with the show in Denver, his manager refused to accept it. Ira's face was now adorned with a quarter-inch of beard growth. He wished once again to be as unrecognizable as possible, as he had wished at the height of the popularity of his film. He had left his apartment only when absolutely necessary in the two weeks since the ill-fated show. When he did, there were always people coming up to him and inquiring as to his well-being, not to mention the people who said nothing, but who were surely looking at him and thinking, "That's Ira Spiro. He fell asleep in the middle of his act."

It is true that people were generally nice and legitimately concerned, but Ira didn't feel like being the object of sympathy, and he certainly didn't feel like being reminded what had happened. He even stopped going to the gym, even though working out had always proven an effective way to boost his mood. He had also canceled all his scheduled performances at the Comedy Den. When he wasn't retreating into the unconscious bliss of a long nap, he spent time watching videos about asteroid strikes, extreme volcanic activity and other possible human extinction scenarios.

Still, Ira did not cut himself off totally from the outside world. He left his phone on and occasionally checked emails, and there were numerous texts and emails from those wondering how he was doing. He responded to only the most persistent among them, including his friend Karen Lee who threatened, via a message on his voicemail, to show up at his apartment if he did not call back. The message ended with a tune, sung by Karen to the melody of Blondie's "Call Me": "Call me Ira Spiro, You can call me any any time. Call me, Ira Spiro, you can call me or a text is fine." Preferring the text option, he wrote her that everything was OK but that he needed some time to himself.

His mother had called only one time in the preceding two weeks, but it had nothing to do with what had happened in Maryland, of which, it seemed, she was completely ignorant. She simply called to notify Ira that the rent had gone up at her condo in Florida and that she would be needing more money from him every month to help with the payment. Apparently, her new boyfriend Frank, who had just moved in with her, was not capable of making up the difference.

Falling onto the couch for his second nap of the day, he received a text message from Dave Rothman - *"Please call me. Got an offer. Not stand up. Big $."* The key phrases in that message were *"Not stand up"* and *"Big $"* and proved sufficient to spur Ira to make a phone call.

- Ira! said Dave, happy hear from his oldest client again.

- Hey Dave.

- How ya feelin'?

- Been better.

- I know. I know. By the way, I sent you back the commission check from . . .

- Yeah I just got it, interrupted Ira. You deserve the money, but I won't argue with you. What's this offer you texted me about?

- It's a little odd. This writer guy wants to work with you on a memoir.

- Memoir? What are you talking about?

- This guy, hold on I wrote down his name. Miles Breakstone. He says he's ghostwritten memoirs for some big people. He can't say who cause I guess when you're a ghostwriter you can't say. Anyway, he's working for this Italian publishing company that's trying to get into the US market.

- I don't know. A memoir? You know I like to keep my life as private as possible.

- They're offering an advance of $300,000.

Entering the Starbucks on 81st street and Broadway, Ira looked around for Miles Breakstone, the ghostwriter. Ira had initially refused the meeting, but Dave had managed to negotiate the offer up from $300,000 to a rather shocking half-million, which was enough for him to overcome his hesitation at the idea of telling the details of his life to the public, although just barely enough.

There was a man wearing glasses sitting by himself in the corner talking on his phone with an iced coffee in front of him. He had on jeans and a Rolling Stones t-shirt, which is what Ira was told Miles would be wearing. Ira walked toward the table. Before he arrived the man noticed Ira and gave him a big wave.

- Sorry. I'm just finishing up a phone call, said Miles.

Miles then uttered a few phrases in Italian before hanging up.

- Nice to finally meet you, Ira. I've been a fan for years.

Ira thanked Miles for the kind words.

Miles Breakstone looked to be in his early fifties. He was about 5'8' and generally thin, albeit with a slight paunch. He looked a bit like a clean-shaven version of Sigmund Freud. Ira, by contrast, was at that moment sporting a three-week beard, which was a far lighter brown, to the point of being almost blonde, than the hair atop his head.

- I like the beard, said Miles.

- It's a new look I'm toying with.

- What do you want? offered Miles. I'm having an iced coffee. It's delicious.

- Nothing actually. I'm fine.

Ira sat down, feeling a bit nervous about the whole affair.

- Alright, began Miles, I'm not sure what your manager told you but here are the broad strokes. I was recently hired by Bartolacci US, a new division of Bartolacci Editore, an Italian publisher.

- I guess that explains the Italian you were speaking when I walked in.

- Exactly. All that Italian I took in college finally found a use. Anyway, they brought me in to help them break into the American market. My experience is ghostwriting memoirs and autobiographies, so that's where we're gonna focus to start.

Miles explained to Ira how the deal would work. The advance would be $500,000 against future royalties, of which the first $100,000 would be paid upon signature of the contract. Miles and Ira would work together on the memoir, and the final version would be subject to Ira's approval. A second payment of $100,000 would be paid to Ira after completion of an initial draft. The final payment of $300,000 would be paid upon completion of the final version of the memoir approved by both parties. Everything discussed between Ira and Miles would be confidential and nothing that did not make the final version would be revealed to anyone by Miles.

At home after the meeting, Ira found nothing online about Miles Breakstone but, as his manager had mentioned, a ghostwriter is by nature someone who flies under radar. There was information on

Bartolacci Editore which was, indeed, a large Italian publisher specializing mostly in novels and short story collections. Ira signed the contract that week in Miles's office in Midtown Manhattan and received a check from Bartolacci US for a hundred thousand dollars, of which he gave ten thousand to his manager Dave as commission.

- This is a really beautiful place, said Miles Breakstone as he walked into Ira's apartment.
- Thanks. My ex made me buy it.
- Is that Moonlight Garden?
- What?
- That lithograph on your wall. It's Miro's Moonlight Garden I believe.
- Could be. Wouldn't rule it out. So, I don't really have an office per se. Why don't we just do our thing here in the living room?

Ira had decided it would be more convenient to have Miles come to him instead of making constant trips to Miles's office. He had alerted one of his doormen that Miles would be coming frequently and that he should in turn tell the other doormen that Miles is authorized to enter the building each time he came. Ira also felt the need to tell him that they were writing something together, lest there be gossip among the doormen as to who this gentleman was that was visiting Ira on a regular basis. Ira would have preferred a building without a doorman for reasons of privacy, but Harlee Shaw had insisted. The doormen provided greater security, which was particularly important to her when she came over.

Miles sat down on Ira's white leather Giorgetti swivel armchair and took out a digital voice recorder which he placed on the absurdly expensive designer coffee table between him and Ira, who was seated on his blue three-seater sofa, designed by Antonio Citterio for Vitra of Switzerland. Ira would have been happy with all Ikea furniture, but, of course, Harlee Shaw and her decorator friend Giovanni decided otherwise.

- That a recorder? asked Ira, a bit surprised.

- Yes, it's a lot easier than trying to write everything down. But as discussed, and it says this in the contract, everything is confidential until approved by you for the final published version of the memoir. I'll take the recordings back to my office and use them to write up each chapter and then, when it's all done, you can make any changes or edits you want.

- What are we gonna call this thing?

- We don't have to decide that yet. Something will come to us I'm sure.

- Alright so where should we start? Where I was born? East Brunswick, New Jersey in 19 . . .

- We don't have to go in perfect chronological order. Also, this is a memoir, not an auto-biography. We don't need every detail of your life. Let's just talk about things as they come up and then we can decide the best order later. Perhaps we can start off by talking about your first time doing stand-up.

- Well, my first time doing stand-up was in 2003.

- Set the scene for me. Tell me about it, as best you can remember.

- Some of the details are foggy.

- Doesn't matter. Not every detail has to be perfectly accurate, as long as the major details are correct. Let's just get the essence of what happened.

CHAPTER 7

IRA SPIRO BEFORE COVID: A MEMOIR - CHAPTER 2

August 21, 2003. I was 23 years old and, after years of dreaming about it, I was about to do stand-up comedy for the first time ever. It's one of the more significant dates in my life and I've used it over the years as a password, including for a couple of pornography sites and my long-defunct Myspace account. For those who don't remember Myspace, it was a social network and the forerunner to Facebook. It actually might still exist. I suppose I could easily go online and verify that, but frankly who cares.

I had been writing jokes for the previous several months and finally had about five minutes of material, which was enough for the monthly New Talent Night at Bleeker Street Comedy Club in Greenwich Village, just a few blocks from its legendary rival, The Comedy Den. My old high school friend Lou Sills had asked to come with me, not wanting to miss my stand-up debut. He was excited and couldn't wait to see me perform. I on the other hand was super nervous and considered turning around and going home as we walked along Bleeker Street toward the club.

After arriving, I checked in with Scott, the manager, who verified that I was on the list of performers for that night and wrote down what I wanted the MC to say for my introduction. Mixed in with the new talent on the lineup were a few seasoned veterans so as to make sure the audience got a decent show. The show had just started, and I was to go on in the middle of the lineup, at about 8:45 pm. My friend Lou paid the ten-dollar cover charge and headed toward the showroom.

- Sit in the back. I don't want to see your face in there, I told him.

- I want to sit in the front, he protested.

- No way. It'll weird me out if there's someone I know sitting up front.

To this day I tell friends and relatives to sit in the back when they come to see me perform. Actually, I tell them to find something else to do. But if they insist on coming, I tell them to sit as far from the stage as possible. I much prefer performing in front of strangers than people I know.

I paid Scott the requisite twenty-dollar fee. Anyone could perform on the New Talent Night show at the Bleeker Street Comedy Club provided they paid the twenty dollars, for which they were entitled to five minutes of time on stage and a DVD of their set filmed with the camera that had been permanently installed at the back of the club. I still have the DVD, and I managed to suffer through watching my awkward first performance in order to present an accurate account of what jokes I did on stage that night. I'll get to that soon.

Several comedians were seated at the bar, which was to your left as you entered the club, just before reaching the door to the showroom. Among the comics seated there was the great Ron Apple, who at the time was already starting to make a name for himself in the comedy game. He was one of the aforementioned seasoned veterans brought in to make sure the show was of reasonable quality.

- Hey Ron. I saw you last week at the Comedy Den. I really love your stuff, I said to him.

- Great, now it's all coming together for me, was his brusque, annoyed response.

62

I had just assumed Ron was only grouchy and hostile on stage. Apparently, it was not just a character. I had been planning to let him know I was about to perform for the very first time and ask him to wish me luck, but I quickly scrapped that idea. I can't even imagine the aluminum baseball bat of sarcasm I would have taken upside the head after telling him that. I decided instead to wander outside and get some air.

I saw a dark-haired girl about my age, perhaps a little younger, smoking a cigarette as I walked out the door. The smoking ban in bars and restaurants in New York City had begun in March of that year, thus forcing people onto the sidewalk to satisfy their addiction. Cigarettes are a habit I never picked up, being too afraid of death to indulge in something so unhealthy.

- Are you performing tonight? she asked me.

I told her I was, and she said that she was performing as well. Then we introduced ourselves to each other. She was Karen Lieberman, and she became my first friend in the comedy world and eventually my opening act on several occasions. Karen is now a veteran headlining comedian with several film and television roles to her credit and goes by the name Karen Lee. At that time, however, she had been doing comedy for only a year and was paying the bills working at a Blockbuster Video store as well as babysitting for rich Manhattan couples. In addition to both day jobs, she's since also ditched her abundant mass of naturally curly hair, opting instead for a daily rendezvous with a straightener.

- You know Ron Apple? I asked her.

- Yeah, Ron and I are friends.

- I tried talking to him a minute ago, and he was a little bit, I'll just say not warm.

- He's terribly weird and off-putting and kind of an asshole sometimes. But he's actually nice deep down believe it or not. What can I say, he's broken, like so many of us.

We continued our conversation, and Karen was giving me detailed information about all the places around town where new comedians could perform to gain experience, when Scott the manager walked outside.

- What the hell are you doing out here? You're on next! he yelled.

- Sorry, I wasn't paying attention to the time.

- I almost canceled your set and put on the guy after you. Next time I won't look for you.

- Kick ass, Ira! Karen shouted to me as I walked into the club. "Break a leg," I would learn, is not a phrase often heard in the stand-up world.

It wasn't fun being reprimanded by Scott, but talking with Karen had distracted me from the butterflies in my stomach which came back with force as I hurriedly walked past the bar toward the showroom. Chuck Fine, the MC, was on stage trying to infuse the audience with as much energy as possible.

- Is everyone having fun? Chuck asked.

The answer was a hearty affirmative in the form of applause and cheers.

- Excellent! Chuck continued. We have lots more comics for you tonight.

The moment was upon me. I was about to go on stage and try to make a group of strangers laugh. My anxiety was manifesting itself with a tingling sensation in my hands and feet as Chuck introduced me. These are the first words you hear on the DVD of my stand-up debut:

- This next comedian comes to us from across the river in Paramus, New Jersey. This is his first time doing stand-up comedy. Please give a warm welcome to Ira Sparrow!

Sparrow, Spiro. Close enough. Maybe he thought I was related to Jack Sparrow, the Johnny Depp character in *Pirates of the Caribbean*. As soon as I hit the stage I noticed that Lou Sills was in the second row stage left. I had told that dumb ass to sit in the back!

- Hi. How is everyone?

A confused mix of "heys," "wooh's" and "hi's" came back at me from the crowd. And there was one loud rebel yell style "yee-haw" from Lou Sills.

- So my father's Jewish, my mother's a WASP. I joined a restricted country club but was only allowed to go every other day.

The response was not the cacophony of laughter I was hoping for to start things off, just a few low-level chuckles, although Lou Sills did let out a deep horse-like guffaw. There were, in fact, a few problems with my opening comedic salvo. By 2003 the "I'm half this ethnicity and half that ethnicity" genre of joke had been done to death. What's more, the idea of Jews not being accepted into certain country clubs was a dated notion. Such clubs may still exist, but if so, no one paid much attention or cared. The third problem with the joke, though unknown to me at the time and likely unknown to the audience as well, is that the basic premise was not new. Groucho Marx was said to have once asked the members of a restricted country club if his half-Jewish daughter could go into the pool up to her knees. So the joke was unoriginal, outdated and irrelevant. What few laughs it got it didn't deserve. Thankfully my second joke did better:

- I was listening to that Billy Joel song before the show. "We Didn't Start the Fire." Everyone know that song?

Most people in the audience responded in the affirmative.

- If you don't know the song, the lyrics are a rundown of the major events of the 20th century. And in one part Billy Joel's singing, "Rock and roller cola wars, I can't take it anymore." Billy Joel is singing about things like assassinations, Vietnam, and the H-bomb and it's the cola wars that pushed Billy over the edge. The U.S. versus Russia, no problem. Coke versus Pepsi, I can't take it anymore!

The joke got good laughs from nearly everyone in the crowd, and it remained in my act for a couple of years thereafter, but it's not up to my current standards. Though they often work well, it's my opinion, and others might disagree, that jokes about song lyrics being ridiculous or not making sense are, quite frankly, too easy. Pop lyrics don't have to make sense. They have to sound good when sung with the corresponding melody. Frequently, lyrics are more of a verbal collage than anything resembling a comprehensible narrative. An extreme example of this would be "Blinded by the Light", written by the great Bruce Springsteen. If you're unfamiliar with the lyrics, you can google them. Perhaps with enough drugs, you can discern a clear meaning within them, but you'd be the first. That said, the "We Didn't Start the Fire Joke" was a relative success, and I was hoping to continue the momentum.

-I gotta rectangle for a chin. Look at this thing. God used a T-square to make this. That's what my name Ira stands for - interior right angles.

As with my first joke, this geometry-inspired comedic turd got a very tepid reaction, except for my increasingly drunk friend Lou Sills who was doubled over with laughter.

- My name is Ira and my father's name is Steve. My father's name is more modern than mine. My grandfather's name was Logan 5.

Logan 5 was a character from a movie from 1975 called *Logan's Run* starring Michael York. The movie took place hundreds of years in the future. The idea of the joke was that my grandfather had a futuristic name and, with each generation, the names became more old-fashioned. The problem, I realized later, was that most people were not familiar with the movie *Logan's Run*, much as I always had great affection for it. Still, the basic idea was a decent one, and an improved version of that joke is the only remnant of my first performance that's still in my act.

I won't bother recounting the rest of my time on stage that night. It was not particularly impressive, though Lou Sills continued to howl after every joke I said, including the last one, a lazy basic misdirection:

- I bumped into my senior prom date the other day. After high school, we lost touch. I only see her at family reunions.

Perhaps I should have been happy that even one of my jokes did well my first time out, but I was brutally disappointed.

- How did it go? asked my new friend Karen as I exited the showroom.

- Awful. It sucked.

- Hey, it was your first time. Have a drink with me.

- I think I'm just gonna go home.

Scott came over and handed me the DVD of my performance. I was going to throw it in the garbage, but Karen convinced me not to, saying that, whatever I thought of the performance, it was an important moment in my life, and the DVD was worth keeping as a souvenir. She said that I'd enjoy watching it one day when I was a big star. As a moderate star, I can say I did not enjoy watching it, but it did come in handy when writing this chapter of the memoir.

- Dude that was awesome, said Lou as he came toward me downing a vodka tonic.

- You see? He thought it was great, said Karen.

- He's my friend. And he's drunk. Believe me, the rest of the crowd disagrees.

My father was on the couch watching television when I got back home to Paramus, New Jersey. I had moved in with my father and stepmother, Carol Spiro, formerly Carol Rosenfeld, after graduating from NYU.

- Well? Are you the next big thing in stand-up comedy? asked my father as I sat down next to him on the couch.

I told him that it didn't go well and that I was having second thoughts about being a stand-up. He was, to my surprise, actually quite encouraging, telling me that it takes time and that if I wanted to do it, I shouldn't give up. He had not reacted positively when I told him about my ambitions as a performer, but seeing that I was upset he rose to the occasion and offered me words of comfort that I never expected from him.

CHAPTER 8

Charlotte Aubertin was seated by herself on a couch at the rooftop lounge of the Marsden Hotel in midtown Manhattan. The lounge offered incredible views of the city as well as the Hudson River to the West. Charlotte, however, was not looking at the view but rather, with her headphones in her ears, was watching a video on YouTube as she sipped her aperol spritz. The video was of Ira doing stand up on *The Tonight Show with Jay Leno* back in 2011:

- I'm seeing this French girl. Sometimes I'm out with her and her French friends and she'll slip into talking French with them. And I don't think it's accidental. Like one time her friend was like (with French accent) "So where did you guys meet?" And she's like "At 'ze comedy club." "You saw him perform?" "Yes. He was on 'ze stage when I saw him." "Was he funny?" *"Franchement, pas vraiment."*

Charlotte let out a loud laugh. She enjoyed Ira's comedy as much as ever, and she especially enjoyed his jokes about the French girl he was seeing because, well, she was that French girl. The incident in the joke never happened, but once or twice she did inadvertently slip into French with her friends in Ira's presence, inspiring the joke. As for Ira's joke about how she would say "come in America" instead of "come to America," it was not approved by NBC standards and practices but did find its way into Ira's HBO special

Charlotte was an exotic beauty owing to the mix between her Sri Lankan mother, who had immigrated to Paris as a little girl, and her white father, who had grown up in Lyon, in the east-central part of France. She was tall and slender with caramel skin, almond eyes and an abundance of jet black hair down to her shoulders that framed her delicate oval face. She attracted attention wherever she went, and several people at the rooftop bar, both men and women, were wondering who this beautiful woman was and who she might be waiting for.

"Is that Ira?" she asked herself upon seeing Ira walk out of the elevator onto the roof. She had never seen him with a beard before. His unique rectangular chin was covered under a mass of facial hair, but it was still hard to mistake that tall lanky body and prominent nose. She put her phone away and called to him.

- Ira! *Coucou!*

Ira smiled and walked over to her as she excitedly got up to greet him. They kissed each other once on each cheek in the French manner and then Charlotte sat back down on the couch. Among the patrons who had been admiring Charlotte, it all made sense to those who recognized Ira. Those who did not wondered how this awkward and unimpressive-looking man in the rumpled "Katz's Deli" t-shirt managed to elicit such a radiant smile from a woman whose face would not be out of place on the cover of a fashion magazine.

Ira decided not to sit right next to her on the couch, but rather on a chair at a right angle to the couch. Sitting side by side was for couples, and it had been years since they'd even seen each other. He would start slow and see how the evening progressed, hoping that ultimately it would end back at her hotel room.

- 'Zis is a new look, 'ze beard.
- Yeah, trying it out. What's that you're drinking?
- Aperol spritz. It is very good I 'sink.

Ira noticed her French accent was thicker than he remembered. It made sense. She had been living back in Paris the last several years. Charlotte had always had difficulty pronouncing the English "th" sound, which does not exist in French, nor in most European or Asian languages. In general, she would pronounce the so-called voiced (using the vocal cords) "th" sound, as in the word "the," as a 'z, and the unvoiced "th" sound, as in "think," as an 's.

- It is nice to see you, Ira.

- Nice to see you too. How long has it been?

- I am back in France since six years so about seven years. So you are doing ok?

- Yeah, things are fine.

- You are sure?

The tone of Charlotte's voice betrayed a certain inquietude.

- I guess you saw that video of me at the show in Maryland, said Ira, upset that the incident he was just starting to put behind him had come up.

- Yes I saw 'zis. I was worrying for you.

- I accidentally took too much Xanax before going on stage. No big deal.

The waiter came over and asked Ira what he'd like to drink. Ira was relieved to have the conversation about Maryland interrupted.

- I'll have, I don't know, I guess a cabernet.

The waiter suddenly gave Ira a look that Ira had come to know well over the years. It was the look of someone who recognized him, but was trying to figure out exactly how.

- Are you an actor?

- Yes. He is a very celebrated comedian and actor of film, said Charlotte, to the great discomfort of Ira.

- Yes, you're Ira Spiro. The beard threw me off a bit. I'm Carl. Nice to meet you.

- Nice to meet you, Carl.

- So, um, how have you been? said Carl with a tone of sincere but unwelcome concern.

- Fine Carl, thank you, retorted Ira brusquely and with sufficient irritation in his voice that Carl understood further questions on his part would be unwelcome.

- I'll get you that cabernet right away.

- I can't believe it's been so long, said Ira to Charlotte as Carl walked away.

- I know. It passes so much fast.

- So, what brings you to New York? Vacation?

- No. I came here to look at apartments.

- What do you mean? You're moving here?

- Yes. I have a job offer doing programming for a tech start-up.

This information changed everything. Ira was hoping for some rekindled romance between him and Charlotte, secure in the knowledge that she would be returning to France. He met Charlotte when she was living in San Francisco and he was in New York. Their past relationship was a long-distance situation with little danger of a serious entanglement. He had never actually thought of her as a candidate for anything more meaningful.

- Are you going anywhere 'zis summer Ira, or you are staying in New York?

- Me and my girlfriend are thinking of spending some time in Vermont.

Ira hadn't been in an actual relationship since Harlee Shaw, but he wanted to firmly establish that he and Charlotte would not be an item upon her move to New York.

- You have someone in your life. It is so wonderful to hear 'zis.

Charlotte was, in truth, a little upset that Ira had a girlfriend, though Ira did not perceive it. Indeed, a platonic relationship with Ira was acceptable to her if not optimal. What she didn't want was the kind of ambiguous relationship they had had in the past. She was older, wiser and in a much different place in her life than when the two were little more than friends with benefits.

- Are you seeing anyone Charlotte?

- No, I am celibate.

Charlotte may or may not have been practicing sexual abstinence, but that is not what she meant. "*Célibataire*" in French means "single," which is what she was trying to say. Ira knew this. Even though it had been years, he was still fairly fluent in Charlotte English. She used to ask him to correct her when she made mistakes in grammar or vocabulary, but he seldom did, as it felt awkward and rude.

- So tell me about your girlfriend. What is her name?

- Stephanie Delsano.

It was the first name that came to mind.

- Can I see some pictures? asked Charlotte, curious about any woman that had managed to lock Ira into a relationship.

Perhaps buried somewhere in his "photos" file Ira had a picture or two of Stephanie, but of course, if Stephanie really was his girlfriend, he would have had several pictures of her readily accessible on his phone. That he did not would have been a dead giveaway that he wasn't being truthful.

- You know what, said Ira thinking fast on his feet, the battery is dead on my phone. He then changed the subject and asked Charlotte to tell him about the apartments she was looking at. Charlotte ignored the inquiry and took out her phone.

- My phone works. Is she on Facebook?

- No, she's not into social media, said Ira, lying once again. He didn't feel liking having to explain why Stephanie's Facebook page said she was single and didn't have any pictures of the two of them together. Of course, neither did Ira's Facebook page, but that could be more easily explained as Ira was almost never on Facebook and, though he still had an account, his last post was several years old.

Ira noticed that on the home screen of Charlotte's phone was a picture of a young boy who looked to be about five or six years old?

- Who's that? he asked.

- Who?

- The kid on your phone?

- Oh. 'Zat's my nephew Sébastian.

- He's cute. He looks just like you.

- Well 'zis is normal. We are in 'ze same family.

- So you're close with him?

- Yes, very close. I spend a lot of time wis' him. I do a lot of babysitting.

- That's great. I'm sure you're a great aunt!

The two spent the next hour chatting about various things such as Charlotte's new job as a programmer in New York, Ira's mom and her odd enthusiasm for President Trump and the dystopian anthology series *Black Mirror* on Netflix, which both adored. Ira also asked, out of curiosity, if Charlotte had had any relationships in the years since they'd last seen each other. She told him about her relationship with a lawyer named René, and how they broke up when, after a year together, Charlotte had the sudden epiphany that they had few interests in common and little to talk about. Then Ira walked Charlotte to her hotel. It turned out that her flight back to France was that evening at 11 pm and she needed to pack and get ready.

-Well, I will be moving here in September, so maybe I will see you 'zen, said Charlotte, standing in front of the Marriott Marquis where she was staying.

They kissed each other once on each cheek and then, after a moment, Ira tried to kiss her on the lips. Looking into Charlotte's eyes in the summer twilight, he wanted her as much as ever. It had been years since they had had sex, but it was better than any encounters he had had since, and there was still time before her 11 pm flight to relive old times.

- What are you doing? she asked, turning her head to thwart Ira's attempt.

- I'm sorry, I thought maybe . . .

- You have a girlfriend Ira, she said, not imagining that Ira had been lying about Stephanie.

- Yes, he said, but we have kind of an open relationship. We can be with other people. We just can't be in other relationships.

Hearing that, Charlotte could not help but let out a subtle laugh.

- *Au revoir*, Ira, she said before turning toward the lobby of her hotel.

Upstairs in her hotel room, as Charlotte was packing her bags for her return flight to Paris, she thought about Ira's proposition. At one point in her life, she would have accepted it. But she was no longer the starry-eyed 24-year-old she was when she met him that night in San Francisco.

CHAPTER 9

IRA SPIRO BEFORE COVID: A MEMOIR - CHAPTER 5

I was sitting at the bar at RJ's Comedy Club in San Francisco on a Saturday night having a glass of red wine of one sort or another and surfing the web on what would have been, at that time, an iPhone 3G, when I heard the big round of applause that indicated that the headliner, a forty-something road veteran named Teddy Mclafferty, had finished performing. It was the second and last show of the night. I could have gone back to my hotel room after my twenty minutes on stage as the opening act but decided to hang out, as I so often did, and try to meet attractive women from the audience. As for Teddy, he lived in the area with his wife and kids and went right home after the show.

- Great show tonight Ira, I'll see you tomorrow, said Teddy, pausing at the bar for a quick goodbye before leaving the club.

- See you then, Teddy.

A couple of minutes later, after paying their checks, the audience started to come out of the showroom. Several people came over and told me they enjoyed the show and some of them asked for pictures, but there were no immediate prospects from a romantic point of view. What constituted a romantic prospect? She had to be attractive. She had to not be there with a significant other, and she had to show overt interest in me. I was then, as I am now, fairly insecure and frankly, I didn't want a girl who otherwise might have thought of me as a funny comedian that she enjoyed watching to instead think of me as an aggressive creep. I was happy to pounce, however, if the signals were clear. You might have noticed that none of the aforementioned criteria had anything to do with a girl's personality. These were criteria for liaisons away from home that were necessarily short-term. A girl could have thought that Hitler was right, and not just about Germany's need for a robust national network of controlled-access highways, but the more controversial stuff too, and it would not have been a deal-breaker. I'm not proud of it, but this is how guys are. Ladies, I assume you already knew this, but if not, sorry to break the news. It's for your own good, though. Knowledge is power.

I was about to give up and go back to my hotel when I saw two absolute stunners making their way towards me from the ladies' room. Both appeared to be in their early twenties. One was a thin blonde and the other had light brown skin and dark wavy hair.

- You were very funny tonight, said the darker-skinned girl with an accent of some sort.

- Thank you so much. What kind of an accent is that?

- We are from France, she said. I am Charlotte and 'zis is my friend Virginie.

- I'm Ira.

- Yes we know 'zis. We just saw you on 'ze stage.

Virginie and Charlotte exchanged some words in French which I obviously didn't understand. Virginie appeared somewhat less happy to meet me than Charlotte, which was fine as I was more attracted to Charlotte anyway.

- I am living here, but Virginie is going back to Paris tomorrow so I am going to show her a little 'ze nightlife.

- We have not seen each o'zer since a long time, said Virginie.

- I understand. You guys go do your thing.

- So you are in San Francisco for how much time? asked Charlotte.

The way Charlotte had been looking at me the whole time should have perhaps been sufficient to clue me in that she was interested, but I was not, at that time, used to getting women at her level of physical attractiveness, so I wasn't absolutely sure. Her asking me "for how much time" I was going to be in San Francisco, however, was enough to give me the confidence to take action.

- Actually, tomorrow is my last night. We just do one show on Sunday. I'll be done around 9. Maybe we can get together after?

- Yes, 'zis would be nice.

I got her phone number and then she gave me a kiss goodbye on the cheek. I thought that was the end of the matter, but then she kissed me again on the other cheek. Apparently, that's how it's done in La France. Her friend Virginie did likewise and then they both left to explore the city.

- Good work Ira, said Ed, the bartender, who had witnessed the whole episode. Looks like you're gonna close this one.

The next day I did what comics often do when they're alone on the road with time to kill. I saw a movie. I believe it was *The Social Network,* a film about the rise of Facebook. As it happens, I was a bit late to the Facebook party having just joined that year, by which time the site had about a half-billion followers, reducing Myspace and other rival sites to smoking piles of rubble.

After the movie, I sent a text to Charlotte asking her to come to the show later. Her reply arrived within seconds:

- *I'll be there!*

The immediacy of her response, coupled with the exclamation point at the end of it, were very good signs indeed. A smiley emoji, particularly one blowing a kiss, would have been even more encouraging, but you couldn't text those in 2010. How far we've come! I was quite glad to hear back from her. It often happens that a girl that seems interested in you at the end of a show can decide in the ensuing hours, once the magic of seeing you on stage has worn off, that you're not that interesting after all. Thankfully, this appeared not to be the case with Charlotte.

I spent the next couple of hours back at my hotel engaged in one of my favorite activities, watching YouTube videos. I was in a '90s music mood and watched a lot of videos from that era, with a particular focus on female singer-songwriters such as Natalie Merchant, Jewel and Sarah McLachlan. After that, I watched a video about the construction of the Golden Gate Bridge, which was visible from my room. I also watched an interview with a guy who had survived jumping from the bridge in a failed suicide attempt. He said that as soon as he jumped, he realized he didn't want to die after all. I've felt sudden regret after casual sex, but this seemed to take the notion of "well that was a bad idea" to a whole other level.

I was about halfway through my set on the Sunday night show at the club when I saw Ed the bartender escort Charlotte into the showroom and seat her in the back. I decided she might enjoy a shout-out.

- Hi Charlotte, I said to her from the stage.

- Allo, she said back in her adorable accent.

- That's Charlotte everyone. I just met her. She's from France.

Then I slipped in a joke that I had thought of that day.

- I was gonna take French in school, but my friend told me to take Spanish instead because it was easier. He told me he struggled with French, but then switched to Spanish and got an A no problem. So I took Spanish and almost flunked. Probably shouldn't have taken the advice of an exchange student from Barcelona on how easy Spanish was.

Charlotte laughed hard, but the joke worked only ok overall. It didn't "crush," as we say in the business. I don't know. Maybe it's a little predictable. That said, I have used it subsequently. It's not a killer, but it comes in handy when performing in situations where I have to work clean and be politically correct and thus am limited in the choice of the jokes in my repertoire I can use. The joke, by the way, is based on reality. I did take Spanish in high school because I had been told it was easier than other languages, but, unlike in the joke, it was American kids that told me that. My parents did too. I don't know where they got that information. I found Spanish incredibly difficult and, though I didn't almost flunk, I was lucky to get a B. To be honest, I think it's a myth born of racism. America has a large Hispanic population and they are generally seen as an underclass. People subconsciously associate Spanish with being easy because they don't respect the intelligence of Spanish speakers. The reality is, it's very hard, and the subjunctive is a total nightmare.

During the rest of my set, I tried to include a few more jokes that Charlotte hadn't already heard the night before, but at that time I only had about thirty minutes of material, and not all of it was good.

- I heard a lot of 'zose jokes already, said Charlotte when I got off stage.

I apologized that I didn't have enough material to give her an all-new show.

- It's ok. I enjoy 'zem 'ze second time just as much.

Perhaps she did enjoy the jokes the second time, but I think she bent the truth when she said "just as much." I asked her if she wanted to stay and watch the headliner. He had hours of material and would likely do many jokes he had not already done on the prior show.

- No, she said. He's funny but, l don't need to watch him. Let's take a drink somewhere.

About a half-hour later we found ourselves at a rooftop bar she had suggested in the Mission District called Moonlight Rainbow.

I found Charlotte quite easygoing and fun to talk to, although she did ask me many of the usual questions people tend to ask when they meet comedians: "Do you write your own material?" (Yes.) "How do you come up with it?" (Living life and observing things.) "Do you get nervous before going on stage?" (Hell yes!) "Do you have another job?" (Not anymore, thank God.) Normally I find these questions annoying as I've been asked them countless times, but Charlotte was so sweet and sincere that I found them downright charming. Also, she was absurdly sexy and I wanted her desperately.

During our conversation, I found out that her mother was from Sri Lanka and her father was a white Frenchman. I wish I could say she offered that information, as it's not terribly polite to ask someone what their ethnic background is. Nevertheless, my curiosity got the better of me, and I asked anyway.

- There are a lot of Sri Lankans in Paris. Have you ever gone in France? she asked me.

"Gone in France?" I guess prepositions can be tricky to master for a non-native speaker. Is there any rational reason, for example, why we sit "in" a car but "on" a bus? And while we're at it, why do we do things "in" the evening but "at" night?

- No. I've never gone to France, I answered, inadvertently correcting her.

- *Merde*! I meant to say "gone TO France." I always do 'zat. Correct me if I make mistakes okay?

- Sure, if you want me to.

Since that moment, I rarely corrected Charlotte's English. Mostly just when I couldn't understand her, or when she mixed up "in" and "to."

She told me that she was a graduate student studying computer science at UC San Francisco. That was quite a surprise. They say you can't judge a book by its cover, and yet, as I've said in my act, if you meet a guy with a neck tattoo, you can be reasonably sure he's never uttered the words "nurse, scalpel." Similarly, in a room full of randomly selected bottle service girls and female computer science students, you'd likely be able to tell which ones were which with a fair degree of precision. Charlotte would be the exception.

After a few drinks, the time had come to go for a kiss. I was not, however, positioned properly as we were sitting at a table across from each other. Rather than simply get up and sit down beside her, I excused myself to go to the bathroom. Upon returning I positioned myself on her left side, eliciting a big smile on her part. After a bit of small talk, I put my hand on her leg. She responded by putting her hand on top of mine and moving it slowly back and forth. And then I kissed her. We made out for a bit, and then she asked me another question I've heard before.

- Do you pick up girls at all of your shows?

I told her the truth, that it happens from time to time. It has never really been that frequent an occurrence for me in large part because, as I've said, I wait for them to talk to me first. Also, I have fairly high standards in terms of physical appearance. That said, Charlotte was well above the minimum level of beauty I need to be attracted to a woman. People in the bar watching us kiss must have wondered how the hell a dork like me was able to seduce someone like her.

Women like funny men, or so they say. I'm not sure why women would have evolved to like a funny man. Yes, it's enjoyable to be with someone that makes you laugh, but would it not be more advantageous, from the standpoint of evolution, to be attracted to a man that is strong, healthy and a good provider and then just hang out with funny friends on the side? Perhaps women are not attracted to funny men. Perhaps women find the men they are attracted to funny. One thing is certain, women are attracted to men they see on stage making a room full of people laugh, and I was feeling immense gratitude for that fact as I sat there kissing a French goddess with the San Francisco Bay stretched out behind us.

I was heading back to New York the next morning. Had I more time, a kiss would have been sufficient for the evening with the hope of something more another night. I prefer to err on the side of taking things slowly with a new woman, so as to not come off as someone who's just interested in sex. However, that option was not available to me. I needed to act fast.

- Do you wanna have a drink back at my hotel? I asked with a modicum of timidity, knowing that this was simply a nicer way of asking "Do you wanna fuck?" and would be interpreted as such.

- We take a drink in your hotel room?

In fact, my plan was that we would have a drink at the bar in the lobby and from there progress to my room at some point. But as she did not seem opposed, why not cut out the extra step.

- Yes, in my hotel room. At the Hyatt Regency. It's not far.

We hopped in a cab and about fifteen minutes later we were sitting on the balcony of my room drinking cabernet from my minibar. She was telling me how her parents met on the Metro in Paris. Her father had stayed on several extra stops before working up the courage to talk to her mother. I told her I wasn't sure how my parents met, but it was likely in a way that was as unromantic as their marriage was short. "Perhaps," I said, "they met in the hardware store and my father's opening line was 'Hey, you know where the plungers are at?'" She laughed hard, spitting out a mouthful of cabernet.

- You know, she said, in French we have an expression: "*Femme qui rit, à moitié dans ton lit.*"

- What does that mean? I asked.

- It means a woman who laughs is halfway in your bed.

That seemed like as good a cue as any. If I've ever heard a better one, I can't recall it. I started kissing her and led her inside the room

84

toward the bed. Must I recount all the details? Everyone knows how this typically goes. There's aggressive kissing and rolling around on the bed followed by grabbing of breasts and butts. Shirts come off first and then bottoms, in my case jeans, in hers a skirt. Soon after you have two naked people and a sex act is imminent. I didn't want to interrupt the flow, but I needed to go get a condom. Turns out we were on the same page in that regard.

- Do you have a *préservatif*? she asked.

- A what?

- I forgot how you say. You put it on to not get pregnant.

- You mean a condom.

- Yes, a condom.

- Yeah, one second. I was just about to go get one.

I went to my suitcase to get the condoms I had packed only to discover I had done something I never do. I had forgotten to pack them!

- You know what, I don't have any. I'll run down to the gift shop and get some.

- Don't take long time!

I quickly put my clothes back on and headed down to the gift shop which, damnit, was closed! I went outside the hotel looking for a place to buy condoms. I had left my phone upstairs and couldn't go online to find a convenience store nearby. Luckily, I stumbled on a CVS drugstore a few blocks away after walking in a random direction. I grabbed a pack of condoms and realized, on my way to the cash register, that, in my haste, I had also left my wallet in the hotel room. I had no choice but to do something I hadn't done in years. I had to shoplift. From a moral standpoint was it even wrong? As far as I'm concerned it's not an easy question. I'm not joking. Maybe I'm half-joking. But I'm half-serious! First of all, CVS is a huge company. What's a few condoms to a corporation with billions of dollars in revenue every year? This may be a controversial statement, but I submit that even if it was a mom-and-pop corner store shoplifting was still, perhaps, justified. There was a beautiful naked French woman in my hotel room waiting for sex. Expecting me to go all the way back there to get my wallet and then return to the store was, it could be argued, unreasonable. Technically it was illegal. But immoral? Philosophers can debate the question, but all I can say is, given the situation, if it were my store I would have understood.

There was a sticker attached to the box of condoms that looked like it might be some sort of tag that would set off the alarm if I left the store without paying. I wasn't sure, but in any case, there was an easy enough solution. I discretely opened the box and put the condoms in my pocket. I breathed a sigh of relief when I made it safely outside. What would I have done if security tried to stop me? I'm pretty fast and I suppose I could have made a run for it. I was not well known then. If I tried such a thing today it would be a lot riskier. The security guard might recognize me and call the police and say, "The dude from *Jackson Taylor's Christmas Party* just stole a three-pack of Trojan reservoir tipped condoms." But in 2010 all I had done TV-wise was five minutes of stand-up on *The Late Late Show with Craig Ferguson*. Another option would have been to simply explain the situation to the security guard and offer to come back and pay after I had, you know, finished up. Again I ask, who could have held it against me? Thinking about it now, the running option would have made more sense. Thankfully it wasn't necessary. I had made it out without attracting any attention. The perfect crime!

No doubt Charlotte was startled when she heard a knock on the door.

- Charlotte, it's Ira. I don't have my key.

Charlotte hid behind the door as she opened it, given that she was still buck naked.

- Why did you take so much time? she asked.

- The gift shop was closed. I had to go to a drugstore. And I forgot my wallet. That's why I had to knock. I don't have my key.

- How did you pay for the condoms without your wallet?

- You taught me a French expression. Here's an English one: "five-finger discount."

- What does that mean?

- I stole them.

We both had a good laugh about my late-night criminal escapade and then resumed our carnal pursuits. The sex was made particularly hot, at least for me, by the fact that she was shouting things out in French. I didn't know what she was saying, but it didn't seem like she was complaining.

The next morning I had to get to the airport, and she had to get home and get ready for a class that afternoon. We had sex one more time, using the last of the condoms. Not sure I could use up a three-pack in one night now, but I was younger then.

Standing outside the hotel we said goodbye and added each other on Facebook. I promised to contact her the next time I was in San Francisco. She promised to do likewise if she found herself in New York, and then we kissed before each getting into a cab.

On my way back to the airport she texted me *"It was great meeting you! The most fun I've had since I came in America!"* to which I responded *"Came TO America. I had fun too xoxo."*

CHAPTER 10

- Okay, what do you wanna talk about today? asked Ira, seated once again on his couch across from Miles.

- Well, let's think. We pretty well covered the show in Denver the last time I was here, responded Miles.

- Yes, it was a lot of fun reliving my panic attack and public humiliation. How about something a little less intense today?

- Perhaps we can talk about your early comedic influences. Were you a comedy fan as a child?

- Yeah. I used to watch it on HBO all the time in the '80s and '90s. I liked Seinfeld, Steven Wright, Howie Mandel, Sam Kinison, Joan Rivers. Was a fan of Eddie Murphy of course. You know what, Woody Allen used to do stand-up. I had a tape of him performing back in the sixties that I listened to all the time. I loved his moose bit. You know that one? Where he brings an actual moose to a costume party and there's a prize for best costume and the moose loses?

- Yeah, that was a great bit! I believe the winners were a couple that was dressed as a moose! When was the first time you saw a comedy show live?

- The first time? Well, when I was seven years old I saw my father. He was performing at a hotel in Poughkeepsie. Guess he couldn't find a babysitter. Anyway, I don't remember much about it.

- Wait a minute. Your father did stand-up? asked Miles, eyes suddenly alight with curiosity.

- Didn't I mention that at some point?

- No. No, you didn't.

Miles leaned forward in his seat looking at Ira with greater intensity.

- What happened with his career?

- He had a kid to support and an ex-wife and he just couldn't make a go of it. So he stopped doing it and started working with my uncle at my late grandfather's formalwear store in New Jersey.

- And when you started to succeed, how did he react?

- I don't know. I never really thought about it.

- You don't remember him expressing pride in your accomplishments? Bragging to his friends about you?

- Nothing like that really stands out in my mind. I think he was kind of indifferent.

Miles remained silent for several seconds, raising his head slightly, his index finger pressed across his lips.

- I'm wondering, he said, now looking directly at Ira once again, if he expressed in subtle, or maybe not so subtle, ways another sentiment, that he was upset that you had succeeded where he had not.

This was not the light and breezy topic that Ira had said he would have preferred to discuss. Miles went on to question him about key moments in his career and how his father reacted. One particular memory suddenly took on a greater significance in Ira's mind than it had in the past.

CHAPTER 11

IRA SPIRO BEFORE COVID: A MEMOIR - CHAPTER 4

My father was in the kitchen making a sandwich when I got home some time after midnight. It had been about five years since I started doing stand-up. Most nights during the week I would perform at clubs in Manhattan and then go back to Jersey. On the weekends I would frequently perform as an opening act at clubs around the northeast and sometimes further away.

- Hey Dad, guess what?

- You got someone pregnant?

- I don't think so. I'm usually pretty careful. No, there's this apartment in Astoria where some comics live, and there's a room that just became available. It would be easier living there since I'm always up late doing shows in the city. So anyway, I'm moving in next week.

- How much is it? The room.

- Not bad, about six hundred dollars a month.

- Gonna be kind of a pain commuting to the store from Queens.

- Well, I'm making enough money in stand-up now that I'm gonna stop working at the store. I mean, it'll be tight, but I think it's time I jumped in full-time.

- So you're just gonna fucking quit the store?

"Wow!" I thought to myself. I didn't expect that response. In any case, I didn't intend to leave him short-handed at Spiro Formalwear.

- Dad, I won't leave right away. I mean, I can stay a couple more weeks. That'll give you time to find someone else.

- Well if the comedy thing goes tits up, I'm not firing your replacement to take you back.

I certainly didn't expect the comedy thing to go "tits up", and even if it did I was sure I could find another gig as prestigious and well paying as renting people ill-fitting tuxes at the family store.

As it turned out the two weeks more I had planned to be in the formalwear game was shortened considerably. About three days later I was in the store talking to a customer about a tuxedo for an upcoming black-tie wedding when a teenager came in with his mother. They were just in the store an hour before picking up a tux for the young man's prom.

- Excuse me, the mother said.

- Oh hello again, I answered. I'm just finishing up with another customer. Everything alright?

- No! she said. You gave us the wrong cummerbund. He wanted the black paisley. You gave us a solid black one. We didn't even notice till we got back home. We live all the way in Ridgewood.

She was talking loudly enough to attract the attention of my father who was in the back office doing some bookkeeping or a crossword puzzle or whatever the hell he was doing.

- Can I help you with something ma'am? I'm the owner, said my father swiftly exiting his office to address the situation.

The woman explained what had happened, that they had ordered a black paisley cummerbund and gotten a solid black one.

- I'm so sorry for the mixup. Come with me. I'll take care of this.

My father took the mother and son up to the register, leaving me to continue showing tuxedo options to the man who had an upcoming wedding. I thought that was the end of the matter until a few minutes later when my father came clomping back towards me, his face flushed red with anger.

- What the fuck's your problem?

It was the second time that week my father had used the f-word in anger at me. The first time that week (or ever) doing so in front of a man searching for a smart but reasonably priced tuxedo rental.

- Dad, can we talk about this in a few minutes?

- You don't give a fuck about this place!

That was three times. My father was able to control his anger long enough to help the prom kid and his mom but not long enough to avoid alienating our other customer, who started walking toward the door, figuring he'd seen enough and would go elsewhere for his formalwear needs.

- That woman had to drive all the way back from her house in Ridgewood because you gave her the wrong cummerbund.

- I'm sorry Dad. I made a mistake.

- You know you're quitting soon, so you don't care.

I wondered to myself if he was right, at least in part. Perhaps I was working less conscientiously at the store knowing that soon I would be a full-time comedian.

- This store is what put a roof over your head and food on the table your whole damn life! Not to mention, it's what paid for your worthless English degree at NYU.

The NYU comment wasn't exactly correct. Not the part about the degree being worthless. He hit the bullseye on that one. But the store isn't where the money came from for most of the tuition. Almost all of it was paid with student loans. I was certainly grateful for the lifetime of food on the table and not being homeless that the store had afforded me, however.

- Tell you what mister big shot comic. You can leave now. I don't need you here.

- No, Dad, I'll stay until you find a replacement like I said I would.

- You're not getting it. I don't want you here. Get the fuck out.

That was the last "fuck" I needed to hear out of my father's mouth that day. Without saying another word, I left.

The room in Queens I was supposed to move into would not be ready for another week, but there was no way I was going to spend another minute at my father's house. I needed to find a place to stay in the meantime. My high school friend Lou Sills lived in a nice one-bedroom on the Upper East Side of Manhattan. Perhaps he'd be willing to let me stay on his couch for a few days.

- Lou it's Ira, I said into my phone while standing in a parking lot down the street from Spiro Formalwear. I had walked there to get out of my father's line of sight.

- Hey Ira, what's new?

- Things are a bit crazy actually. What ya' up to?

- Not much. Chillin' out.

- Lou, I kind of had a fight with my father. I was wondering if I could stay at your apartment this week. Just this week. I'll be moving to a place in Queens after that.

- Oh shit, said Lou. I'm not in town right now. There'd be no way for you to get into the place.

- Where are you?

- At my brother's lake house in Connecticut for the weekend. Hanging here with my girlfriend.

I wondered why he didn't mention being at a lake house when I asked him "What ya 'up to?". I was tempted to get all "suspicious girlfriend" on him and ask him to text me a photo of him in Connecticut, preferably holding that day's paper. Of course, friends don't ask each other to do such things. To this day I don't know if he was lying to me or not, but I get it. Not everyone likes house guests, and a week is a long time.

Next, I called my manager, Dave. He agreed to let me stay with him. He lived with his wife and son and daughter in a nice house in the 'burbs with a spare room. The only problem was, it was out on Long Island and a lot less convenient to the comedy clubs, but I didn't feel like making any more phone calls begging for housing.

This was in the days before Uber and Lyft, so I called Paramus Taxi to go back to my father's house to pick up some clothes and my laptop. Then I took New Jersey Transit to New York City and the Long Island Railroad out to Roslyn, Long Island where Dave lived. My post-Jersey life was about to begin.

CHAPTER 12

Ira was covered with sweat after having done thirty minutes on the StairMaster. As he stood by his locker changing out of his clothes, he saw that the area of redness on the tip of his penis had not gone away. In fact, it seemed to have grown somewhat larger. When he first noticed it a few days prior he paid it little mind, but at that moment he was feeling more concerned. He decided to try to find some answers online.

Googling symptoms is always a risky proposition when you're a neurotic individual, but perhaps he would quickly find out that a penile rash was never a sign of anything serious, and he could then enjoy one of his favorite activities, the steam room. Ira probably spent more time in the steam room than any other member of Equinox fitness. It's true that most people had family or work obligations that limited the time they could feasibly spend immersed in steam like a pot of mixed vegetables, but more than that, few people loved it as much as Ira. He would sit there until he could no longer tolerate the heat and then go take a cool shower before returning for more. On one occasion he repeated that process four times, racking up a total of an hour and twenty minutes of steam time.

Ira took his phone and sat down on the bench next to the lockers with a towel wrapped around his waist. He entered "rash & penis" into the search bar. WebMD listed several possible explanations for a penile rash, including something called balanitis, an inflammation of the head of the penis. It said nothing about the prognosis, so Ira had to then google "balanitis" which lead him to other websites which, thankfully, indicated that balanitis was typically not serious and easily treatable and in any case was uncommon in circumcised males. So far so good!

Other possibilities according to WebMD were psoriasis and allergic reactions. Also on the list: genital herpes! Ira thought of the sexual encounter he had had several weeks before with a young lady he met on Tinder. According to her profile, she was a student at NYU, Ira's alma mater, looking to make some extra money to pay her tuition. Women providing escort services are not rare on Tinder, though it is not the main purpose of the app. There was reason to doubt her story of being an NYU student, however, given that when Ira asked her if she liked Greenwich Village she replied "I don't really go there much." This was slightly suspicious considering that NYU is located in Greenwich Village. But whether or not "Tess" was a fellow "Bobcat" or not was of little importance to Ira. Two hundred dollars seemed like a good deal for a young redhead with huge breasts, educational credentials notwithstanding. Then again, perhaps it wasn't such a good deal. Might she have given him herpes? He clearly remembered using a condom. Ira never had sex without a condom and he certainly wouldn't have done so with a stranger, particularly a stranger who exchanged sex for money.

Yet another Google search was necessary. Ira entered "condoms & effectiveness & herpes." Again according to WebMD, condom use cuts the odds of getting genital herpes by thirty percent. It seemed like an unimpressive number and certainly a lot lower than the one hundred percent Ira was hoping for. Despite his use of a condom, Tess could still have given him herpes. "But wait", he thought to himself. "If I had herpes, would my only symptom be a rash?"

"Herpes & initial symptoms" was his next search. He was now waist-deep in the quicksand of hypochondriacal obsession, as he had been many times in his life. He discovered that the early symptoms of a first episode of genital herpes included, among other things, fever and flu-like symptoms followed by an outbreak of blisters. Ira had none of these symptoms and was satisfied he did not have genital herpes. Phew!

Ira went back to the results of his initial search, "rash & penis", to see what other information he might glean. Scrolling down through the search results he saw a particularly disquieting article from The Sun, a publication from the UK: "11 Signs YOU could be suffering penile cancer." Number four on the list - A rash on the penis! Could this be the only symptom of penile cancer, at least in the beginning stages? The article was not clear on this point. More research was needed.

Ira found little comfort in the fact that all of his health scares in recent years had turned out to be false alarms. He once had a suspicious-looking mole on his finger that turned out to be a blood blister. An episode of late-night chest pains he thought was a heart attack was, in reality, caused by gastrointestinal reflux, as he was told upon showing up in the emergency room. He had also once experienced several days of intermittent blurred vision that, though the cause was never determined with certainty, was not a tumor on his optic nerve or anything that threatened his life or eyesight.

Ira decided to head home, abandoning his steam room ambitions for that day.

- Oh my God, Ira Spiro! I love *Jackson Taylor's Christmas Party*! exclaimed a bookish-looking thirty-something male who was heading into the men's locker room as Ira was heading out. Even at the height of his fame, Ira was seldom bothered at Equinox. It was a high-end club and its members were not prone to, or at least pretended to be not prone to, getting excited over a show biz personality. At any rate, Ira was still reading medical articles on his phone and did not even hear the young man who surely thought Ira was arrogantly ignoring him, feeling himself too important to acknowledge a fan. He was certainly far from imagining that Ira was distracted by thoughts of a possible penectomy.

- I'm really not into working on this memoir today, said Ira, coming back from his kitchen with a bowl of vegan pistachio ice cream. Ira wasn't a vegan, but his lactose intolerance precluded him from eating real ice cream, and certainly not with a guest in the house! One time on stage Ira compared freedom of speech in America with his ability to consume milk products. Theoretically it existed, he said to the audience, but not without the potential for severe consequences.

- You do seem distracted, said Miles. Would you like to talk about it?

Miles was still a virtual stranger to Ira, but his tone of voice was so calm and he was always so understanding and without judgment in their discussions that Ira felt more and more at ease with him.

- I may have cancer.

- Why do you think that? asked Miles, his measured tone of voice unchanged.

- This is awkward, but a few days ago I noticed a rash on the tip of my penis.

- Well, that could be any number of things. Maybe you have psoriasis.

- Yeah, but I don't have it anywhere else. And it doesn't itch.

- I don't think you have penile cancer.

- Well how do you know? You're not a doctor. I read online that the initial symptoms can be simple discoloration.

- I highly doubt it's anything serious. Is there something in particular going on in your life right now?

- Why don't you think it's anything serious?

- It's a very minor symptom. It could be anything. Is there anything stressing you out right now, I mean, besides thinking you have cancer?

- Why are you asking that?

- I think it's relevant.

- If you must know I have to go to Bermuda next week for my mother's 60th birthday. Her boyfriend is organizing a birthday vacation at a resort there.

- Bermuda is beautiful. You're not looking forward to it?

- Not in the least.

- Why not?

- You wouldn't ask that if you knew my mother, answered Ira in a serious and somber tone that stripped the response of all its potential humor.

- I think maybe you're stressed about spending time with her and you're dealing with it by focusing your attention on other things. The anxiety is attaching itself to this fear of having cancer.

- You're starting to sound like a therapist.

- I've worked with a lot of artists on memoirs. Believe me, that can be like therapy. I think we should talk about your mother. And again, if you don't want it in the final version of the memoir, we can take it out.

- My mother's an alcoholic. I mean, she's been sober for a few years, but it's still in her.

- You're afraid she's going to start drinking again?

Ira remained silent for a long moment, seeming to withdraw into the meanders of his mind.

- But if it is cancer, I should get it looked at as soon as possible, right?

- I don't think it's helpful to go down this road and feed your obsession.

Ira took out his phone and dialed a number.

- Hi, this is Ira Spiro. I'd like to make an appointment with Doctor Chang, he said into the phone.

- Hold on, let me look at his schedule, answered the receptionist. Okay his next available date is September 22nd.

- That's not for three weeks. He has nothing sooner?

- If you can come right now, he can see you at 2 pm today.

- Okay great. On my way.

- Ok, let's check down 'dere, said Dr. Joseph Pai-Sun Chang as Ira stood in the examination room in his underwear. Dr. Chang was a small-framed man of about 45 who, despite his nearly thirty years in America, still spoke with a slight Taiwanese accent.

- How long have you had 'dis redness 'dere?

Dr. Chang's serious tone as he posed this question worried Ira, forgetting that Dr. Chang always spoke in a serious tone.

- Well I first noticed it like a week ago, but it seems to have spread a bit since then.

- Ok, so 'de red area seems to be getting bigger?

- Yeah a little bit, said Ira, fearful as to where this line of questioning was heading.

- It seems like you have some psoriasis 'dere.

Ira was relieved he was not faced with a more serious diagnosis. "Breakstone," he thought, "apparently was right."

Dr. Chang told Ira to buy some over-the-counter cortisone cream at the drugstore and apply it to the area twice daily. As Ira was heading toward the reception area to pay, he abruptly headed back to the examination room, catching Dr. Chang returning to his office.

- Dr. Chang sorry, just one quick question. You said, "It seems like psoriasis." Does that mean there are other possibilities, and if the cream doesn't work it may be something else, or it's definitely psoriasis?

- You have genital psoriasis. I am sure of 'dat, answered Dr. Chang, trying to be as reassuring as possible as he was well aware he was dealing with a man in the throes of obsessive thinking.

Dave Roth was in the city that day, and the two had planned to meet for lunch after Ira's appointment. Naturally, the lunch date was contingent on what the doctor said, as Ira would have been in no mood to socialize had he gotten bad news.

- Hey Ira, said Dave, answering his phone. So do you have cancer?

- I'll put it this way, let's eat! exclaimed Ira as he headed out of the doctor's office toward the elevators, a renewed spring in his step.

- Great. Leo's Crab House 1:30?

- See you there!

Dr. Chang's diagnosis had put an end to Ira's obsession with his penile rash, at least for the moment.

CHAPTER 13

Ira was impatiently awaiting a call from Dr. Chang as he sat at Gate 42 of the American Airlines Terminal at John F. Kennedy International Airport. His phone finally rang as the boarding process for his flight to Bermuda began. As a first-class passenger, he was entitled to board immediately, but needed to talk to the doctor first.

- Dr. Chang?

- Yes, Ira. I received a message 'dat you called. Is every'ting ok?

- Yeah, I just had a question. I was reading about psoriasis online, and it said that it increases the risk of type 2 diabetes.

Ira was not only anxious about the four days in Bermuda with his mother that was now imminent, but he was also a nervous flyer and there was heavy rain and wind in New York which promised to render the take-off and climb quite turbulent. If Miles's supposition was to be believed, all this anxiety was expressing itself in a cascade of obsessive-compulsive symptoms. Before leaving his building that morning he went back to his apartment twice to make sure the stove was turned off. This despite the fact he hadn't used the stove in well over a month.

- Yes 'dere are some studies 'dat suggest 'dis, said Dr. Chang in response to Ira's question. But 'dere are many more important risk factors for diabetes than psoriasis, and if you get diabetes it can be managed.

- So are you saying you think I'll get diabetes?

- I'm not saying 'dat, responded Dr. Chang calmly with well-practiced patience. Like I said, 'dere are other risk factors 'dat are more important. Family history, obesity and lack of exercise are 'de most important.

- Okay, well, I don't have those. But how big a risk factor is psoriasis?

- Different studies say different 'tings. But the risk is linked to 'de severity of 'de psoriasis and how much of the body it covers. In your case 'de psoriasis is very limited.

- Okay. And the other risk factors are more important anyway?

- Yes, 'dat's right.

- And even if I got it, you're saying diabetes is not that big a deal anyway, right?

- I didn't say 'dat. I said it can be managed. But I don't see you being at risk for 'dat right now.

- Cause I don't have the other risk factors?

- Yes, exactly.

- Okay. Thank you, Dr. Chang.

Ira hung up the phone, took a Xanax from his freshly prescribed supply and boarded the plane.

Arriving at his room at the Elbow Beach Hotel in St. George's Bermuda, Ira headed straight to the bed for a nap. He hadn't slept well the night before and was still a little groggy from the Xanax as the two-hour flight time from JFK was insufficient for the drug to wear off.

As Ira was dreaming, as he often did since the beginning of his career, about being on stage and forgetting all his jokes, his mother, Eileen Deridder, her sister, Ira's spinster Aunt Sally Deridder, and Eileen's boyfriend Frank Dornan were in the hot tub enjoying a cocktail. Eileen's cocktail was a virgin daiquiri as she had been sober since her last slip off the wagon two years before. Rounding off the birthday group were Frank's two children, Eric and Abigail. They were both in their early twenties and, not thrilled to be hanging around with the older folks, had gone off to the beach to go jet skiing.

- Can you take our picture, said Eileen to a young Bermudian man who was handing out towels to hotel guests. It's my birthday!

- Happy birthday ma'am, he answered, in his Bermudian accent, best described as something midway between an American and English accent with nuances of West Indian.

She handed him her phone and then loudly ordered everyone to make some sort of funny face. Eileen stuck her tongue out and used her two fingers to make devil horns on the top of her head. Frank put his hands on either side of his face and pushed back on his cheeks, tightening his skin and simulating the effects of a really strong headwind. Aunt Sally just continued drinking her piña without changing expression until reprimanded by Eileen at which point she halfheartedly pushed her front teeth in front of her mouth feigning a rabbit-like overbite.

- You going to put this on Instagram, asked Frank?

- Of course, answered Eileen. Should get a lot of "likes."

Ira was about an hour into his nap, by this time in the middle of another recurring dream wherein he's driving a car that keeps accelerating no matter how hard he brakes, when he was awakened by a pounding on his door

- Who is it? he shouted groggily as he opened his eyes.

There was more pounding at the door as Ira slowly transitioned into full wakefulness.

- It's the birthday girl!

Ira, seriously vexed by the interruption, reluctantly slid out of bed. Wearing boxer shorts and a t-shirt, his hair in disarray, he made his way to the door and opened it.

- Well you're a mess, said Ira's mother.

- I was sleeping. I had an early flight.

- You grew a beard again. Looks weird. Doesn't match your head.

- So I've been told.

- Let's take a picture.

Eileen put her arm around her son and snapped a quick selfie.

- What the hell are you doing? shouted Ira. Are you gonna post that online?

- Maybe.

Ira grabbed the phone out of his mother's hand.

- Give me my phone back!

- As soon as I delete the photo. You're not posting a picture of me online in my underwear.

Ira gave his mom back her phone, having deleted the photo in question.

- You're 60 years old, Ira continued. You're not supposed to be posting pictures on Instagram.

- Still 59 for another two days. And I look much younger. Everyone says so.

Indeed people often told Eileen Deridder that she looked younger than her years, but it was said only in the spirit of politeness. The decades of alcoholism were not without their effects on her appearance. Yet despite the deep lines in her face and the spider veins characteristic of heavy drinkers, one could still discern the beauty she once was. Tall and slender, she still had the delicate sharp features that inspired so many stares and so much attention in her younger years.

- We have a tennis court reserved. Me and Frank versus you and Aunt Sally.

- I'm not playing tennis, protested Ira. I'm going back to bed.

- Bullshit. We're playing tennis. Get dressed and grab your racket.

- I didn't bring a racket, said Ira, before jumping back into bed, letting his head fall between the two pillows.

- We have extra rackets, said Eileen.

She grabbed his arm and vainly tried pulling him out of bed, but it had been many years since she was able to physically maneuver her son.

- Fine, said Eileen in frustration. I'll see you later for dinner. We're eating at 6, she said before leaving the room.

Eileen was able to convince Eric Dornan, Frank's son, to round out the foursome and join Sally Deridder in a game of doubles against her and Frank. It didn't last long, however, as Eileen, upset when Eric called one of her shots wide, wrongly in her opinion, stormed off the court. Frank tried to talk her out of leaving but to no avail. She remained convinced that Eric could not be trusted to play fairly. Thinking it best to remain with his girlfriend, Frank left with Eileen, leaving Sally and Eric alone on the court. Eric, a former college player, took it easy on his opponent. Yet, even playing at only a fraction of his normal level of tennis, Sally was not able to get a single point off him in three games and decided, in turn, to abandon the court for that afternoon. That suited Eric well enough because, though not at all enjoying himself, he was too polite to tell Sally that playing against her was a complete bore.

Ira meanwhile, after another half hour of napping, headed off for a quick swim in the ocean followed by some time in the hot tub. It was not quite as satisfying to him as the steam room at the Equinox in Manhattan, but it would have to suffice as there was no steam room at the hotel.

In the bathroom of Ira's hotel room, there were two mirrors angled in such a way that when Ira walked past them on his way to get into the shower he noticed a mole on the right side of his upper back. Was that a new mole? Ira didn't know, but it looked bigger than his other moles. Upon closer inspection, it seemed slightly asymmetrical in shape, with one side convex and the other looking flat. In the course of previous mole obsessions, Ira had learned that moles that are asymmetric have a greater chance of being melanoma. Just as he was about to fall prey to another hypochondriacal episode, he remembered that Dr. Chang had given him a full-body skin check at his recent visit, before examining his penile psoriasis. Certainly, he would have mentioned it had he seen any suspicious moles. Ira still harbored a slight concern that Dr. Chang may have missed it, but he was able to put it out of his mind, at least for the time being.

Ira spent the rest of his time before dinner in his hotel room watching music videos on his phone. Of late he had been on a Bruce Springsteen kick. He had recently finished reading Bruce's autobiography on the recommendation of his manager Dave, himself a huge Bruce fan. He so enjoyed reading about Bruce's rise from humble working-class New Jersey roots to the summit of rock and roll superstardom that he wished to continue the Bruce experience by watching him in interviews and listening to his songs.

Dinner that night was at a restaurant called Stephano's. It came highly recommended by the concierge at the hotel. Customers dined outside on a deck right on the beach. The whole group was there: Ira, his mother Eileen, Aunt Sally, Frank, Eric and Abigail. The sun, still high in the sky, afforded the group a lovely view of the aqua-marine Bermudian waters and the unique pink-tinted sands.

Looking at the menu, Ira noted that the prices were steeper than he would have guessed. He had agreed to split everything 50/50 with Frank — the airfare, hotel rooms and meals for everyone. Thus he was somewhat annoyed when he had heard Frank planned to bring his two kids, who had little if any relationship with Ira's mother.

Eileen was in good spirits, uploading to her Instagram account the several pictures the waiter had just taken of the group toasting "to family and friends," Eileen with her Diet Coke, Frank, Eric and Abigail each with a glass of Chardonnay, and Ira with a Sprite. Ira generally did not feel comfortable drinking alcohol in the company of his mother.

- Eric, began Eileen, Frank says you love seafood. My friend Dayna was here last year. She said the shellfish trio is incredible.

Apparently, Eileen had forgiven Eric since her false allegation of cheating. This was typical of Eileen, who was given to sudden childish rants that were forgotten a short time later. Ira noted that the shellfish trio was a fifty-dollar entree, but his aggravation was somewhat mitigated by the fact that he had already come to accept that it was going to be an expensive meal and an expensive trip in general.

The dinner conversation was inoffensive enough at first. All were in Bermuda for the first time and discussion revolved around the beauty of the island and the friendliness of the people. They spoke of their plans for the next day. Frank had chartered a boat for a snorkeling excursion that would take up most of the afternoon. There was also talk, inevitable when adults with jobs and established lives come in contact with people in their early twenties, about what Eric and Abigail were doing career-wise. Eric, 22, was waiting tables in Fort Lauderdale and preparing to take the LSAT's, hoping to start law school the next year. Twenty-four-year-old Abigail was living in Chicago working at a large marketing company whose clients were mostly fashion and luxury brands.

If Ira was hoping to get through the meal without any conversation directly related to him, such hopes met with an abrupt end as everyone was about midway through their entrees.

- Ira, said Eileen, looking up from her beef tenderloin. I meant to ask you, what the hell happened in Maryland? I heard you fainted or something on stage?

- Eileen, I don't think he wants to talk about that, offered Frank.

- You're the one who told me, Frank. How did you find out anyway?

- I heard Eric and Abigail talking about it. I know I told you, but I didn't mean for you to bring it up in front of everyone.

- Frank is right, said Ira, I don't wanna talk about it, his tone of voice betraying a mix of anger and embarrassment.

- Ok fine. Sorry. Geez, Ira, you're so sensitive. How's that Chardonnay, Frank?

- It's really good. In fact, I'm gonna order another bottle.

- You know what, I need a wine glass. I wanna try a little.

- No fucking way! screamed Ira loud enough to startle several people in the restaurant and a young couple walking by on the beach.

- He's probably right, said Frank. You shouldn't be drinking.

- Not probably. Not a chance she's having a drink!

Ira was upset with Frank's tepid reaction, but then Frank had not experienced his mother as a raging alcoholic.

- Come on Ira, it's my birthday vacay! I'll just have half a glass.

- Alright, goodbye everyone, said Ira getting up to leave.

- Where are you going, asked Eileen?

- I'm not going to stay here and watch you drink.

- Ok ok, she said. Sit down. You're such an uptight Jew.

- Yeah, very funny, said Ira sitting back down at the table.

Eileen came over to Ira and gave him a hug.

- Don't be upset. You're my favorite uptight Jew. Look at that gorgeous Jewish nose. You look just like your father.

Ira was uncomfortable with his mother's not unprecedented Jewish comments, but at least the worst had been averted. Eileen would not put an end to her sobriety that night at Stephano's. After dessert and coffee, the group headed back to the hotel. Eric and Abigail opted for a nighttime swim. Eileen, Frank and Sally went for a walk along the beach and Ira headed back to his room.

Ira spent an hour or so fitfully switching between reading *The Count of Monte Cristo*, which he had recently downloaded to the kindle app on his phone after seeing the 2002 version of the film, and watching more Bruce Springsteen videos. He was still, however, preoccupied with his mother's behavior at dinner and decided to head over to the lobby bar and try to relax with a drink.

- Mind if I join you?

It was a voice Ira recognized and was certainly surprised to hear in such a context. Looking up from his glass of cabernet he saw Abigail Dornan standing there swirling the stirrer straw in her Mojito.

- Yeah sure, said Ira, with slight hesitation. Where's your brother?

- Not sure. Probably in his room masturbating. How you enjoying Bermuda so far?

- Well, it's beautiful that's for sure. You know I read that when the first British settlers arrived here in the 17th century, there was no native population.

- That's cool, she replied, with utter indifference. Another mojito please, she said, calling out to the bartender while placing her recently finished glass on the bar. So Ira, you dated Harlee Shaw?

- That I did. For about a year and a half.

- You still talk to her?

- No, not since we broke up.

- I'm sorry. Is it bad that I'm asking about her?

- No, it's ok.

- I love her. She's so gorgeous. Is that your thing, Ira? Blonde hair and big tits?

- Well, I'm not offended by it. I like a lot of different types.

- Me too. I'm all about variety. How did you meet her? Like at a glamorous Hollywood party or something?

- No. Never went to many of those. Believe it or not, I called her agent and left my number. Only time I ever did that.

- Very interesting. Tell me more.

- It was after she broke up with Dean Perna. Or maybe it was Steven Danziger.

- She went through a lot of male celebrities from what I read. Never lasted too long with any of them. Guess you like a challenge.

- Wasn't really thinking about it that way. I found her attractive, and I told her agent to tell her that if she wants to have dinner she can call me. To be honest, I never thought she'd call. I was kind of shocked when she did.

- I'm not shocked she called you. Women like funny guys.

Ira had suspected it at first, and now he was fairly certain. His mother's boyfriend's daughter was flirting with him. The idea of a sexual encounter with her was certainly intriguing. She was very pretty — she had a tall willowy form and long silky dark hair. Her face was somewhat reminiscent of Stephanie Delsano, perhaps because they were both of partial Italian ancestry mixed with Northern European. Adding to the temptation was the fact that Abigail lived in Chicago, far from New York, where Ira lived. From that fact it could be deduced with reasonable certainty that she was not looking for anything serious. There was the potential awkwardness that might arise if the two saw each other at other family events, but such events were likely to be few and far between.

On the other hand, it was still a potentially treacherous path upon which to embark. Yes, Abigail was an adult and he was not trying to manipulate her in any way, nor encouraging her in the slightest way to continue drinking. Her father, on the other hand, might not see it that way were he to find out. He might not view with an understanding eye a 38-year-old sleeping with his much younger daughter, who was no doubt a little star-struck. His mother, also, would be upset. Eileen and Abigail were not close. There was no mother-daughter type of relationship between the two. The problem lay elsewhere. They were in Bermuda to celebrate the glory that was Eileen Deridder. That Ira had opted not to spend more time with her after dinner was bad enough. That he had chosen instead to engage in carnal pursuits with Frank's daughter would no doubt render her furious. Everything was supposed to revolve around her that week and no one else.

Processing all of these factors, Ira still could not decide for or against a nighttime frolic with Abigail. All he knew is that he would not make the first move. If Abigail, on the other hand, made an overt gesture in a sexual direction, he would then have to make a decision. Such an overt gesture was not long in coming. At some point in the midst of her third mojito, after having interrogated Ira about all the other people he knew in Hollywood besides Harlee, she made her thoughts as clear as the waters surrounding the island.

- You wanna go to your room? she asked, sensually biting her lower lip.

- My room? Ira repeated, unprepared for such an overt proposition.

- Or my room. Either way.

- Well, I'm not sure, to be honest.

- Why not? You have a girlfriend?

- No it's just, I'm not sure it's a good idea. You know what I mean?

- Don't worry, Ira. I won't tell anyone.

Ira sat there for several seconds not saying a word. Abigail, sensing the persistence of his misgivings, sought to put his mind at ease.

- So do you know what I did when I was a student at the University of Florida for spending money?

- Tarot card readings?

- No, answered Abigail with a laugh.

- Corporate diversity consultant?

- I was an escort.

- Really?

- Yes really. So I kinda know how to be discrete.

Ira wasn't necessarily sure that Abigail having a past as an escort was a guarantee of discretion. It was, however, a turn-on for him, as he imagined Abigail would be adventuresome in bed. It was sufficient, at the very least, to tip the balance away from indecision and toward "yes."

- Well I guess my room, he said.

Ira was not terribly concerned about Abigail seeing his penile rash. It had diminished considerably since he started using the cream Dr. Chang had recommended, and it wouldn't be noticeable in low lighting anyway.

Arriving in his room, Ira went into the bathroom to grab a condom out of his travel kit. He wasn't expecting to need them on his trip to Bermuda, but he had packed them nonetheless, just in case. Abigail was already completely nude and lying on the bed by the time Ira walked out. Ira found her body perfect in every way, though he was surprised not to see any tattoos, assuming that a former sex worker would certainly have at least a couple. Ira generally liked tattoos on women, not for aesthetic reasons, but simply because they implied a certain lack of prudishness. Regarding Abigail, however, that lack of prudishness was already well established, and Ira was happy to see a girl lying before him with nothing on her body not intended by nature to be there. With such an appetizing feast before him, he eagerly indulged in some oral preliminaries before moving on to more serious matters.

One of Abigail's kinks, Ira soon found out, was being insulted during the act of intercourse. Ira, always open-minded in matters of sexuality, was happy to hurl words like "slut" and "whore" at Abigail as they experimented with various positions. He was enjoying the experience well enough although he, as was so often the case, did not find the reality quite at the level of his expectations. As for Abigail, she seemed to be pushing the limits of the human capacity for pleasure, at least judging by the volume of noise she was making. Ira shushed her several times fearing that her passionate squeals and moans would somehow, against all logic and physical laws, find their way to the other side of the hotel and up the three floors to Frank and his mother's room, not that they would necessarily recognize Abigail's voice at that pitch.

Abigail got dressed immediately after it was all over. They were both, it seemed, of a similar mind as far as not wishing to extend the evening any further.

- Well, it was nice hanging out with you. Certainly the highlight of the Bermuda trip, she said.

- Don't speak too soon. We have the snorkel excursion tomorrow.

- That's right, I forgot about that, she said before heading toward the door.

- Wait hold on!

Ira insisted on checking the hallway first to make sure the coast was clear, lest anyone see Abigail leaving his room that shouldn't.

Walking into the bathroom the next morning to take a shower, Ira again noticed the mole on his back that had been a brief source of worry the day before. A new thought occurred to him. What if the mole was normal during his recent skin check, but had changed in the days since? Or perhaps it wasn't even there when Dr. Chang did the skin check. Perhaps it was a brand new mole Dr. Chang didn't even see!

Ira entered "normal mole & size" into the search bar of his phone. It was not technically his first medical-related Google search of the day. He had woken up in the middle of the night, several hours after Abigail had left, with a disquieting notion swirling around in his brain. He turned on his phone and entered "'HIV & oral sex." Abigail had been a sex worker and therefore at elevated risk for HIV. Ira had been with sex workers before but he had never gone down on one! The risk of transmission was small, according to Ira's online research, especially since he had no abrasions or cuts in his mouth. Ira had not completely dismissed the idea of having contracted HIV, but his mind was put sufficiently at ease to allow him to go back to sleep.

A normal mole is less the six millimeters across, or about the size of a pencil eraser, according to the American Cancer Society website. Ira's mole was certainly not as big as that, but there was still the matter of the lack of symmetry. Ira figured a picture of the mole itself, rather than a picture of the reflection of the mole in the mirror, would provide a more precise image for him to analyze. He reached over his shoulder with his phone in his hand and tapped the screen several times with his thumb until he finally succeeded in hitting the white circle which engaged the camera. He repeated this awkward procedure a few more times until getting a picture with the mole in frame. The mole was as he remembered from the day before. Flat on one side and convex on the other. Ira found a picture online labeled "normal mole." That mole was also not perfectly symmetric, but somewhat more symmetric than the one on his back that he was looking at, in enlarged form, on his phone. "How symmetric is symmetric enough?" wondered Ira. After all, is anything perfectly symmetric? Perfect symmetry may exist as a Platonic ideal, but does it actually exist in nature? In atoms and subatomic particles perhaps, but probably not in anything larger and certainly not a mole.

Ira continued googling to try and ascertain exactly what the chances are that an asymmetric mole, otherwise normal in terms of size and color, was cancerous. Unable to get that information, he contacted Dr. Chang's office to make another appointment for after he got back to New York. He then began reading about survival rates for melanoma. The fact that, at its early stages, it was highly curable offered Ira only small comfort. The idea of a cancer diagnosis was terrifying whatever the odds of beating it might be. He likely would have spent all morning online looking at medical websites, but it was time to meet everyone in the lobby to go to Blue Hole Hill Park for snorkeling.

The snorkeling expedition broke Ira out of his obsession and proved a satisfying experience for the hard to satisfy Ira. They explored a coral reef and even a shipwreck of a steamboat that sunk in 1863. The *Montana* was built in Glasgow and served as a blockade runner during the American civil war. Carrying supplies for the Confederacy from the UK to North Carolina, it foundered in shallow water off the coast of Bermuda where it intended to stop and take on coal. The crew and much of the cargo were saved but the ship was lost, destined no longer to serve the cause of Southern independence, but rather that of Bermudian tourism. The wreck had been heavily colonized by coral, but the bow was still mostly intact and its two paddle wheels clearly recognizable.

Abigail's behavior toward Ira that afternoon was the same as it had been the night before at dinner — polite but mostly indifferent. Indeed there was nothing to suggest that anything had happened between the two, and Ira was happily convinced that she would not reveal their secret. The only acknowledgment of what had taken place the night before was when Abigail, just before plunging over the side of the boat upon reaching the site of the shipwreck, briefly took the snorkel out of her mouth and said to Ira, who was seated nearby, "Midnight your room. Be there."

That night they all had a late dinner at Eagle's Bistro, a restaurant near the hotel. Eileen was reasonably well behaved and thankfully she did not bring up Ira's gig in Maryland again or threaten to have a drink. It was the eve of her birthday, and though she found the prospect of turning 60 upsetting, she was excited because the picture of herself in full snorkel gear with the caption, "Aqua-Chick," was getting a lot of "likes" and positive comments on Instagram.

Other topics discussed that evening included everyone's thoughts on the shipwreck they had seen, which all agreed was fascinating, and Eileen's opinion on global warming. Eileen revealed that, in her gut, she felt that man-made global warming was nonsense. Ira countered that most climate scientists were in agreement that it was real, to which Eileen responded that scientists are often wrong, citing as an example a new study she had read about which concluded that, despite what the scientific community had been saying for years, red meat might not be bad for your health after all. Ira didn't feel like continuing the argument but thought to himself that although climate scientists might conceivably be wrong about global warming, they are a lot less likely to be wrong about it than a retired dental hygienist with an Instagram addiction. Ira felt the same way about the existence of anthropogenic global warming as he felt about John Bonham being the all-time greatest drummer in rock. He lacked sufficient knowledge to draw that conclusion from his own analysis, but if that's what all the experts said, he figured it's likely correct.

Ira's skin cancer obsession had returned after arriving back at his hotel room, and he was in the middle of looking at images of melanoma online when Abigail knocked on the door. It was midnight. Abigail was right on time. Ira put down his phone and cracked a slight smile as he thought about the covertness of their affair. "The only words we exchanged at dinner was when Abigail asked me to 'pass the tomatoes and burrata'," thought Ira. "And now, here she is at my hotel room to get her ass smacked and to be called names."

After a brief exchange of "hellos", Abigail finished the Maker's Mark on the rocks she had with her, and then the two got physical without further small talk. Ira was still somewhat distracted and would have preferred to be left alone to continue his research on melanoma, but he did not wish to insult Abigail by rejecting her. This time, however, he did not perform cunnilingus on her. He hoped she did not take it personally. Unfortunately, he had set the bar very high the night before with ten solid minutes of vigorous oral stimulation. Abigail did not seem to be bothered by this deviation from the previous evening's itinerary, and as they started things off in the missionary position her moaning was hitting decibel levels even greater than those from their first time together. As he had the night before, Ira urged her to modulate her vocal output and again his words were ignored.

A minute or so later there was a knock on the door. "This is embarrassing," thought Ira, imagining that another hotel guest was signaling them to keep the noise down.

- Shhh, said Ira. I told you you're being too loud.

Another knock followed a few moments thereafter.

- One second, said Ira, as he got dressed and went to see who was at the door.

- It's Mom! said the voice on the other side.

- Get in the bathroom, whispered Ira to Abigail as he ran back to the bed. It's my mom!

- Shit, is my father with her?

- I don't know. One second, Mom! called out Ira to Eileen as Abigail grabbed her clothes from off the floor and headed into the bathroom.

Ira hurriedly put his clothes on, wondering to himself whether his mother knew what he had been doing with Frank's daughter just moments before. He was happy that Abigail had been enjoying the experience, but did she have to be so loud?

- It's after midnight. Wish me a happy birthday! said Eileen as Ira opened the door.

Clearly, she was unaware of Ira and Abigail's activities, but Ira was no longer concerned about that as he noticed the drink in her right hand. He stood there in silence as Eileen raised the glass to her lips and took a sip.

- What is that?

- Ginger ale!

- That's not ginger ale. You're drunk. I can tell just looking at you! shouted Ira.

- Whatever, I can't have a vodka tonic on my 60th birthday?

- You can do whatever you want, but not around me.

- Ira don't be a party pooper. Here, have a sip, she said with a laugh as she extended the glass to Ira.

- Please, Mom, just go.

- Ira baby, it's just a little birthday drinky drink, she said as she reached out to try and hug her son.

- Sorry, Mom. I need you to go, he said pushing her away.

- Ira please! she said as Ira closed the door in her face.

Ira looked through the peephole to make sure she had left before telling Abigail she could come out of the bathroom, from which she then emerged fully dressed.

- Sorry about all the drama, Abigail.

- It's ok. Not your fault. Anyway, I'm gonna head back to my room now, she said, correctly anticipating that Ira would have no desire to continue what they had started.

- Ok. Well, thanks for stopping by, said Ira, unable to think of more appropriate words.

- By the way, I wasn't really an escort back in college.

- No?

- No, that was kind of a big fat lie. My job in college was working at the Banana Republic near campus.

-Your secret is safe with me.

Abigail let out a slight laugh before turning toward the door. Ira stopped her, once again insisting on checking first to make sure there were no prying eyes in the hallway before letting her walk out.

A moment later Ira's phone rang. It was his mother. Ira declined the call and turned his phone off. He then took a Xanax, took his clothes off, and got into bed. Within fifteen minutes the Xanax had calmed all the agitation Ira was feeling from the confrontation with his mother and five minutes after that he was asleep.

For the third time that morning, Ira looked at his phone and saw an incoming call from his mother, and for the third time he ignored the call. It did, however, serve as a reminder to put his phone on airplane mode as he settled into his first-class seat by the window of the American Airlines 737 for the return flight to JFK. Ira had decided to change his flight and leave that day. He felt no guilt. His mother made her choice when she decided to have that drink. She would have to spend the day of her birthday without him.

Ira had spent three days in Bermuda with his mother, and what he had feared most had happened. She fell off the wagon. Now that it was all over, however, and he was returning home, he felt almost euphoric. His preoccupation with the mole on his back all of the sudden seemed silly to him. After all, the doctor had given him a complete skin check the week before and found no problems. The chances that in the time since the appointment he had suddenly developed a melanoma was infinitesimal and the mole in question was, in truth, no different than numerous other moles on his body. Ira's new writing partner Miles was right apparently. His bout of hypochondria was a psychological reaction to the stress of spending time with his mother.

Thanks to the wifi onboard the aircraft Ira was able to use the internet, but not for health related-research, which he was now free of the urge to engage in. Thinking about the previous day's snorkeling trip spurred Ira's curiosity about Civil War-era shipwrecks. He spent a good portion of the flight watching a documentary on YouTube on the *Hunley,* a primitive submarine belonging to the Confederate navy which sank in 1864 for as yet unknown reasons after first sinking the Union ship *USS Housatonic* with a torpedo. The wreckage was found in 1995 and raised in 2000 at which time the crew members' remains were found still at their posts.

Such was the extent of Ira's good mood that he was barely bothered by the turbulence while descending toward JFK airport. Shortly after landing, he called Dr. Chang's office to cancel his upcoming appointment.

CHAPTER 14

It was a brisk November day as Miles and Ira walked toward the Comedy Den, picking up the pace as a light rain was starting to fall, neither of them having had the foresight to bring an umbrella.

- How are you feeling? asked Miles.

- I'm ok. Little nervous. Haven't performed in a while.

It had taken Miles several weeks, but he finally succeeded in convincing Ira to get back on stage. Ira's concern was that the other comics would bring up his performance in Maryland, something he desperately did not wish to discuss. His even greater fear was confronting the audience, most of whom would likely know what had happened. The time had come, however, for Ira to face the public once again. He would have to do so eventually. Abandoning performing completely was not a viable option as it was his only reliable long-term source of income. He didn't have a scheduled set at the Comedy Den, but he had called Brian Rezack, the owner, and was told, as always, that he could come whenever he wanted and go on stage.

- I don't believe it! exclaimed Ira as they approached the club.

- What is it? asked Miles.

- That new store across the street.

- Méli-Mallow? asked Miles, reading the sign above the store.

- Yeah. They sell nothing but marshmallows. There's one in my neighborhood. I wondered how they would stay in business. Now they're expanding! Only in New York!

- Near where I live there's a place called The Carrot Cake Store. It's packed every day!

- How ya doin', Ira, said Ron Apple, a notoriously unsocial comic who was seated alone at the bar with a Stoli on the rocks when Ira and Miles walked into the Sunrise Cafe, the restaurant above the Comedy Den.

Instead of lifting his glass to his mouth to drink his vodka, Ron was lowering his head to the glass and drinking, like a deer slaking his thirst at a mountain lake.

Ron, 45 years old with thinning hair increasingly dominated by gray strands, was well known, but not nearly as well known as most comics thought was appropriate given the quality of his edgy, absurdist humor. Ira was not of that mind. Not that he wasn't a fan. Ira always thought Ron was hysterical, but it had been so long since he had abandoned the notion that one's level of fame was correlated to one's ability, that he barely noticed even the most flagrant examples of that lack of correlation.

- That's Ron Apple! exclaimed Miles. Would you mind introducing me? I love his work.

- No can do, said Ira.

- Why not?

- It's for your own good. He's kinda cold to fans. Not great with friends either.

Miles, undeterred, approached Ron at the bar.

- Ron, hi. Just wanted to say I loved your last album, *Live from LA*.

Ron, his head in mid-descent toward his glass of Stoli, did not hesitate to respond with a well-placed arrow from his quiver of sarcasm.

- Well, I guess it was all worth it then.

126

- You warned me, admitted Miles, slinking back toward Ira after his ill-fated attempt at talking to Ron.

At the corner table of the Cafe, Brian was once again provoking, as he so loved doing, a political debate with several comics. Included in the discussion were Karen Lee, Canadian comic Jeff Bunton, guitar comic Stu Healy and Vivi Liu, an Asian-American comic in her late twenties.

- So you don't see it as a problem? asked Karen, that there are people with billions of dollars and other people that can't afford food?

- Of course it's a problem, said Brian. But that's a problem of poverty, not income inequality. If everyone has enough, then who cares how much the people at the top have. How is income inequality in itself bad?

- Ok, said Stu, but the rich have more political influence than the poor, so income inequality kind of distorts democracy.

- There's logic to that, conceded Brian, musing to himself that Stu's points were generally more astute than one would imagine from someone who wrote "Sniffing panties that she wore, stained or one-color I adore. With or without poo. With or without poo." But from what I've read, Brian continued, the evidence suggests that that's not what's happening. As income inequality has increased, we're not really seeing an increase in policies that are bad for the poor. Social programs have not decreased with increasing numbers of the super-rich.

- Ira Spiro! shouted Karen, seeing Ira approach the table with Miles.

Karen got up from the table and ran toward Ira, giving him a big hug.

- So good to see you!

- Hi Ira, said Vivi Liu. We've never met. I'm Vivi. I'm a huge fan!

- Thanks, Vivi. Everybody, this is my friend Miles. We're working together on my memoir.

- That's so great, said Karen. What ya' gonna call it?

- We don't have a name for it yet, but we'll come up with something.

- How about calling it *Ira Spiro Superhero*?

- Whatever we call it, Karen, I promise it won't be that.

- We're talking about income inequality Ira, said Brian. As far as I'm concerned, what people at the top are making is not the issue as long as the people at the bottom have what they need.

- I'm just glad I make enough in stand-up not to have to wait tables at my parents restaurant, said Vivi. Yes my family is a stereotype thank you.

- I'm with you Vivi, offered Ira. I used to work at my father's formalwear store. The Jews are more about dry goods than restaurants.

- I think it's scandalous that you have all these rich people in the United States and there's no universal healthcare in this country like we have in Canada, said Jeff.

- I'm in favor of universal healthcare, said Brian. But again, that has nothing to do with inequality. You can have universal healthcare and still have multi-billionaires, as they do in Canada. What are your thoughts, Miles was it?

- Yes, it's Miles. Well, income inequality could lead to unhappiness because people compare themselves to those who have more, but I don't know if we want to tailor our economic policies around such a toxic human instinct as envy. And, of course, there are numerous other reasons people envy each other. I would imagine, and you comics could probably speak to this, that in show business talent might be a more significant source of envy than money. No doubt there are people who have achieved great fame and wealth who are not

128

regarded as particularly talented who would be jealous of someone who makes far less money but who is more respected.

- Probably true, but I'm jealous of anyone who can eat real ice cream, regardless of talent, quipped Ira.

- That's the real problem in America, lactase inequality, joked Karen.

Everyone present either knew that lactase was the enzyme responsible for the digestion of lactose, or got the general idea from the context, allowing Karen to extract additional laughs from Ira's initial joke.

- Karen's really "milking" Ira's premise, added Jeff Bunton, followed by a chorus of groans and boos from those at the table.

- You sound like a psychologist, said Brian to Miles, addressing Miles point about jealousy.

- Not professionally, responded Miles, but I'm an observer of people and their behavior.

- So Brian, about what time would be good for me to go on stage? asked Ira.

- You can go on third on the 9 pm show, just after Vivi if you want, answered Brian.

- Perfect.

There being no more room to sit down at Brian's table, Miles and Ira grabbed a booth in the middle of the restaurant and ordered some much-needed dinner. Ira was glad neither Brian nor the comics mentioned his show in Maryland. Surely it was on their mind, but luckily they resisted the temptation to bring it up.

- How's the salad, asked Miles, as he bit into a juicy cheeseburger.

- It's a salad, Ira snapped back. How good could it be?

Ira ordered the salad because he had had a barbecued pulled pork sandwich and fries that afternoon and felt he needed to compensate the unhealthy nature of his lunch with a healthy, if not entirely satisfying dinner.

- I need to address the elephant in the room straight away, asserted Ira. I was thinking I'll say something like, "Hey what's up everybody. Gonna do about ten minutes of stand-up for you. Of course, unlike the last time I did ten minutes on stage, this time I'm only scheduled to do ten minutes."

- Yeah, that's funny said Miles laughing. You got any other new jokes you're trying out tonight?

- Yeah, I got one. I'll run it by you. Ok here it goes: So I'm kind of a hypochondriac. Mostly because I don't believe in God. I mean, if I thought that after we died an eternity of bliss awaited us in heaven, I wouldn't give a shit about my health. And, of course, I'd obey the commandments to make sure I went to heaven. Two places you'd never see me in again, the gym and my neighbor's wife.

Miles let out a hearty laugh, almost choking on his cheeseburger. Ira was certainly glad that Miles liked the joke, but the real test would be on stage. The opinion of one person, particularly a friend, and indeed Miles and Ira were becoming friends, was of limited value for judging a joke.

- I really like that. How did you come up with it?

- Well, the hypochondria angle comes from my life obviously, in particular my recent obsession with that rash thing, which by the way is all cleared up. Anyway, for a while I've been toying with the notion that I wouldn't make any effort to live longer if I believed in heaven as a premise for a joke. The other day I was thinking "hey if I believed in heaven, and therefore God, I'd also behave differently in terms of obeying the Bible." So it was a matter of finding a funny connection between those two ideas — obeying the Bible and not taking care of myself.

130

- Lawrence Hummel in the house, shouted Tony Powell, once again addressing Ira using the name of his character from *Jackson Taylor's Christmas Party*.

- Hey Tony?

- "Hey Tony?" That's all I get after all this time I haven't seen you. Get up and give a brother a hug.

Ira obliged Tony's request for a more affectionate greeting and sat back down.

- Tony, this is my friend Miles.

- What's up, Miles. How long you know Ira?

- Just a few months.

- That's it? Ten years I've known him! Love Ira Spiro!

- He's a great guy, said Miles in agreement.

- He's a funny N*** too isn't he.

- He's a funny man indeed, answered Miles.

- Ira, asked Tony, why's your beard so much lighter brown than the hair on your head?

- I don't know. It just grows in like that.

- Well you look like a chocolate mousse cake. We were worried about him, Tony remarked to Miles. He hasn't been here since that show in Maryland.

Ira felt a slight pang of anguish at the mention of the Maryland show. Of course, he knew that one of the comics was bound to bring it up sooner or later and that that comic was likely to be Tony. Tony had a huge heart but was not necessarily known for discretion.

- Karen here? asked Tony. I need to check up on her. She needs supervision.

- She's at the back table, answered Ira. Brian has one of his debates going.

- What's today's topic?

- Income inequality.

- That reminds me, said Tony. Brian! When we getting that raise? he shouted across the room as half the customers turned to look at him. A hundred bucks a set is 2010 money N***, he continued as he walked toward Brian, Karen and the others at the back table. And I don't see any Diesel jeans up in here.

Ira and Miles sat in the back corner, stage left, of the Comedy Den showroom as Vivi Liu was performing. It was a full house as usual.

- My parents own a restaurant, said Vivi to the crowd. Yes. My parents have the most stereotypical job possible for Chinese people. Well, stereotypical because it's a Chinese restaurant. It wouldn't be stereotypical if the customer came in and my father was like, (in a Chinese accent) "Hello, welcome to Xing Liu House of Falefel."

- She's funny, Miles whispered to Ira.

- Yeah, very funny, said Ira who, after having been immersed in comedy for so long, was hard to impress.

At that moment Ira noticed a man seated in the audience on the other side of the room that looked very familiar. "Oh shit", he thought to himself. "Is that Matt Schefter?" The room was dark and Ira's vision wasn't what it was when he was younger, but it certainly looked like Matt Schefter. The same round puffy middle-aged face and bald head. And next to him was a skinny blond woman who seemed to be in her twenties, Matt's preferred demographic for extra-marital female companionship.

- Miles. Is that Matt Schefter? whispered Ira.

- Matt Schefter the director?

- Yeah. Over there, on the other side of the room. Back row.

- Looks like him, said Miles, after taking a quick look.

- Could you do me a favor. Go over there and make sure. Just pretend you're going to the bathroom or something.

As Miles set forth on his mission, Vivi Liu continued her set.

132

- As a young Asian woman, I'm afraid to walk alone in certain neighborhoods in New York City. I'm afraid some white couple might try to adopt me. I go to the Upper East Side, I get nervous. You white people love adopting Asians. I saw an Asian girl on St. Patrick's day with a t-shirt that said, "Kiss My Parents, They're Irish." I went to school with a Chinese kid that was adopted by a Jewish couple. Some kid was making fun of him. He was like "Stop calling me Chink you fakakta schmuck."

- That's definitely him, said Miles, after returning to his seat next to Ira.

- Ok, let's go, said Ira.

- What?

- We're outta here.

Ira got up out of his seat with Miles, a bit confused, following behind. Walking out into the hallway next to the showroom they saw Doug Greco who was MC'ing the show.

- Ira, said Doug, Vivi's got like two minutes left and then you're on. By the way, Matt Schefter is here.

- Yeah I saw.

- I heard he's here to watch Vivi. He's thinking of working with her on a show.

- Hey look Doug, I forgot I have something to do uptown. I can't do the set.

- You sure?

- Yeah, sorry about that.

- All right, I guess I'll put on Bunton.

- Perfect. Catch you later. Come on Miles, let's go.

The two then walked out of the club for an inevitable soaking in what was now a heavy thunderstorm.

Miles, leaning forward in Ira's expensive Giorgetti armchair, turned on the digital recorder.

- Why don't we talk about what happened last night, he said.

- You wanna put that in the memoir? asked Ira.

- It's up to you what goes in the final version, but I imagine whatever happened between you and Matt Schefter would be of interest to anyone reading an Ira Spiro memoir.

- Well, years ago we were working on a TV series together. Ultimately the project fell apart and never made it to the air.

- You were working on a series together? How did that come about?

- Matt contacted me a few months after the disastrous Colorado gig. You remember we spoke about the Colorado gig. It was the first time I couldn't finish my performance. Anyway, Matt was a fan of *Jackson Taylor* and wanted to talk to me about possible projects we could pitch to HBO, which was looking to develop something with Matt as director and producer. He asked if I had any ideas for a television series. I met with him and we brainstormed a bit. I told him about this idea I had come up with for a show about a comedian in the future. Figured there could be a lot to play with there. A show where a comedian makes jokes about life in the next century. Why not? I would play the comedian, Charlton Choudhury.

- Charlton Choudhury? Interesting name. You came up with it?

- Yeah. His parents named him Charlton after President Charlton Talbert who kept America together during the west coast secession crisis of 2055. Kind of a nod to Charlton Heston, who I always associate with the future, you know, cause he starred in *Planet of the Apes*.

- Great movie.

- Yeah, one of my favorite sci-fi flicks. That and *Logan's Run*.

134

- Never saw it. So what about Chouhdury? Isn't Choudhury an Indian name?

- Yeah.

- You were going to play an Indian? You don't exactly look Indian.

- Charlton was only a little bit Indian. His great grandfather Manoj Choudhury was Indian. He came to America in the late 1990s and became a citizen in 2015, just a few years back. Charlton would walk around with a video of him at his citizenship ceremony on his Mirsviyaz phone.

- Mirsviyaz?

- It's a Russian brand. Bestselling phone in the world in 2100.

- Well it sounds like an interesting idea for a show.

- Yeah, who knows. Might have worked.

CHAPTER 15

IRA SPIRO BEFORE COVID: A MEMOIR - CHAPTER 10

Matt Schefter liked my series idea, and he especially liked the name I had come up with for it, *Charlton Choudhury - Modern Times*. The next step was to go to Los Angeles to spend time working on the idea with him and then pitch it to the execs at HBO. I was happy to go. I'm not one of those east coasters who look down on Los Angeles, considering it to be full of uncultured narcissists. It is of course, but there are plenty of those in New York as well, and Los Angeles has the stunning natural beauty of the desert hills and canyons and, of course, the great weather.

I spent my first day in LA just hanging out at the pool at the Marriott in Santa Monica where I was staying. I needed the day to recover from the fatigue of travel and the jet lag. At about 9 am the next morning I hopped in my car and drove off to Matt Schefter's house in Malibu to start working.

I had rented a Mercedes C 300 sedan from Hertz. Living in New York City, I don't drive often, and I rather enjoy the experience when I get the chance. However, I derive little if any extra pleasure from driving a Mercedes as opposed to a far cheaper car. But I was an Oscar winner, and were I to be seen stepping out of say, a Honda Accord, it would look a little bizarre and I might be thought an eccentric cheapskate. Next thing you know there'd be rumors circulating on social media that I would fill bags with shampoo bottles and soap from the housekeeping carts at hotels and take them home to save money. It was for the same reason that I always fly first class, even on shorter flights where a coach seat would be sufficiently comfortable.

The driving distance from Santa Monica to Malibu is about twenty miles and I arrived at Matt's house in a little over a half-hour. I had never seen his house before but it was, as expected, palatial. I had done better than most in show business, but Matt Schefter, at 45 years old, was becoming a titan in the industry. Most would not recognize the face, but few are unfamiliar with the name. Though at the time not yet a force in series television, he had produced, directed, and written or co-written three of the top five highest-grossing comedy movies of the previous decade.

Schefter lived in a ten thousand square foot Mediterranean-style mansion perched on the bluffs overlooking the ocean with, needless to say, a pool and tennis court. The gate opened as I pulled up to the house allowing me access to the driveway. I assumed that was why Matt had asked me the make and model of the car I was driving. He, or whoever was in charge of the gate, must have seen me on a monitor as I arrived and pressed the appropriate button. As I rolled up toward the house Matt came out to greet me.

- Ira, great to see you again, he said, as I exited the C 300, which seemed wholly unimpressive, parked as it was next to a limited edition Bentley Mulsanne.

- I'm really excited about working together. Like I said to you last week in New York, I'm a huge fan of *Jackson Taylor's Christmas Party* and also your stand-up.

- Thanks. And, obviously, I love all your films, I responded.

The truth is, I didn't love all of his films. I hadn't even seen all of his films. Of those I had seen, my opinions varied. I did very much enjoy *The Doorman*, the blockbuster romantic comedy about a love that blossoms between a New York City doorman and a beautiful resident of the building he works in. The script has a lot of fun with the relationship between doormen and their tenants. As for me, I would prefer to live in a building without doormen. They know more about my life than I'd prefer and are one of the reasons I've cut down on the number of call girls I invite over. Yes, I can ask them to dress casually, but when a young woman comes to your apartment at 11 pm and leaves a half-hour later, no one is likely to think she's the cleaning lady. And then there are those awkward moments when the laser-focused look on my face as I briskly and silently walk past a doorman en route to the elevator is a clear indication that I need to get to my bathroom, and fast. But my ex Harlee Shaw liked the apartment and insisted that I buy it so, for now, hookers and diarrhea are not as much of a secret as they could be.

I also liked *Professor Millions,* the film about the English professor who wins a big lottery jackpot and tries to keep it a secret so as not to be harassed for money by friends and family. On the other hand, *No Pain No Jane* was awful. Jane is a young lady who only falls for men who are, in some ways, suffering and broken. The premise is reasonable, but the execution is a mess and if you haven't already seen it, it is not on my recommended list. Incidentally, *No Pain No Jane* is part of a long Hollywood tradition of films whose titles are altered versions of common phrases and expressions. Examples include *Me, Myself and Irene, Knight & Day*, *Bee Movie* and *Legally Blonde*, where golden-haired actress Reese Witherspoon plays a seemingly ditzy, but ultimately quite intelligent young woman who is accepted as a student at Harvard Law School. The name of the film is, of course, a play on the term "legally blind," which, given the proximity of O to I on the QWERTY keyboard, could well have started off as a typo to which a script and several big-name actors were ultimately attached. By far my least favorite Matt Schefter film was *Gulliver*. How that hunk of shit about a talking Iguana managed to even make the modest profit it did at the box office is a question for the ages.

I never even saw the inside of Matt's house, nor met his wife and two sons. We went immediately to a small guest house, also in the Mediterranean style, which Matt used as an office. I sat at Matt's computer writing down ideas as the two of us brainstormed. I found it difficult at times to not be distracted by the spectacular view of the Pacific Ocean and the mountains to the North out of the three enormous arched windows which composed nearly the entire west-facing wall of the guest house living room. The opposite wall was covered with framed posters of Matt's various films. Notably absent from the wall was a poster of *Gulliver*. Matt's opinion of that film was, apparently, not that different from mine.

We spent a total of seven hours or so over the course of two days outlining the show. I managed to convince Matt that the show would work better as a subtle comedy with dramatic elements as opposed to the farcical comedy he had had in mind. My vision was to try and convey the idea that whatever technological advancements the future brings, human beings will still have the same problems and frustrations they have always had.

Once we felt confident with the outline that we had written, Matt called HBO and scheduled a meeting for the next day at their LA headquarters, which were in Santa Monica at the time. Normally when you pitch a show to a network you start off with executives lower down within the hierarchy and, if they like it, you work your way up to, eventually, pitching the show to the ultimate decision-makers. Given Matt's power in the business, however, we were able to avoid all that and start right at the top.

Matt picked me up at my hotel in his Tesla Model X for the quick trip over to HBO. Quickly after arriving, we were ushered into a conference room where Dave Seethaler, the head of programming, his assistant Alicia and Andy Mason, head of development, were seated. After a brief exchange of "hellos" and some small talk, we started the

140

pitch. Matt and I took turns discussing various elements of the show, *Charlton Choudhury - Modern Times*. I began by explaining the general idea. I would play the character of Charlton Choudhury, a stand-up comedian in his thirties living in the year 2100 who is a keen observer of the world around him. A rising star, Charlton jokes about many of the same things people joke about today such as relationships, money and religion. Human nature, I remarked, hasn't changed in thousands of years and certainly won't change by the end of the century. Charlton also talks about current events on stage, for example, the recent addition of the former Canadian province of New Brunswick as the 52nd state (Puerto Rico was the 51st) and jokes about the latest technology, such as, perhaps, hypersonic travel and bionic body parts.

Dave, the head of programming, asked if the effects of global warming would be addressed in the show. Matt and I had discussed this, and I had an answer at the ready. I explained that global warming was causing more and more problems through the mid-21st century, but increasing use of renewable energy and ultimately the development of fusion power by 2070 were able to attenuate the worst effects.

Matt filled in some of the show's finer details, in particular the other main characters in the series. There was Charlton's girlfriend, Aida, who works in holographic advertising. The family patriarch, Manoj Choudhury, who came to America from India in the late 20th century as a child, is 115 and still going strong. Because of the latest medical technology, Matt explained, Manoj has the looks and mental acuity of a man in his 70's today. He is very close to his great-grandson Charlton and follows his comedy career closely. Their connection is in large part due to the fact that Manoj himself had tried his hand at stand-up as a young man in the 2020s and '30s and is delighted to see his descendant becoming such a success at it. Retired from the hotel business, Manoj goes to Charlton's shows frequently.

Other characters included Charlton's brother, Eldrick Choudhury. Eldrick lives with Charlton as he lacks motivation and has difficulty making a living. He finds work from time to time walking dogs. People, of course, still have dogs in 2100 and those dogs need to be walked. In our imagined future, robots, though quite capable in certain areas, are not up to that particular task. They lack the intuition to perceive potential health issues with dogs that a human might perceive and, of course, dogs have evolved to need and appreciate human company. Doggy doo dissolving chemicals, however, have been perfected and are in wide use.

I then began discussing the story arc for the first season of the series. It revolved around the relationship between Charlton and his girlfriend Aida. As season one begins, Charlton is about to embark on his first big comedy tour, "The Turn of the Century Tour." He explains to Aida that he was going to be away a lot and felt they should take a break and see other people as their relationship would surely be strained by his frequent absences. Secretly Charlton, getting his first taste of success, was motivated by a desire to take advantage of the many sexual opportunities that would no doubt be available on tour. Matt jumped in and explained that over the course of the season Charlton realizes he has made a mistake. Aida has moved on and found another boyfriend, whereas Charlton fails to find a real connection with anyone else and comes to understand how important Aida was to him.

I finished off the pitch by emphasizing that the show will be unique in presenting characters that, though they live in a high-tech world of the future, will be just like people are today. The frustrations, disappointments and human foibles will be largely the same, and though they might live longer on average, will still complain that life is too short and wonder what the point of it all is. The series would be generally comedic in tone but would have no shortage of dramatic and emotional moments. Was presenting people from the future as similar in their basic nature to people today really a unique idea? Probably not. Who cares? When you pitch a show you always talk about how unique it is. It's like selling a car. Whatever the reality might be, you tell the customer it's got the best handling in its class.

Dave and Andy, the two execs, seemed to really like the idea. They excitedly suggested possible actors that could be contacted to play the other roles and talked about the timeliness of the idea in a world where people seemed more obsessed about the future than ever, exhibiting both incredible optimism about the possibilities and at the same time profound wariness about what lies ahead. The problem is that network suits are always enthusiastic at pitch meetings. Had we pitched a show about a man sitting in a room drooling from the opening to the closing credits during every episode, they would have said they loved the idea and excitedly talked about the possibility of marketing tie-ins with tissue companies. "Alicia!" one of them would have shouted. "Set up a meeting with Ed at Kleenex." Until a TV executive makes a decision to write a check to produce a show, you cannot gauge what they really think. It was time to head back to New York and wait.

CHAPTER 16

IRA SPIRO BEFORE COVID: A MEMOIR - CHAPTER 11

Eight episodes! HBO ordered eight thirty-minute episodes, a full season, of *Charlton Choudhury - Modern Times*. In fact they were sufficiently excited about the idea to order the episodes without making a pilot first. A pilot is a sort of test episode that television executives look at to determine whether they think the show would make a successful series. Am I over-explaining? Does everyone know this already or just show biz people? Anyway, there are thousands of pilots that have been made for shows that were never produced. Most of them were no doubt utter crap, but many of them might have been wildly successful series, including a lot of the ones that were utter crap. My friends Karen Lee and Tony Powell insisted on taking me out to dinner to celebrate the good news.

- To *Charlton Choudhury*, said Tony, lifting his glass.

I in turn lifted my glass of, in all likelihood, red wine, my go-to alcoholic beverage. Karen did likewise with whatever she was drinking, and we toasted to my future television show about, as it happens, the future. Karen and Tony picked Il Mulino, an upscale Italian restaurant, for the celebratory dinner. Il Mulino has three locations in Manhattan. We elected to dine at the original one, located in the West Village.

- Now Ira, said Tony, is there a role in the show for me? I always wanted to play a future N***.

145

- Oh, and I could play your sister, said Karen. Korwenly Choudhury.

- Korwenly? I asked, not sure I heard right.

- Yes. Korwenly will be a very popular name in the future, joked Karen. Spelled with a K, like my name.

- As it stands now, Charlton doesn't have a sister, but I will suggest both of you for any roles that are appropriate after the scripts are written.

- Thank you, Ira Spiro superhero.

Karen never got tired of calling me Ira Spiro superhero, though as for me, I was tired of the nickname the first time she used it almost ten years before.

- Don't get your hopes up Karen, he ain't putting us in his future-com.

- Look, guys, the casting won't be up to me, I said, as the waiter came over with the appetizers. It's up to Matt and the execs at HBO.

- It's ok, Spiro. We can stay friends anyway.

- Are you excited about it? asked Karen.

- I don't know. To be honest, I'm not sure Matt Schefter and I have the same artistic sensibility. I have mixed feelings about his work.

- You got a shitty attitude, Spiro, said Tony. Don't sabotage this.

- Why would I do that?

- Cause you're afraid of success.

This was the first time someone had accused me of being afraid to succeed. I protested that the idea that I would sabotage this opportunity was beyond absurd. Seeing I was uneasy with the topic, Tony changed the subject.

- There gonna be flying cars in your show? he asked.

- Not sure about flying cars. Maybe personal helicopters.

As a kid in the mid '80s, I imagined we'd have flying cars by now, complete with built-in cassette tape players. That didn't happen, of course. Flying cars never came to be, and cassette tape players are obsolete. It's not easy to predict the future. One future event I did correctly predict, however, was that Karen and Tony would not offer the slightest protest when I offered to pay for the meal. Yes, it was they who had offered to take me out to dinner, but given that I had a lot more money than they did, protocol dictated that I foot the bill.

I have found that those who succeed in show business are particularly prone to generosity towards their friends because of the sense that success or failure is largely a question of luck as opposed to the sole product of hard work and talent. In my case, had Clementine Witt, one of the most successful independent producers in the business, not been a close family friend of Lawrence Roberts, a classmate at NYU who read and liked my script, she likely never would have seen my first draft of *Jackson Taylor's Christmas Party*, let alone wanted to produce it. That said, I do believe, rightly or wrongly, that I have more talent than my average colleague, but, of course, having talent is a question of luck as well.

In any case, had I been dining out with Jerry Seinfeld, whose net worth was close to a billion dollars, he would no doubt have treated, but since my dinner companions were of means somewhat less vertigo-inducing than that, it was me who'd be expected to cover the check. Yes, they half-heartedly reached for their wallets, but everyone knew it was just a formality. We had ordered several courses and plenty of drinks and the bill that night was north of five hundred dollars for the three of us. Not a problem. It was a good meal, and they would have done the same if the situation were reversed, probably.

The next day I was again off to Los Angeles to get started on the writing of the first season of *Charlton Choudhury,* with casting and production scheduled to begin three months later. I rented a little two-bedroom house in Studio City with a view of the San Gabriel mountains to the north.

Everyone was already there when I arrived early on a Monday morning in February on the fourth floor of an office building in Century City that served as the headquarters for Matt Schefter's production company, Head Chef Productions. When I walked into the conference room, Matt was having a conversation about some topic of minor significance with the writing staff he had hired to work with us on the project. The youngest of the group was 23-year-old Taylor Gold. In the two years since graduating from Harvard, he had written on staff for a couple of short-lived sitcoms. Ali Talbert was in her early thirties and had spent the last five years writing sketches and monologue jokes for various late-night talk shows. Finally, there was Josh Benson, a man in his mid-forties. Josh was a former stand-up comic and had co-written the screenplay for the awful *No Pain No Jane* with Matt.

Matt and I explained the basic idea of the show to everyone and outlined the characters and story arc for season one. It was basically a replay of the pitch we had done for the HBO execs several months before. After that, it was time to start talking about ideas for the first episode. Matt suggested starting the series off with Charlton Choudhury doing a stand-up show at a theater in a new colony on Mars.

- I even thought of a couple of jokes, he said. "Hey, good to be here on Mars. I've been saying it for years but now it may actually be true — I'm the best comic on the planet."

- I love that! shouted Josh Benson, literally applauding in his seat like the suck-ass he was.

- I got another joke, continued Matt. "Do you guys use different expressions now that you live on Mars? Like, if you hear an original idea do you say, 'It's like a breath of fresh compressed oxygen.'"

- No! No! No! No! No! was my less than enthusiastic response.

- What's the problem? said Matt, more than a little annoyed by my passionate rejection of his idea.

It wasn't the jokes that I objected to. I mean, they were bad, but my opposition was based on other issues.

- So Charlton Choudhury, a civilian, is going to spend eight months each way in a spaceship going to Mars to do a stand-up show? I objected.

- Maybe by the year 2100 we'll be able to get to Mars faster.

- It will still likely take months to get there. And I don't think we're gonna have colonies on Mars by then anyway.

- Sorry, I didn't realize we had the head of NASA here among us.

- Look, I've seen documentaries about this. The atmosphere is toxic, and the average temperature is minus 80. And where will the food and water come from to supply a whole colony?

- You don't think between now and the next century it's at least possible we'll resolve these problems?

- Yeah, come on Ira. You really can't rule it out. And it would be a cool way to start the episode, said the 23-year-old Taylor Gold, jumping into the debate.

- Excuse me, what did you say, junior?

Yes I know, I went too far with the "junior" comment, which is why I immediately offered an apology, which Taylor readily accepted, at least with his words if not with his heart. Ultimately we agreed on a compromise. The episode would start off with Charlton performing at a space-hotel in low Earth orbit. Josh Benson excitedly noted that we could still use the compressed oxygen joke.

There were other conflicts during that first week in the offices of Head Chef Productions. Among other things, Matt and I clashed over the question of, believe it or not, flying cars.

- Anything that looks like a car can't fly! I yelled, startling Ali and causing her to spill her coffee. You need a lifting surface to fly, which means wings or a rotor. And winged vehicles require a runway for takeoff and landing.

After showing Matt and the others a couple of related articles online I succeeded in convincing them of the correctness of my position. Personal transportation in Charlton's world, at least for medium to long distances, would be the province of personal helicopter-like vehicles with sufficient computer power to operate autonomously without the input of a trained pilot. This is, in essence, what I had said to Tony at our pricey dinner at Il Mulino.

The Thursday of that week Matt suggested a slight change in our initial conception of the rupture between Charlton and his girlfriend.

- Here's an idea. Just throwing it out there. Might be dramatically more interesting if, instead of Charlton breaking up with Aida before going on tour, Aida makes a surprise visit to him on the road and catches him with another girl. Then she breaks up with him. Thoughts?

- Stupid fucking idea! I grumbled, offering my thoughts as requested.

- Can I speak to you for a second, in private?

I followed Matt out into the hallway where he proceeded to holler in my face.

- Don't you ever speak to me like that again!

- You want Charlton to cheat on his girlfriend in the first episode? You want our main character to be brutally unlikeable from the get fucking go?

- I was throwing out an idea. You don't like it we can have a civil discussion, which I've been noticing you seem to have trouble with.

Despite the harsh reprimand, I ultimately won that argument as well, and we agreed that Aida would not catch Charlton cheating.

The next day, however, we had an argument I would not win. I suggested that in one of the episodes we have Charlton go to Washington, DC for a show, only we reveal that, in 2100, the nation's capital is no longer called "Washington, DC." I didn't have another name in mind, but I felt that a future, more diverse US population, would be less willing to venerate the slave-owning founding fathers, even the once untouchable George Washington. Ali, Taylor and Josh thought the idea interesting, but Matt was categorically against it. He felt the topic was too sensitive. So many Americans felt, and feel, that the history and heritage of this country are under attack, and Matt did not want to broach the topic. He especially did not want to provoke those who were insisting, with increasing fervor, that a demographic change in the country would fundamentally change our culture and that further, this change was a bad thing.

I felt that there was another factor influencing Matt's decision. I was not a fan of President Trump, but I did not spend too much time thinking about him and could not muster up the energy to actively hate the man. Matt Schefter, on the other hand, detested Donald Trump and refused to even say his name, simply referring to him as "the fool in the White House". He spent an inordinate amount of time writing anti-Trump posts on social media, especially Twitter. In the context of a recent debate as to whether statues of Confederate soldiers should be removed from public spaces in the South, Trump had expressed concern that hostility toward Confederate soldiers might ultimately lead to attacks on men like Jefferson and Washington, both also believers in the superiority of white people. "Is it George Washington next week, and is it Thomas Jefferson the week after? You know, you really do have to ask yourself where does it stop?" Trump had said at a press conference. I imagined that the last thing Matt wanted to do was imply that Trump might actually be right about something. If, in our imagined future, the founding fathers had lost their central place in the American pantheon, then Trump's prediction could be said to have been borne out.

Upon hearing Matt's objection, Josh, Ali and Taylor quickly changed their minds about the future renamed Washington, DC. I, on the other hand, had no such change of opinion.

- So we're just gonna avoid anything potentially controversial? You know what, I'm just not in the mood for this. I'll see y'all Monday, I said as I headed out the door.

Matt ran out after me and grabbed me by the arm, squeezing hard.

- Where are you going?
- First of all, let go of my arm.

Matt let go, and the enraged look on his face seemed to increase in intensity as if to compensate for the anger he was no longer manifesting with the tight grip of his hand.

- You're gonna get back in there and act like an adult or I will shut this whole fucking thing down. I will pull the plug on this whole series. I do not fucking care.

I wasn't sure if he was serious or not, but I went back into the conference room and behaved reasonably well for the rest of the day. We finished outlining the first episode of the show. I would write the first draft of the episode over the next week while the others would work on outlining the second episode, for my eventual perusal.

"No question, in terms of natural beauty, Los Angeles has it all over New York," I thought as I sat in the backyard of my rented home in Studio City for about an hour, admiring the hilly rugged terrain surrounding the house and watching the sun as it made its descent towards the mountains in the distance. It was a stressful week, and I thought about how I might best spend my weekend. I thought of going to one of the local comedy clubs to see who might be hanging out, but the idea had limited appeal to me as I knew few of the LA-based comics personally. In fact, I really had no close friends in Los Angeles.

Ultimately thoughts drifted into my head, as if on the warm desert breeze, of Charlotte Aubertin. I had not spoken to her since she had abruptly gone back to France two years before. So much had happened since then, notably the success of *Jackson Taylor* and my relationship with Harlee Shaw. If only she were still in San Francisco. I could take a drive up there and spend the weekend with her. That not being an option I spent the next couple of hours watching the movie *Sully* which had come out the year before, though I hadn't yet gotten around to seeing it. It was about Chesley Sullenberger, a US Airways captain who landed his Airbus A320 on the Hudson River in 2009 after losing power to both engines as the result of a bird strike. There were no fatalities and it was dubbed the "Miracle on the Hudson."

I'm not a very calm flier under the best of circumstances, and I no doubt would have literally shit myself had I been on board that day, though surviving such an event might have been good publicity for me at the time. I can imagine the interview. "We're here with Ira Spiro. He was one of the passengers of flight 1549. Can you tell us what happened in those final minutes of the flight?" "Well," I would say, "there was an eery silence in the cabin after the engines had stopped, and then the captain announced 'brace for impact'. Whatever our mundane thoughts had been just seconds before, we were all now wondering if the final moments of our lives were at hand. By the way, my DVD, *A Side of Chuckles,* is available on Amazon and iTunes. An hour of hilarity for only $9.99."

After watching the movie, I took a hot bath and then listened to music videos on YouTube with a particular emphasis on songs related to Southern California, my new home, at least for a while.

The rest of the weekend was similarly uneventful, though I will confess to treating myself to the services of a five hundred dollar an hour escort. As usual, the anticipation was more exciting than the experience itself, but it was nice to be able to simply open the front door for her rather than endure that awkward moment when you have to tell your doorman "Yeah, it's ok. You can send Destiny Renée up."

By Thursday I had finished a first draft of season one episode one of *Charlton Choudhury - Modern Times*. Matt had a few notes and comments about it, including one involving a scene with Charlton and his 115-year-old great-grandfather Manoj. I am able to reproduce the scene exactly as I had originally written it because I happened to find it on an old USB drive at home. No need to rely on vague, reconstructed memories as, I must confess, I have done from time to time in writing this memoir. Anyway here it is:

INT. CHARLTON'S APARTMENT – DAY

Charlton and Manoj are in front of Charlton's computer watching a nearly century-old video on YouTube (Yes, YouTube is still around in 2100. Why not? There are brands that old. Jack Daniels has been causing fights and bad decisions since 1875).

MANOJ: I just found this video of me performing back in 2016. I had forgotten I went by the name Manny Charles back then.

CHARLTON: Wish we could watch it in holography.

MANOJ: Not with a video this old! You'd have to convert it to HJAX-3, if that's even possible.

154

*The video is titled "Manny Charles at Edgar's Pub - New York City."
A young Manoj is on a makeshift stage performing in front of a half-
filled bar.*

*YOUNG MANOJ ON STAGE: My family has a Holiday Inn franchise.
A lot of Indians in the hotel business. Whether you're American Indian
or Indian American you're dealing with reservations.*

*The joke was followed by mild laughs in the bar on the video and no
laughs at all from Charlton in front of the computer.*

MANOJ: I know. Not a great joke.

*CHARLTON: It's not bad. There are still a lot of Indians in the hotel
biz.*

*MANOJ: Yeah, but used to be a lot more. Now it's mainly people from
the former North Korea.*

*YOUNG MANOJ ON STAGE: My grandfather just came from India to
live with us. He's 90 years old. If you asked him what day it is he
couldn't answer you. Not Alzheimer's, he doesn't speak English.*

*Another round of barely audible laughter in the bar. Charlton doesn't
even get this joke.*

*CHARLTON: What exactly is Alzheimer's? All I know is you're
supposed to get vaccinated for it after 50.*

*MANOJ: Alzheimer's disease was a disease a lot of older people used
to get. It made you lose your memory. As it got worse you wouldn't*

recognize your own family members. You'd even start to forget
common words.

CHARLTON: Forgetting common words? That would be a real, you
know, night . . . something or other.

Manoj laughs.

END SCENE

- I like the idea of watching an old video from when Manoj did
stand-up, said Matt. But you gotta get rid of the Alzheimer's stuff. Find
something else.
- What's the problem with the Alzheimer's stuff exactly? I
responded.
- Alzheimer's is not funny. It's a horrible disease.
- It's something comedians joke about. And Manoj's jokes
aren't necessarily supposed to be funny. That's why he went back into
the hotel business!
- Charlton makes fun of it too. When he pretends to forget the
word "nightmare."
- Charlton lives in a post-Alzheimer's world. To him it would
be more than fair game for a joke. Would you find a leprosy joke
offensive?
- Change it. Conversation over.
I was pissed off, but knowing I was on thin ice with Matt, I let
it pass and agreed to make the changes. Early the next week, as I was
staring at my computer reworking the script, I noticed Riley Ann
Rogers leaving Matt's office.

- Hey Ira, she said as she walked past the cubicle where I was working. Looks like we may be working together. Anyway, gotta run. Ciao.

I had met Riley years back at Harlee Shaw's Birthday party at the Hollywood Roosevelt Hotel. As I recall Harlee didn't really like her, but since Riley was a successful young Hollywood actress, she felt the need to invite her. As for Riley, she felt the need to accept the invitation, given that Harlee was similarly a successful young Hollywood actress.

- What was Riley Ann Rogers doing here? I asked Matt as I walked into his office.

- We're talking about her playing Charlton's girlfriend, Aida. She wants to get into series television. Then again, who doesn't these days? Crazy how all of a sudden TV series are becoming more prestigious than films. Anyway, we'd be lucky to have her so hopefully we can make it happen.

Certainly having Riley on board would be a big deal. Having big names attached to a project cannot guarantee success, but it gets people talking about it and can certainly help attract big ratings initially. Plus, having one big name can attract others.

- Well, I guess we'll see what happens with that. Fingers crossed. By the way, did you have a chance to look at Karen Lee's script?

The week prior I had given Matt a copy of a spec script that Karen Lee had given me. In order to get a job writing for a TV show, especially if one has never written for a TV show before, it's necessary to submit a writing sample. Karen had written an episode of a TV series idea she had thought of involving a woman who runs a personal matchmaking service. I told her we'd likely be hiring more writers once the show was in production, and she asked me to pass her script along to Matt.

- Yeah I read it, he said.

I knew at that moment that he had found it underwhelming. Had he read it and liked it he would have told me immediately. That he didn't mention it meant he was trying to avoid an unpleasant conversation, knowing that Karen was a good friend of mine.

- So you didn't like it?

- She has potential. I think she needs a little more experience as a writer.

- Really?

- I'm sorry Ira. I know she's a friend of yours. I just wasn't all that impressed.

Once again I controlled my emotions and simply walked out of his office without any further words. I spent the rest of the day at my computer being deeply and profoundly unproductive, at times bouncing around the web, at times doing nothing but thinking about what nerve Matt had to dismiss Karen's script as he had. I certainly thought it was good when I read it, even laughing out loud several times. Granted, writing is subjective, but I had the feeling that, as is so often the case with producers, Matt's opinion of the script was based less on its actual merit and more on the fact the Karen was neither a famous comic nor an accomplished writer. Had the same script been written by some young hotshot, say Ali Talbert, who was at that moment working with Taylor Gold and Scott Benson on the outline for episode two, he probably would have heralded it as a work of genius.

Back at my rented house that night, once again in the back yard watching the sun disappear behind the mountains, I felt increasingly angry about, well, pretty much everything related to my working relationship with Matt, but in particular about Karen Lee's script. I knew he wouldn't wish to be contacted outside of work, but such was my frustration that I did it anyway.

- Why are you calling me? We can talk about this tomorrow, barked Matt into the phone.

-Actually, I wanna talk about it now. Did you even read the script or just google Karen's name and decide she's not any good because she hasn't won any stupid awards?

- You saying I'm a liar?

- Hey, we're all liars. I'm saying you lied about reading that script. Or maybe you're just too stupid to recognize good writing!

- Fuck you, he said, hanging up the phone.

- No fuck you, I said after calling him back.

- I told you, I will pull the plug on this whole fucking thing. Don't fucking call again.

No, I didn't have the nerve to call a third time. What I did do, however, was write and send him the following email:

Hey Matt, I rewrote that scene with Charlton and Manoj. Here's the revision:

YOUNG MANOJ ON STAGE: Hey I saw a movie yesterday called No Pain No Jane. *Who saw it?*

Bunch of "Yeah's" from the audience in the bar.

YOUNG MANOJ ON STAGE: What a pile of shit that was, huh?

Huge laughs in the bar.

CHARLTON: What's No Pain No Jane?

MANOJ: That was a movie by this marginally talented, overrated, bald director named Matt Schefter. He was famous when I was young.

159

CHARLTON: It wasn't a good movie?

MANOJ: It was terrible but far from his worst. He had another movie about a talking iguana named Gulliver that pushed the boundaries of awfulness.

CHARLTON: That does sound horrible.

MANOJ: Sure was. Changing semen-stained sheets at our Holiday Inn was more fun than sitting through that.

Charlton and Manoj share a hearty laugh.

MANOJ: Oh and also, it was kind of an open secret in Hollywood that he cheated on his wife with young actresses who naively thought it would help their career.

END SCENE

The email he sent in return, several hours later, told me not to come in the next day as the series had been officially canceled. I managed to put an end to a multi-million dollar production in about two weeks, make enemies of HBO, Matt Schefter, Taylor Gold, Ali Talbert, Josh Benson and, evidently, Riley Ann Rogers who sent me a text the next day with just one word: "*Asshole*."

CHAPTER 17

Charlotte Aubertin's one-bedroom apartment on the third floor of an early 20th-century apartment building in the 17th arrondissement of Paris was beautifully decorated for the 2018 Christmas season. Charlotte's Sri Lankan mother grew up in a Hindu household and her French father was a lapsed Catholic. Charlotte herself had little use for religion, but she loved the traditions of Christmas and always took great pleasure in creating a welcoming, festive environment in her home every year at holiday time. A red ribbon spiraled its way from the gold star at the top of her big tree to the base, cutting a path through the white lighted bulbs and angel figurines present in abundance among the green needles. There were also white lights surrounding the living room windows that looked out on Rue Poncelet. A wreath was hung on the adjacent wall below which, written in green and white glass balls, was the word "*JOIE*," French for "joy."

Charlotte was single again that Christmas. She had gone on several dates in the previous months with various men she had met through friends and online, but none had succeeded in sparking her interest in the slightest measure. Her last date was dinner with an attractive engineer named Didier from Aix-en-Provence whom she had met on Meetic.fr. Things were going well enough that she considered the possibility of a second date until, at some point mid-entree, Didier said, "*D'habitude les Indiennes me plaisent pas, mais toi t'es vachement jolie en fait*" (Normally I'm not attracted to Indian women, but you're actually really pretty). Without another word, Charlotte put enough money on the table to cover her portion of the meal and walked out, leaving Didier wondering what he had done wrong.

Charlotte was curled up on her couch indulging in some macarons purchased at the boulangerie across the street from her apartment and watching what was still one of her favorite films, *Jackson Taylor's Christmas Party*, made even more enjoyable given the time of year. Normally Charlotte watched English-language films with the French subtitles activated in case there was something she didn't understand, but she had seen this film enough times that she was familiar with almost every word.

Jackson Taylor's Christmas Party, co-starring and written by Charlotte's old boyfriend, or fuck-buddy or whatever the hell Ira Spiro had been to her, was the story of a slightly eccentric middle-aged novelist named Jackson Taylor who had a Christmas party every year at his New York City apartment. Each year many of the same colorful and eclectic characters would show up, often after having not seen each other since the party the year before. Jackson Taylor was played by Colin Rory, an English actor who did an American accent well enough to play the Manhattan-born and bred Jackson, though now and again an "ah" sound in words like "bath" and "glass" would betray his origins across the Atlantic. Ira played Lawrence Hummel, an awkward young law student who meets Jackson randomly on a flight and winds up on the writer's invite list. At his first Jackson Taylor party, he meets Julianne Dunn, a beautiful aspiring actress played by Marlise Warner Stewart, a young theater actress in her first big film role. Charlotte always thought Marlise somewhat resembled her, albeit a caucasian version, and she was not wrong on that account. Their facial features were quite similar, notably their high foreheads and cheekbones and narrow straight noses.

In the film, Lawrence and Julianne see each other over the years at the party and eventually fall in love, break up and, of course, fall in love again. The film is, at its heart, a romantic comedy and adheres to the necessary structure of the genre. As for Jackson, he tragically dies of an opioid overdose at what is naturally his last Christmas party. The final scene of the film is a Christmas party at Julianne and Lawrence's home in Los Angeles, which they share together as a married couple. By this time Julianne is starring in a major motion picture and Lawrence has abandoned his job at a New York corporate law firm and embarked on a career as a television comedy writer.

On her television screen, Charlotte was watching a scene about twenty minutes into the film where Julianne is walking along seventh avenue in New York with her friend Zoe. It is Christmastime and there are lights and decorations everywhere.

ZOE: Do you wanna go see Atonement?

JULIANNE: I've already seen it. It's really good though. Keira Knightley's in it.

ZOE: I know. I love her!

JULIANNE: Oh look. A party.

From the street, Julianne notices a party in full swing through the window of Jackson's apartment on the fifth floor of an elegant brick prewar building. There is a huge Christmas tree in the apartment as well as a Hanukah Menorah and people are milling about talking and drinking. Nearer the window, an odd-looking small-statured man wearing a top hat is talking to a tall thin modelly looking blond woman.

Deciding the party looked like more fun than a movie, Julianne convinces Zoe to crash the event. They buy a couple of Santa hats from a street vendor and a bottle of white wine from a liquor store figuring

163

that, dressed as St. Nick and bearing gifts, the doorman wouldn't question them when they said, "We're here for the Christmas party"! Indeed he did not question them and simply said, "OK, apartment 5C."

- *Qu'est-ce que tu regardes?* said six-year-old Sébastien, walking into the living room.

- Did you say somes'ing. I cannot 'ear you, was Charlotte's response in her French-accented English.

- What you are watching?

- Now I 'ear you better. I am watching a movie called *Jackson Taylor's Christmas Party*.

Charlotte had a strict rule with Sébastian. Whenever they were alone together they would speak English. This would allow Charlotte to practice her English, still quite imperfect even after the five years she had spent living in the United States, and also allow Sébastian to learn the language, albeit with a French accent and imprecise grammar.

- Can I watch 'zis wis' you? he asked.

The film was rated R, thus not necessarily appropriate for someone as young as Sébastian, at least, according to the American rating system. The French, however, tend to be somewhat less rigid in that regard, and Charlotte, in particular, was largely unconcerned about such things.

- Of course you can, said Charlotte, gently patting the couch with her hand, inviting Sébastian to sit next to her.

Sébastian jumped up on the couch, resting his head on Charlotte's shoulder.

On the screen, Jackson opens up the door and sees Julianne and Zoe in their Santa hats. Julianne is holding the bottle of wine they had just purchased.

JULIANNE: *Hi!*

JACKSON: Hi! Merry Christmas!

JULIANNE: Merry Christmas!

JACKSON: I'm having trouble placing you. Might you be friends of my ever so lovely and charming girlfriend Ella?

JULIANNE: Well, to be honest, we were just kind of walking by and noticed there was a party going on.

JACKSON: And indeed there is. Come on in!

Julianne and Zoe wander in amongst the revelers. The man in the top hat is seen seated in a corner of the living room getting a caricature of himself drawn by a young male artist Jackson had hired for the occasion.

- She's pretty! said Sébastian.
- Which one?
- 'Ze one that looks like you Maman!

When Charlotte had gotten together with Ira a few months prior, during her trip to New York to look at apartments, and Ira had seen a picture of Sébastian on Charlotte's phone, she told him he was her nephew. But indeed, Sébastian was her son and he looked just like her and, to a lesser extent, like Marlise Warner Stewart, the actress who played Julianne.

- What does my fa'zer look like?
- We've talked about 'zis Sébastian, said Charlotte. Let's watch 'ze movie.

165

Charlotte had explained to Sébastian many times that she wanted to have a baby, but could not find the right daddy, so she went to a special place, kind of like a store, where a woman can go to buy the seeds from a man to make a baby. She told him she had never seen the father, but that she knew he was handsome and smart.

- Sébastian, 'zis is 'ze part where Julianne meets Lawrence for 'ze first time at 'ze party.

LAWRENCE: How do you know Jackson?

JULIANNE: Who?

LAWRENCE: Jackson Taylor. This is his party.

JULIANNE: Oh. Well, I don't really know him. I think I met him at the door. You?

LAWRENCE: I sat next to him on a plane from Chicago. I wouldn't be here if I hadn't missed an earlier flight because of a fender bender on the way to O'Hare.

JULIANNE: Funny how it all works. I wouldn't be here if the blinds over there were closed.

At that moment Julianne's friend Zoe comes over toward her looking distraught. She is staring at a black Motorola Razr flip phone.

ZOE: Paul hasn't texted me back and he's not answering. I know he's fucking that girl from the gym.

- That mean what Maman? Fucking? asked Sébastian.

- That means *"embrasser."*

"Embrasser" is French for "to kiss," which Charlotte thought captured the idea well enough, not wishing to explain the real meaning of the word to a child of six years old. Perhaps, she thought to herself, it wasn't a good idea to let Sébastian watch the movie after all. Oh well, she had already invited him to join her on the couch. There was no turning back. Anyway, it was always a good thing for him to be exposed to more English. He'd no doubt learn some more words and not just the naughty ones.

JULIANNE: Maybe not Zoe. He could be doing anything. Try not to think about it. Enjoy the party.

Zoe starts to cry.

ZOE: Can we please go. I don't feel like being out right now.

Julianne says a quick goodbye to Lawrence and she and Zoe walk off, leaving him there with his drink. They will not see each other until the next year's party.

- *Est-ce qu'elle lui plait, Maman?*
- Sorry, I don't understand French.
- Does he like her? 'Ze man in 'ze movie. Does he like 'ze woman that look like you?
- Yes, he like her very much.
- He want to fuck her?

That Sébastian instinctively knew the appropriate form of the verb "to fuck" to use in that sentence was an impressive testament to the instinctive facility children have with languages. Nevertheless, it

167

was an awkward moment and Charlotte thought it best to answer the question quickly and move on.

- *Oui*, Sébastian, she said, inadvertently violating her English-only rule.

Charlotte was likely never to forget this moment. Not because Sébastian had said a bad word. Because, rather, it was the first time Sébastian had laid eyes upon Ira. Whether Ira had been a boyfriend or merely a so-called "friend with benefits" Charlotte was not certain. What he was without question, however, was the father of her child. All her talk of sperm donation, or going to a "store" as she explained it to Sébastian in terms she felt more appropriate for a child, was, in fact, a complete lie.

After finishing watching the movie she picked up Sébastian, who had fallen asleep about halfway through, and tucked him into his bed, which was next to her own in the apartment's only bedroom. She turned off the bedroom lights, leaving illuminated only the Santa Clause nightlight, as Sébastian preferred not to sleep in total darkness. She then returned to the living room and poured herself a glass of Prosecco, which she took with her into her bathroom for a hot bubble bath. Leaning her head back in the tub and closing her eyes, her thoughts traveled back in time the six-plus years separating that moment from the night Sébastian was conceived.

In 2012 Charlotte and Ira had known each other for two years. Ira was living in New York and Charlotte was in San Francisco. There would be periods where they would text each other frequently and talk on the phone and periods where there was little communication between them. They would, however, always make an effort to get together whenever they found themselves on the same coast. Though the nature of their relationship had never been explicitly defined, Charlotte did not consider it an exclusive arrangement and she was certain, rightly so, that neither did Ira. She would have happily committed to something more serious and even moved to New York, but Ira never seemed to be of that mind.

By coincidence, they happened to both find themselves, in March of that year, in Las Vegas, Nevada. Ira was doing shows at a comedy club at the MGM Grand Hotel and Charlotte was in town for an information technology conference. Though she had a room at the Mirage, she spent most of her time with Ira at the MGM Grand.

After Ira's Saturday night late show they had done some bar hopping as well as a little gambling and ended the night in Ira's luxurious suite overlooking the hotels of the strip and the desert beyond.

- Shit!

- What is there? asked Charlotte.

She was directly translating the French phrase "*qu'est-ce qu'il y a*" into English. Though "*qu'est-ce qu'il y a*" usually does mean "what is there?" it is also used to express the question "what's the matter?"

- It broke, answered Ira.

- The preservatif?

- Yes, the condom.

- I 'sink it's ok. My period was just over so I don't 'sink I get pregnant.

- Can you take the morning-after pill?

- Ok, I go get some tomorrow.

- Actually, I have some.

- You have 'ze morning-after pill?

- Yeah. I have it with me just in case.

Charlotte found this somewhat odd, but then again Ira had always been extremely careful regarding birth control. She recalled one time when he threw out a pack of condoms because he had left it in the bathroom while he was taking a shower, and he had read that shower steam could weaken them and reduce their effectiveness.

Ira got a pack of morning-after pills from out of his suitcase and handed one to Charlotte.

- Ok I go to 'ze bas'room and take 'zis.

Charlotte went to the bathroom with the pill. She turned on the faucet as if she were filling up a glass of water with which to take the pill. Instead, she simply flushed it down the bathroom sink drain. She had no intention of taking the morning-after pill. She had taken it once in her life, after an encounter with a man named Jean-Michel in the south of France, and suffered awful side effects from it including dizziness and headaches. The subterfuge was simply to put Ira's mind at ease. If she did get pregnant, and she highly doubted that she would, she would decide on the best course of action.

A few weeks later, back at her apartment in San Francisco, Charlotte noticed the first signs. Her breasts were sore and she had morning sickness. A home pregnancy test revealed that indeed she was pregnant. A tiny Tamil Sri Lankan, French, Jewish, Dutch (and other sundry European ethnicities) human being had begun to grow within her. She had never been pregnant before but had always felt that if it happened while she was not married, or at least in a serious committed relationship, she would not keep the baby. Now that she was actually in that situation she was not so sure. One thing was clear, however. Ira was not interested in being a father. As if the fact that he handed her a morning-after pill from his own personal stash was not clue enough, he had mentioned on several occasions that procreation was not in either his immediate or long-term plans.

Over the weeks that followed she struggled with what to do. She knew she would be a great mother and she adored children, but perhaps it would be best to wait until the stars of parenthood were more properly aligned. Before saying anything to Ira she decided it would be

170

best to talk about it with her parents back in France. As it turned out, they were thrilled at the idea of being grandparents, even if the circumstances were less than ideal. They told her she could come back to France, and that they would happily give her all the help she needed with the baby.

The decision, seemingly so difficult before, had become easy. She would have the child. But what about Ira? A thought crossed her mind that, at first, she dismissed as absurd, but that seemed more and more reasonable as she analyzed it from every angle. What if she did not tell Ira? He did not want to be a father. Would it not be better for all involved if he didn't know? The best thing would be, as her parents had suggested, to raise the child in France surrounded by an adoring family. What good would it do Ira to know he had a son or daughter that he made it clear he did not want? Perhaps, out of a sense of obligation, he would visit but, given that they'd be separated by thousands of miles, those visits would certainly be few and far between. And what good would it do the boy or girl to have a father who came to visit so infrequently, if at all? She was not discounting the necessity of a father in a child's life, but the youngster would not be without male influences. There would be his or her grandfather and also uncle, Charlotte's older brother Laurent.

She was still, however, considering the possibility of telling Ira the truth when, a couple of weeks later, she saw an incoming call from Ira on her phone.

- Hi Ira. 'Ow are you?" she said, answering the call.

- Good, what's up with you?

- Not much. I am just at home taking a coffee. What you are doing?

- At home too. Was listening to music. So how is everything?

Charlotte found the tone of the question a bit more serious than the standard "how is everything?"

- Fine, she said.

- So, um, you're not pregnant or anything?

- Why do you ask 'zis?

- Well, you know, because of what happened. I mean, I was just reading online that the Plan B pill is not . . . It doesn't always work.

- It's fine Ira. I'm not pregnant. Look, I'm meeting a friend for lunch. Can we talk later?

Charlotte had no lunch planned with a friend, but it was not a conversation she wished to continue. That settled the matter. Better her baby has no father than one that had no interest in being one. "Neither one," she said to herself, "would know about the other."

Two months later Charlotte was in Paris living with her parents. She found a job at a French financial firm and, eventually, moved into her own apartment a short time after Sébastian was born. As the months went by she watched, from across the Atlantic, as Ira became more and more famous. There was no anger or bitterness on her part. Whatever his faults, she had fond memories of the times they had spent together, and he had given her Sébastian, whom she loved more than anyone in the world. She was genuinely happy to see him succeed, and she and her old friend Virginie were at the famous Grand Rex cinema in the 2nd arrondissement the night of the *Jackson Taylor's Christmas Party* Paris premiere. She loved the film and was anxious to see the original English version, which she did as soon as it was available on DVD. Charlotte was an exception, but the French have little tolerance for subtitles and prefer to watch American films dubbed in French. Americans, by contrast, prefer not to watch French films at all.

One day, as she was walking down Rue Gaultier heading to her office in La Défense, the major business district at the western edge of Paris, her attention was caught by the cover of the magazine Paris Match at one of the news kiosks that are ubiquitous in the French capital. *HARLEE SHAW N'EST PLUS UN COEUR A PRENDRE*, read the headline, accompanied by a picture of the beautiful blonde actress walking arm in arm with Ira Spiro along Beverly Boulevard in Los Angeles. Harlee Shaw, according to a literal translation of the headline, was "no longer a heart to be taken," or as it might read, with admittedly less poetic flourish, in an English publication, Harlee Shaw was off the market.

The article, which Charlotte felt compelled to read, spoke of the new couple being seen together all over Hollywood and how friends of the actress said they had never seen her so happy. Charlotte had never thought of Ira as a man who was interested in any sort of relationship. He had certainly never broached the subject with her, and now here he was in mad passionate love, at least according to what she was reading, with a woman who, best as she could tell, was a vapid Hollywood actress.

Charlotte was hurt. She would never have predicted that she would be, at least not to that extent. She would not have imagined that seeing such news would result in the welling up of tears, but there they were, flowing down her caramel cheeks onto the pages of the latest issue of Paris Match. Luckily the sadness didn't last too long. Charlotte was never one to stay submerged by negative emotions more than a short while, and in the days ahead she had managed to put it behind her. If that was the kind of woman Ira preferred, it was his problem, not hers. Whatever lingering anger she had toward him dissipated over time and soon enough she was even able to once again watch and enjoy her DVD of *Jackson Taylor's Christmas Party*.

Charlotte got out of her bathtub, put on her soft pink robe and walked into the bedroom where she stared at Sébastian for a while as he lay sleeping. His physical resemblance to his father was subtle and included his square chin and his height. At 5 foot 4 inches, he was very tall for his age, and would surely be as tall as Ira one day. As Charlotte slid into bed it dawned on her that this would be their last Christmas in that apartment. Soon they would be moving to New York City.

CHAPTER 18

IRA SPIRO BEFORE COVID: A MEMOIR - CHAPTER 8

If you watched the Academy Award broadcast the year I won for "Best Original Screenplay," or perhaps even if you didn't, you know that I was not even at the ceremony that night. It wasn't because I thought the Oscars were silly or in some way beneath me as, perhaps, Woody Allen had thought every time he didn't show up when nominated. Granted, the Oscars are political and very subjective. How can one judge what film is the best, or what actor or screenplay is the best? It is kind of silly when you think about it. But that's not why I wasn't there.

Winning an Academy Award was something I had fantasized about for much of my life. I was planning on going and even had a speech prepared in case I won. In the speech, I thanked my agent Carl Edson at the Creative Artists Agency, my manager Dave Rothman, my mother, my late father, Clementine Witt the producer, Lawrence Roberts, who was my roommate from college who had given my script to Clementine, and Harlee. I had also planned to remark that, though I considered myself more Jewish than anything else, I wrote *Jackson Taylor's Christmas Party* because I felt *Jacob Teichman's Hannukah Bash* wouldn't have had the same potential at the box office. That would have likely gotten good laughs in the Jew-rich environment of the Dolby Auditorium on Oscar night, though I'm not sure how it would have gone over with the average viewer at home.

175

The reason I wasn't there was, as had been reported in the media, I simply wasn't feeling well. Though I didn't reveal specifics at the time, I had had intermittent bouts of nausea in the days leading up to the event and that evening I felt particularly ill. None of this made my girlfriend at the time, actress Harlee Shaw, particularly happy.

- I can't believe we're not going. I was dying to wear that new dress.

The white form-fitting ecru Christian Dior dress, studded with pearls, that Harlee was referring to had a price tag north of about seventy grand. Harlee did not actually buy the dress. The fashion house let her borrow it for the evening. By Oscar dress standards it wasn't even that expensive. In 2013 Jennifer Lawrence had worn a pink strapless gown that retailed for four million dollars. No, I didn't know this information offhand! I had to look it up online. But I did know that celebrities wore astronomically expensive dresses to the Academy Awards.

- I can't even go to all the parties after, she whined.

- Why not? You don't need me to go to the parties.

- Yeah, that would be a good look, she said sarcastically. I'll be seen out partying while you're home not feeling well. Everyone will think I'm a shitty girlfriend.

Was Harlee Shaw a shitty girlfriend? I would say that yes she was, about half the time. I guess that means that indeed, she was a shitty girlfriend. If you were a doctor that misdiagnosed half the patients that came to see you, you'd quickly be fired for incompetence, hopefully before someone wound up dead. That said, I never fired Harlee. I stayed with her until she finally quit.

- Sorry Harlee. It wasn't my idea to get sick.

- You're not sick. It's all in your head.

- Really? Is that your diagnosis? Where did you go to med school again?

176

- Have you seen a doctor? she asked, shifting tone from outright hostility to a limited degree of actual concern.

- I'm going tomorrow.

- Ok good. I'm glad.

As I said, Harlee's concern was limited. She left me there alone that night on the couch in the living room of her four thousand square foot home in the Hollywood Hills to go watch the Oscars with her friend Giovanni, the interior designer who decorated my apartment in New York at her insistence. If you're wondering whether I was jealous that my girlfriend would be spending the evening at another man's house, let me repeat. He was an interior designer! There may be some men in that profession who aren't gay, but they are few in number and Giovanni was not one of those rare few. In fact, I don't believe Harlee ever cheated on me. To be honest, she was not an overly sexual person. In the course of our relationship, she never initiated sex and showed at best moderate enthusiasm during the act itself, not to mention a profound lack of creativity. Attention and adoration were what she craved most in life, far more than physical passion.

I didn't watch the Oscars that night. I didn't watch anything. I just lay on the couch trying to will myself to not be nauseous. I have always had a terrible fear of nausea and vomiting. I'm not alone. There's actually a word for this phenomenon — emetophobia. In junior year of high school, I felt slightly ill after eating a Big Mac, and have not been able to walk into a McDonald's since. This phobia is why food poisoning so readily came to mind as an excuse for abruptly ending my show that night in Denver.

As the nausea got worse I started to panic, worried that I might have to throw up. Literally shaking at the thought, I got up and walked in circles around the living room. As getting up and moving around was not diminishing the panic, I decided to resort to pharmaceutical assistance. Harlee had a prescription for Xanax, a drug I had of course heard of, but never actually seen until meeting her. I'm not sure how many milligrams the pills were or how many I took, but my next memory was waking up on the couch the next morning. Thankfully I had not thrown up in my passed out state. In fact, the nausea was gone, but it would no doubt be back, as it had been plaguing me on and off all week.

There were dozens of texts on my phone congratulating me on having won the award for best original screenplay. Among numerous others, there were texts from my agent, my manager, comedians Tony Powell, Karen Lee and Doug Greco, my mother, Brian Rezack and Lou Sills. There were also voicemail messages and emails, including one from my old friend Charlotte Aubertin who wished me a hearty *"Félicitations pour ton Oscar."* However, I didn't need to read those texts and emails or listen to those voicemail messages to find out that I had won. I knew immediately when Harlee lovingly presented me with a magnificent breakfast of strawberries and cream and brioche french toast upon waking. Granted, she didn't make any of it herself. That task fell to Eleanora, her full-time chef. Still, it was a gesture she would not have made had I lost.

- Good morning honey, she said, placing the tray on the coffee table next to me. Hope you're feeling better. I made you something to eat!

- Yeah I feel better thanks, trying not to chuckle at her claiming to have made my breakfast. Did I win?

- You didn't watch?

- No, I didn't do much of anything last night.

- Yes you won. I knew you would!

- That's cool, I said, more concerned about the nausea which was starting to make its presence felt once again than my new status as an Oscar winner.

- Hello, I'm Dr. Rostow, nice to meet you, the doctor said as I walked into his office later that morning.

I'm not sure if he knew who I was or that I had just won an Academy Award the night before, but if so, I was grateful he made no mention of it. A doctor should be a man of science. Ideally, I had come to believe, he should be completely uninterested in show business people and unimpressed by them. If he holds them in contempt that's okay too. It's certainly better than worshipping them. A doctor, in my opinion, should not be watching award shows in his spare time but rather reading medical journals or, if he must turn his attention away from the science of healing for a few moments, listening to classical music or reading great works of literature.

Needless to say, I had already done research online about the potential causes of my symptoms. Ruling out pregnancy, other possibilities included infection, gastroesophageal reflux disease, peptic ulcer, and, most worrisome of all, a cancerous bowel obstruction. Over the next week, I underwent blood tests, an upper GI series and abdominal X-rays. Dr. Rostow was happy to tell me that there was nothing physically wrong with me and that it was his considered opinion that the cause was another possibility that I had come across when I googled "chronic nausea & causes" — a psychological issue. In other words, his opinion was in accord with that of Harlee Shaw, whose medical training was limited to a role early in her career as a nurse in a vampire film called *Undead on Arrival.*

Having Jewish ancestry, and what's more, having grown up in the New York area, one would think I'd have had some experience with psychotherapy. Yet I had, up to that point, never been to a psychologist or psychiatrist. I never had the inclination to reveal my innermost secrets to a stranger on a regular basis for what I assumed would be of little or no real benefit. My skepticism grew after becoming a comedian and seeing so many of my colleagues who, despite years in treatment, were, to say the least, far from paragons of mental health. Perhaps, looking back, they hadn't found the right therapist. Or perhaps they had found the right one and, as screwy as many of these comics were, they would have been far screwier with no therapy at all! Perhaps, without therapy, Ron Appel would not merely be distant, cantankerous and unable to make eye contact with people, but would be living in a shack out in the woods scribbling Nostradamus style predictions about the end of the world.

A few days after my final visit with Dr. Rostow I returned to New York. Harlee stayed back in LA, planning to come east in a few weeks. The nausea had by this time dissipated entirely. Perhaps indeed it was all in my head. Adding credence to Dr. Rostow and Harlee Shaw, aka Nurse Harker's, diagnosis of psychosomatic illness was the fact that the misery of nausea was soon replaced by the misery of a spate of obsessive-compulsive symptoms including an uncontrollable urge to verify several times that I had locked the door before leaving my apartment and the need to knock on a piece of wood every time I said something involving death or illness.

- By the way, can you text me Dr. Levin's number? I asked Karen Lee in the middle of a phone conversation about an audition Karen was getting ready for.

- I just asked him about another friend of mine. He says he's not taking any more patients right now.

- Oh, ok. Not a prob.

- But maybe that's just for the average nobody. If I tell him it's you, maybe he'll find room.

- No thanks. Just say you have a friend looking for treatment and ask him if there's another therapist in New York he could recommend.

Dr. Kweskin, a portly man who looked to be about 50, walked out of his office to greet me as soon as I walked into the waiting room. I had booked two sessions with him. The 1 pm to 1:55 pm slot and the 2 pm to 2:55 pm slot. I planned to see him from 1:30 to 2:25, a standard 55-minute session with a sufficient buffer before and after to make sure I didn't bump into other patients who were leaving or waiting to go in. I was now officially famous and preferred to be discrete about the fact that I was seeing a shrink.

- Hey, congratulations on the Oscar, were the first words he said to me after I sat down in the large armchair opposite his.

An inauspicious beginning as far as I was concerned, but I was ready to give this new experience a fair chance. My first hour with Dr. K., as he insisted I call him, was spent telling him what had brought me to his office that day. I explained to him that I had always been an anxious person, but that I had become even more so over the past couple of years and I spoke to him about the recent episode of nausea for which the doctor could find no physiological explanation and about my current obsessive-compulsive symptoms.

During the next few sessions, he asked me questions about my childhood and in particular about my relationship with my parents. I avoided talking about the more painful memories and often changed the subject to talk about a book I was reading or a film I had just seen. This, of course, defeated the purpose of why I was there in the first place.

Dr. K. seemed particularly fascinated by my relationship with Harlee Shaw, inquiring about our sex life on more than one occasion. It made me uneasy discussing this with him and, although sexuality is no doubt an important component of human psychology, I wondered if he wasn't getting a certain pleasure out of hearing about life in the bedroom of a Hollywood couple.

- Who are Harlee's friends in Hollywood? he once asked me.

Was this a legitimate question or was Dr. K. just interested in show-biz gossip?

- Dr. K, I gotta ask. What does that have to do with my psychological problems?

- It's relevant to know what kind of person she is since she's the person you chose to be with. Her friends are a reflection of who she is. Who she is is a reflection of who you are.

I still wasn't convinced of the legitimacy of the question, particularly because he had asked it in a tone that seemed to me to betray an unhealthy curiosity, and his eyes widened each time he mentioned Harlee's name. I spoke to Dr. K about Giovanni the interior designer as well as some of Harlee's other non-famous friends, leaving out her close relationship with the well-known actress Iris Winterfeldt, as I did not wish to reward what I felt in my gut was an inappropriate curiosity about celebrities.

About a month into my life as a psych outpatient I walked into Dr. Kweskin's office and saw a stack of printed pages with two brass brads inserted in holes along the left side, which is by convention the way screenplays are bound.

- Is that a screenplay, I asked him?

- Oh yes, he said as he took the pages off his desk and put them in his briefcase.

- Why was there a screenplay on your desk? I asked, feeling very uneasy about the possible response.

- It's just something I'm working on. Actually just finished it. It's my third script. Hopefully, I'll sell one of them one of these days.

This was the worst possible answer he could have given. The best answer would have been that it wasn't a screenplay at all but something else entirely, perhaps a study from the National Institute of Mental Health. An acceptable answer would have been, "Yes it's a screenplay. One of my patients wrote it, and he wanted me to read it."

That Dr. K. was an aspiring screenwriter, however, was extremely upsetting.

- It's actually about a psychologist, he continued.

I certainly did not ask what the damn thing was about, but apparently, he was determined to tell me.

- Turns out one of his patients is a bank robber, and the two of them do a heist together. Don't worry, I would never rob a bank with one of my patients, he added with a laugh. Anyway, tell me about your week.

There wasn't much to tell. It was a rather uninteresting week. I spent a fair amount of time at the gym. And I had been listening to a lot of Prince music since his death the week before. I was wondering aloud to Dr. K. if I'd feel as anxious on stage if I were a musician as opposed to a comedian. It seemed to me that if you have a song that people love, you know the response will be positive. As long as Prince hit the right notes on "Little Red Corvette" what could go wrong? A comic, by contrast, is generally presenting an audience with jokes they've never heard before. Fans want to hear the songs they know and the jokes they don't.

- By the way, said Dr. K., seemingly not even listening to my thoughts on performing music versus comedy, if you know anyone that might be interested in my script maybe you could pass it along.

I could barely believe he had just asked me that question and felt the need to verify that I had heard him correctly.

- You want me to help you sell your script?

- No not at all. I'm saying if you happen to know someone who might be interested, maybe you could give it to him. I don't think it would be right for you. You're a comedy guy and it's not a comedy. But I'm saying if you know someone.

In other words, he wanted me to help him sell his script.

- Our work is done here, I said angrily as I got up to leave.

- I'm sorry. Maybe I shouldn't have asked you that.

Without even responding to his apology, I walked out of his office never to return and swore off therapy for good.

CHAPTER 19

IRA SPIRO BEFORE COVID: A MEMOIR - CHAPTER 12

Thinking back on my life, I don't recall my father ever taking much joy, if any, in my victories or accomplishments. He did not even call me to congratulate me after my first appearance on *The Tonight Show*, hosted at the time by Jay Leno. To this day I'm not even sure he saw it. The appearance, as it happens, went very well. The only joke that didn't get roars from the crowd was my bit about past lives:

I went to a past life hypnotist. Under hypnosis, I saw myself lying in an old-fashioned hospital bed wearing a torn Confederate uniform with a bandage around my head. That's right. It turns out in my past life I was an extra in Gone with the Wind.

Gone with the Wind is obviously a classic film, but it came out in 1939 and with each passing year fewer and fewer people were familiar with it. But one of *The Tonight Show* executive producers had seen me do the joke at a club in Los Angeles and loved it. He insisted that I do it on the show. It didn't outright bomb, but like I said it didn't get roars. All the other jokes did, however, and Jay loved the set.

There were a couple of occasions where mere indifference would have been welcome, as opposed to the outright contempt my father demonstrated after I did something other parents might have found praiseworthy. In addition to the ones I remember, there are likely more such occasions lost in the haze of memory. Some I might one day recall, finding them tucked away in some hidden corner of my consciousness like a note waiting to be found in the pocket of an old garment. Others perhaps are completely gone, like the pages of a book burned to ashes. Hey, those were some good metaphors. I'm starting to get the hang of this literary shit!

There was the time, as a 15-year-old sophomore, when I brought home my best report card ever since starting high school. It was straight A's, with the exception of a B in Algebra 2. "I guess this makes you a genius then?" he said angrily before leaving the house to head to the formalwear shop.

Then there was what I call, in the privacy of my inner thoughts, the "tennis incident." My father had been a life-long tennis player and it was one of the few activities we did together regularly. When I was little we would just hit the ball around without keeping score. Eventually, we started playing actual sets, generally the best of three. My father beat me easily enough at first, but over the years I started closing the gap, in part because my skills were getting better, and in part because my father was getting older and more out of shape. He had put on a lot of weight in the previous few years. In those days I didn't think about how much someone weighed in terms of the actual number of pounds. I thought of weight rather in terms of three general categories. You were either a complete blimp, a run-of-the-mill fatso or a normal person. Picturing my father's body in my mind, the curve of his stomach and the girth of his arms, he was probably about 180 lbs. which, for a guy that was 5'9," is well overweight and definitely in the fatso category.

I beat him for the first time when I was 13. It was a summer day, and I had just come back from three weeks at a fancy tennis camp in Massachusetts, paid for by my maternal grandparents. We played all day, every day at the camp, and my game had greatly improved.

"Alright, let's see what you got," he said to me when I proposed a match at the public courts not far from our house in Paramus.

It was, as I recall, a perfect day for tennis. Sunny but not too hot and best of all no wind. The one element of my game that had improved the most at camp was my serve, and my father was not able to win a game against it once. I was also able to place my shots with a lot greater accuracy in general, and I had my father running around chasing balls all over the court, which, for a guy carrying around all those extra pounds, was a formidable challenge. He became frustrated and angry, and after losing game point of the first game of the second set he threw his racket against the fence surrounding the courts, drawing curious looks from the four people playing mixed doubles next to us. They no doubt couldn't believe this sort of infantile poor sportsmanship coming from a grown man, but it was even worse than they thought, as they had not seen the particular point that precipitated the tantrum.

Had my father been frustrated because he missed an easy shot, say by hitting a ball that came right to him into the net, his reaction might have been somewhat more understandable. But he lost the point because, after a strong serve, I had come to the net and hit a well-placed volley into the corner of the court that he never could have gotten to even if he had been in the best shape of his life. In other words, he was not angry because he had played the point poorly. He was angry because I had played the point well. I assume with some confidence that most fathers would have reacted to my winning volley with a "great shot son" or an "atta boy" rather than by launching their racket like a javelin across the width of the court.

I suggested to my father that I was feeling tired and that perhaps we could finish the match another time. Obviously, I was lying about feeling tired, and my father knew it. He was surely feeling tired, but as for me, I had plenty of fuel left in the tank.

- Bullshit, he said. We're gonna finish the game. And you're gonna play your best, he added.

Indeed, the thought of losing the match on purpose had crossed my mind, but I played my best as instructed, afraid to win, and afraid to lose, lest I be accused of throwing the match. Several cursing fits and another racket throw later I won the second set for a final score of 6-4, 6-2. As we drove home in the car we did not exchange a word. I tried turning the radio on, and he immediately turned it off as if not wanting any distractions from his simmering resentment. As I think about the "tennis incident" today I can perhaps better understand the dynamics at play.

My father was traversing a difficult moment in life. He was divorced and alone, having not yet met his second wife. What's more, he was no longer performing stand-up comedy. His career had been stalled for years. The only TV appearance on his resumé was a five-minute stand-up set on a show called *Evening at the Improv* that he had taped in the early '90s. My father was funny, but he was not extraordinary. Of course, one can succeed in show business with moderate talent, and many people do, but that requires a healthy dose of luck, and my father didn't have that either. Rather than continuing to tread water in the business, he decided it would be less of an assault on his ego to simply stop performing altogether and work full time at the family formalwear store, which he eventually took over when my Uncle Al, who had made some smart real estate investments, retired to Florida in '97. By contrast, my life was just beginning. While my father was losing hair and gaining weight, I was growing taller and stronger each day. The ideal father would have rejoiced in my development as a person despite his personal travails. He was not the ideal father.

All of this analysis was certainly beyond the understanding of the 13-year-old I was at the time. But I did feel sympathy for him and guilt about having won the match.

- You know dad you would have won easily if you weren't so heavy, I offered in an attempt to soothe his ego.

He did not respond right away, but as his face became increasingly red and his lower lip started to tremble I knew I had said something I should not have.

- So I'm fat, is that what you're saying?

- No I wasn't saying that.

- Maybe that's what happens when you're 42 and your life is a mess. You eat and you get fat. Maybe if I were 13, with no responsibility and nothing to do all day but run around and play, I'd be skinny like you!

At the time I didn't quite understand the connection between lack of responsibility and being thin. Of course, now I well realize the link between stress and self-medication with food and, though I've never been overweight, I have, from time to time, found solace in needless calories.

My father retreated back into silence and I assumed the matter was over until he turned off onto a side street that was not on the way to our house and stopped the car.

- You know what, you're in such good shape, why don't you just walk home.

I wasn't totally sure if he was serious or not.

- Get out!

Would he have grabbed me and physically removed me from the car if I had just stayed in my seat? My father yelled and screamed a lot but never moved beyond the verbal in expressing his anger. Still, I thought it better not to put him to the test, and I exited the car. I maintained some hope that he would motion me through the window to get back in and then laugh telling me it was all a joke. Instead, he just drove away.

The walk back wasn't that long, perhaps a mile or so, but it was an inhospitable walk. American suburbs are generally not designed with pedestrians in mind. Absent an actual sidewalk, I had to cross the street frequently in my constant search for stretches of flat and unobstructed grass on the side of the road. At times I had little choice but to walk on the pavement with cars whipping by me at high speed.

When I got back to my father's condo he did not mention a word of what had just transpired. He simply said that there was pizza in the kitchen if I was hungry. Apparently, he had picked it up after abandoning me back on Durand Place. By the way, in case you were curious, the answer is no. My father and I never played tennis again.

CHAPTER 20

When one is a young child, not only do the years go by slowly, but the hours do as well. Sébastian Aubertin had already watched several episodes of *Les Aventures de Tintin* on his iPad and, though it was one of his favorite cartoons, he was starting to grow tired of it. His fascination with the intrepid young Belgian reporter Tintin, his dog Milou and their friend Captain Haddock was giving way to the agitation of being confined in a small seat for over seven hours. Fortunately, the Air France 787 was nearing its destination, and Sébastian's first transatlantic flight would soon be over.

    - *Maman, on va arriver bientôt?*

    - I am sorry. I do not speak French. You know 'zis, said Charlotte.

    The passenger seated next to them in seat 16A, a blonde-haired American woman in her twenties who, like Sébastian, had just emerged from several hours cut off from the world with sound being delivered directly to her auditory canal via earphones and the images on her iPad occupying nearly the totality of her visual field, could not help but smile upon overhearing the woman with the thick Parisian telling her son that she could not speak French.

    Sébastian, fatigued and not terribly enthusiastic about making the extra effort required to communicate in a second language, let out a growl of frustration. Charlotte did not relent, refusing to answer Sébastian's question until expressed in the language of Shakespeare.

- Are we almost 'zere Maman? he said with evident exasperation.

- Yes, we will be landing in not much longer. You see over 'zere, said Charlotte, pointing to the Manhattan skyline that had just become visible through the window as the aircraft descended below a low cloud layer. 'Zat is New York City.

- *C'est où on va . . .*, I mean, 'zat is where we will be living Maman?

- Yes. You see 'zat building over 'zere, said Charlotte referring to Freedom Tower in lower Manhattan. 'Ze one 'zat is much taller 'zan all 'ze o'zer ones around it.

- Yes I 'sink so.

- Our new apartment is not so far from 'zat. It is in a neighborhood called 'ze financial district.

- So, this is your first time in New York? the blonde American woman asked Sébastian, addressing her row 16 neighbor for the first time during the flight.

- Yes. 'Zis is my first time in 'ze America.

- Not "'ze America," Sébastian, just "America," said Charlotte, gently correcting him.

Sébastian's error was attributable to the fact that in French the names of countries are preceded by the French equivalent of the English word "the," as in *Vive **LA** France*."

- And you're coming to New York to live? asked the blonde, revealing that she had been listening to their conversation.

- Yes, we will be living in 'ze, Maman what is called 'zat neighborhood?

- 'Ze financial district.

- We will be living in 'ze financial district, said Sébastian to the American woman, struggling a bit with the pronunciation of "financial."

- You're going to love living in New York City. My brother and I grew up there. Do you have any brothers and sisters, or is it just you and your parents?

A more aware person would not have assumed that Sébastian had two parents. Certainly, there was only one parent on the plane. If there were a second one, he would likely have been sitting with them, and if for whatever reason he was seated elsewhere on the plane, he would have certainly come over to speak with them at some point during the flight.

- It is just me and Maman, said Sébastian, a hint of sadness in his voice.

The blond girl knew she had made a mistake, but at least had the good sense to let the conversation drop.

- *Maman*, Sébastian continued, turning toward Charlotte, *je vais rencontrer mon papa un jour? L'homme dont tu as acheté les graines au magasin?* (Mommy, will I meet my father one day? The man whose seeds you bought in the store.)

Charlotte did not reprimand Sébastian for speaking in French given the overly curious ears of the American seated in their row.

- *Un jour peut-être Sébastian.* (Perhaps one day Sébastian.)

Charlotte looked out the window toward lower Manhattan, the neighborhood they would soon be inhabiting, and wondered what lay ahead for her and her son in the city they would soon be calling home.

Miles was not seated on the chair next to Ira's couch as he normally would be, but on the couch itself to the right of Ira, as this allowed him to speak with Ira and at the same time look out the window at the thick flakes of snow that had begun to fall outside.

- In the course of a lifetime there are only so many snowfalls like this in New York, said Miles. I'd hate to miss one.

- In half a billion years, declared Ira, the sun will have become so hot that the oceans will evaporate. I guess that'll be the end of rain and snow.

- Perhaps there will be snowfalls on some moon or another planet somewhere else in the universe. Maybe there'll even be conscious beings living there that have the privilege that we have to witness it and be moved by it.

Miles stared toward the window saying nothing for a long moment.

- Miles, did I mention Charlotte's living in New York now?
- The French girl?
- Yeah. She got a really good job here, and she moved into an apartment in the financial district.
- You saw her?
- No. We spoke briefly on the phone. She asked if I had any shows coming up at the Comedy Den. Told her I'd let her know.
- You never wanted to have an actual relationship with her?
- I think we were always better just as friends.
- Well, it was more than a friendship I'd say.
- I suppose, but less than a relationship.

Ira spoke to Miles about some of the moments he and Charlotte spent together. He spoke of the time he invited Charlotte to join him down on the island of Saint Barts where he had been hired to perform for a group of hedge fund employees on a corporate retreat. Charlotte was able to take a few days off from her job as a software engineer at Airbnb and flew from California to meet Ira in New York. The next day the two flew to St. Martin, followed by a ten-minute shuttle flight to St. Barts. As the island has no large international airport, it was impossible to fly there direct from the United States on a commercial flight.

Ira was being paid fifteen thousand dollars for a forty-five-minute set, the most he had ever been paid for a single show before *Jackson Taylor* came out. His manager Dave Rothman also managed to negotiate an extra day at the hotel so he could enjoy the island after having already done the show.

The fact that his audience would be a relatively small group, about fifty people, lessened his normal pre-performance anxiety somewhat, but not dramatically, in part because he was being paid so much, and felt pressure to justify his price. Also, Ira was not thrilled that the show was to be outside. They had set up a tent on the grounds of the Hotel Christopher where everyone, including Ira and Charlotte, was staying. An outside show was never optimal as the sound is not as good as it would be at an inside venue.

Nevertheless, the show went quite well and after a brief meet and greet with the top execs at the hedge fund, Ira and Charlotte took off for dinner at the Mango Beach Club, one of the restaurants at the hotel. Ira was generally quite hungry after an important show because, inevitably, he had eaten little if anything before the show due to his high stress level. Once the stress of the show was behind him, his hunger sprung forth like an animal released from a cage. The exception to this rule was when a show went so poorly that Ira's distress at having embarrassed himself on stage killed his appetite for the rest of the evening. A notable and extreme example of this was the time he had a panic attack during his show in Denver. He also didn't have anything to eat after he finished performing in Ocean City, Maryland for the Warren insurance group, but that was because he was passed out from having taken too much Xanax. That said, he didn't eat much the day after either.

Ira and Charlotte went on a jet skiing excursion on their free post-show day in St. Barts. After that, they took a private guided tour of the island by convertible. St. Barts is a French-speaking island, and from time to time Charlotte inadvertently slid into French when speaking to their tour guide, Olivier, at which point Ira would yell an expression he had learned for the occasion, "*Parlez Anglais putain!*" (Fucking speak English!) which never failed to make both Olivier and Charlotte laugh heartily.

At the end of the day, they found themselves drinking daiquiris and watching the sunset at the breathtaking Gouverneur Beach on the south side of the island.

- I don't want to leave tomorrow. Can we stay a couple days more Ira?

- I'd love to, but these rooms cost a thousand dollars a night. If I had Jerry Seinfeld money we could spend the week here. Or even Ron Appel money.

- Who is 'zis?

- Ron Appel? He's a kind of sort of famous comic. Anyway, I don't wanna go back either. It's beautiful here. And I hate flying.

- 'Zat is weird because I always see you look up whenever a plane fly overhead.

- Well, they kind of fascinate me. I just don't like being in them.

- I don't like it also. Especially in class economy, I mean economy class. Do you 'sink one day 'zey will be able to do 'ze teleportation? You can just instantly go from place to place like sending an e-mail?

- No, I don't think that'll ever happen.

- Ever? Not like in a million years?

- Well, I doubt our species will still be here in a million years, but if we are, no. I don't think there'll be teleportation.

- Why not?

- They'd have to break you down into atoms and molecules and then send them through space and put them back together at the destination exactly as they were before in order to recreate you. I'm predicting never.

- Maybe they re-put you together better than before?

- That's an interesting idea. There may be a joke there. Can I use it?

- How much you pay? I'm kidding. Of course you can.

- You could be like, "One-way teleportation to Cleveland please, and could you not teleport the herpes," Ira said, improvising a possible punchline.

Ira was in the middle of talking about himself and Charlotte on the beach together in St. Barts when Miles interrupted him, now standing at Ira's window staring toward the skyscrapers in midtown which were only partially visible, their upper floors disappearing into the low clouds that were still releasing their store of snow onto the city below.

- I remember that teleportation joke, he said. You did it on *The Tonight Show*. But I think you said "could you not teleport the back hair" instead of "the herpes."

- Yeah, I changed the joke. I thought "back hair" was funnier. Plus it's a better fit for corporate shows without the STD reference. Impressed you remember that.

- I actually just watched it again on YouTube. Sounds like Charlotte and you work well together.

- Well, that was the only joke she ever helped me with.

- It's a good one. You guys really had a nice time together, didn't you?

- Yeah I guess so.

Once again Miles stopped talking. He gazed out the window with such an intensity that one might have wondered whether even a single snowflake escaped his attention as it fell, following a diagonal path dictated by wind and gravity, toward the east. He was devouring the scene with his eyes as if it were a sort of visual last meal.

- I wanna talk more about you and Charlotte, he said, finally breaking the silence. I think it's a really interesting aspect of your life.

CHAPTER 21

IRA SPIRO BEFORE COVID: A MEMOIR - CHAPTER 13

One tends to remember, in strikingly vivid detail, the moment one finds out one's father has died. It was a hot and humid evening, and I was content to stay inside in shorts and no shirt with my anemic air-conditioner on the highest setting possible, struggling to cool my apartment. I was living in a handsome but modest studio on the third floor of a walk-up building in the Hell's Kitchen neighborhood of Manhattan. Seated at my desk in front of my computer, I was listening to music while writing one of the early scenes of *Jackson Taylor's Christmas Party*. It was the scene where my character arrives at Jackson's apartment for the first time.

- Lawrence! So glad you could come celebrate the season with us. This sublime creature you see before you is Ella, the love of my life. And this dashing man in the top hat is Brent. He's been to every one of my Christmas parties. Ella and Brent, this is Lawrence Hummel, law student, life student, dreamer of a better world, I wrote, just as I heard my phone ring. It was my stepmother, Carol.

"Why," I wondered, "would she be calling?" I paused the song that was playing on YouTube, a Dixie Chicks cover of "Shower the People" by James Taylor, and answered the phone. I suspected bad news. I suspected right.

At the age of 57, my father had died of a heart attack in front of the television watching the latest episode of season four of *Breaking Bad*. His smoking and terrible diet had finally caught up with him. He likely also had a genetic predisposition to heart disease as his father had also died of a heart attack, though I believe Grandpa Hal was in his sixties. Thankfully, my blood pressure and cholesterol levels are quite good. Knowing this provides me with a measure of confidence in my cardiac health such that my hypochondria generally focuses on other issues, though there was that time a particularly brutal episode of chest pains caused by acid reflux made me go to the emergency room fearing the end was near.

In the years before my father's death, I seldom saw him and spoke to him only from time to time on the telephone. I never brought up my career, mostly because he never asked about it. Had he been alive when I won the Academy Award for *Jackson Taylor* he probably wouldn't have asked about that either. Despite our lack of contact, I felt devastated when I received the call from my stepmother that he was gone. He was my father after all, imperfect though he was.

His funeral was at Temple Sholom in our hometown of Paramus, New Jersey. Among those present at the service were Carol, of course, as well as my Uncle Al who had come up from Florida. Al's son David and daughter Ellen were there as was my father's sister Myrna who made the trip from Ohio with her husband Sam. Their daughter, my childhood crush cousin Shari, had not made the trip.

I hadn't seen my cousins David and Ellen in many years and would certainly never have recognized them were it not for the fact that I was seeing them at a family event. Were it anywhere else I might have thought "That's interesting. Those two chubby thirty-somethings look a bit like my father and my Uncle Al." A few people that worked at the formalwear store were also there in addition to my father's old friend Harry Rosen, whom he had grown up with in Brooklyn. From the world of show business Tony Powell, Karen Lee, Brian Rezak and Dave Rothman had come to offer me moral support.

It was my first time giving a eulogy. It was certainly difficult, but at least I was not under pressure to get laughs as I usually am when speaking in public. Needless to say, I didn't mention the time that my father fired me from the store, or for that matter the "tennis incident", the time he snapped at me for bringing home good grades or any of the other contentious episodes that were too common in our relationship.

I talked a bit about his stand-up comedy and how he was an unrecognized genius. He was certainly unrecognized, but I exaggerated the genius part. I also spoke of his generosity with waitstaff. He always left large tips at bars and restaurants. I leave big tips as well, in part because people know who I am. As for my father, as I would mention in the eulogy, he once told me he left big tips to dispel the stereotype of Jews being cheap. I spoke of how my father was always concerned with not reinforcing negative Jewish stereotypes and of the joke in his act about never picking up a quarter after dropping it except, he said, when he was in Israel, where, comfortably surrounded only by Jews, he walked the streets with a metal detector. My father's metal detector in Israel joke got big laughs that day at Temple Sholom, although it was likely already familiar to most of the people there. It's the sign of a quality joke when people laugh at it even after having heard it before!

Shiva, a Jewish ritual where friends and relatives gather in the days following a funeral to comfort each other and, typically, stuff themselves with deli sandwiches and cake, was held at Carol's house. The first day of shiva was the day of the funeral but not immediately after. I had a few hours to head back home and change out of my dark blue suit, which I rolled up, put into a bag with the black wingtip shoes I was wearing and threw down the garbage chute in my building.

On the second day of shiva, I was having a pastrami on rye listening to Al Rosen talk about my father's prowess on the wrestling team in high school when I saw Charlotte Aubertin walk into the living room with a box of assorted cookies she had brought for the occasion.

I had told Charlotte my father had died, but neither asked nor expected her to come all the way from San Francisco. I excused myself from Al and walked over to greet her.

- Oh my God. I can't believe you're here, I exclaimed, taking her box of cookies and putting them on the coffee table before giving her a proper embrace à la Francaise, one kiss on each cheek. No sooner had I placed the cookies on the table than Dave Rothman stealthily moved in, walking off with no fewer than three of the delicious baked treats before anyone else even knew they were there.

- I'm sorry I couldn't make 'ze funeral, said Charlotte, but I saw 'ze address for 'ze shiva in 'ze obituary and wanted to come. I got in last night.

- How long are you in town? Do you need a place to stay?

- I'm at a hotel near 'ze JFK Airport. It's easier because I'm going back tomorrow. I have to get back for an important meeting at work.

I could not believe she had traveled across the country just for the day, but I was certainly glad to see her. After about a half-hour of eating and mingling, I suggested to her that we go for a drive. I was getting tired of well wishes from people I barely knew, mixed with questions about show business, and I couldn't imagine she was having any fun being asked repeatedly about her accent and ethnicity, the kinds of questions you'll recall, I asked her when we first met.

As I've said, I tend to enjoy driving as I have little opportunity to do it living in New York City. Charlotte and I got in my rented Toyota Corolla and headed out onto the roads of New Jersey with no particular destination in mind. Negative stereotypes about my native state notwithstanding, Bergen County can be quite a lovely little corner of the world on a warm summer's day. We drove for a while along the Palisades, a twenty-mile line of high cliffs affording a view of the Hudson River that Charlotte found *"magnifique!"*

- Hey Charlotte, have you ever played miniature golf?

- I don't 'sink I have played 'zis.

- You want to? It's fun!

- Ok, I am down to it.

I entered "Philly Mini Golf" into the GPS which instructed me to "Continue on Palisades Parkway South to Exit 9W." Charlotte took a glance at the "Time to Destination" on the GPS.

- An hour and fifty-four minutes? 'Zere is no'sing more close?

- This is a good place. Anyway, we're not in a rush.

I turned the radio on to Sirius '80s on 8. I needed to hear some '80s tunes at that moment. The '80s were not just a relatively good time in my life, they also represented the best years in terms of my relationship with my father. Even songs from the end of the '80s, after my parents' divorce and my mother's worsening alcoholism, tended to evoke good memories given their association with an otherwise decent decade.

I recall one of the songs that played during our trip was the Bangles "Manic Monday." It sticks in my memory because, by a weird coincidence, we were on the New Jersey Turnpike passing by Newark Airport when the lead singer, Susanna Hoffs, sang the line "And if I had an airplane I still couldn't make it on time." At that moment an airplane was taking off on the runway that parallels the highway, runway 22L if my googling is correct. I don't remember which airline, but it could not have been Air France. That would have stuck in my memory all the more given the nationality of the person sitting next to me in the Corolla. I also recall Charlotte singing along to the chorus: "It's just ano'zer manic Monday, wish it was Sunday."

- You know this song?

- Of course I do. I love it.

Turns out Charlotte knew most of the big hits of the '80s. She was generally unfamiliar with the hair bands like Poison and Twisted

Sister, and heartland rock acts like Bruce Springsteen and Bob Seeger, but was impressively knowledgable with regard to new wave music and big pop acts like Whitney Houston, Madonna and Michael Jackson.

The French listen to a lot of American music and English language music in general. Of course, the French have their own popular music of which we in America know basically nothing. Unlike the French and other Europeans, we here in America have little regard for music with lyrics in another language. The German song "99 Luftballons" was a top 40 hit in the United States in 1984, but that was a rare exception.

Charlotte played me some French songs she had downloaded onto her iPhone. She was somewhat disappointed that I found none of them to my liking. It wasn't just that I didn't understand the lyrics. They were, in my opinion, melodically uninteresting. My thought at the time was that French music sucked. I've since been educated on the matter, however. I've learned, for example, that Frank Sinatra's "My Way" is a translated version of a French song called "Comme d'habitude" and that "I Can't Help Falling in Love with You," made famous by Elvis Presley, is based on a classical French melody called "Plaisir d'amour." There are some other good French songs as well. So I was wrong. To paraphrase a line from the 1987 film *The Princess Bride*, French music only "mostly sucks".

Philly Mini Golf is located in Franklin Square Park in Center City Philadelphia. Each hole features a Philadelphia landmark such as Independence Hall or the Liberty Bell. As mini-golf courses go, it's probably one of the better ones. I'm sure, however, I could have found a suitable course closer to Paramus, NJ, but I would not have been able to putt a ball across a miniature Ben Franklin Bridge at those other courses. More importantly, they would not have been the location of one of my more pleasant childhood memories.

When I was about seven my father's stand-up career was on an upward trajectory. It was a modest upward trajectory that would never ascend much higher, but my father didn't know that at the time and, buoyed by the hope that things would continue to improve, his good moods were far more frequent than his bad ones. One weekend he took me with him to Philadelphia where he was the headliner at the Chestnut Street Comedy Club. The show was not suitable for children. My father, like myself and most other comedians, made use of occasional curse words and references to drugs and sexuality. So while he was onstage I hung out outside the showroom with my handheld electronic football game while the woman who collected the tickets before each show kept watch over me. The rest of the time that we were in Philly my father and I spent together swimming in the hotel pool, watching movies in the room and eating like pigs at local restaurants.

On the day of his last show, he took me to Franklin Square Park where we played a round of mini-golf. Nothing of monumental significance happened during our outing, but I remember being filled with the pure joy that is the unique preserve of childhood. I remember my father proudly cheering me on as I made each shot and lifting me up in the air and spinning me around when I got the ball in the hole. It was probably not every time I got the ball in the hole, but it definitely happened. Given my father's distant and unaffectionate nature, this actually was indeed, upon reflection, of monumental significance.

The memories of that weekend occupied my thoughts as we putted our way through eighteen holes of Philadelphia culture and history. Charlotte played terribly and we both laughed uncontrollably as she struggled to get the ball through the crack in the mini Liberty Bell, or "Bell of Liberty" as she called it, on the last hole. After beating her soundly, as my father had beaten me soundly back in the '80s, I insisted that we do what my father and I had done after our game, ride the nearby Parx Liberty Carousel and then stuff our faces.

Charlotte slept most of the way back to her hotel near JFK airport. No doubt she was exhausted from having flown cross country just the day before and then waking up early to get to New Jersey for the shiva. Being tired myself, I stayed with her in her hotel room rather than heading back to Manhattan.

I got back to my apartment early the next morning and headed directly to the exorbitantly expensive mahogany bookcase in the living room that Harley Shaw and Giovanni the decorator insisted I could not live without. My step-mother had given me a photo album on the first day of shiva, right after the funeral. I took it off the shelf and turned the pages. Images of my childhood passed in front of my eyes — pictures of me with my parents actually looking happy to be in each other's company, school photos, summer camp photos, me on a bicycle learning how to ride. Then I saw, right next a picture of me dressed as a pirate for Halloween carrying a plastic pumpkin waiting to be filled with candy, a picture of my father and me next to a miniature version of Independence Hall at the Philly Mini Golf Course. We had our golf clubs crossed as if we were dueling knights, with huge smiles on our faces, sharing the kind of moment that was all too rare between us. As I stared at that photo I started crying. It was a long hard cry. I am crying also, as I write these words.

CHAPTER 22

Ira opened his locker at the gym and started changing out of his workout clothes back into his regular clothes. It was something he had done a thousand times before, but this time was a little different insofar as his t-shirt and shorts had not an ounce of sweat on them. He was hoping the sadness he was feeling would evaporate once he started running, but after no more than three strides he turned off the treadmill. Realizing he did not have the energy or attitude required for any sort of productive activity, he headed back downstairs to the locker room. The steam room, he noticed, was closed for maintenance and so he decided to just go home.

- That was fast, Ira, said Tina, the young lady working at the front desk of Equinox Fitness, as Ira walk past her on his way toward the door.

- Yeah, I actually have a meeting. I had completely forgotten about it, said Ira, responding with the first lie that came to mind before exiting the gym and heading to his apartment.

As Ira walked into the beautiful newly renovated art deco lobby of his building, he saw Carlos the doorman and, though Carlos didn't say a word, Ira assumed he was surprised to see him back in the lobby so soon after having left with his gym bag. Being Ira, he felt it necessary to justify himself and offer an explanation.

- You know what Carlos, I was at the gym and I remembered I have a conference call. I had completely forgotten about it.

Ira thought about the fact that he could have avoided the burden of having to lie to his doorman if he did not have a doorman in the first place and again felt resentment toward Harlee for pressuring him into buying the apartment. He also could have avoided having to lie to the doorman by simply realizing that he was under no obligation to lie to the doorman. He could have just walked past him without saying anything, but that was simply not a realistic option for Ira. The compulsion to justify oneself in these types of situations is hardly rare. As Ira quipped in one of his earlier pieces of stand-up material, "Every day in America dozens, perhaps hundreds, of people exit elevators seconds after having entered, unable to resist the need to explain why, by mumbling a completely unnecessary 'forgot something' to a bunch of strangers." Ira had done exactly that a half-hour before when leaving his apartment building for the gym, though, in that case he hadn't really forgotten anything. He just wanted to verify, for the third time, that he had locked the door.

Ira was feeling extra heavy as he sat down on his couch as if the gravitational attraction between himself and the Earth had suddenly increased. He briefly wondered whether the physical laws of the universe might have somehow suddenly changed. After all, Ira reasoned, since no one could explain how those laws arose in the first place, could we rule out the possibility that from time to time they underwent some sort of metamorphosis? Perhaps such a metamorphosis took place every 13.8 billion years or so, which was about the length of time that had elapsed between the Big Bang and Ira settling onto his couch with his chilled bottle of coconut water.

The more likely explanation, Ira figured, was that this sensation of heaviness was a physical manifestation of his psychological state. Ira was struggling under the weight of sadness and loss brought about, not by recent events, but by memories of slightly more distant ones. Talking the day before with Miles about the death of his father had brought to the surface thoughts and emotions he would have preferred to keep submerged. He thought about his father's life. It was a relatively short life and one full of disappointment. His dreams had gone unrealized and there seemed to be, in his 57 years, a profound dearth of truly joyful moments, at least as far as Ira could recall.

Working on the memoir, though frequently pleasurable, was just as often forcing Ira to confront an often difficult past. He had entertained the thought of turning his back on the project altogether, but his financial situation made that option impractical, especially given the phone call he received later that day from his high school friend Lou Sills.

- Ira, Hi.

- Hi Lou, what's up.

- Ira, I have some bad news about The Fallout Zone.

Upon hearing that ominous statement exit Lou's mouth, Ira immediately knew he had just lost two hundred thousand dollars. Two years before Lou had introduced Ira to a bar owner he knew named George Witkoff. George was looking to raise money to open a place in Ft. Lauderdale, Florida that would have billiards, ping pong and a supply of board games that people could sit down and play. It would also have a full bar and occasional live music. George would be the managing partner but was searching for investors. Ira was hesitant, but Lou convinced him it would be a great investment. Lou himself was putting in a lot of money.

- What happened, Lou? said Ira, dreading the response.

Lou explained that George had embezzled money from the business and that his inappropriate behavior toward female employees had resulted in several costly lawsuits. The Fallout Zone would be filing for bankruptcy.

- How do you feel about that? Do you have any anger toward Lou? asked Miles at their next writing session.

- I'm more angry at myself. I should have done some research on that guy George Witkoff instead of taking Lou's word for it that he knew what he was doing. Or maybe not put my money in an investment having anything to do with nightlife. Shit is risky.

- Like comedy clubs I guess.

- Actually, comedy clubs in New York do alright. So many great comics live here and they all need to get on stage to test jokes so they're willing to work cheap. As I've told you, when I started I used to actually pay to perform, even after I didn't completely suck. And a club doesn't have to be fancy. The market's a bit glutted now, but I still think if you can find a space with cheap rent and run it right, it can be profitable. I'd never want to own one though.

- Why not?

- Comics are my friends. I wouldn't wanna get into arguments with them about money. And the ones I didn't book to perform would hate me. Anyway, we're getting sidetracked. To answer your question, I'm not mad at Lou. Maybe I would be, but to be honest, he's made me a lot more money than he's lost me.

- Really? With other investments?

- No, it was Lou who gave me the idea for *Jackson Taylor's Christmas Party*.

- He came up with the idea?

- No. Well, in a way he did. He used to have Christmas parties every year for a few years in the late aughts through the early 2010s after he started making good money on Wall Street. I would see a lot of the same people there each year, mostly people I only saw there. Sometimes we'd continue conversations right where we'd left off the year before. So I used that as the basis for the script, made the partygoers a little more eclectic and threaded a love story through it.

210

- I really enjoyed the love story aspect of the film, said Miles, his voice taking on a joyful tone as he thought about the film. I loved all the kooky characters and the comedic aspects of it too, but for me, the best part was the chemistry between Lawrence and Julianne. When are you gonna find your Julianne? he asked after a brief pause.

- I don't know. Not every Lawrence finds their Julianne.

- Are you looking?

- I'm open to it.

The truth is that there was little evidence to suggest Ira was looking for anything real in the romantic arena. He had only had one relationship in his life that lasted longer than a year and it was a relationship that made little sense at all. Harlee Shaw never truly appreciated Ira. She knew he was funny because everyone said he was funny. She laughed occasionally at his jokes but was at best lukewarm in her enthusiasm for his humor. In a bizarre way, she felt it gave her a certain cachet to be dating someone less famous and less beautiful than her usual boyfriends. "Wow," she imagined people saying." "Harlee Shaw is a deeper person than we thought. She cares about personality and chemistry, not about looks or money." There was also the fact that Harlee was sure that Ira's star was rising, which of course, it was at the time.

- Are you really open to it? asked Miles.

- Why wouldn't I be open to it?

- I have some ideas.

CHAPTER 23

IRA SPIRO BEFORE COVID: A MEMOIR - CHAPTER 7

From my earliest years, I can remember my mother being, essentially, two different people. At times, she was the most affectionate and loving woman imaginable, at other times angry and hostile. It wasn't until about the age of eight or so that I began to make the connection between these profound changes in her personality and those beverages she loved that I was never allowed to try. Generally, she would start drinking after work and then continue throughout the evening until she finally passed out, often in her bed, sometimes on the couch and a few times on the floor. Even on days she wasn't working, the pattern would generally be the same — she would start the day sober and hit the sauce by late afternoon.

My parents, after years of constant fighting, finally got divorced when I was nine years old. At the time my parents had shared custody of me. I would spend every other week with my mother at the house where I grew up in Paramus, New Jersey, which she got in the divorce settlement, and every other week with my father at a two-bedroom apartment he rented in the same town.

After the divorce, my mother's drinking seemed to get worse. If she found life with my father difficult, she seemed to have had even greater difficulty adjusting to life without him. One day after school, several months after my father had moved out of the house, I was in the kitchen in search of a snack. There was a box of Oreo cookies on a high shelf in the cupboard and, not yet having hit my growth spurt, I struggled to reach it. My mother, home early that day from the dental office where she worked as a hygienist, was in her room, probably, I thought to myself, having a glass of wine. The wisest course of action was to try to get the cookies myself. Rather than pull a chair over to the counter, I decided instead to make use of the broom leaning against the wall next to the dishwasher.

I used the broom to slide the box of Oreos off the shelf, and as it fell to the counter it knocked a serving plate onto the floor. The noise made by the breaking china brought my mother out of her bedroom. She didn't have a drink in her hand as she came into the kitchen, but I intuitively knew, even if unable to articulate why at that age, that she probably had already had at least two glasses. Likely her gait was unbalanced and her eyes had taken on a lightly glassy look. I just remember knowing that I had picked a bad time to break a plate.

- I'm sorry mommy. The box of Oreos fell and knocked the plate onto the floor.

- They just fell, all by themselves? she asked rhetorically. Her voice was slightly elevated, but she seemed less angry than I had anticipated. That would soon change.

She started picking up shards of glass with her hand and tossing them into the garbage.

- Mommy you shouldn't be using your hands for that, I said, handing her the very broom that was the proximate cause of all the trouble.

- Goddamnit! she screamed. Look what you made me do!

She had cut the tip of her left index finger picking up one of the pieces of the broken plate.

- You gonna stand there like an idiot or are you gonna get me a band-aid? she screamed.

As I went to the bathroom to get a band-aid out of the medicine cabinet, I could hear her continue her tirade. It consisted mostly of swears and words like clumsy, worthless and good-for-nothing. Though I don't precisely remember the context, I also distinctly remember her uttering the words "your Jew father."

After putting on the band-aid that I had gotten for her, she grabbed me by the by arm and lead me to my room.

- You're going to your room and you're gonna stay there until I say you can come out, she shrieked, almost yanking my shoulder out of its socket as she pulled me toward my prison cell.

She pushed me into my bedroom with sufficient force that I almost lost my balance, and then she slammed the door closed. As was typically the case when my mom went off the rails, I did not feel anger. I blamed myself, wondering what I had done wrong. I had broken a plate. I should have been more careful, I thought, as I sat on the edge of my bed, wondering how long my confinement would last.

I heard my mother making grunting noises interspersed with more cursing outside my bedroom. It sounded, in fact, like she was struggling to move something heavy. I laid down in front of my bedroom door and looked through the space between the bottom of the door and the floor to see what was going on. Indeed she was struggling with something heavy! My mother was sliding the coffee table from the den along the carpeting and positioning it in front of my bedroom door. This was a first. My mother had sent me to my room before but had never tried to barricade me in. It didn't make much sense considering my bedroom door opened inwards, but the message was clear enough. I was not to leave that room under any circumstances.

There wasn't much for me to do. The television in my bedroom was no longer working and there was no computer. Not that a computer would have necessarily done me much good. It was 1989. There were primitive video games you could play on a computer if you had the software installed, but there was no web to surf or YouTube videos to watch, and you couldn't chat with friends on social media. If I had wanted to write a research paper or configure a spreadsheet, I suppose a computer would have been useful, but not for much else. As far as the entertainment options that were available to me that day in my room there was only one, and for an eight-year-old boy it was a decidedly bad one — books! There wasn't much of a selection in any case. There were some children's versions of classic novels my father had bought for me at a yard sale. I believe *Oliver Twist* and *The Red Badge of Courage* were among the titles. There was also a book of aerial photos from Holland that my mother's father, Grandpa Deridder, had gotten for me, thinking I might enjoy getting in touch with my Dutch heritage. The pictures were quite lovely and there were some utterly spectacular shots of tulip fields in various colors, but it was of little interest to me at the time. Apart from the books, there were some board games in my room but they, of course, required more than one person to play. There was also my old beach playset, but that wasn't particularly useful indoors.

I ended up curled up on my bed with a recent edition of the *Guinness Book of World Records*. I had already perused the book many times, but I always found it enjoyable. As a kid, I liked reading about and looking at pictures of things like the guy with the super long fingernails and the world's tallest man. Other world records I found interesting were the world's highest IQ and the most cigarettes ever smoked at the same time. I assume it's never happened, but it would be interesting if those two records were held by the same person. If I had the world's highest IQ, I'd at least attempt to stuff one hundred sixty cigarettes in my mouth. "As long as you're here," I'd tell the Guinness guy after having taken the IQ test, "let me try for another record."

I've always been fascinated with extreme human longevity and no doubt took a glance at the section of the book that listed the oldest people of all time. I had to look this up while writing this memoir, but in 1989 the world record for longevity would have been held by

Shigechiyo Izumi of Japan who died in 1986 at the presumed age of 120 years, 237 days. The record was later invalidated when research indicated he might have actually been 105 when he died. The real all-time world's oldest person in 1989 would have been Fannie Thomas from Illinois, who lived from April 14, 1867 until January 22, 1981. This woman was born during the post-civil war reconstruction period, nine years before the Battle of the Little Bighorn, and made it all the way to season four of *The Love Boat*. Sorry if this kind of stuff doesn't interest you, but it's my memoir and I'll digress if I want to!

After finishing with the *Guinness* book I spent some time lying on my back and throwing a tennis ball up in the air and catching it as it came down. After about a half-hour of that, I killed a chunk of time with a game called Labyrinth that I had forgotten about but was glad to find in my closet. The game consists of a wooden maze that can be moved vertically and horizontally with two knobs. The object is to guide a metal ball through the maze using the knobs without the ball falling into one of the holes spaced throughout.

Dinner time was approaching and I was getting severely hungry. As you recall, my earlier efforts to satiate myself with an Oreo cookie failed spectacularly, resulting in my current situation. Normally when my mother confined me to my room, she let me out after a couple of hours, but it had been close to three and still, there I sat, alone and scared, not knowing when or if I'd ever be let out.

- Mom! I called out softly while knocking on my door from the inside.

No response. I called out to her again, this time a little louder, but still failed to attract her attention.

- Mom!!! I called out, now as loudly as I could.

- God damn it, what? came the screaming reply.

- Can I come out? I answered timidly. I'm hungry. It's dinner time.

The request was met initially with silence and then I heard the grunting noises and cursing that I remembered from hours earlier. This time I did not have to look under the door to know what was going on. My mother was moving the coffee table. This surely could mean but one thing — my liberation was at hand! My mother opened the door. She had a glass of wine in one hand and a can of Campbell's soup in the other.

- "Here's your fucking dinner she said," as she threw the can of soup at me. "You can choke on it you piece of shit."

In my memory, the iconic red and white Campbell's soup label melded into a pink hue as it spun towards me. If I had a can of Campbell's in the house perhaps I'd spin it to test the possible validity of that recollection, as I'm not sure of its accuracy. I do know that it narrowly missed my face and hit the back wall of my room before landing on the floor. My mother then slammed the door closed after which I heard another door slam, presumably the one to her room where she no doubt went to continue her drinking. She didn't bother to move the coffee table back in front of the door, perhaps this time realizing it was useless to do so.

Had the soup hit me it certainly would have hurt like hell. Luckily I had the reflexes to avoid the metal projectile and my wounds were purely psychological, although nonetheless terrible. "You can choke on it you piece of shit." I don't recall what kind of soup it was or whether it contained any large chunks of meat or vegetables that would have rendered it choke-on-able. Nevertheless, her words were so hurtful that I no longer felt like eating anyway, not that I would have or could have eaten a can of unheated soup with no means to open it.

I lied in my bed staring at the ceiling for a long time, again blaming myself for my mother's reaction. By this time I had to go to the bathroom. I had no desire to provoke my mother's wrath yet again and held it in as long as I could. Eventually, however, the time came when I simply had to relieve myself. I was not willing to take the risk of leaving my room and being caught by my mother. Instead, I opened my window and urinated into the bushes on the front lawn from my room on the second floor of our split-level ranch. Luckily, I wasn't a girl, or I might have had to resort to the sand bucket from the aforementioned beach playset.

Sometime later, after managing to occupy myself for a couple more hours with the *Guinness Book of Records* and my tennis ball I went to sleep. I woke up the next morning and got dressed for school. My mother, I thought, was likely sound asleep in her room as she always was early in the morning. I just needed to make it out of the house without waking her. My father would be picking me up at school, and I was scheduled to stay with him for the next week.

Leaving my room I noticed the coffee table next to the door. My mother had not bothered to move the stack of magazines on the table nor the picture of her taken some time in the late '60s with my Aunt Sally and my grandparents at Disneyland. What a contrast between the young girl with the radiant smile and the mouse ears on her head and the broken woman in the next room.

I went to the kitchen to get something to eat, my hunger having returned. The Oreo cookies were still on the floor, as were several shards of glass and some streaks of blood from my mother's cut finger. I grabbed the box of Rice Krispies that was on the counter and headed out the door for the half-mile walk to school, devouring the Rice Krispies as I went.

I explained what happened to my father when he picked me up at school that afternoon. Shortly thereafter, my mother lost custody of me and from then on only had visitation rights. Her first attempt at sobriety was two years later. It lasted about six months.

As for the book *Holland From the Air*, I still have it. It's in my seldom-used guest bathroom off my seldom-used guest bedroom. I no longer have the *Guinness Book of World Records* from that day, though I do have the 2017 edition on my bookshelf. It is between Charles Dickens' *David Copperfield*, which I didn't finish, and Stephen Hawking's *A Brief History of Time*, which I didn't understand. I maintain, and have always maintained, that, although the book was marketed to the general public, no one without a PhD in physics understood it, and those who say they did are lying.

By the way, the oldest person of all time listed in the 2017 edition of the *Guinness Book of World Records* is Jeanne Calment, who died at the age of 122 years, 164 days in 1997. She was a French woman. As far as I know she never, in her twelve decades of life, came in America.

CHAPTER 24

Charlotte and Sébastian were seated on the couch in front of the television in their new one-bedroom apartment in the Financial District of Manhattan. They were watching *Jackson Taylor's Christmas Party*. It was Sébastian's idea. Though he was too young to fully appreciate the film he had a certain affinity for it, in particular the main character Lawrence Hummel.

They were watching the scene where Jackson was having his yearly party on a yacht that he had chartered. The yacht was sailing up the East River under the Brooklyn bridge. Sébastian was giggling watching the diminutive man in the top hat flailing about as he was being hoisted aboard the yacht from a motorboat. The operation was rendered more difficult by the fact that it was a windy day and the water was choppy.

JACKSON: Brent, I thought you weren't coming this year!

BRENT: Have I missed one of your parties yet?

JACKSON: Not in the fifteen years I've been doing it!

BRENT: Well then you should have known I'd be here. Sorry I'm late. (to the driver of the motorboat as he sails away) Thanks for the ride, Dave.

- Brent porte ce chapeau chaque année Maman! (Brent wears that hat every year Mommy!)

- Je sais. Ce chapeau lui plait. (I know. He likes that hat).

- Comment il connait Jackson? (How does he know Jackson?)

- Tu t'en souviens pas? Ils ont travaillé ensemble au restaurant, avant que le premier livre de Jackson sorte. (Don't you remember? They worked together at the restaurant, before Jackson's first book was published)

- Oui. C'est vrai. J'avais oublié. (That's right. I had forgotten)

The film cuts to the other side of the yacht where Julianne is at the railing looking towards Long Island City. The water is getting rougher and the boat is rising and falling. Lawrence approaches her.

LAWRENCE: Julianne!

JULIANNE: Lawrence. Hi! How are you?

LAWRENCE: OK. Wish the water were a little calmer?

JULIANNE: Yeah, we're really bouncing around. You weren't at the party last year.

LAWRENCE: No. I was tied up working on a case.

JULIANNE: Anything exciting?

LAWRENCE: Two brands of yogurt with a similar logo. Lawsuit ensues.

JULIANNE: Too bad you couldn't make the party. You'd have gotten one of these.

Julianne shows Lawrence her watch. It's a Movado.

LAWRENCE: Wow, a Movado!

JULIANNE: Isn't it pretty? It was in the gift bag last year.

LAWRENCE: Gift bag? These parties are getting a lot more lavish since Jackson's last book became a bestseller.

JULIANNE: I know. I wonder what'll be in the gift back this year.

Julianne, Lawrence and everyone else are almost knocked off their feet as the boat hits a big wave.

LAWRENCE: I'm hoping Dramamine.

Sébastian knew a joke had been told because the character Julianne was laughing as was his mother. Once Charlotte explained to him that Dramamine was a medicine used for seasickness, he laughed as well.

JULIANNE: Who's that girl I saw you with on the dance floor?

LAWRENCE: Nina? We're actually on a date. I met her on Tinder.

JULIANNE: What's Tinder?

LAWRENCE: It's a new online dating site. Well, not really a site. It's an app for your phone. You scroll through pictures of single people in your area. If you like them your press "heart", if not you press "X."

JULIANNE: Not terribly romantic.

LAWRENCE: No, not terribly.

JULIANNE: So how's the date going? Are you gonna see her again?

LAWRENCE: Probably. It's not that big a boat.

This time Sébastian laughed immediately, getting the joke without explanation.

- It's almost 7. I have to get ready, said Charlotte.

- *Vous allez où pour votre rencard?* (Where are you two going on your date?)

- *On va dîner et peut-être prendre des verres apres.* (We're going to have diner and maybe drinks after.)

- Are you going to fuck him *Maman*?

As Sébastian clearly wasn't going to forget that word, Charlotte had no choice but to explain to him that it did not mean "kiss" as she had told him previously and that he should not use it. What it actually did mean she declined to say. That task accomplished, Charlotte got up to prepare for her evening out.

Charlotte had recently purchased a sexy new burgundy mini dress and was happy for the chance to wear it. She had just finished putting on her makeup when Meghan the babysitter arrived. She was a 21-year-old female college student that was recommended to Charlotte by a friend from work.

224

- You guys are watching *Jackson Taylor's Christmas Party?* said Meghan. I love that film!

- You can watch it wis' me! said Sébastian excitedly. It's 'ze part where 'zey are on 'ze boat.

- I have such a crush on the guy who plays Lawrence, said Meghan to Charlotte. I like awkward guys.

- Yes, 'zey have some charm. So here's 'ze rule. Sébastian can finish watching 'zis movie, and after 'zat he can watch whatever he want but only if it's in French.

Since they were now living in the United States and Sébastian was at school with Americans, Charlotte was no longer concerned about Sébastian learning English, but was now concerned about him forgetting French. Thus, she no longer insisted that they speak English together. They would often switch between the two languages, and she encouraged Sébastian to watch movies and TV shows in French.

Charlotte's date that evening was none other than Ira Spiro. They had dinner at a high-end Japanese restaurant and then went to Paola's, a wine bar on the Upper East Side.

- You look good, Ira. I'm glad you shaved your beard. I like you better 'zis way.

- Thanks. The beard was getting mixed reviews.

- My babysitter has a crush on you , said Charlotte, taking a sip of her Malbec.

- Babysitter? Why do you need a babysitter?

Charlotte had come dangerously close to revealing her secret and needed to think fast.

- I'm sorry. You know sometimes my English gets not so good after a few drinks. I did not mean babysitter. I meant my, you know, what is 'ze word?

Charlotte searched in her mind for a word that could have plausibly been confused with "babysitter."

- My baby sister. 'Zat is 'ze word I meant.

- Sandrine?

- Yes. You remember her name. I am impressed. 'Zat's funny how in English a baby sister doesn't have to actually be a baby. Anyway, we were talking today and she said she has a crush on you.

- Well, that's flattering, but I can only handle one Aubertin woman at a time.

- Hey, did you guys see the new Dave Chappelle special on Netflix, said a sandy-haired stocky guy in a Yankees baseball hat to his two friends who were standing next to him at the bar, not far from Ira and Charlotte.

The group of three guys all looked to be in their early to mid-twenties. They were speaking very loudly and Charlotte and Ira, as well as most of the patrons in the bar, could easily hear what they were saying.

- Yeah, it was fucking great, said one of the stocky guy's friends, a short guy with a noticeable beer belly.

- Chappelle's funny but I still prefer Louis CK, said the third member of the group, similar in build to the stocky guy in the baseball hat but with a more ethnic-looking face, indicating perhaps Jewish or Italian ancestry.

- Fucking CK makes me shit my pants, said the guy with the beer belly.

- These guys are comedy fans, said Ira to Charlotte. I hope they don't recognize me, he continued, tilting his head down to hide himself from view.

- Not in 'ze mood to talk to fans?

- Not these guys. I know the type. I can imagine the conversation. "Hey, it's fuckin' Ira Spiro." "Yes I am. How you doing." "Dude let me buy you a drink." "Oh, no thanks, I appreciate the offer though." "What the fuck dude? You don't wanna have a drink with me?" "Sorry not right now. I'm with a friend ." "You're a fuckin' douchebag!"

Charlotte laughed at Ira's interpretation of his would-be exchange with the young men sitting about ten feet away.

- You 'sink it would be like 'zat?

- I know it would be like 'zat, said Ira, playfully mocking Charlotte's inability to pronounce the English "th" sound. I've had pretty much that exact conversation before. More than once. Maybe I shouldn't have shaved my beard.

- You were pretty recognizable even wis' 'ze beard, I 'sink.

- You guys wanna go to the Comedy Den this weekend, said the stocky Yankees fan, once again loud enough for all to hear.

- Fuck yeah, I love that place, said the Jewish or Italian (or other Mediterranean ethnicity) guy.

- Shit. They're Comedy Den regulars, said Ira. Good chance they know me.

- Maybe 'zey don't want to have a drink wis' you because 'zey 'sink you're not funny, said Charlotte with a laugh.

- Ouch. Maybe, but I can't take the chance. Let's get out of here.

Ira settled up with the bartender and he and Charlotte discretely made their way to the exit. Ira attempted to hide his face by looking towards the wall opposite the bar as Charlotte walked between him and the three twenty-somethings with whom Ira was assiduously trying to avoid eye contact.

The short, rotund member of the trio noticed Charlotte's pleasing form as she and Ira walked past and was moved to comment on it.

- Dudes check it out, he said, trying to be discrete but failing terribly.

- Crap, said Ira to himself. I hope they don't say anything inappropriate.

- Whoah, said the Yankees fan, also failing miserably to speak softly. I would do all kinds of naughty things to that.

Ira brusquely turned away from the wall toward the bar.

- Hey, have a little respect, snapped Ira.

- Hey it's Ira Spiro, said the ethnic-looking one.

- Dude, I fuckin' love you! said the round one. Have a drink with us!

Ira and Charlotte continued walking toward the door, obviously not anxious to accept the drink invitation.

- Come on, don't be a dick, continued the round one, insulting Ira after having just expressed his love for him moments before.

Ira and Charlotte continued to ignore them and exited the bar.

After having a quick drink at another bar, Ira and Charlotte decided to take a nighttime stroll through Central Park. They didn't pay too much attention to where they were going, heading in a general westerly direction toward the Upper West Side. Though Central Park is far less busy at night, more than a few people were taking advantage of the unseasonably warm March evening to walk and bike ride in what some refer to as New York's backyard. Ira and Charlotte even passed a man on a unicycle as they made their way past the Loeb Boat House located next to the Central Park Lake.

- I need to sit down. I have no more legs.

- What do you mean you have no more legs? responded Ira, amused as always at Charlotte's occasional lapses in communicating in English.

- My legs are tired. I have no more legs. You don't say 'zat?

- No we don't.

- In French when our legs are tired we say *"j'ai plus de jambes,"* I have no more legs. What you say in English?

- We say "my legs are tired." Why don't we go sit down?

Ira and Charlotte took a seat on the wide sweeping staircase that descended toward the iconic Bethesda Fountain and the lake just beyond. The familiar black cast-iron lamp posts that light up Central Park at night were relatively scarce in the vicinity of the fountain, which was, as a result, barely visible from Ira and Charlotte's vantage point. One could, however, easily hear the rush of the water as it fell from the angel statue at the top into the fountain's ninety-foot diameter main basin.

From where Ira and Charlotte were seated you could look in all directions without seeing any building or structure from outside of the park. It gave the impression of being out in the country, though if one hazarded a gaze upward, the lack of stars, even on a cloudless night, rendered less tenable the illusion that one was anywhere but in the middle of a huge city filled with electric lights.

- Have you been here before? asked Ira.

- I've been to Central Park, but never 'zis place.

- Really? This is a great spot. One of my favorites in the park. I used to come here a lot to write. Came up with a lot of ideas for *Jackson Taylor* sitting here staring at the fountain and the lake. Here and in the steam room at the gym.

- 'Zat remind me of some'sing.

- What's with you foreigners? It's really that hard to pronounce "th?" You just put your tongue against your upper front teeth?

- Shut up! I have some'sing to give you.

- Some'sing good I hope.

Charlotte couldn't help but laugh at Ira's playful imitation of her pronunciation, giving him a playful gentle push in simulated protest.

- Anyway, I know you have a 'sing where you don't like birs'days, but I believe you had one last week.

- You're right. I don't like them, and I made sure to ignore all the texts and emails I got. But thank you for remembering.

- I got you a present.

Charlotte opened her Louis Vuitton handbag and took out Ira's gift, wrapped in brown paper with twine around it tied into a bow. A plain white card was glued onto the wrapping on which was printed *"Joyeux Anniversaire"* with each letter in different colors of the rainbow.

- I assume "joyeux anniversaire" means happy birthday?

- You are so smart.

- Well, it looks like a book.

- Maybe.

- A cookbook?

- You don't cook.

- Fair point. I'm not even sure my stove works. Book of dirty limericks?

- No, Charlotte responded with a giggle.

- Well if it's Stephen Hawking's *A Brief History of Time,* I already read it and couldn't understand a word. "No prior knowledge of cosmology necessary" my ass!

- Nope. Zero by 'sree.

- Zero by three?

- 'Sree guesses. Zero correct.

- I think you meant "zero for three."

- Shit. Yes. Zero for 'sree. I was back in France all 'zat time, and my English got worse.

- It's ok. Prepositions are tricky. Alright, let's see what we got here.

Ira pulled the card off the wrapping and then tore the wrapping from the gift, revealing a *The Little Prince*-themed notebook from Montblanc. It was bound in brown leather with embossed gold foil images from the Saint-Exupéry novella. The cover featured the Little Prince himself, an airplane and several little stars.

- It's beautiful, said Ira, leafing through the lined gold-edged pages. Thank you so much.

- You can write your ideas down for your jokes or your next movie. Or maybe some dirty limericks!

- I haven't written much of anything in a while.

- You must write. You're too talented for your voice not to be heard.

Ira smiled, feeling genuinely moved by Charlotte's faith in his talent.

- Do you still have "no more legs" Charlotte?

- I 'sink I maybe have 'zem back.

Ira and Charlotte got up to continue their walk westward through the park on that moonlit night.

- So, how does it feel to be 40 years old?

- I try not to think about it.

- You don't look it.

- Thank you, but as it happens, I am it. Statistically speaking, I've strutted and fretted about thirty minutes of my hour upon the stage.

- What?

- *Macbeth* reference. I'm saying my life is half over. And since time seems to go by faster and faster as you get older, the finish line is well in view.

- 'Zat is weird how it goes faster and faster.

- What if medical technology allows us to live to like 800 years old, wondered Ira out loud? Would it continue to go faster and faster? Would the last hundred feel like a week?

- I 'sink 'zat is interesting. You could make it into a joke. Write 'zat down in your new notebook.

Charlotte handed Ira a pen from her handbag.

- Here, write it.

- I guess that's an order then?

- Yes.

Ira opened up the notebook to the first page. He wrote down: "Older = time passes faster. Live till 800 - last 100 fly."

Continuing their walk past the Naumburg Bandshell, frequent site of outdoor concerts in the summer, Ira asked Charlotte how her new job at TeaBrick was going. TeaBrick was a hot new startup headquartered in Midtown. It was an online lender using artificial intelligence to analyze whether or not a borrower is a good risk. Tea bricks, Charlotte explained, are compressed blocks of tea that, in addition to being used to make tea, were once used as currency in China and Tibet.

- So, what now? mused Ira as they reached Central Park West, the street that borders the park on, as its name suggests, its western edge. A drink back at my place?

- I need to get home Ira.

- Just one drink? You know I'm a lightweight anyway.

- Ira! she said, her tone of voice sufficient to convey her sentiments without further words.

- What? exclaimed Ira, insisting on clarification anyway.

- I don't want to jump back into a casual sex relationship. You said you were open to some'sing real 'zis time.

- You bought that shit, joked Ira.

- Very funny. Let's take it slow, ok?

- Ok Charlotte. I understand.

Ira and Charlotte kissed briefly on the street, and then he put her into a cab and watched it pull away, whisking Charlotte to her new Manhattan apartment and, unbeknownst to Ira, their son.

CHAPTER 25

Miles lived in an enormous, stately renovated 1829 three-story federal-style townhouse on a quiet tree-lined block in Greenwich Village. Deciding to make productive use of a Sunday afternoon, he ambled into his well-appointed, mahogany-walled study on the top floor, carrying three partly written screenplays which he placed on his desk before sitting down in his soft brown leather chair. He clicked on the classical music playlist on his phone and Mozart's "Violin Concerto Number Three" started playing softly through the cylindrical Bose Bluetooth speaker on top of the bookshelf against the wall several feet to his right.

As he was about to pick up one of the scripts, his eight-year-old white terrier/poodle mix scampered into the room, sliding along the dark brown wood floor and wagging his tail vigorously in a clear expression of unbridled joy.

- Yes I know Sig, I love Mozart too, said Miles picking up the dog and holding him, arms outstretched, above his head before lowering him slowly towards his face.

The dog wasted no time in showing his affection as soon as he was in licking range.

Miles put the dog on his lap and started gently stroking his head, eliciting the low pitch grunting that signaled his complete contentedness.

Mile's wife Adele appeared in the doorway smiling at the sight of Miles and the dog. Adele was a petite and slender woman who, like Miles, was in her early fifties.

- There you are Sigmund. Enjoying some playtime with Daddy I see.

- We're listening to our favorite concerto.

- You both have good taste, opined Adele.

- I never tire of this piece.

- Classical music usually means you're doing some reading.

- I was about to, but Sig insisted on being paid attention to, and I couldn't refuse.

- What are you reading? asked Adele. Looks like a book manuscript.

- Actually, these are movie scripts.

- Movie scripts? Well that's a first.

- Yes it is. This performer I'm working with wrote some screenplays, and I asked him if I could take them home and have a read. They're all scripts he started and never finished.

- Why not?

- He said because they're shit, though I'm skeptical about that. Writers always have doubts about their work, but I'm wondering if he sensed they might in fact be good, and that's what made him uneasy.

- Ah, very interesting. I see a lot of that kind of thing in my practice, said Adele. I have one patient who works in finance. She's very brilliant and very capable but every promotion sends her into an emotional tailspin. She eventually recovers, but then it happens again the next time.

- What do you think is causing this? asked Miles.

- I think she's torn. She wants to be appreciated for her abilities, but at the same time she feels that being a successful woman will alienate men.

- That's certainly not an uncommon feeling among women, said Miles, while putting the dog on the floor in preparation to start reading.

- True, though her case is fairly extreme.

- Well, this is a male writer so he doesn't have that particular fear. With him, there are a few factors at play, but I think it's mostly to do with his relationship with his father.

Miles stood in the living room of Ira's apartment looking out the window towards Amsterdam Ave.

- Wow, what a clear day, he remarked. You can see across the Hudson River and probably twenty miles into New Jersey.

- Can you see Spiro Formalwear?

- It still exists?

- I think it's a bank now. You know, there was an identical apartment to this for sale on a lower floor. Less of a view but a lower monthly maintenance charge. But Harlee insisted on the twentieth floor so here I am with New Jersey still in my life.

- Just don't look west, joked Miles.

- I have to, or I can't see the river. And I must admit, I do have a certain affection for New Jersey. There were some good memories mixed in with the bad. And if it's good enough for Bruce Springsteen, who am I to besmirch it.

- I'm in full agreement with that sentiment, said Miles. The Boss's judgment should not be lightly dismissed.

Miles continued to stare out the window for a few moments before turning around and taking his usual seat next to the couch.

- So I read your scripts. Or should I say your partial scripts. Your unfinished symphonies if you will.

- Well, as I told you they're not particularly interesting. Not sure why you wanted to read them.

- I actually quite enjoyed them.

- You're just saying that to be nice. You won't hurt my feelings. What do you really think?

- I liked them. All three. The first one I read was the time travel one. I thought it was a lot of fun.

Miles was referring to *Spring Back*, a story about a group of 21st-century college students who steal a physics professor's time machine in order to spend their spring break traveling through time.

- Ah yes. My attempt at a high concept Hollywood blockbuster. I even named it *Spring Back*. As much as I have a pet peeve about film names that are plays on words, I figured it would appeal to the studios.

- Why didn't you finish that one?

- I thought it was silly. At the end of the day, my heart wasn't into a broad comedy like that.

- Like I said, I thought it was fun. I enjoyed the part where the character Zachary is trying to use his smartphone and he gets frustrated and screams, "Shit, there's no reception in the '80s!"

- Yeah, I guess that was an ok line.

- Well, what about the script about the guy spreading his recently deceased friend's ashes in his favorite spots around the country? Pretty original idea I thought.

- Not really. If you google it, it turns out there are several ash-spreading movies out there. In fact, it's a whole sub-genre. That's one problem with the internet. You discover how unoriginal your ideas are. I remember writing a joke about the fact that March is women's history month. The punchline was that it makes sense to choose March to celebrate women's history because it comes in like a lion and goes out like a lamb. In other words, March has mood swings. To make sure it hadn't been thought of already, I googled "women's history month & lion & lamb." Found out someone had tweeted pretty much word for word what I had come up with.

236

- Well, said Miles, I'm pretty sure *Hope from History* is original. It was my favorite of the three by the way.

Hope from History was about a famous actor named Brian Lowe who is in a turbulent relationship with his model/actress girlfriend Jamie Beck. Back in high school, Brad's English teacher, Mr. Antinori, made him and the other students write in a journal every day. Reading through the journal twenty years later, after discovering it while visiting his parents' house, he realizes that his high school crush, Hope Anderson, actually liked him. He was too awkward and inexperienced to know it at the time, but reading about their interactions that he had written about in the journal made him realize that she was indeed sending him signals all those years ago. In the last scene that Ira had written, Brian goes online and googles "Hope Anderson."

- I assume, said Miles, that Brian ultimately breaks up with Jamie and gets together with the pretty girl from high school who liked him when he was a shy nobody.

- Yeah, I suppose that's where it was headed.

- Well, why did you give up on that one?

- I don't know. Does the world need another romantic comedy?

- I think so. If it's a good one. But I don't think that's why you stopped writing.

- Then why did I?

- I think, perhaps, you might have an idea.

CHAPTER 26
IRA SPIRO BEFORE COVID: A MEMOIR - CHAPTER 16

I came to realize that my many career setbacks, the panic attack on stage in Colorado, my constantly picking fights with Matt Schefter as we were working together on *Charlton Choudhury - Modern Times* and my failure to finish my various writing projects were tied to an unconscious desire to ruin my own career. Perhaps I even took too much Xanax before that gig in Maryland on purpose, albeit without fully realizing it. My friend and fellow comic Tony Powell saw this propensity for self-sabotage in me long before I did. Others perhaps saw it too. I, on the other hand, was blind to it.

Examining my life, there were examples of this tendency manifesting itself even before I got into show business. After the "tennis incident" I eventually gave up the sport, but not right away. I stopped playing against my father but continued playing with school friends on public courts around town. I also took semi-private lessons once a week, courtesy of my mother's parents. During my freshman year in high school, I joined the tennis team. I started off as a junior varsity player. After beating all the other kids on the junior varsity squad, the coach suggested I try for a varsity spot. In order to do that I had to play a best of three set match against a varsity player and win.

On a warm spring day after school, I played a match against Alex Chapman. As the lowest-ranked member of the varsity team, Alex was obligated to play against me if challenged. Alex was a good player, but I rose to the occasion and won the first set making few, if any, unforced errors and even winning several points at the net, though volleys were normally the weakest part of my game. In the second set, I quickly rose to a two-game lead. I was four games away from making varsity, which would have been a pretty big accomplishment for a freshman.

Sports, like anything in life, has a strong psychological element to it. Regardless of one's physical abilities, one cannot achieve victory without being in a victory frame of mind. After winning those first two games in the second set, I remember running full force into a wall of anxiety I couldn't quite explain. My game fell apart piece by piece starting with my serve, which I was only able to make half the time. Even my normally strong and consistent forehand eventually abandoned me. I lost the next two sets and my shot at varsity glory. I quit the tennis team altogether and barely played the game at all after that.

What I understand now, but did not at the time, was that although I was upset to have lost, I was even more scared of winning. To be on the varsity team, especially as a freshman, would be an assumption of my own power as a tennis player. My father had clearly expressed, given his hostile reaction after I defeated him during our last match, his antipathy toward that power.

Of course, it went beyond just tennis. As I've said, my father never rejoiced in my successes in life, especially successes in those areas where he himself had failed. One of those areas, of course, was show business. My father had hoped to be a famous stand-up comedian and, I would imagine, to get the film and television career that so often went with that. Yet he would spend his life renting tuxedos for proms and weddings, not wearing them for red carpet interviews at awards ceremonies.

A psychological battle raged within me that was no more obvious to me on a conscious level than such physiological processes

240

as the metabolism of glucose in my cells or the filtration of blood in my liver. My desire to become a big-time comedian was at war with a subconscious desire to languish in obscurity. I was at relative peace with the idea of earning a living touring and writing and even selling my screenplay for *Jackson Taylor's Christmas Party* was not too destabilizing at first. But the unexpected success of the film and my increasing fame disrupted the fragile stalemate of opposed psychological forces and brought with it increasing uneasiness.

My father's death was difficult for me, but of perhaps equal or greater significance was a first heart attack he had suffered about fifteen months before his fatal heart attack. This first attack didn't kill him, but it was serious and resulted in the insertion of a stent to relieve arterial blockage. At the time, I was in Los Angeles for something called "pilot season." It's the time of year, generally between January and April, when networks cast and film their pilot episodes for TV series that may or may not get picked up for broadcast in the fall. Since most of the casting and filming takes place in Los Angeles, I decided I'd have a better chance if I went out there rather than auditioning remotely by sending videos, which was less common then than it is today.

When I heard about my father's heart attack, I booked a red-eye flight back east and arrived the next morning in New Jersey in time to accompany my stepmother to bring my father home from the hospital. I spent the next couple of days at the house with them as my father rested and recovered. My roommate, an actor I met online who paid the bills answering phones and making coffee at a talent agency, was no doubt happy to have our crappy apartment in Hollywood to himself for a while.

The conversations between me and my father were quite matter-of-fact. There were no heartfelt "I love you's" exchanged, nor were there, as it happens, any emotionless "I love you's" exchanged either. Our conversations revolved largely around the weather and what had

241

been going on at the formalwear store. My father had, apparently, just hired a teenager to work there part-time named, if memory serves, Jeff Pernice.

- So this 16-year-old kid, Jeff, recounted my father, he says to me the other day, mind you he just started working in the store. I barely know him. He says "Mr. Spiro, have you seen the movie *The Hangover*?" I said to him "No, I haven't seen it, why?" He says he wanted to know if it's worth the ten bucks a ticket for him and his boyfriend. Amazing how much things have changed since I was a kid.

- Yeah, those ticket prices have really gotten expensive, I joked, managing to elicit laughter from my father even in his weakened condition.

- Obviously, there were gay kids when I was in school, he said, but it was kept under wraps. Maybe the New York City kids were out of the closet but not in the suburbs like now.

- But that's a good thing don't you think Dad? That gay kids aren't ashamed to be who they are?

- Yeah it's a good thing. Though not as good as me winning the lottery. I mean, if you gave me the choice.

And with that, my dad in turn made me laugh. He was a funny man. Certainly, there have been no small number of less funny people that became famous. Then again, there have also been far funnier people that similarly went nowhere. The same, it should be noted, can be said of me. There are people more talented than I who have not achieved what I have. That, as the saying goes, is show business.

The heart attack had not changed the distant nature of my relationship with my father to any significant degree, though I did call him from time to time to check on how he was doing. A few months later my stepmother called me. She explained to me that dad's cardiologist had advised him to make numerous lifestyle changes to prevent a second heart attack, including a better diet and more physical activity. He had also been prescribed statins to lower his cholesterol. She said she had been making sure he was taking the medication and was preparing healthy meals for him, but that he was still eating poorly outside the home and, as much as she hounded him about it, he was not exercising. In truth, he seemed to be doing less physical activity than ever and was even gaining weight. In tears, she asked me if I would talk to him and try to encourage him to take better care of himself. If his wife couldn't convince him to take his health seriously, I had serious doubts that I could, but nevertheless, I told her I would try.

It was bound to be an awkward conversation and I was not looking forward to it, but rather than putting it off, I decided the better course of action would be to get it over with as quickly as possible. To that end, I called that very evening at about 9 pm New York time when I knew my father would be at home, finished with dinner and available to talk. The conversation started with yet more small talk about the weather and the store before I abruptly transitioned into the delicate heart of the matter.

- So Dad, I said nervously, Carol was telling me . . .

- When were you talking to Carol? he interrupted.

- Earlier today. She called me up.

- You two talk on the phone now?

- Well, she called me up to tell me about the diet and exercise regime the doctor recommended for you.

- She did, huh? he growled.

My father was not making this discussion easy.

- So we think you should, you know, do what the doctor says.

- Oh yeah? Why?

- Well, so you can be around longer.

- Be around longer for what? To continue living a mediocre life?

The rest of the conversation continued more or less in that vein. I tried to convince my father that he should try to stay healthy, and he complained about his life having been largely a failure and hardly worth the effort to prolong it, even adding at one point that he had a good insurance policy and that if something happened my stepmother would be better off without him. Finally, he told me he wanted to watch the news, said a brief goodbye and hung up.

My father had clearly stated that life held such little charm for him that he was at best indifferent to it continuing. For me to flourish and prosper would be to provoke a sort of survivor's guilt I would have a hard time dealing with. This was all the more the case after he died the following year.

CHAPTER 27

Miles's friend Harry Solomon looked very much like him. They were both of shorter than average stature and both had a long narrow face, close-set eyes and an aquiline nose, though Harry's hair was a lighter, slightly reddish, brown. The two were seated next to a window having lunch at Pret A Manger, a sandwich shop on Broadway a few blocks from Columbus Circle.

- I've been doing a lot more cognitive behavioral therapy for my patients with seasonal affective disorder, said Harry.

- In conjunction with light therapy? asked Miles.

- Yes, although I try to avoid it when — hey that guy over there. Isn't that, I can't think of his name. He's a comedian. He was in that Christmas party movie.

- Where?

- Over there on line waiting to pay for his food.

- Oh shit, exclaimed Miles looking over and seeing that the comedian in question was, as suspected, Ira Spiro.

- There a problem?

- He may come over here. I know him.

- Really? asked Harry with excitement. How?

- I'll explain later. Just ah, don't say anything. Whatever I say, follow along.

After paying for his mozzarella and sliced tomatoes on a baguette at the counter and taking a quick selfie with a middle-aged female fan standing behind him online, Ira surveyed the dining area looking for an open table when he spotted Miles and immediately headed over towards him.

- Hey Miles! Crazy random sighting. What's up?

- Hey Ira. Good to see you. Ira this is my friend Harry.

- Your friend? Funny, I was actually about to ask if that was your brother.

- Yeah, we get that sometimes.

- Hey, what was the name of that movie you were in? asked Harry.

- *Jackson Taylor's Christmas Party*, responded Ira.

- Right, *Jackson Taylor's Christmas Party*. Sorry, I forgot the name. It was a good movie. I really liked it. I didn't know movie stars ate at Pret A Manger?

- As far as I know, they don't, said Ira, whose personal definition of "movie star" required appearances in more than one film.

- Ira, Harry and I are friends from college, said Miles.

- Oh cool. Where did you go to college, Miles? I don't think we ever discussed it. We're always focused on my life.

- Dartmouth.

- Good school. Certainly better than NYU where I went. So you went to Dartmouth as well? Ira asked Harry.

- Yes, we both went to Dartmouth, interjected Miles, before Harry had the chance to answer for himself.

- You live around here, Ira? asked Harry

- No. I'm on my way to the gym. Grabbing a quick snack before heading over there.

- That would explain the gym bag you're carrying, quipped Harry.

- Wait, your gym is near here? asked Miles.

- No, not normally. But the steam room at the Equinox I usually go to is closed for maintenance again. So I decided to try out the

246

Columbus Circle one. They got a pool there so I may have a swim for a change. Why don't we grab a table for three and I can join you guys.

- Actually, said Miles, we need to run. Harry, we're gonna have to finish our lunch on the way. We're gonna be late for the movie.

Miles gave Harry a light kick under the table as a reminder that he was to follow Mile's lead as previously instructed.

- What movie you guys going to see?

- What movie? Ah, *Spiderman: Far from Home*, said Miles.

- Never imagined you were into superhero flicks.

- Like you said, we're always focused on your life.

Miles grabbed the uneaten half of his tuna salad sandwich and got up from the table.

- Come on Harry. Let's go!

Harry, looking slightly confused, likewise got up, his mostly untouched yogurt and fruit parfait in hand.

- Good seeing you, Ira. Talk soon.

- Nice meeting you, said Harry as he followed Miles toward the door of the Pret A Manger.

"Something bizarre just happened," thought Ira as he sat down to eat his sandwich. It was clear that Miles didn't want him interacting with his friend Harry, who seemed completely taken by surprise when Miles announced that they needed to leave to catch a movie. Not to mention that two grown men, both in business casual clothing, catching a Spiderman flick on a weekday afternoon seemed unusual in itself. Ira went on the internet to see where *Spiderman: Far from Home* was playing. It was 1 pm. At all the theaters in the area, there were no showings of the film before 2 pm, rendering suspect the notion that they needed to hurry to catch the film. There was a 1:30 pm showing at Williamsburg Cinemas in Williamsburg, Brooklyn. However, Manhattanites seldom travel more than a couple of miles to see a movie, and they certainly don't cross a river. It was bizarre indeed.

- How was the movie? texted Ira that night after having thought about the encounter all day long, including while working out at the gym and during his precious steam room time.

- Pretty good, came the response a few minutes later. *A nice afternoon diversion.*

- What theater did you go to?

- The one near the Pret A Manger.

That settled the matter. As Ira had discovered online that afternoon, none of the showtimes for that film at the theaters near Columbus Circle justified a precipitated departure, unfinished sandwich and parfait in hand.

The question Ira was asking himself at that moment was this: "Who was Miles Breakstone?" He had found no trace of the man online after their initial meeting. It seemed logical at first. If Miles were a ghostwriter, he would, by definition, not be a credited author on any of the projects he had worked on. Yet, might a ghostwriter be involved in other projects? Would he not also have written things under his own name? There was nothing. Not so much as an archived article in the Dartmouth student newspaper. What about the social media? Ira had never used Instagram, which he thought to be an electronic temple of grotesque narcissism and, though he did not believe in the god of the Old Testament (or any other god), the endless duckface selfies and boomerang photos seemed to him justifiable grounds for another Great Flood. He had abandoned Twitter after the panic attack in Colorado. He still had a Facebook account, though he seldom used it. Perhaps Miles could be found there.

As it happened, there was only one Miles Breakstone on Facebook, but it was an elderly man who lived in Portland, Oregon. He tried entering "Breakstone & Dartmouth" in the Facebook search bar. People usually list their alma maters on Facebook and perhaps Miles might be found under a different first name. Maybe Miles was his middle name or a nickname. However, that search yielded no results at all. The search "Breakstone & New York" showed a couple dozen results. Ira looked at all of their profiles, but none were the man with whom he'd been working on his memoir for over a year.

Also absent from the internet was Bartolacci US, the name of the company that appeared on the check Ira had received from Miles. It was, according to Miles, a brand new division of Bartolacci Editore, the publishing company that was publishing Ira's memoir. The lack of an internet presence for a newly created division of an Italian publisher might not, in and of itself, arouse suspicion, but coupled with the recently raised doubts about Miles's identity, it was time for Ira to take his investigation a step further.

Ira, like most people, seldom deleted contact information once entered into his phone. There were several people he no longer even remembered in his list of contacts. There were even more people that he remembered but hadn't the slightest intention of ever speaking to again. One of those people was Harlee Shaw's decorator friend Giovanni Monterisi. Nevertheless, intentions change.

- Allo Ira, how are you? said Giovanni in his Barese accent, answering the phone after one ring.

- No doubt he thinks I need his expensive decorating services, thought Ira. That would explain the upbeat tone in his voice.

- Hey Giovanni. I'm good. Been awhile.

- Yes it has been some time. What I can do for you? responded Giovanni.

- Well, actually, I need someone who speaks Italian.

Ira explained to Giovanni that he needed him to call Bartolacci Editore and find out if there was a Miles Breakstone working for them or if anyone was working for them on an Ira Spiro memoir. He offered Giovanni four hundred dollars for the job. Ira figured the only way to get Giovanni to do it, and to do it quickly, was to give him the same exorbitant rate he charges for an hour of decorating. Giovanni accepted the deal, and Ira sent him the money right away by Venmo.

Giovanni called back the next day at around noon.

- Hey, Giovanni.

- Ira, *ciao* my friend.

- So, did you speak to them?

- Yes, I speak to 'dem. No one know what I'm talking about. I speak to someone in the editorial department, the contracts department, some more people. No one has heard of 'dis man, Miles Breakstone. And 'dere is no Ira Spiro memoir in 'da works.

- Thank you, Giovanni. I appreciate it.

- Ira, have you redecorated your apartment recently. Give it a new look. It's good to do it now and again.

- Maybe in the New Year, Ira said, with precious little sincerity.

- Ok, we will talk at New Year. *Ciao.*

- *Ciao.*

Ira's next phone call was to Miles, after spending a few moments trying to grapple with the fact that he had been the victim of some sort of scam. Yet it was the oddest sort of a scam. One that left him several hundred thousand dollars richer.

- No one at Bartolacci Editore knows who you are! screamed Ira into his phone.

- Why don't we get together and I'll explain everything.

Miles was already there and seated at a table when Ira arrived at the 81st and Broadway Starbucks where they had first met. Ira sat down to join him and cut to the chase without any "hello's" or small talk.

- What the fuck?

- My name is Miles Bregman, responded Miles firmly and without hesitation, wishing to get his confession over with quickly. Dr.

Miles Bregman. He continued. Breakstone was a guy I knew at summer camp in the third grade.

- Dr. Miles Bregman, Ph.D., Columbia Department of Psychology, said Ira, reading one of the entries that appeared on his phone when he googled "Miles Bregman & Doctor."

- Yes. That's me. I'm a psychologist and psychotherapist. And Harry, the person you saw me with at Pret A Manger, is a colleague of mine. I was afraid if you joined us, he would inadvertently reveal who I really was.

- I'm thoroughly confused.

- I've been a fan of yours for years. Since well before *Jackson Taylor's Christmas Party*. Here. Look at this.

Miles showed Ira the modestly followed Twitter account @IHeartIra on his phone.

- This is my account. @IHeartIra. I've had it for years.

Ira scrolled through the account, reading the occasional tweet such as "I have a feeling Ira will be back on stage soon!", which he had posted a few weeks prior. "Who misses Ira Spiro?" "Met a guy from Bulgaria. Thought of Ira's joke about how slow a news day it would have to be for anyone to hear about the Prime Minister of Bulgaria!" "Favorite *Jackson Taylor* scene - The year Jackson held the party on the chartered yacht." Ira kept scrolling and noticed a tweet from many years before that said, "Just finished watching *Ira Spiro - All In*, highly recommended."

- That was my first stand-up DVD.

- I know. I'm waiting for you to come out with a second.

- I was so new in comedy at the time. You liked it?

- I'll go one step further.

Miles unzipped his blue windbreaker to reveal a t-shirt with Ira's face behind a stack of poker chips and the words "Ira Spiro - The All In Tour."

251

- I got this at your show at the "Laugh Emporium" comedy club in Morristown, New Jersey.

- So, this memoir we've been working on. No one actually wants to publish it?

- I think someone will. I think it will be great and we'll find a publisher. And you'll make money.

- And you'll make money too, obviously.

- No. You would keep it all. The money I've given you already and any residuals. I had no intention of taking anything. I did this just to help you.

- To help me financially?

- Yes, but not only that.

- What else then?

- I saw how you were struggling. There was the show in Colorado. You said it was stomach flu, but then you stopped doing stand-up altogether. And then I heard about the show in Maryland. I couldn't just contact you and say, I'm a therapist, and I think I can help you.

- Why not?

- I had read in an interview that you did years ago in *People* magazine that you were a skeptic when it came to psychotherapy, and even if you weren't, no doubt you would have found it bizarre to be approached like that. What kind of therapist telemarkets?

- So these writing sessions are basically therapy sessions?

- Yes. I was actually working on my own memoir. I'm not sure anyone would be interested in reading about my life, but I enjoyed writing it. And I found it therapeutic, and that gave me the idea of contacting you.

- And Bartolacci US?

- I'm Bartolacci US. It's just a company I created. Bartolacci Editore really exists as you know. I chose an Italian publisher so that it

252

would be harder for you to verify. Harder, but not impossible, obviously.

- What about that office I saw you in? It said Bartolacci US on the door.

- Part of the ruse, alas.

Ira looked at his phone and started reading online about this man he had known all this time, but not really known at all. Miles Bregman's list of accomplishments was impressive. A graduate of Dartmouth, he wasn't lying about that, he got his master's and Ph.D. at Columbia University before joining the faculty there. Perhaps he was not a ghostwriter to the stars, but he had indeed written several books including *Cognitive Therapy and PTSD* and *Depression - Confronting A Modern Epidemic*. It certainly made sense. Miles looked and spoke like a therapist and seemed to know more about the science of psychology than the average person. The only thing about him that didn't seem stereotypical of a shrink was his Twitter fan account.

- I think we're writing a great memoir, said Miles, ending the several minutes of silence that had passed between them. And I think you've been making progress, both professionally and personally.

- So you expect me to believe that you did this all to help me. You gave me all that money out of your own pocket and you had no intention of making any money on this book?

- Believe it or not, yes. I don't need the money, Ira.

- Things booming in the psych biz? said Ira, sarcastically.

- They're going alright. Google "Bregman Textile."

Bregman Textile Inc, as Ira discovered online, was one of the largest textile manufacturers in the country.

- My grandfather founded that company, said Miles.

- Annual sales of eight hundred million dollars! said Ira, reading the company's Wikipedia entry.

- It wasn't quite that much when my grandfather sold his interest in the '80s, but not far off when adjusted for inflation. But Ira, even if I was in it for the money, you'd stand to benefit a lot more than me.

Ira and Charlotte were having an argument at Ira's favorite spot in Central Park, the Bethesda Fountain next to the lake. It was not a particularly acrimonious argument, however, as both parties wanted only what was best for Ira.

- So 'zat is it? You are going to quit writing 'ze memoir wis' Miles?

- Yes, I can't continue working with that guy. He's a weird, obsessed fan. And no one's gonna buy that memoir anyway.

- I 'sink 'zey will.

- I doubt it. And certainly not a lot of people, if it even finds a publisher, said Ira as he watched a plane fly overhead.

- You are wrong. But it doesn't matter, because Miles is helping you. I see it in the way you are with me. You are more open.

Charlotte was right about that. Ira had been, of late, opening up to her in a way he never had when they first knew each other, talking in particular about his parents and all the difficult times he had growing up. It was Charlotte, not Ira, who had been keeping secrets of late. Moreover, Ira was loving his time with her even though they hadn't slept together since that night in Vegas. He had never enjoyed spending time with a woman that much in his life.

- I'll think about it, said Ira.

- Good.

- Can we have sex?

- No.

CHAPTER 28

Alari Aubertin, née Rajan, was, like her daughter Charlotte, a woman of great exotic beauty. Though she was in her mid-fifties, this child of Tamil Sri Lankan immigrants to France still managed to turn men's heads wherever she went. This might be upsetting to some husbands, but for hers, Baptiste Aubertin, it was a source of pride. There was scarcely a wrinkle or line on her medium-brown skin and she had, on more than one occasion, been taken for Charlotte's sister.

Alari and Baptiste had come to New York to spend a few days visiting their daughter and young grandson. It was a sunny Saturday afternoon, and Baptiste had taken Sébastian out to the neighborhood playground, leaving mother and daughter behind in Charlotte's apartment.

- *T'as pas encore parlé à Ira de Sébastian?* (You haven't talked to Ira about Sébastian yet?) asked Alari.

- *Non, pas encore.* (No not yet.)

- *Pourquoi pas?* (Why not?)

- *On en a parlé mille fois. Je veux être certaine qu'Ira sera un bon père. Je veux pas que Sébastian s'attache à lui et finisse par avoir le coeur brisé. Franchement, il n'a jamais voulu avoir d'enfant.* (We've talked about this a thousand times. I want to be certain that Ira will be a good father. I don't want Sébastian to get attached to him and wind up heart broken. Frankly, he never wanted kids.)

- *C'est ridicule. C'etait une chose quand vous étiez separés d'un océan, mais vous vivez dans la même ville! Et en plus vous sortez ensemble!* (Thats ridiculous. It was one thing when you were separated by an ocean, but now you live in the same city. And moreover you're seeing each other!)

    - *Peut-être que t'as raison.* (Maybe you're right.)

    - *Je l'ai!* (I am!)

That evening, Ira invited Charlotte to come hang out with him at the Comedy Den and Sunrise Cafe. This was the first time Ira had planned to go to the Comedy Den since narrowly avoiding an awkward encounter with Matt Schefter. Matt had been there that evening to watch Vivi Liu with an eye toward working with her on a TV pilot. Though the possibility of running into Matt again at the Comedy Den was highly unlikely, Ira was nonetheless concerned about it, knowing from the Comedy Den website that Vivi was scheduled to perform that night. Ira got Vivi's number from Brian Rezack and texted her to ask if Matt had planned to be there again. She texted back that she and Matt were no longer in contact and were not working together on any projects. Ira was relieved. Clearly, there was no chance then that he'd be showing up to talk to Vivi. Hopefully, thought Ira, he wouldn't show up to see anyone else either. Ira was, as was his tendency, being overly neurotic. More than likely Matt was in LA anyway, where he spent most of his time.

Charlotte had dinner with her parents and Sébastian at an Italian Restaurant in Greenwich Village and, after putting them in a cab to return to her apartment, headed to the Comedy Den. She found herself with Ira at the corner table at the Sunrise Cafe with Brian Rezack, Stu Healy, the guitar comic, Vivi Liu and Karen Lee, who had brought her new boyfriend Tod Landers, a straight-laced looking management consultant whom she met in yoga class. Brian had once again brought the conversation around to political matters.

- I think the Second Amendment, Brian said, can reasonably be read to guarantee an absolute right to bear arms, even outside the context of an organized militia.

- What are you talking about? It says right in the amendment, "well regulated militia," said Karen Lee. Am I right Tod?

- I believe so, answered Tod.

- Tod's a very bright young man. He went to Duke, said Karen.

- To me the key clause is where it says the right to keep and bear arms "shall not be infringed," said Brian. The preceding clause about a militia being "necessary to the security of a free state," as I read it, is simply added as the reason that the right to bear arms shall not be infringed. If everyone has the right to keep and bear arms, that will make it easier to create a well regulated militia.

- Okay, said Ira, jumping into the discussion, but what if the stated reason for the right to bear arms no longer applies. Like, what if, instead, the amendment said "Given that the United States has no standing army, any motherfucker can bear arms." Once the United States formed a standing army, would the Amendment be automatically null and void? And so the question then becomes, are militias still necessary to our security?

- That's an interesting point, ceded Brian. I think the best solution is to have a constitutional convention and clarify the amendment.

- What y'all talking about, interjected Tony Powell, coming up from the showroom downstairs.

- The Second Amendment, said Stu Healy.

- None of y'all mental cases should have guns. Some of y'all shouldn't have shoelaces.

Everyone laughed except Charlotte, who had seemed stressed and distracted since arriving.

- What's your name? Are you a comic? asked Tony, addressing Charlotte.

Charlotte, not even realizing she was being asked a question, didn't answer.

- Charlotte, Ira said, Tony's asking you your name.

- Oh, sorry. I'm Charlotte.

- She's not a comic, added Karen Lee. She's Ira's special someone. A lovely flower from Paris, France.

Karen followed up these kind words with a poor imitation of Edith Piaf singing *"Non, rien rien. Non, je ne regrette rien."*

- That was awful Karen, said Tony. You should feel an overwhelming sense of shame. So you're from France! he continued, now talking to Charlotte. *Tu vit où maintenant?* (Where do you live now?), he continued in reasonably well accented French, to everyone's surprise.

- Oooh, French. *Très* sexy, said Kevin the red-haired waiter as he passed behind Tony with a plate of piled-high Mozzarella sticks.

- *Ici à New York* (Here in New York), responded Charlotte to Tony's question.

- *Depuis longtemps?* (For a while?)

- *Non, quelques mois.* (No, a few months)

- Did anyone know Tony spoke French? asked Ira. Where you learn it, Tony?

- Took it in college Spiro. History major. French minor.

- Ira underestimates you cause you're black, quipped Brian.

- Stop making trouble Brian! exclaimed Tony. Obviously you're right, but stop making trouble. Ira what time do you wanna go on?

- You're MC'ing this show, Tony? You never MC.

- I know it. Doug Greco called in sick last minute, and I was the only comic here when the show started, so Brian asked me. And as you know, I'm not famous enough to say "fuck you, Brian."

- You say it all the time, said Brian.

- I'm not famous enough to say it and mean it.

- You don't like MC'ing? Brian asked.

- No!

MC'ing a comedy show at the Comedy Den involved performing for ten minutes at the start of the show in front of an unwarmed-up audience, some of whom were still taking their seats and settling in. The MC also had to introduce each comic and do a few minutes of jokes between them. The problem was, it was hard to build up any momentum in those minutes between comics, and the jokes often fell flat. Moreover, if audience members needed to use the bathroom, it was during the MC's time on stage they typically chose for that task. Some comics enjoyed the extra challenge it presented, most did not.

- Well alright, I won't ask you to MC again. Unless someone calls in sick and you're the only non-famous person here, said Brian letting out a big laugh.

- Alright Brian you got me. That was funny, said Tony, joining Brian in his laughter. So Ira, when should I bring you up?

- Who's scheduled to go next?

- Stu's next.

- Okay, I guess I'll go after him.

- Perfect. You can follow the skid-marked panties song. And don't run away this time N*****.

Ira laughed uncomfortably at Tony's reference to what had happened the last time he was at the Comedy Den.

- Actually, said Stu, I think I'm gonna close my set tonight with my new song, "Chest X-Ray."

- Look forward to hearing, responded Tony.

- I'm gonna go outside and get some air before my set. Come with me, said Ira to Charlotte as he got up from the table. I'll be outside Tony.

- Noted.

- Everything alright? Ira asked Charlotte as they stepped outside of the Sunrise Cafe onto the sidewalk.

- I'm ok.

- You're not ok. You've barely said a word since we got here.

Charlotte briefly considered continuing to deny she was distressed but knew it would be a vain attempt. It was clear to all she was distracted and hardly herself.

- Well, my moh'zer hasn't been feeling well. She's going for some tests tomorrow.

- Oh no! I'm sorry Charlotte. I hope everything turns out alright.

- Thank you. I hope so.

Though curious, Ira thought better of asking any further questions about Charlotte's mother's health, simply letting her know that if she wanted to talk about it, he was there for her.

- Ira, you're up in five minutes, said Tony, walking outside to let Ira know it was almost time for him to head down to the showroom. You've seen Ira do stand-up before, right? Tony asked Charlotte.

- Yes. A lot of times.

- You gonna come watch him tonight or enough is enough?

- Yes, I come down.

Ira, Tony and Charlotte walked down into the Comedy Den via the exterior stairs leading from the street into the club. Ira walked Charlotte into the showroom and sat her down in one of the seats in the back designated for comedians and their friends. He then took the seat next to her.

- Keep the applause going for Stu Healy, said Tony to the crowd, as Stu put his guitar in his case and exited the stage. I got Stu's song in my head now, Tony continued. Chest X-Ray, cause I smoke pot several times a day, sang Tony, to the tune of the Beatles "Yesterday." How does the rest of the verse go Stu?

Stu sang from offstage, finishing the verse: "Is showing signs of some severe decay. But who needs good lungs anyway."

- McCartney would be proud, enthused Tony. Ok, we're running a little behind schedule so I'm just gonna bring up the next act without any more in-between shit. This next comic, good friend of mine, wrote and starred in *Jackson Taylor's Christmas Party*, done a bunch of other crap, make it loud for Mr. Ira Spiro.

The applause was robust, letting Ira know that his level of fame, though not that of a true A-lister, was holding steady.

- Thank you, said Ira to the crowd, as Tony handed him the microphone and walked off the stage. What other crap have I done Tony? Pretty much just *Jackson Taylor* by my recollection.

- *Tonight Show*, stand-up DVD, HBO special, shouted Tony from offstage.

- Yeah I guess so. But let's face it, it's been downhill since *Jackson*.

- You'll be back, N****!

- Round of applause for your MC Tony Powell everyone, said Ira to the crowd.

The crowd gave Tony a round of applause as he walked out of the room and headed back upstairs.

- Don't pass out! shouted a conservatively dressed man in his twenties sitting in the back row with two of his similarly attired friends.

The awkward heckle did not garner large amounts of laughter from the others in the audience, not even from the two friends of the heckler. Firstly, not everyone was aware of what had happened to Ira

261

in Maryland and secondly, those that were aware rightly assumed that it was an unpleasant subject for Ira and didn't wish to contribute to what was seen as an attack.

- I'll try not to, but thank you for the advice, Ira said, addressing the young man. For those of you who don't know, I passed out during a show in Maryland a while back. The main reason is that, unfortunately, no one was there to tell me not to pass out. Where were you, sir, when I needed you? Ira asked, again addressing his foil in the back row. It never would have happened if only someone told me not to pass out. Oh, and also if I hadn't taken all that Xanax before the show!

The crowd laughed and cheered, loving the way Ira managed to make light of what had happened to him in Maryland and handle the heckler in a gentle non-hostile way.

- They don't warn you about that on the Xanax bottle. It tells you not to drive or operate heavy machinery, but it doesn't say anything about doing shows for insurance company executives, all dressed like you, by the way, Ira said, once again addressing the heckler, who was happily laughing along with the others.

The young man had, in reality, done Ira a favor by yelling out "Don't pass out." Such interruptions are generally unwelcome by comics, but the comics often use them to their advantage. Ira was planning on addressing the incident in Maryland anyway, and the unexpected remark gave him an effective way to do it.

- Turned 40 recently. Hard to believe. Should probably go to the doctor for a full checkup. Anyone know a good doctor in New York? People review their doctors online, like on Yelp and stuff. I saw one review online: Dr. Shapiro, one star, worst psychiatrist ever. Not only did he misdiagnose me as having paranoid delusions, but he's selling my personal information to the government. I try to take care of myself. Mostly cause I'm an agnostic. If I were convinced that after we die we spent an eternity in paradise, I wouldn't give a shit if I lived a long time since I got heaven waiting for me. And I'd obey the commandments to make sure I went to heaven. Two places you'd never see me in again, a health food store and my neighbor's wife.

In the original version of the joke, the punchline was "the GYM and my neighbor's wife" but in thinking about the joke earlier that day Ira decided to replace "gym" with "health food store." Health food, as a general concept, was funnier to him than the gym. "Is there anything funnier," Ira had wondered, "than carob, wheatgrass, and other awful tasting things people eat to try and put off their inevitable decline?" Once he had decided to use "health food store" in the joke, he also changed what had been "I wouldn't give a shit about my health" in the original version to "I wouldn't give a shit if I lived a long time," thus avoiding the double usage of the word "health." Repetition of words tends to undercut the potency of jokes, and Ira tried to avoid doing so whenever possible. He had never actually tried the joke in its original version, so he would never know what the reaction would be, but the reworked version of the joke worked quite well and Ira was satisfied with the response.

- The years go by a lot faster as you get older. My twenties went faster than my teens. My thirties went faster than my twenties. What if one day medical science allows us to live a lot longer? Would it keep going faster and faster? You're 900 years old chatting with some dude at work, "Hey, how old's your kid? Must be like five by now." "He actually just turned 100." You're thinking, "Wow. These centuries are really flying by."

The crowd enjoyed the joke. When Ira looked over towards Charlotte, however, he noticed that she did not seem to react at all despite the fact that the joke was based on the premise that she had insisted he write down in the *Little Prince* notebook that she had given him for his birthday. "Shit, why the hell am I talking about aging and death when Charlotte's mother is sick," thought Ira. "I'm such an idiot." Ira changed gear and joked about less serious matters for the rest of his set, ending with his bit about how the French girl he was seeing says "I'm coming *in* America" instead of "coming *to* America." Looking over at Charlotte, he noticed she had little reaction to that joke either.

Charlotte and Ira went upstairs to the Sunrise Cafe after Ira got off stage. As Ira headed toward the corner table where Brian Rezak and the others were seated, Charlotte suggested they sit by themselves elsewhere, so they grabbed a booth by the window near the exit.

- 'Zat went well. 'Ze crowd was laughing a lot.

- Yeah I guess, responded Ira, refraining from mentioning that Charlotte seemed unmoved by his performance.

- So I have to tell you some'sing. My muh'zer is not really sick.

- Oh, well, that's good, said Ira, relieved that Charlotte's mother was alright but wondering why she had lied to him.

- Nice job Spiro, you were killing it when I walked back in, said Tony walking past the table where Ira and Charlotte were seated.

- Thanks, Tony.

- *Salut mademoiselle*, said Tony to Charlotte.

- *Salut Tony*.

- *Ira a bien fait rire le public, non?* (Ira really made the audience laugh, didn't he?), continued Tony.

- *Oui, comme toujours.* (Yes, as always.)

- *Il est bien talenteux ce N***** (He's a talented N****), said Tony. Have I heard that "Coming in America" joke before, he asked Ira?

- You might have. I've done it on HBO.

- Good joke. That about you? Tony asked Charlotte.

- Yes, I 'sink so.

- Don't let Ira make fun of how you speak English. It's a lot better than his French. This N**** don't know *c'est la vie* from RSVP.

With that Tony walked off, assuming Ira and Charlotte wanted to be alone since they weren't at the same table as everyone else.

- Isn't N**** a word for a black person? asked Charlotte. Why he call you 'zis?

- He calls everyone that. By the way, just so you know, you should never say that word. Only black people can say it, and you're not black. Brown, but not black.

- Yes, but I was only asking if it was a word . . .

- I know, interrupted Ira, but you're still not supposed to say it, even if you're quoting someone else. I never say it. If a black guy tweets it, I won't even click "like". Say "the N-word" if you need to refer to it. Just an FYI.

- Ok. That means what FYI?

- It means "for your information." It's an acronym, like RSVP.

- You know what, in France we don't much use RSVP.

- Really?

- Yes. It is kind of old-fashioned. We mostly say *"Reponse Souhatée,"* meaning "response desired."

- *Très* interesting.

- So, began Charlotte nervously after several seconds of silence, 'ze reason I told you my muh'zer was sick was, well, you asked me what was wrong, and I didn't want to tell you 'ze truce, at least, not before you went on stage. I didn't want to affect your show.

Ira assumed that Charlotte was about to break up with him. It would certainly be upsetting. He was very fond of Charlotte. However, though they had known each other for years, them being an actual couple was fairly new and, though he'd prefer it did not end, he could handle it.

- So, Charlotte continued. 'Zis is kind of hard, she said, taking a deep breath. I haven't been honest wis' you.

- She's seeing someone else, thought Ira. If she's found happiness, perhaps it's for the best.

Charlotte showed Ira a picture of Sébastian on the home screen of her phone. It was a photo of Sébastian smiling brightly while riding a merry-go-round at the Jardin du Luxembourg in the 6th arrondissement of Paris. Ira recognized the face. It wasn't the first time he had seen a picture of this child.

- Hey, that's your nephew. You showed me his picture before. What's his name again?

- His name is Sébastian, but he's not my nephew, Ira.

Ira took Charlotte's phone to examine the photo more closely. He noticed that Sébastian bore, it seemed, certain subtle resemblances to him. His lips curved slightly downward at the corners when he smiled, as did Ira's, and Sebastian's chin was a less sharply rectangular version of his.

- How old is he? asked Ira.

The question was more than one of simple curiosity.

- He's seven.

At that instant, Ira knew. It had been seven years since Vegas. Ira remembered it well. She had gone to the bathroom to take the morning-after pill, but he had never seen her take it.

- Excuse me Ira said. I'll be right back. I need to make a phone call.

Ira went outside where the reception was better. He had a lot to sort out and there was one person that immediately came to mind as someone he needed to talk to.

- Miles, it's Ira. Can we meet tomorrow? I wanna continue working together.

CHAPTER 29

IRA SPIRO BEFORE COVID: A MEMOIR - CHAPTER 20

After the bomb that was dropped on me that night at the Comedy Den, I needed a few days to work things through and process everything. I got together with Charlotte and told her that I was unsure about our remaining together as a couple. She had kept the secret of our son from me for so many years. She had her reasons it's true, but still, given the magnitude of the deception, how could I trust her going forward? "Go fuck you," was her response. Her years back in France had definitely lead to a deterioration in her English, and her heightened emotional state didn't help.

Despite her anger at me, she was agreeable to me spending time with Sébastian, which I had told her I very much wished to do. Yes, it's true, the idea of having a kid had never excited me. In fact, it had petrified me. I had trouble taking care of myself. Throwing another sentient being into the mix seemed unimaginable. And yet here he was, and I decided I wanted to get to know him.

Hearing that I was interested in a relationship with Sébastian, Charlotte finally told him about me and we got together for lunch on a Friday afternoon after school. Charlotte was at work, and her new nanny Alice from Mali dropped him off at Salvatore's Brick Oven Pizza near their apartment. Alice and I had a brief, cordial chat and she mentioned that Sébastian was allergic to shrimp, though that wouldn't be an issue at this particular restaurant, which offered only the traditional pizza toppings. The first thing I noticed upon seeing him in person was that he seemed tall for a seven-year-old. Clearly, he inherited his stature from me and by extension the Deridder side of the family.

- So I should call you Ira or Papa? he asked timidly in his Parisian accent as we sat down to eat.

I'm assuming it was a Parisian accent since he's from Paris. It was some sort of French accent that resembled his Paris-born mother's accent, so I put two and two together.

- Your choice. You can call me "Ira" or "Papa" or you can call me "Daddy," which is how we say "Papa" in America.

- I 'sink I call you Ira.

Calling me Ira did seem the best choice. After all, we had just met!

I enjoyed learning a bit about my son that day over our half-pepperoni, half-sausage pie. He was a second-grader at the Spruce Street School, a public school in lower Manhattan which, according to what I read online, had an excellent reputation. He said sometimes the kids made fun of his accent, but the teacher told him it wouldn't take very long before he was talking like all of the other kids. His favorite subject was science, and currently they were learning about chlorophyll which, as Sébastian explained to me, is the green chemical that plants use to make food. The "green" part I was aware of. The "make food" part certainly seemed right, based on my faded memories from my own school days. Sébastian, I learned, also enjoyed sports, and was taking, of all things, tennis lessons once a week at the Sportime Tennis Center on Randall's Island. He was also a big fan of the cartoon *The Adventures of Tintin* which I had never heard of but was apparently a big thing in France.

- So you are living wis' Julianne? he asked as we were waiting for our cheesecake to finish off the meal.

- Who?

268

- Julianne, from 'ze Christmas Party. At 'ze end she was your girlfriend and you were living toge'zer.

Apparently, to my surprise, Sébastian had seen *Jackson Taylor's Christmas Party*.

-That was a movie Sébastian. We were just making pretend.

- I know it was a movie, but sometimes a movie is true story I 'sink.

- You're right Sébastian, but in this case it's pretty much entirely made up.

- You don't live wis' anybody?

- Nope. All by myself.

- You are not lonely?

- Sometimes. But you know what's great? If I don't clean up, no one yells at me!

Sébastian smiled and agreed with me that that was certainly a great thing.

We ate our dessert, and I dropped Sébastian off at his apartment building feeling quite pleased with how our first encounter went and looking forward to seeing him again. That evening I watched a video on YouTube on bilingual children. According to the video, given his age and level of immersion, Sébastian would be speaking English like a native in a short time. Though his accent was adorable, it was obviously not good for his self-esteem to be so noticeably different from the other children. I don't know when my dermatologist, Dr. Chang, had arrived in America from Taiwan but, unfortunately for him, it was clearly after the age where it's possible to lose one's foreign accent, having diagnosed the redness on my penis as a "psoriatic lash." I also learned from the video that if a child doesn't speak his first language regularly, and in various contexts, he could easily lose it. It dawned on me that Charlotte was likely attentive to this consideration given that Alice, the nanny she had hired, was from Mali, a French-speaking nation.

Over the weeks that followed, we got together a few more times for walks, lunches and visits to the ice cream parlor, and I learned more about my newly discovered son. For example, I found out that his best friend at the Spruce Street School was a boy named Enrique Berni whose father was a doctor from Buenos Aires, Argentina and who spoke Spanish at home. I learned that his favorite song was, of all things, "What's Up" by 4 Non Blondes. The song, which by the way I've always liked as well, is part of the soundtrack to *Jackson Taylor's Christmas Party*, and that's where Sébastian first heard it. We're certainly not the only fans of the tune. I just checked on YouTube, and the video is closing in on a billion views! I enjoyed the fact that he so loved a song that was part of my movie, but then felt a little uneasy when I remembered that it was the song that was playing when Jackson was in his bedroom snorting a mountain of cocaine. It was certainly not a movie geared for people in his age group. With any luck, I thought to myself, the less kid-friendly scenes went over his head entirely.

I noticed, as well, at some point during that initial period in our relationship, that Sébastian was a lefty as am I and as my father had been. Charlotte is a righty. Yet another genetic connection to his father's side of the family? Perhaps, although I've read that handedness is a complex phenomenon involving a variety of factors. I found out also, after having directly asked, that Sébastian indeed spoke to his mother, as well as to Alice the nanny, in French, unless they were with people that didn't speak French, so as not to be rude.

On one particular weekday afternoon, he had come over to my apartment on the Upper West Side. I showed him my Oscar, for years largely ignored in my guest bedroom. The little gold statue held little interest for him, though. What kid that age cares about the Oscars anyway?

- You can stay here any time you want, I said.

- Ok thanks, he responded with little excitement.

The idea of a sleepover in my apartment did not appear to fill him with great enthusiasm, but then I couldn't blame him. We were still virtual strangers.

- Do you wanna go for a bike ride? I asked.

- Yes, 'zat would be fun! I love riding bikes!

I myself wasn't a frequent bike rider, but I did have a Citibike membership. If you don't live in New York, Citibikes are shared bicycles that, for a small annual membership, can be picked up and dropped off at any number of parking stations around the city. They are clunky and heavy, but if you don't need to go fast, they do the job. However, the Citibike program is restricted to people 16 and over so, having planned this outing in advance, I bought a small Schwinn bicycle for Sébastian, which I kept in my closet. He was excited to learn that it was for him to use any time he came over, with adult supervision of course.

- Can we take an ice cream after? he asked.

Obviously, it would have been more correct to say "have an ice cream" or "get an ice cream" or "down an ice cream like the pigs we are," but I let it slide. I had seldom corrected Charlotte's English and felt even less inclined to correct Sébastian's, given that I knew he would master the language soon enough. His mother, on the other hand, would probably continue making the same mistakes until she died, and if there actually is an afterlife, perhaps for several centuries more.

- Of course we can, I said, causing Sébastian to let out a high-pitched cheer! We can go to Van Leeuwen. They have dairy-free for me.

We headed downstairs with our helmets and the Schwinn. I told Sébastian to ride slowly, stay in the bike lane and stop at all intersections until I say it's ok to cross.

271

- Any violation of the above rules and we're not getting ice cream!

- No ice cream?

- Ok, we can get ice cream, but you can only get pickle flavor.

- Ewww, he exclaimed, followed by an adorable giggle.

- Or salmon flavor.

- Salmon ice cream! 'Zat is gross!

The comic in me went for the laugh with the pickle and salmon ice cream lines, but I realized this was something not to be treated lightly.

- Seriously Sébastian I mean it, I continued in a more severe tone. If I see you not being careful we're going right home, and no ice cream.

There was a Citibike station right across the street from my apartment building. I inserted my Citibike key in the slot in the bike dock to release the bike and we were on our way. I told Sébastian that we were going to head to Central Park where there were plenty of places to ride and no cars. He had heard about Central Park but had not yet been there and was excited to see it. It was a gorgeous day, warm and sunny with a slight breeze. There are a limited number of such days per year in New York and the city's residents make sure to take full advantage of them. The streets were crowded with people walking and biking and riding their electric scooters, which were becoming increasingly popular in the city. The outdoor seating areas at the coffee shops and cafes were full or nearly full. It was a weekday afternoon, and there were plenty of unfortunate suckers stuck in offices, but anyone that could be outside was.

We headed down West End Avenue and made a left on 78th street heading east toward the park, Sébastian riding a few yards in front of me and, as instructed, stopping at intersections and waiting for me before crossing. As we crossed Amsterdam Ave., heading past the marshmallow shop on the corner toward Columbus, there was a cab stopped in the middle of the block to let off a passenger. The cab was blocking a grey Mercedes sedan whose driver was honking his horn like a lunatic as the female passenger of the cab struggled to slide a box out from the cab's back seat. She had, evidently, just purchased a rather large item of some sort and opted against home delivery. The driver of the Mercedes apparently decided he couldn't wait another few moments for the woman to remove the box and for the cab to drive away. He pulled into the bike lane in order to go around the cab.

- Sébastian, I yelled out, as he braked his bicycle as hard as he could to avoid running into the rear of the Mercedes.

The bike skidded and toppled over to the side sending Sébastian to the pavement. The driver of the Mercedes, unaware or unconcerned, continued along toward Columbus Avenue. I ran over to Sébastian as he was screaming and crying and rubbing his right knee. I lifted up his pant leg and saw that, though he was a bit scratched up, he was likely more frightened than physically hurt. I grabbed him in my arms and softly repeated "it's ok" into his ear.

- Is your son alright? asked the female cab passenger, standing beside the box which she had placed on the sidewalk so she could rest a bit before attempting to carry it home.

- Yes, I think so. Just scratched up a bit.

- Thank goodness. I can't believe what that idiot did!

I looked over and saw the Mercedes turning right on Columbus, but it was too far away to make out the license plate. There was another cab heading towards us, and the illuminated cab number on the roof indicated that it was available. I raised my hand and the cab stopped. I put the two bikes on the sidewalk and grabbed Sébastian's hand.

- Let's go, I said as I opened the door to the cab.

- Where are we going?

- We're getting in the cab.

- What about my bike?

- We'll come back for it. If it's not still there I'll get you another one. Go to Columbus and make a right, I said to the cab driver, an East Indian man with a beard and mustache.

- You have no address, sir?

- No just make a right on Columbus for now.

- Where are we going, Ira? asked Sébastian once again.

- We're gonna try to find that idiot that cut you off and get his license number.

The driver made a right on Columbus and I looked for the car in question.

- What kind of car are you looking for? asked the cab driver.

- Grey Mercedes sedan.

- 'Zere is one Ira, said Sebastian, pointing to a gray Ford Fusion.

- That's the wrong kind of car Sébastian. And that car is behind us. Look in front of us.

- Is that him sir? asked the cabbie, indicating a car turning right a couple of blocks ahead on 65th street.

Indeed it was a grey Mercedes sedan. Though I wasn't sure of the exact model we were looking for, I recognized the narrow rectangular taillights and the tacky black rear spoiler.

- Yeah, I think that's him. Turn right.

At that moment the light just in front of us turned red and we could not make the turn. It seemed to stay red longer than usual, although I guess it always seems that way when you're in a hurry.

- Okay, let's go, I said when the light finally turned green.

We turned right and headed west on 65th street. Traffic was slow going cross-town and there were more red lights to deal with. It was seeming like a hopeless endeavor, and I was about to give up the chase when I noticed a police car stopped on West End Ave. with lights flashing, and just in front of the police car was our friend in the Mercedes.

- Make a left! Make a left! I shouted to the cabbie. That's him!

We stopped behind the police car, and I got out my phone to enter the license plate number in my notes app. I decided it would be even better to talk to the cop directly. Perhaps a reckless driving charge in addition to the ticket for speeding, or whatever he was being pulled over for, would teach him a lesson about cutting off children on bicycles.

I told the cab driver to wait and asked Sébastian to come with me to talk to the police officer. As we were exiting the cab, I noticed the cop reach into the car and pull something out, apparently the keys. He threw them to his partner who had by this time stepped out of the police car. The partner then opened the trunk of the Mercedes. The next thing I knew the cops had their guns drawn and the driver was pulled out of the car. As they were putting him in cuffs I grabbed Sébastian and got back into the cab telling the driver to return us to 78th and Columbus where he had picked us up.

After reading about the arrest online later that day, I decided not to report the license plate number to the police. I didn't think it was necessary: "Hey you know that guy you arrested in possession of a hundred lbs. of crystal meth and several illegal firearms? Well if you really wanna send him away for a while, he also illegally crossed into the bicycle lane on 78th street." The plate number, 6TY JFG, is still in my notes app, souvenir of a crazy day with the kid.

In the cab on the way back to where the incident all started I explained to Sébastian exactly what had happened and why I chased the man that had made him fall off his bike.

- Have you done 'zat before? he asked me. Have you chased a car like 'zat?

- No, I haven't, I responded.

"Why" I wondered, "did I do it this time?" What made me take such an action? "Because," I said to myself, "he was my son." Something in me took over when I saw him on the ground crying, knowing he could have been severely hurt, or worse. I cared about him more than I even knew and, though I had only known him a short time, would probably have given my life for his, if ever it came to that. He continued to call me Ira after that day, but had he switched over to "papa" or "daddy" I would have felt worthy of it, or almost worthy. The bikes were still there when we got back to 68th and Columbus, though we both decided we had had enough biking for the day. It was time to take some ice cream!

CHAPTER 30

Ira and Sébastian continued to spend time together and both were generally enjoying the experience. Their relationship was becoming more and more like that of father and son, with the exception that Ira did not feel that he had the authority to discipline Sébastian or even raise his voice to him. It would have taken a serious transgression of appropriate behavior on Sébastian's part to evoke a stern reaction from Ira, but, fortunately, transgressions of that type were not part of the child's personality.

Sébastian enjoyed playing tennis and inspired Ira to pick up a racket for the first time in over twenty years, and the two would play on the courts in Central Park. Sébastian had been taking lessons and showed great skills on the court for a child his age. Ira, well remembering the last time he had played against his own father, made sure to encourage Sébastian and compliment his game. Though rusty after so many years, he still had to make an effort not to hit the ball too hard for Sébastian to return it. Sébastian wasn't able to win any points off Ira unless Ira made an unforced error, but even in those instances, Ira congratulated him on keeping the ball in play. "You wore me down." he would say. "You're like a brick wall!"

Ira had decided he should reach out to his mother and tell her she had a grandson, and the two spoke again for the first time since the fateful birthday trip to Bermuda. Eileen Deridder swore, though she had fallen off the wagon during the Bermuda trip and for a short time thereafter, that she was sober again and hadn't touched a drop of alcohol in over a year. She said she wanted to come to New York and meet Sébastian. Ira was okay with that, but no way could he tolerate her staying with him in his apartment. He agreed to pay for a hotel for a few days while she was in town. Ira told his mother several times to avoid comments in Sébastian's presence about the boy's ethnicity. "Even if you don't mean anything by it," he said to her, "it's not appropriate." Ira hoped that, if he was clear enough with his mother about this matter, emphasizing it repeatedly, there was an ok chance she might actually listen.

Sébastian was recounting his recent adventure with Ira to his grandmother over lunch at the Acropolis Diner on the Upper West Side.

- And 'zen we got into 'ze cab to find 'ze guy in 'ze car 'zat made me fall over on my bike.

- Did you find him?

- Yes Eileen, we found him and 'ze police were 'zere and 'zay had 'zeir guns out.

- Mom, it turns out this guy was a wanted drug kingpin, interjected Ira.

- Wow. Sounds scary!

- I wasn't scared, said Sébastian proudly.

-Ira, that reminds me of something that happened when you were about two years old, said his mother. We were driving somewhere, I think we were taking you to the museum. Anyway, a car hit us from behind and your father got out. He started yelling, 'My kid's in the car. You could have fuckin' killed him.'

Sébastian started giggling, being by now familiar with the "F word," its various variations and uses, and its forbidden nature.

- Then next thing you know he hits the guy and knocks him down. Your father ended up spending the night in jail.

278

Ira had never heard this story before and, though his father had a temper, he was unaware that he had ever been physically violent. In a way, it was nice to hear. His father had been passionate about his safety, to say the least.

- That was your grandfather, Eileen continued. He's dead now. Heart attack.

- 'Zat must have made you sad.

- Not that much. We were divorced. His name was Steven Spiro. He was Jewish. So you're part Jew. Did you know that?

- No, responded Sébastian, never even having heard of either Jews or Judaism.

- Your father's half Jewish so that makes you what? Do you know? What's half of a half?

- Is my mom actually using Sébastian's ethnic background as the basis for a lesson in fractions? wondered Ira.

- You're one-quarter Jewish, said Eileen, after Sébastian failed to respond to her question. Now I'm Dutch, English and Scottish so you have that in you also. What else? Eileen wondered out loud. Ira, didn't you tell me Sébastian was part Indian?

- His mother's mother is from Sri Lanka.

- Right, I knew it was one of those places. That's why you have that beautiful beige tint Sébastian. Ooh, let's take a picture, said Eileen grabbing her phone and clicking the camera icon.

- Put the phone away! yelled Ira. My son is not an Instagram prop.

- I wasn't going to post it, protested Eileen.

- Bullshit. No pic.

- You're no fun, grumbled Eileen, her lips forming an infantile pout as she put her phone back in her handbag.

Sébastian was ignoring all this drama, focusing instead on his plate of onion rings. Ira was getting angry. He had told his mother to avoid talk of the child's ethnicity. It's true his son didn't seem bothered by her comments, but who knew what might come out of her mouth next.

Not wanting to verbally scold his mother in front of Sébastian, Ira figured he'd send her a text message reminding her to keep the child's "beige tint" out of the conversation. Before he could do so, however, he noticed an incoming call. It was Miles. They mostly communicated by text, and Ira wondered why he was receiving an actual call from him.

- Sorry, it's my friend Miles, he said to his mother and son. Shouldn't be long. Hey Miles, he said into the phone.

- Hello is this Ira? asked a female voice on the other end of the line.

- Yes, who's this?

- This is Adele Kaufman-Bregman. I'm Miles's wife.

- What's going on, said Ira nervously, suspecting that the reason for this call was not likely a happy one.

- Miles is going to have to cancel again tomorrow. He won't be able to get together to work on the memoir.

Miles had canceled the week prior. He had sent a text saying he wasn't feeling well.

- Is everything ok?

- I'm afraid the answer is no. Miles is in the hospital. He has cancer. A brain tumor.

- Oh my God! exclaimed Ira.

- Ira, I'm sorry to be giving you this kind of news. I have to go now, but if you need to call me later, I'll be around.

- What's the matter? asked Ira's mother after he hung up the phone.

- I just found out my friend Miles has a brain tumor.

- What's a brain tumor? asked Sébastian.

- It's a lump on your brain, Sébastian. And it's very serious, said Ira.

The plan for that afternoon had been for the three of them to go and see the musical *Aladdin* at the New Amsterdam Theatre on Broadway. After lunch, they would head down to the theater district to walk around a bit before the show and perhaps go shop for souvenirs.

- I'll be honest guys, I don't really feel up to seeing *Aladdin* right now.

- What does "feel up to" mean? asked Sébastian, trying to understand the unfamiliar phrasal verb, one of thousands in the phrasal verb-rich English language.

- It means I really don't want to right now. I don't feel like it.

That's what Sébastian had thought it meant, but he held out hope it meant something else.

- But you promised! protested Sébastian.

- Sébastian, I'm sorry. We'll go another time.

- It's ok Ira, I can take him, and afterward, I'll drop him off wherever you want me to, said Eileen.

- You want to take Sébastian without me?

- Yeah. We can have a little grandmother/grandson time.

- Can Eileen take me, Ira? Please!

- I'll tell you what, I'll go. Let me pay the check and we'll head over there, said Ira.

- Yay, we are going to see *Aladdin*! shouted Sébastian joyfully.

- You don't want me to be alone with Sébastian? asked Eileen, suspicious of Ira's abrupt change of mind.

- It's not that Mom, it's just . . .

- Because two seconds ago, interrupted Eileen, you were gonna scrap the whole thing, and then I suggested I could take him myself, and all of the sudden you've decided you'll go after all.

- Mom, I'm sorry. I mean, I just want to be really careful with him.

- You think I'm gonna fall off the wagon this afternoon at the play? Maybe knock back a few shots at intermission?

The thought had crossed Ira's mind that his mother might have a drink, but he was also concerned she might say something inappropriate without him being there to monitor the situation.

- Mom, come on. Let's forget about it. Let's go to the play and try to have fun.

- No that's ok. I'm heading back to the hotel. If you feel like apologizing you can give me a call. And by the way, I know you fucked Frank's daughter Abigail in Bermuda.

It was the second time a form of the "F word" had come out of Eileen's mouth that afternoon at the diner, this time used in its literal sense, which Sébastian understood, at least in a vague way. He knew that it had something to do with a boy and girl being naked together. This time he did not laugh, however, having sensed the tense nature of the situation. Ira was curious as to how his mother knew about him and Abigail, but he did not wish to pursue the conversation, especially with Sébastian present. Eileen, however, was happy to elucidate the matter without Ira inquiring.

- After you left the hotel, Frank and I went to the front desk and asked to move to your room. It had a better view of the water than ours. Well, guess what Frank found in the space between the wall and the nightstand? Abigail's ring. The one that Frank had given her when she graduated college. That's the reason Frank didn't come with me to New York. He wants nothing to do with you. Neither do I, she added, before leaving the diner.

"I guess when Frank says he wants 'nothing to do with me,' that doesn't include me sending my mother rent money for the apartment he lives in with her", thought Ira. Ira had continued to send his mother money, even during the period after the birthday trip when they weren't talking.

- Is Abigail your girlfriend Ira?

- No she's not, said Ira, with a brusqueness that discouraged any further related questions.

Ira and Sébastian stood on the sidewalk in front of the New Amsterdam Theater on 42nd Street between 7th Avenue and Broadway waiting for Karen Lee. Ira decided he would go visit Miles in the hospital but didn't want to deprive Sébastian of the show he was looking forward to seeing. It so happened that Karen was available and happy to take Ira's ticket and act as babysitter. As for Ira's mother's ticket, Ira would have to eat the $150 he paid for the orchestra seat as no refunds were available.

- When's she coming, Ira?

- She'll be here soon.

- Is she nice?

- Yes, she's very nice. A bit quirky.

- What is "quirky?"

Ira took out his phone and went online to Google translate. He entered the word "quirky" to find the appropriate French translation.

- It means "excentrique" said Ira, trying his best to approximate a French accent when pronouncing the word.

- What is "excentrique?"

Turns out it was not a language barrier issue but an everyday vocabulary issue. Most American-born seven-year-olds wouldn't know the word "quirky", and it made sense to Ira, upon reflection, that Sébastian wouldn't know the French equivalent.

- It means she's a little strange but in a good way, said Ira.

- You are quirky I 'sink.

- As it happens Sébastian, a lot of comedians are.

- Is Karen your girlfriend?

- No!

- Ira Spiro superhero! yelled Karen as she got out of a cab in front of the theater and walked towards Ira.

- Hi Karen. Karen this is Sébastian.

- Hello Sébastian. Nice to meet you.

- 'Ello Karen. Nice to meet you also.

- Oh my God you're so cute, she gushed.

- 'Sank you.

- Here you go, said Ira, handing Karen the two tickets and a hundred-dollar bill.

- What's this? asked Karen, referring to the money.

- A little something for helping me out.

- You don't have to.

- It's the least I can do. Just take it.

- Thanks Ira, you're the best, said Karen, not feeling the need to push the issue given the disparity between her financial situation and Ira's.

- You excited to see the show Sébastian? asked Karen.

- Yes, I am very excited.

- Let's go let's go it's time to see the show, sang Karen, making up a melody on the spot.

- You're quirky, said Sébastian, with a giggle.

- I certainly am. And that's a good word. What a vocabulary!

- Thanks again, Karen. Have fun Sébastian, said Ira picking him up and giving him a quick squeeze.

Hospitals and serious illnesses were not things with which Ira was particularly comfortable, and he felt a slight shortness of breath as he stood outside Miles's room at New York-Presbyterian/Weill Cornell Medical Center on the Upper East Side. After waiting a few moments to collect his thoughts, he walked into the room where he was greeted by Miles's wife who stood up from the chair she was seated in beside his bed.

- Hi. I'm Adele Kaufman-Bregman.

- Ira Spiro. Nice to meet you.

Ira looked over at Miles and was relieved to see that, though he was noticeably thinner than the last time he had seen him, and his face was adorned with several days of beard growth, he looked more or less like himself. His left arm was hooked to an intravenous solution attached to a stand beside the bed. The IV was composed of various vitamins and antioxidants to combat fatigue, nausea and other side effects from Miles's recent radiation therapy session.

- Hi Ira, said Miles in a soft, strained voice.

- He's a little tired, said Adele. He just had radiation.

- How's everything going with the kid? asked Miles.

- Pretty good. He's with my friend Karen right now seeing *Aladdin* on Broadway.

- You didn't want to go?

- I wanted to come here.

- I'm honored.

- Well, if I had had tickets to *Bruce Springsteen on Broadway* I wouldn't have come.

Miles let out as much of a laugh as he could given his tired state.

- Speaking of sons, you just missed my son Lenny. He's a psychologist too, as is my wife.

- So much I don't know about you.

For the next few minutes, it was Ira that listened to Miles while he talked about himself. He spoke of how four years prior he had been diagnosed with what's known as a grade III astrocytoma of the parietal lobe. What followed was nearly a year of aggressive treatment with chemotherapy and radiation as well as a seven-hour brain surgery.

Miles told Ira that during that time he found comfort in laughter, and in particular in listening to Ira's stand-up as well as other comics like the late Mitch Hedberg, Chris Rock and Marc Maron. But Ira, he insisted, was his favorite.

With the full arsenal of 21st-century medical technology unleashed upon it, the cancer went into remission leaving little in the way of permanent damage other than a diminution in hand-eye coordination, which Miles joked, he did not possess in abundance in the first place. It was as good an outcome as could be hoped for, yet Miles was told that recurrence was probable and that if the cancer did come back, it would likely come back in a more aggressive form.

- And so it's come back, said Ira.

- Yes, and as predicted, it's really pissed this time. The treatment might give me some extra time, but I won't likely beat this again.

- You knew all along you would never profit from this memoir we've been working on?

- I told you. It was never my intention to make any money from it. Even if I live to see it published, it was never my intention to take a cent. It was all to help you. After all, you helped me, during that awful year when I was being bombarded with x-rays and injected with toxic chemicals. When I was fighting headaches and seizures you helped keep me laughing.

Ira had reached the limit of his impressive capacity to hold back tears and they began to fall. As for Miles, even as he lay there in his hospital bed, a tumor laying siege to his cerebral cortex, he remained ever the psychologist.

- Tell me about what you're feeling, Ira.

- I'm feeling sad. D'uh!

- Why? Are you sad because you won't see me anymore? Is all this reminding you of your father's death? Your own mortality?

- All of the above, I imagine.

- What about Charlotte? Do you miss her?

- I think so. I don't know.

- Why don't you call her?

- Charlotte doesn't want to talk to me.

- Why not?

- Because I can't give her what she wants.

- What does she want?

- She wants us to be a couple.

- And why can't you give that to her?

- She lied to me.

- I lied to you, and yet here you are.

- It's not the same.

- That's true, it's not. You have a son with her and I think that fact makes any relationship with Charlotte seem like a marriage. And that scares you.

- Hi David, said Adele, who had quietly been reading a book on her kindle all this time, as a smartly dressed man in his late twenties walked into the room.

- Ira, said Miles, this is my other son David.

- Is he a psychologist as well?

- Lawyer.

- Like your character in *Jackson Taylor's Christmas Party*, said David. Except I never quit the profession. Still stuck doing it. Great movie by the way.

- Thank you.

Ira felt the arrival of David was a good time to say his goodbyes and head back home. He thought it best to leave Miles with his family and, in any case, Charlotte was in Washington, DC at a conference and, in a father and son first, Sébastian would be staying with him that evening. Ira had purchased Legos, toy trucks and an indoor portable basketball arcade game to make his apartment a suitably attractive destination for the boy.

When Karen dropped Sébastian off at Ira's, he was wearing an *Aladdin* baseball hat and carrying an *Aladdin* sweatshirt, and he was also in possession of an assortment of goodies from the M&M store in Times Square.

- Karen, did you spend the whole hundred I gave you spoiling my son?

- I couldn't help it. He's such a sweetheart.

Ira felt compelled to hand Karen another hundred.

- You don't have to. But thanks, she said, putting the bill in her pocket. She gave her new friend Sébastian a high five before heading off toward the subway.

Later that evening, after Sébastian had gone to sleep, Ira decided to make a phone call.

- Charlotte, hi. It's Ira. How's the conference going?

- It's fine.

- So Sébastian is here. Everything's going well.

- Yes, he told me he had a good time today.

- I had to leave him with my friend Karen, but she's great.

- I know 'zis. He told me Miles is sick. I'm sorry.

- Thank you. Yeah, it's crazy. So how's everything been?

- Every'sing is fine.

- So, what's the conference all about?

- Ira, I can't do 'zis wis' you.

- Do what?

- I can't be in your life only when you feel like it. Maybe 'zat worked before but not now. If it's about Sébastian we can talk, but apart from that, I cannot do it. Bye, Ira.

288

CHAPTER 31

It was the 10 pm show on Thursday night at the Comedy Den and, despite his past protestations, Tony Powell was enlisted to MC as, apparently, no one else was available.

- So they're investigating Trump's phone call to the Prime Minister of Ukraine, said Tony from the stage in front of the Comedy Den's usual full house. You think he's getting impeached?

A large number of enthusiastic cheers and "yeah's" emanated from the crowd in response.

- Yeah, and I bet y'all thought he was gonna lose the election in 2016 too. Trump's not getting impeached, stop dreaming. He's got a worse chance of getting impeached than I have of getting a cab tonight after the show.

Most of the crowd laughed except for a few foreigners who were unfamiliar with the fact that in the United States cab drivers are often hesitant to pick up young black men. Adding to the effectiveness of the joke was the fact that Tony was wearing a "hoodie". Adding further to the effectiveness of the joke was the fact that on the front of the hoodie was the word "BLACK" with a clenched fist in place of the "A."

- Gonna bring up the next act now. He was the star of the movie *Jackson Taylor's Christmas Party*. He's a friend of mine, a very funny guy, although a complete idiot when it comes to relationships. Please make some noise for Ira Spiro.

Ira walked on stage, accompanied by the usual chorus of applause. He was carrying the *Little Prince* notebook Charlotte had given him which he put on the stool next to the microphone as he shook Tony's hand.

- Keep it going for Tony Powell, everyone. He calls things as he sees them, folks. Tony, Brian made you MC again? I thought you told him you didn't wanna do it?

- Racism, joked Tony, now at the back of the room.

Ira started his set with his joke about the psychiatrist Yelp review and then did the bit about the Bulgarian guy telling him Bulgaria has just elected its first female Prime Minister. That was followed by a few other time-tested jokes, and then Ira let the audience in on the big news.

- So, I'm a father. Yeah. I have a seven-year-old son. Did anybody know that? I didn't either until about four months ago.

The crowd laughed tentatively, not knowing whether or not Ira was serious.

- It's true. I'm not kidding. He was born in 2012 and I didn't know he existed until this year. That's why I didn't give him a shout-out at the Oscars when I won. Also, cause I wasn't there. That was the main reason. I suppose I'm gonna have to start posting pictures of him online every two seconds like other parents. Last month on Instagram everyone was posting back-to-school pictures of their kids. People are using their kids to get attention for themselves on Instagram. And everyone clicks "like" to be polite, but the truth is, there's nothing less interesting than seeing a picture of your friend's kid going back to school. That's why before social media no one ever said to their friend, "Hey are your kids back in school yet?" "Yeah, why?" "What do you mean 'why?' let's see some pics! Come on, I've been waiting all summer for this!" On a related note, you know what else never happened before social media. No one ever called their friend and said,

"Dude, I gotta know. How long you been sober? I need constant updates!"

That Instagram "back-to-school pics" joke with the "how long you been sober" tag was another old crowd-pleaser. The only new element was that Ira introduced the topic by talking about taking pictures of his own kid. Ira opened up his *Little Prince* notebook. Many comics will bring a notebook onstage to reference when testing new material. Although Ira never did so before, he had more new material than usual to try out and didn't wish to forget anything. He opened to a page in the notebook where, written in large capital letters, were the words "JOKES ABOUT SON", and underneath the heading was a series of bullet points with keywords for each individual joke. Ira glanced in his notebook and saw "french, first word, not daddy" written next to the first bullet point.

- So my son grew up in France. His mother tongue is French. So, uhm, I guess that's another reason why his first word wasn't, uhm, "daddy."

The joke got a medium level of laughter. Not bad but probably not enough for Ira to keep it in his act. However, he stuttered a bit while delivering the punch line. He would try it again another time. With a more fluid delivery, it would likely work much better. Ira looked over at his notebook at the next bullet point: "love his French accent, lose it, selfish."

- He lives in New York now, my son. He still has a French accent though. His teacher here in New York says he'll lose the accent soon. That makes me a little sad because I love his accent. It's so cute! Sure, he's looking forward to having an American accent so he doesn't get made fun of by the other kids, but that's a little selfish don't you think? What about my needs?

That joke did quite well, and Ira took a quick look at the keywords for the last couple of new bits he wanted to try out.

- So, my son looks a bit like me. He's tall like me. He has my eyes. He's a lot better looking though. He has very delicate features. Kind of feminine features. Now that I think of it, I've never seen him naked. He might be trans. I'll love him either way. I'm just thinking out loud.

That joke got a very mild response, and Ira thought to himself he likely would never try it again. In fact, he wasn't even sure why he thought it was worth trying in the first place. He looked over and saw a red light illuminated above the door of the showroom with Tony standing next to it. The light meant he was almost finished his allotted time on stage.

- So, in the past when people asked me if I had kids I'd say "no". Now I say "at least one." Cause I figure maybe some other woman had my kid without telling me.

- Harlee! yelled out a young man from the audience.

- Harlee doesn't have any kids, responded Ira. If she did everyone would know it. There'd be paparazzi taking pictures of it. You'd see it in magazines with captions like "Harlee Shaw shopping on Rodeo Drive with little Sunrise Windchime," or whatever ridiculous Hollywood kid's name she gave it.

The audience enjoyed that little improvised detour in Ira's act. It's always fun to hear a movie star being mocked, especially by someone who knows them personally.

- But maybe some other woman I had sex with had my kid. To be honest, that particular group of women is a real mixed bag. Decent chance the kid would be a disaster. I'd find out about him one day watching the news. "Police are on a manhunt for an alleged serial killer. The suspect is described as a white male, narrow build, looks like a younger version of that dude from the Christmas party movie. Whatever happened to him anyway? He ain't done a damn thing since."

292

In the interest of ending on a laugh, Ira had planned to finish up by segueing from jokes about his son, who was from France, to his old joke about his French girlfriend, the child's mother, switching between English and French when talking to her friends in front of Ira. However, the serial killer joke worked well enough, and he decided it was a good way to finish the set.

- Thank you, everyone. Back to your host Tony Powell.

- Ira Spiro everyone, said Tony, grabbing the microphone as Ira walked off stage. Yes, that's right. White people have baby mama's too. Or as the French say, *les mama de baby*. Ira, you left your notebook up here.

Tony picked up Ira's *Little Prince* notebook and opened it to a random page.

- "Premise for joke," said Tony, pretending to read from the book. "My attraction to high school girls." Ira, I didn't know you were into the youngsters?

Ira walked back up to the stage to retrieve his notebook, laughing along with everyone else at Tony's prop-assisted ad-lib. Ira then walked over to the showroom exit where his phone was attached to the doorframe with a phone mount he had brought with him.

- Did you tape your set, Ira? asked a waitress named Julie as she passed by on the way to the service bar off to the side of the showroom.

- No, I never tape my sets, said Ira, leaving Julie wondering why else he would have his phone mounted on the doorframe facing the stage.

Ira took his phone and walked outside to the front of the club. He looked at the screen and saw a frail-looking Miles Bregman looking at him from his hospital bed. By this time, Miles's cancer was no longer actively being treated, and he was receiving only medications necessary to keep him comfortable and pain-free.

- Loved it. Awesome, said Miles in a low hoarse voice, giving Ira a thumbs up.

- Glad you enjoyed it. The new jokes worked pretty well. Most of them anyway.

- It was great. So glad I could see it.

It was painful for Ira to see Miles in such a weakened state, but he did his best not to let his emotions show.

- Well, I'm feeling kind of tired, Ira. I'll speak to you soon.

- Ok, Miles. Speak soon, said Ira before ending the FaceTime video call.

The last thing Miles did before going to sleep that night was make the following tweet from his @IHeartIra account: Saw Ira tonight at the Comedy Den in New York. He gave us a glimpse into his personal life, and it was marvelous!

In fact that brief conversation over FaceTime video were the last words exchanged between Miles and Ira. Miles slipped into unconsciousness later that evening and died four days after that.

Ira gave his condolences to Miles' wife Adele and his sons Lenny and David as they stood in front of the Frank E. Campbell Funeral Chapel on Madison Avenue after the service.

- Thank you, Ira, said Adele. Miles wanted me to give this to you, she said as she handed Ira a white envelope with his name on it.

It was a sunny and cool afternoon in mid-November and Ira decided to walk home from the funeral chapel to his apartment on the other side of Central Park. Along the way, he reflected upon the curious relationship he had had with Miles Bregman. How might his life have been different, he wondered, had he had a father like Miles? A father who wanted nothing more than to see him flourish. Was Miles like that with his own sons? Ira didn't know. Certainly, he thought, at least some of the qualities of Miles the friend were present in Miles the father.

294

When he got home Ira took off his suit, which he restored to its place in his closet, and got into some casual clothes before opening the envelope that Adele had given him. Inside was a cashier's check for four hundred thousand dollars, the amount left under the deal he had signed with Bartolacci US, the company created by Miles expressly for the ruse with Ira. Also in the envelope was a USB flash drive. He inserted the drive into his computer and clicked on IRA_SPIRO_MEMOIR, the only file on it. The text of the memoir was preceded by a letter from Miles.

Ira,

Well, here it is. Your memoir. It still doesn't have a title. I'm sure you'll come up with something interesting! It's mostly taken directly from the conversations we had at your apartment with little in the way of real input from me. You're of course free to make whatever changes you want, though I would appreciate it if you didn't include me in it in any way. I would like my reputation to be preserved after I'm gone and, let's face it, the psychology community might look askance at the subterfuge I used to procure your involvement in this project. I don't know if what I did was right. I do know that it was an honor and a privilege to work with a great talent, and a great person, such as you. It made my last year and a half on this Earth a truly special time. I thank you for that. You and I are similarly skeptical about the existence of a life beyond this one, but perhaps we will meet again. If so, don't forget to bring me an edited copy of the book! You'll find me in some quiet corner looking at the world below and watching the snowfall. It's always falling somewhere. Goodbye Ira. Your greatest adventures await you.

Miles

Ira spent the next few days reading through the memoir. Any corrections and edits would come later. He just wanted to get familiar with the book. Once again he relived the many important moments in his life. Once again he was a little boy not understanding the effects of his mother's drinking. Once again he faced the anger and jealousy of a father whose dreams had never come true. Once again he became a father, seven years after the birth of his son Sébastian. Once again he laid eyes on Charlotte Aubertin for the first time, dumbstruck by her angelic face and once again he struggled with his feelings toward her. There were twenty chapters in the Ira_Spiro_Memoir file on the flash drive. The events of the next couple of months prompted Ira to add one more.

CHAPTER 32

IRA SPIRO BEFORE COVID: A MEMOIR - CHAPTER 21

Charlotte Aubertin was a woman of staggering beauty. She was also smart and accomplished and, despite all the foregoing, appreciated and admired me. It was for these reasons that I had a history of pushing her away. I didn't want to take the chance of loving her too much and risk devastating heartbreak. The Freudian explanation, which I have come to believe has a lot of merit, is that my mother's instability had made me fearful that women will ultimately betray me. Moreover, my parents' relationship with each other did not offer me a positive example of what a true, loving partnership could be.

I was in my apartment in late November of 2019 watching music videos on YouTube when I decided that Charlotte was a risk worth taking. To add a more romantic flourish to the whole episode I could say, I suppose, that I'd had a sudden epiphany while listening to some French love song. In reality, it was a slow realization that had been building for days and reached full intensity in the middle of the video for "Safety Dance." I picked up the phone and called her. It was not easy, but with sufficient apologies and promises, I was able to convince her to let me back into her life.

She was quite busy at work, but over the next month we were able to get together a couple of times a week and we talked almost daily on the phone. After a short time, Charlotte told Sébastian that we were seeing each other, as she had started to trust that things might actually last between us this time. In my opinion, it was a premature trust given my track record, but perhaps she sensed that I was finally ready, at 40 years of age, for a real adult relationship, or at least ready to try. As a sort of celebration Charlotte, Sébastian and I went out to dinner at Bangkok 52 in Midtown Manhattan. It was the first time all three of us spent time together and it felt truly wonderful. Sébastian was bursting with enthusiasm as he told me and Charlotte about his virtual voyage around the solar system on a recent school field trip to the Hayden Planetarium.

- You were exploring outer space like the Little Prince, I said.
- Who? he asked.

Apparently, not every French kid is weened on the Little Prince. Go figure.

- Not important, I said. What do you want to eat?

Sébastian was starting to sound more and more American and he had finally mastered the "th" sound. He demonstrated this new skill admirably when, reading the menu, he mispronounced "pad thai" as "pad thigh."

- Mommy and I are gonna watch *Incredibles 2* tonight. Are you coming, Ira?

Before answering Sébastian's question, I looked toward Charlotte for guidance. I wasn't sure if she wanted me crashing their movie night and did not wish to presume.

- Yes Ira, why don't you come watch it wis' us?

Animated superhero movies weren't my favorite genre of film, not to mention the fact that I had never seen the first *Incredibles*. Nevertheless, I was happy to extend our family time, not that we were officially a family.

- Sure. Sounds fun, I said.

Back at Charlotte's apartment, I didn't pay much attention to the film, though I did enjoy the ice cream and donuts we had purchased to eat while watching it. As I was the only one bravely living with lactose intolerance among the three of us, I had a pint of non-dairy almond-milk-based peanut butter caramel swirl to myself. Not as good as the real thing, but a reasonable approximation. Charlotte did not invite me to stay over afterward. In fact, when the movie ended she immediately asked me how I was getting home, making her position on the matter clear. She was not comfortable with a man spending the night in her apartment with Sébastian there, even if that man was his father.

Charlotte had planned to spend Christmas and New Year's in France with Sébastian at her parents' house in Neuilly-Sur-Seine, a town just outside of Paris. I floated the idea of joining them, at least for part of the time that they would be there. I had never been to France, and I thought it would be nice to be with Sébastian over the holidays. Charlotte agreed on the condition that I stayed in a hotel, which was fine with me as I didn't wish to impose on her parents. I planned to do some sightseeing on my own and pop over to Neuilly once or twice to visit.

I won't go into great detail about my days wandering around Paris exploring the city. Suffice it to say I went everywhere you're supposed to go when in Paris for the first time: Montmartre, the Eiffel Tower, the Louvre Museum etc.. Like everyone else I found it to be a beautiful city with incredible architecture. And they really go all out for the Christmas season. Everything is covered in twinkling lights rendering the city a vast canvas splashed with incandescent blue, green and crimson.

I guess it's worth mentioning that I did stand-up while I was there. Tony Powell had put me in touch with a guy named Henry Witter, an English comic living in Paris who produced weekly English-language shows at a small theater in an area of Paris known as Montparnasse. I had assumed that the audience would be mostly composed of people from America, England and other English-speaking nations that were living in or visiting Paris. That would be an apt description of myself and the other comedians on the show. The audience, however, turned out to be mostly French people who felt that true stand-up comedy is meant to be enjoyed in the language in which the art form originated. Given that they often overestimated their own ability to speak and understand English, however, I found myself needing to talk as slowly and clearly as I could and using the least amount of slang and idioms possible. I would, for example, say "I'm going to" instead of "I'm gonna," and I certainly avoided the even more laconic "Imma."

I did my joke about having a more old-fashioned name than my father. It didn't work because the French, apparently, do not know that "Ira" is more old-fashioned than "Steve," as these are names they don't have there. I did, however, get big laughs with the following joke I had written a few days before, after Lou Sills told me that he had stumbled on an obituary for Mr. Morales, our 9th-grade health teacher:

In America, we learn about sex in 9th grade, the first year of high school, but our teacher was fired. First day of school he said to the class, "I'm going to demonstrate how to put on a condom," which in France you call a préservatif. Anyway, he said "I'm going to demonstrate how to put on a condom. That is why I have this banana with me, cause I can't get an erection on an empty stomach."

Thankfully, people use bananas to demonstrate putting on condoms all over the world. Keep in mind that this joke, like most of my jokes, is fiction. The late Mr. Morales was never fired and was never inappropriate. May he RIP.

I also killed with this joke I came up with based on a sign I saw riding on the number 4 line of the Paris Metro:

I saw a sign on the metro. It says the seats closest to the door are reserved for wounded veterans. But it doesn't say which army! Imagine you're sitting on the metro and some 90-year-old with a German accent starts yelling at you. "Can't you read 'ze sign! 'Zis is mein seat!"

I had texted Charlotte the joke beforehand and asked her to search online in French to make sure no French comic had a similar joke. She said she couldn't find any indication it had been done before, which surprised me as it seemed like a fairly obvious idea.

On Christmas Day I took a cab out to Charlotte's parents' house, a beautiful home on a quiet street next to the river. I would have taken the train in the continuing interest of experiencing France like a native, but I was encumbered by a bottle of red wine for the Aubertin's and Christmas gifts for Charlotte and Sébastian.

The Aubertin's were an impressive family. Charlotte's mother Alari was an obstetrician and her father Baptiste was an engineer who worked for a French electronics company. Apples don't fall far from the tree or, as the French say, *"les chiens ne font pas des chats"* ("dogs don't make cats"). Her younger sister Sandrine, who was at the house as well that day, had followed her mother into the medical profession, working in the emergency room at the Hôpital Européen Georges-Pompidou in Paris and, of course, Charlotte herself was making a name for herself in tech. Her older brother Laurent, who was in Belgium at his wife's family's house for Christmas, was a partner at a major law firm in Paris.

I arrived at the house in time to join everyone in opening presents. Charlotte gave me a much-appreciated pair of Bose noise-canceling headphones, and I gave her a leather backpack I had purchased the day before at a store called "La Maison des Bagages" near my hotel. As for Sébastian, I bought him seven presents. It seemed a fitting gesture given that I had missed his first six Christmases. I had set the bar high and no doubt he would expect retroactive gifts on his birthday in May as well.

- What's this, Ira? asked Sébastian, having just opened a small box with nothing in it but a picture.

- Well, I couldn't bring Disney World with me so I just brought a photo. I booked a trip for us in March!

- March is so far away.

- Your mother wants to come and she can't take time off before then.

Sébastian didn't even listen to my explanation as he had already moved on to the next present I had gotten him, a new junior-sized tennis racket. My other offerings were various toys and games including a map of the USA jigsaw puzzle and a telescope for kids. For children, and adults as well, the euphoria of new possessions wears off quickly, but he was thrilled for the time being and it was a great pleasure for me to witness it.

Charlotte's family was very welcoming to me. I was the father of their grandson and nephew and I suppose that carried a good deal more weight than had I just been some random person who was dating their daughter. None of them spoke English as well as Charlotte. Alari and Baptiste in particular struggled greatly with it, but they avoided speaking French the entire time I was there so that I would not feel excluded.

- Sébastian, you are going to so much amuse yourself at Disney World, said Baptiste, as Sébastian was finishing up opening his presents.

- Yes, I can't wait, responded Sébastian.

Sébastian was now sufficiently bilingual to find other people's idiomatically awkward English a source of humor and had to suppress giggling at his grandfather's attempt at the language.

- Ira, said Baptiste turning towards me, you wish to light your, how you say *bougies* in English?

- *Bougie* is candle Dad, said Charlotte.

- Yes 'zat's right. I forget 'zis. Ira, you can light your candles when you will want.

I had bought a menorah and some Hannukah candles at a shop in the Jewish section of the Marais District and asked Charlotte if it would be alright if I brought them in order to introduce Sébastian to a little bit of Judaism. It's something I used to do with my father as a kid, and I always enjoyed it. Charlotte thought it was a lovely idea. Her family celebrated Christmas, but her mother grew up Buddhist and they were open to any sort of religious tradition. I didn't know this offhand, but a quick online search told me it was the fourth night of Hannukah, so I put four candles in the Menorah and held Sébastian's hand as he lit each one with a lighter. There's a Hebrew prayer you're supposed to say while doing it, but I didn't know it and couldn't have pronounced it even if I looked it up. I simply yelled "Happy Hannukah" and everyone enthusiastically repeated the words with varying intensities of French accent united into one resonant Gallic cheer.

On my last night in Paris, I went with Charlotte and Sébastian on a dinner cruise along the Seine. It was Sébastian's idea. He got the idea from the boat cruise scene in *Jackson Taylor's Christmas Party*. Just as in the movie there was a live band on board, although this band played French songs mixed in with the English ones. One highlight of the evening was dancing with Charlotte with Sébastian joining in, one arm around each of our waists, as the band filled the boat with the strains of a tune called "Le Prince des Villes." It was one of several French songs I enjoyed that evening and I was forced to concede to

Charlotte that French music was perhaps better than I thought. Not great. But better than I thought. A second highlight happened during dinner when, passing under Le Pont de la Concorde, Charlotte asked me "Are you glad you came in France?" Sébastian started laughing, and in a gorgeous moment of father/son complicity, I added my own laughter to his. It took Charlotte a few moments to realize what was going on.

- Shit! I mean are you glad you came to France?

Charlotte and Sébastian were still in Paris on New Year's Eve 2020. I had been back in New York for several days, and after my last stand-up set of the year at the Comedy Den, I went upstairs to the Sunrise Cafe and awaited the arrival of the new year. Brian Rezak was at the corner table leading a discussion about the impeachment of President Trump, defending the position that an impeachable offense required criminal conduct and that Trump's veiled threat to withhold aid to Ukraine unless they investigated his political rival's son did not qualify. Not being a Constitutional scholar I couldn't argue the merits of that point of view, but I expressed concerns about a religious conservative like Vice President Pence becoming President if Trump were forced to leave office.

Karen Lee wasn't paying much attention to the conversation, busy as she was scrolling through the pictures of Sébastian I had taken in Paris. Each photo provoked stronger and stronger reactions culminating in a thunderous "Oy gevalt he's so cute I could die!" upon seeing a photo of him hugging a Cockapoo we had encountered on the Champs-Elysées. Her boyfriend Tod seemed to look a bit nervous, perhaps realizing that Karen might soon be looking to have her own children and he could find himself on the receiving end of a "propose to me or leave" ultimatum.

Tony Powell was at another table in conversation with Gisele, a woman he had recently started dating who worked as a private math tutor. African-American herself, she was highly disapproving of Tony's liberal use of the N-word, both on stage and off. As proof of his affection for her, Tony stopped using it even when she wasn't around. He felt it best to break the habit altogether rather than take the risk that it would slip out when she was in earshot.

At midnight I made the rounds with my glass of champagne wishing a happy new year to the Comedy Den staff and the other comedians. Most of the regulars were there — Tony, Karen, Stu Healy, Doug Greco, Ron Apple and Vivi Liu were all booked that night. Jeff Bunton was off doing a show in his native Toronto. Ron Apple, seated at the bar as the bartender put down a glass of vodka in front of him, briefly turned around and shouted "Happy New Year everyone" before turning back to enjoy his first drink of 2020 the same way he had enjoyed his first drink of 2019, by himself.

- Bring it in dude, said Tony, putting his arm around me and locking me in a tight embrace. It's gonna be a big year. I can feel it!

I don't believe he had ever called me "dude" before but, like I said, there was a certain word he was trying to not use and I guess he needed a substitute. At about ten minutes after midnight, I sent the following text to Charlotte: *HAPPY NEW YEAR! I LOVE YOU!*. It was the first time I had ever said "I love you" to a woman, at least, in a romantic way. Perhaps I had said it to my mother as a small child, though I could not recall a specific instance. Forty years may not be a record, but I think it's an impressive length of time to have spent without falling in love. It was 6 am in Paris and I did not expect Charlotte to be awake, but a few seconds later I received a text: *HAPPY NEW YEAR. JE T'AIME!*. She followed that text with: *I love you feels more real to me in my native tongue*, to which I responded: *JE T'AIME*.

305

2020 started off like a normal year, but it didn't stay that way for long. At first, nobody paid much attention to a dangerous, sometimes fatal, virus called COVID-19 that had originated in China sometime in late 2019. In January and February, while here in the United States the Trump impeachment hearing occupied the national attention, the virus was spreading from its point of origin in Wuhan to other regions of China, and to Europe and elsewhere. Even in late February, as the virus started to ravage Northern Italy, there was little concern here. Meanwhile, I was continuing to spend time with Charlotte and Sébastian, sometimes together, sometimes separately, and the words "I love you" and "Je t'aime" were exchanged amongst the three of us often and in all directions. I had also returned to working on a screenplay I hadn't looked at in years called *Hope from History*, about a famous actor that reconnects with his unrequited crush from high school. I had abandoned it thinking it wasn't very good, but reading through it again after all this time I had a renewed appreciation for the project and spent a good deal of time on it, continuing where I had left off.

By the second week in March Covid-19 had reached nearly every country on Earth and had been officially declared a pandemic, the center of which was shifting from China to Italy where thousands were dying despite a strict lockdown in the most affected parts of the country. With cases rising sharply in the U.S., the NBA suspended the 2019-2020 season on March 11. On March 12 all Broadway theaters were closed. Brian Rezak, who had been following the pandemic since January, closed the Comedy Den on March 14 and went into hiding in his country house in Skaneateles, in upstate New York. Our trip to Disney World, one of Sébastian's Christmas presents, was put on hold indefinitely when the park closed on March 16.

New York City went into lockdown on March 22. All restaurants, bars and entertainment venues were closed as were all stores, except those that sold essential items such as food and medicines. Schools and offices were closed as well and New Yorkers were encouraged to leave their homes as infrequently as possible. Public transportation was running but on a limited schedule.

If you saw *Jackson Taylor's Christmas Party,* you know how it ended. Lawrence Hummel and Julianne Dunn were living together. The final scene was at a Christmas party at the home they shared in Los Angeles. This memoir does not end in the exact same way, nor does it end at Christmastime, but rather a few months after. There is, however, a point in common between the two. I asked Charlotte if she, Sébastian and I might all spend the lockdown together, rather than seeing each other rarely if at all given the pandemic. She agreed, and since I had the more spacious apartment they moved in with me, and Charlotte subletted her place downtown. It was another relationship first for me. I had never lived with a girlfriend before. Needlessly to say I'd never lived with a son before either. I imagine all this would have happened soon enough, but Covid-19 hastened things. It also gave me a cool title for my memoir.

Fairy tales end with the words "And they lived happily ever after." In Hollywood movies, these words aren't explicitly stated, but they are often implied. No one doubts that Lawrence Hummel and Julianne Dunn both continued to flourish professionally and realize their grandest dreams and that they would love each other until they'd breathed their last breath. This, however, is a memoir. It is about a real person's life, and in a real person's life, there is no certainty. The coming chapters of my story are unknown to me. All questions about the future remain unanswered. Will Charlotte and I continue living together after lockdown? Will we stay together as a couple? Get married? Have more children? Will my career see a resurgence or will I fall back into old patterns of self-sabotage? Perhaps there will be another memoir when the answers to these questions are known. All I can say with any certainty is that there will be good moments and bad, but overall, I'm optimistic.

CHAPTER 33

Ira and Charlotte got along quite well in Covid quarantine. Their sex life was robust, their conversations were animated and engaged and their arguments were few and relatively minor. These arguments generally revolved around Ira not doing one of his agreed-upon chores, like cleaning the bathroom, with sufficient meticulousness. Ira generally accepted the reprimands, which were sometimes harsh, with little protest, grateful that Charlotte had let him back into her life and knowing that, overall, he'd be hard-pressed to find someone better.

On weekdays, while Charlotte was doing her programming work for TeaBrick from the apartment, Ira was tasked with home-schooling Sébastian. Since the schools were closed during the pandemic, parents were responsible for teaching their children, following guidelines established by the school board. The parents were not left completely on their own. They were aided by online materials including numerous videos. Ira, of course, was a big fan of watching online videos but found them less fascinating when they involved things like arithmetic, spelling and cartoon leaves singing about chlorophyll.

Ira had other things that kept him occupied as well. He devoted an hour or more each day to working on his screenplay for *Hope from History.* He also spent considerable time obsessing about the Covid-19 virus, how it was transmitted and what effects it could have. He would frequently read accounts online of otherwise healthy people who wound up in the emergency room with pneumonia and low blood oxygen as a result of the virus, and, to calm himself down, searched the internet furiously for other accounts of people whose symptoms, by contrast, were mild. Once a week or so he would feel slightly warm and, fever being the typical first symptom of Covid, was relieved when, upon taking his temperature, the thermometer read a normal 98.6 or thereabout. In fact, any time he perceived even the slightest physiological abnormality, real or imagined, he would go online to verify that it was not a Covid-19 symptom. His browser history was dotted with searches such as "itching & covid," "throat tickle & covid," "tingly feet & covid," "dry fingertips & covid," "urine lighter than normal & covid" and, the strangest one of all, "'momentary gingerbread taste in mouth & covid."

Ira went outside for occasional walks and to go shopping for food. Incredibly, despite wearing a mask, he was recognized a couple of times at the supermarket by fans. They did not ask for selfies, however, in the interest of keeping the CDC-recommended six feet away from other people.

Charlotte did the cooking, and it was the first time the stove in Ira's apartment had been used in over a year. She was a quite competent cook and that, combined with the fact that all the gyms in town were closed, caused Ira to add several pounds to his frame, though he still remained relatively willowy. Charlotte always insisted on French music playing in the background at mealtime, in large part so that Sébastian would maintain ties to French culture. Ira discovered one or two more French songs he could tolerate and one that he really enjoyed called "La Voix Du Silence", which might have led him to completely change his opinion about French music were it not just a French version of Simon & Garfunkel's "The Sounds of Silence."

As for stand-up comedy, though the clubs were all closed, Ira did a few shows sponsored by the Comedy Den via the teleconferencing software Zoom. He and other comics would sit in front of their computers and perform while being watched by audience members that were in their homes sitting in front of their computers. The performers could see the faces of the audience members in little boxes on the screen and could hear them, provided their mics were not put on mute. It was usually a good idea, when doing a Zoom comedy show, to leave a few people's mic's unmuted so the comic could hear laughter, but not have too many unmuted mics because when people are watching from home, as opposed to in a club or theater, they're more likely to talk to whoever they're watching with, without necessarily realizing that everyone else can hear. There's also the possibility of dogs barking or babies crying.

A fan of Ira's who had seen him at the Comedy Den contacted him through Brian Rezak and asked if he would do sixty minutes via Zoom for family and friends to celebrate him and his wife's 30th wedding anniversary. His offer for the show was ten thousand dollars. It was far less money than Ira had received for a private show in years, but Ira felt ready to get back into doing long headlining sets outside the comfort of the Comedy Den. He had not done one since the debacle in Maryland. This seemed like a good way to rebuild his confidence. He would feel less pressure working for less money and being at home would help put him at ease as well. He called his manager Dave Rothman to tell him about the gig. Under his agreement with Dave, he owed commission for all shows, even those that Dave did not obtain or negotiate for him. They hadn't spoken for a while, and Dave was happy to hear from Ira and happy he was going to be doing the performance.

Ira insisted that Charlotte sit near him while he performed, albeit out of the frame of the camera. Having her near calmed his nerves before his first hour-long show in over a year, and he was at a manageable 2.5 on his personal anxiety scale as he logged into the video conferencing site. Ira decided to start things off with a couple of jokes about the current situation. A comic simply can't do a show remotely by computer during a worldwide pandemic without addressing the situation.

- So I'm here in quarantine with my son. I'm sure a lot of you watching are locked down with your kids. It's not easy. This has never happened before. No parent signed up for this. If you were planning to have a kid and someone said, "one day the kid might have psychiatric problems or turn to crime," you'd say "if it happens we'll work through it." If they said, "Oh, and one day you might be stuck with them for months in quarantine," you'd be like "I'll get the condom."

This joke was not strictly based on experience. Fatherhood was still a novelty for Ira, and so far he had been enjoying having Sébastian with him nearly 24/7, challenging though it could be. However, he had certainly heard complaints from other parents.

Ira's anxiety was diminished by the success of his opening joke, and with confidence he moved on to his bit about his parents making him go to summer camp so they could get some peace and quiet, introducing the bit by saying that he hopes camps are not going to be closed in 2020 because of the virus. After that, he did a joke about a new concept that was on everyone's lips, "social distancing."

- It's crazy. People are keeping away from each other to avoid spreading the virus. No one is even shaking hands. "Social distancing" they call it. I spoke to my mother on the phone today, but I haven't hugged her since before the pandemic. Since about thirty-five years before the pandemic.

That joke also worked and things continued to go well throughout the performance. Ira had thought of a joke about recently seeing a street ventriloquist, but that his act wasn't that impressive because, given the pandemic, he was wearing a mask. However, after googling "ventriloquist & mask & covid," he discovered dozens of other comics, and quite a few non-comics, had come up with the same idea, so he scrapped it.

At one point during the at-home performance, Ira retried the joke he had done at the Comedy Den about how Sébastian was raised in France and thus, that was another reason why his first word wasn't 'daddy'''. He delivered it flawlessly this time and as hoped, it worked like a charm.

Sébastian, in fact, made a brief appearance on the show when he came out of the guest room, which was now his bedroom, and screamed, "When's dinner I'm hungry!" which got an even bigger laugh from those watching than many of the actual jokes.

- Sorry everyone. That's my son Sébastian. I was talking about him earlier. You can make him something to eat if you want, he said to Charlotte, feeling confident and no longer needing her by his side. I'll eat after.

The audience didn't mind the brief interruption and actually enjoyed a glimpse into the home life of a comedian well known to many of them.

When Ira felt as though he had done about an hour he glanced at his phone. Sixty-three minutes! Ira did it! He made it through the hour panic attack-free. He thanked everyone for listening and then finished as he had started, with a joke about the lockdown.

- It's been so much fun doing this show for you guys, though it is always a bit weird doing comedy at home in front of my computer. Especially cause I live in a building with thin walls. Last time I did a show my neighbor pounded on my door and screamed, "Keep it down in there! Or at least do some new jokes!"

After the show Ira received a text from Dave Rothman, who had watched from his house while devouring a box and a half of Cheez-Its: *"Loved it – You're Back!."* Ira was encouraged that the show went well. Still, he was at home and it was a relatively low-pressure gig. He wondered how things would go the next time he was in front of a large audience in a theater, whenever that might be.

In addition to the occasional show on Zoom, the *Hope from History* script, his Covid-19 research and dealing with Sébastian", Ira also spent considerable time finishing up his memoir. By early May he had completed, revised and proofread *Ira Spiro: Before Covid*. He cut out some of the stuff he thought was of little interest or importance and punched the book up with more humorous moments and anecdotes. He also added a few things that required some research. For example, the information about the world's oldest person in 1989 and the price of Jennifer Lawrence's Oscar dress were details that were added to the memoir while in lockdown.

In its final form the book was organized as follows:

Chapter 1 - Ira's show in Denver and his onstage panic attack.

Chapter 2 - Ira goes to the Bleeker Street Comedy Club to perform stand-up for the first time ever. His performance is not stellar, but he does not lose his motivation to continue doing stand-up.

Chapter 3 - Ira navigates the world of open mic's and slowly but surely becomes a competent comedian.

Chapter 4 - As Ira starts to have modest success, his father fires him from Spiro's Formalwear, where Ira was still working, after he gave a customer the wrong cummerbund.

Chapter 5 - Ira meets Charlotte at a show in San Francisco and is blown away by her beauty. The two wind up in bed together before the weekend is over.

Chapter 6 - Ira's movie, *Jackson Taylor's Christmas Party*, is an unexpected success. He and actress Harlee Shaw start dating and form one of Hollywood's more unlikely couples.

Chapter 7 - Ira speaks of the time as a young child when his mother had a drunken fit and locked him in his room overnight.

Chapter 8 - Ira wins the Oscar for Best Original Screenplay for *Jackson Taylor's Christmas Party*. He does not attend the ceremony due to psychologically induced intermittent nausea which continues for weeks and is soon joined by other obsessive-compulsive symptoms. Ira seeks the help of a therapist for the first time in his life, but things don't end well.

Chapter 9 - Ira and producer Matt Schefter discuss possible show ideas to pitch to producers.

Chapter 10 - Ira and Matt Schefter pitch their series idea, *Charlton Choudhury - Modern Times,* to television executives in LA.

Chapter 11 - Ira goes to LA to work on the first eight episodes of *Charlton Choudhury - Modern Times*. His bad attitude and animosity toward Matt Schefter ultimately sink the project.

Chapter 12 - The memoir returns once again to Ira's childhood and the time his father blew up at him after Ira beat him in tennis. Ira calls the episode "The Tennis Incident."

Chapter 13 - Ira speaks of the death of his father from a heart attack and how Charlotte unexpectedly showed up at the shiva. He takes her on a pilgrimage to a mini-golf course in Philadelphia where he and his father had shared one of their better moments as father and son.

Chapter 14 - Ira recalls his fling with aspiring actress Stephanie Delsano, whom he met at the Comedy Den. She was drunk when he met her, and on most of their encounters thereafter.

Chapter 15 - Ira does a show in Maryland that ends with him passing out after ten minutes on stage.

Chapter 16 - A year prior to his death Ira's father has a first, non-fatal, heart attack and seems to have little desire to prevent a second.

Chapter 17 - Ira goes to Bermuda for his mother's 60th birthday where he has a sexual adventure with his mother's boyfriend's daughter. He leaves the vacation early when his mother falls off the wagon.

Chapter 18 - Ira reconnects with Charlotte, now living in New York. One night at the Comedy Den she confesses to him that they have a son together.

Chapter 19 - Ira recalls the night in Las Vegas his son was conceived and how he asked Charlotte to take a morning-after pill after the condom broke, which, Charlotte would later confess to him, she never took.

Chapter 20 - Though having broken up with Charlotte, Ira wishes to have a relationship with his son Sébastian. They meet and get to know each other. One day on a bike ride a car almost hits Sébastian. Ira gets in a cab and pursues the reckless driver.

Chapter 21- Ira and Charlotte reconcile. They spend time in Paris together over Christmas and a couple of months later Charlotte and Sébastian move into Ira's apartment as New York goes into Covid-19 lockdown.

Ira had never felt at ease about revealing details of his life to the public. His stand-up act itself seldom delved too deeply into his personal life. Nor, at this point, did Ira feel desperate to make money. He was now confident he could rebuild his career. He was excited about the screenplay he was working on and he had recently pulled off that hour-long performance with little difficulty. He was cautiously hopeful that, when the Covid-19 crisis was over, he could make good money again in live performances, and thus he ended up donating the half-million dollars he had received from Miles, minus the commission he gave to Dave Rothman, to a charity for brain cancer. He would have felt guilty keeping it anyway, given the circumstances.

As for the memoir, he decided against looking for a publisher and opted simply to self-publish it. He designed the cover himself. It was a simple design. It said "Ira Spiro: Before Covid - A Memoir" in black letters below which was a minimalist black line drawing of his face that had been sent to him by a fan years earlier. The title and drawing were set against a light blue background. That was it for the cover and there was nothing on the back but his picture and a brief bio. He had a mere ten copies printed, nine of which he put on the bookshelf next to the *Guinness Book of World Records*. Perhaps he would give copies to Karen, Tony, his manager and maybe some others. He might even send his mother a copy, though they hadn't spoken since that day at the diner with Sébastian. He tried calling her to make sure she was being careful to wash her hands and limit going out in the wake of Covid-19, but she never called him back. Regarding Sébastian, Ira didn't even tell him about the book, lest he get curious and try and read something completely inappropriate for his age.

Charlotte read the memoir in one sitting the day the copies arrived.

-Ira, I finished 'ze book, she said just after midnight as Ira was watching the World War One movie 1917. He paused the film to hear what Charlotte had to say about it.

- I really enjoyed it, she said, but 'zere is something I want to talk to you about.

Ira felt slightly concerned that she might have a problem with his admission of having occasionally used the services of prostitutes, which is something he had never discussed with her before. That, however, was not what was bothering her.

- You wrote 'zat you don't correct me most of 'ze time when I make a mistake in English.

- It would break up the flow of the conversation to correct you constantly.

- Constantly? I make 'zat many mistakes?

- No, but, I just don't wanna make you insecure about your English.

- Correct me whenever I will make a mistake!

- Okay, from now on I'll correct you, said Ira, neglecting to tell her it's "whenever I make a mistake" not "whenever I will make a mistake" nor having the slightest intention of correcting her any more than he had done in the past.

- Good. Don't forget.

Other than Charlotte, by the next week, one other person had read *Ira Spiro: Before Covid* as well.

- Okay Sébastian, I need your room, ordered Ira. I have a doctor's appointment by Zoom.

- Can't you do it in the living room, Ira?

- No I need privacy. And I can't use our room. Mom's in there working.

Sébastian grabbed some legos and his iPad and left Ira alone as requested. Ira opened up his laptop and made himself comfortable at the desk that Sébastian used for schoolwork. He logged into Zoom and, on his screen, popped up the face of the sixty-something Dr. Simon Levin, seated in a large chair in front of a bunch of diplomas and awards. Ira had called Adele Kaufman Bregman a few weeks earlier requesting the name of a therapist. It so happened that Miles, before he died, had told Adele that Dr. Levin would be a good person for Ira should he ever inquire.

- Hello, Ira, it's Dr. Levin. Nice to meet you.

- Hi, Dr. Levin. Nice to meet you too. You came highly recommended by Adele Kaufman Bregman.

- That's very nice to hear. She's one of the best in her field, as was her late husband Miles. I believe you knew him.

- Yes, he was a comedy fan.

- Interesting. I didn't know that about him. Well, normally I ask a lot of questions about a patient's personal background but in your case, I read your memoir. I'm glad you sent it to me. So Ira, what do you wish to get out of therapy?

- Happily ever after.

- Well, as you wrote in your book, that's for films and fairy tales. But we'll try.

- Let's do it.

About the Author:

Dan Naturman is a stand-up comedian and actor who has appeared on "America's Got Talent", "Late Show with David Letterman", and "The Conan O'Brien Show" and was also a regular on the HBO series "Crashing". Dan has an undergraduate  degree from the University of Pennsylvania and a JD from the Fordham University School of Law, though he has never practiced. In his spare time he enjoys studying French and trying to acquire a reasonable level of competence on guitar. He lives alone in New York City and has issues with close relationships.